Clare Connelly was [...] amongst a family of [...] of her childhood up a [...] hand. Clare is marrie[...] and they live in a bungalow near the sea with their two children. She is frequently found staring into space—a sure-fire sign that she's in the world of her characters. She has a penchant for French food and ice-cold champagne, and Mills & Boons continue to be her favourite ever books. Writing for Mills & Boon is a long-held dream. Clare can be contacted via clareconnelly.com or her Facebook page.

Taryn Leigh Taylor likes dinosaurs, bridges and space—both personal and the final frontier variety. She shamelessly indulges in clichés, most notably her Starbucks addiction—grande six-pump whole milk, no water chai-tea latte, aka: 'the usual', her shoe hoard (*I can stop any time I... Ooh! These are pretty!*) and her penchant for falling in lust with fictional men with great abs. She also really loves books, which was what sent her down the crazy path of writing in the first place. Want to be virtual friends? Check out tarynleightaylor.com, Facebook.com/tarynltaylor1 and Twitter, @tarynltaylor.

If you liked *The Season to Sin* and *Secret Pleasure*
why not try
Undone by Caitlin Crews
My Royal Surrender by Riley Pine

Discover more at millsandboon.co.uk.

THE SEASON TO SIN

CLARE CONNELLY

SECRET PLEASURE

TARYN LEIGH TAYLOR

MILLS & BOON

All rights reserved including the right of reproduction
in whole or in part in any form. This edition is published
by arrangement with Harlequin Books S.A.

This is a work of fiction. Names, characters, places, locations
and incidents are purely fictional and bear no relationship to
any real life individuals, living or dead, or to any actual places,
business establishments, locations, events or incidents.
Any resemblance is entirely coincidental.

This book is sold subject to the condition that it shall not,
by way of trade or otherwise, be lent, resold, hired out
or otherwise circulated without the prior consent of the publisher
in any form of binding or cover other than that in which it is published
and without a similar condition including this condition
being imposed on the subsequent purchaser.

® and TM are trademarks owned and used by the trademark owner
and/or its licensee. Trademarks marked with ® are registered with the
United Kingdom Patent Office and/or the Office for Harmonisation
in the Internal Market and in other countries.

First Published in Great Britain 2018
by Mills & Boon, an imprint of HarperCollins*Publishers*
1 London Bridge Street, London, SE1 9GF

The Season to Sin © 2018 Clare Connelly

Secret Pleasure © 2018 Taryn Leigh Taylor

ISBN: 978-0-263-26658-0

MIX
Paper from
responsible sources
FSC® C007454

This book is produced from independently certified FSC™ paper
to ensure responsible forest management.
For more information visit www.harpercollins.co.uk/green.

Printed and bound in Spain
by CPI, Barcelona

THE SEASON TO SIN

CLARE CONNELLY

MILLS & BOON

To the Romance Writers of Australia:

the best group of creative, talented and supportive writers in the whole wide world.

I'm so glad to be a part of the tribe.

PROLOGUE

Were all stars to disappear or die,
I should learn to look at an empty sky
And feel its total dark sublime,
Though this might take me a little time.

—*WH Auden*

I DREAMED OF her again last night. Of how she'd been on that last morning, her pale face blotchy from tears, her eyes holding apologies and lies, begging me to forgive her.

How could I, though?

She was leaving me. Just like everyone else.

I dreamed of my foster mother Julianne, and the dream was so real that in it I was able to reach out and hug her, to fall into her hug, to smile at her. To pull back through time and space and change the way the day had actually unfolded—to undo the way I had shouted at her and shoved her when she'd tried to draw me close.

In my dream I didn't swear at her.

In my dream I didn't refuse to go near.

It was just a dream, though: powerful enough to drag me from my fitful sleep, but futile in allowing me to change the past.

The past is a part of me and there is no escaping that.

CHAPTER ONE

THERE IS ONLY one word to describe the way he's looking at me. With disdain. There is a hint of boredom that curves his lips, lips that I have looked at far too often in the five minutes since Noah Moore walked into this bustling café, just around the corner from my office.

I've heard of him, of course. Who hasn't? Self-made billionaire, one half of the tech empire that's completely taken over the world as we know it. In the last ten or so years he's gone from strength to strength, his professional successes only outdone by his frequent outings in the society papers—for all the wrong reasons. Along with his business partner, he's renowned for his ruthless instincts and fast-paced lifestyle. Luxury. Glamour. Wealth. Success. Wild parties on yachts in the Mediterranean, the after-party they throw every year at the Cannes Film Festival that draws all the big-name celebrities. They might have made their money in the tech industry, but they're the epitome of Hollywood cool—the gritty, bad boy kind.

Yes, Noah Moore is a quintessential bad boy and, as if I needed any further proof of that, he arrived at our meeting in a leather jacket, black jeans, his dark hair a little longer than it should have been, stubble on his angular and symmetrical face, his brows thick, his lashes thicker, and with a hint of alcohol lingering around his very buff, very distracting frame. And it *is* distracting me. All six and a half feet of him, all muscled, *big* and tanned all over—or so I imagine—is making me forget that I am a professional.

'This isn't an appointment. I don't need a shrink. I just…want to talk.'

It had been a confusing declaration, given that he'd called me—a shrink—but I'd made the appointment with him regardless, despite my growing waiting list. Curiosity, you see, got the better of me.

I didn't get to be twenty-eight and divorced without learning that I have a predilection for bad boys. Specifically one—and he burned me, badly. Bad boys are my sinkhole, my quicksand. The longer Noah Moore looks at me with that scathing contempt, the more my pulse flutters at my wrist, hammering me in a way that makes me uncomfortably aware of the way he's sitting, his legs spread wide, one arm bent at the elbow supporting his head, the other resting close enough to his cock that I know I can't look anywhere near his hand. His gaze doesn't waver from my face. He has a magnetic quality. He's drawn the attention of most of the women in this place, and not because he's well-known. It's purely because of *him*.

I summon all my strength to hold his stare. 'Well, Mr Moore.' His lips flicker at the formal use of his name. I can't help it. I feel I need every tool at my disposal to keep him at arm's length. 'We've covered the basics. Why don't you tell me why we're here?'

'Why we're here?' Noah Moore is Australian and, though his accent has been flattened by the years he's spent here in the UK, there's still that hint of lazy sunshine in his inflection, enough to warm me unconsciously. 'Isn't it obvious?' He lifts his brows, waiting for me to answer, turning the tables on me. His eyes, a green that would blend into the Mediterranean, narrow.

'Usually, my patients complete a pre-appointment form,' I say. 'You didn't email one back.'

His gaze doesn't shift. Curiosity sparks in my gut.

'You didn't complete it?'

'I'm *not* a patient.'

A frown pulls at my lips and I instantly wipe it from my face. I don't show emotion when meeting prospective clients. This process isn't about me and my feelings—it's about them. 'I see,' I say, nodding calmly. 'So why did you call me, then?'

He compresses his lips. 'To talk. To see what this is all about. I explained that on the phone.'

'Right.' I resist an impulse to respond sarcastically. 'I'd still like to have some of your details on file. Do you mind?'

'By all means.' He drags his fingers through his hair and then casts a glance at his wristwatch. It's not a fancy, expensive timepiece like you'd expect.

It's a smart watch. Is that what they're called? You know, the ones that count your steps, forward your mail and lock your house.

I lift out my phone, opening the secure app I use to record confidential patient information. 'Here you are.' I hand it over to him, but he makes no move to take it.

'You fill it out,' he says with a shrug.

Rudeness has reached astronomical levels.

Now, I've been doing this a long time. I know I'm good at this. That's not ego speaking; it's the line of awards from the Guild of British Psychologists I've received; it's the magazine articles; it's the waiting list as long as your arm to get an appointment; it's the fact I can charge what I want—though rarely do. Because what I love most of all is to help people, and seeing my success in the way my patients' lives change—that's why I do my job.

It's why I agreed to see Noah for this 'audition', when I have far too much to do as it is. He sounded like someone who needed help. I want to help him.

Patients with trauma and severe trauma disorders, like PTSD, should be handled gently. Even the ones like Noah Moore, who seem as though they can handle anything, are only ever one distress away from bolting. From fleeing a therapy that is too hard to process.

Of course, I can only guess, at this stage, that he's affected by a trauma—he's not exactly giving me much to work with. Except for the 'tells', the small signs that indicate to someone like me that he's using every cell in his body to push me away, right down to insisting that this isn't a normal appointment, that he's not a 'patient'.

'If you'd like,' I say, with a soft nod and a smile that is my professional version of *But we both know you're being an asshole.*

Out of nowhere, I picture Ivy and warmth spreads through me. I work long hours, and God, I miss her so much. I have a picture of her on my desk, back in my office, because it helps to tether me to the other part of my life—the love of my daughter and the need to make her safe.

She looks just like I did as a child—like me as an adult, really. Our hair is the same shade of blonde, so fair it's almost white, though hers has been cut—at her request—into a bob whereas mine is long, halfway down my back, and I tend to wear it in a plait over one shoulder. We both have ice-blue eyes and our smiles are the same. She has her father's nose, straight and lean, whereas mine slants up at the end in a way that my dad used to call a 'ski jump' when I was a kid.

'Age?' I prompt, finger hovering over the appropriate box on the electronic form.

'Thirty-six.'

At least he's answering. I had expected him to prevaricate.

'Previous treatment history?'

His eyes narrow, and I know he's fighting an urge to tell me that this isn't 'treatment' either. 'None.'

'I see.' I tap 'nil' on the screen, then lift my attention to him once more. And freeze. He's watching me unapologetically, taking advantage of the fact I'm distracted by the form, and his eyes are roaming over me as though I'm a painting on display in a gallery.

My skin prickles with goosebumps.

Noah Moore is dangerous.

He has all the markers I have trained myself to avoid—he is rough and arrogant, ruthless and feral—and yet I stare at him for a moment, our eyes locked, and a surge of something forbidden rampages through my system. For the first time in five years, a slick of desire heats my blood, warming me from the inside out. I thought I'd never feel desire again after Aaron. I unmistakably feel it now.

'Can I get you something to drink, folks?' The waitress stands beside me and I flick my phone off automatically, discreetly hiding any information she might otherwise have seen.

'Piccolo latte,' I say.

'Nothing,' Noah says with a shake of his head. I frown. He suggested we meet for coffee and yet apparently has decided he won't drink one.

'Why are you here, Mr Moore?'

'Is that *you* asking, or your form?'

My smile is tight. 'Both. It will save us time if we cut to the chase.'

He makes a slow, drawled *tsk*ing sound. 'But where's the fun in that, Holly?'

He rolls his tongue around my name, making it sound like the sexiest word in the English language. 'Do you find this fun, Noah?' I return his challenge, inflecting his name with a hint of huskiness. I see it hit its mark. His eyes widen slightly, his pupils heavy and dark, and speculation colours his features.

'No.' It's over, though. He's sullen and scathing once more.

'You didn't want anything to drink?' I say when the waitress returns with mine.

'Don't think this place serves my kind of drink,' he drawls, and I surmise he's referring to alcohol.

'Do you drink every day?'

'Some days,' he says with a lift of his broad shoulders. 'Some nights.'

'Is that why you asked to meet me?' I prompt. 'Do you think you have a drinking problem?'

His laugh is short and sharp. 'If I say yes, can we end this charade and both go home?'

'No one's forcing you to be here. It's just a "conversation", remember?'

He looks at me with barely concealed impatience and I am curious as to the reason for that.

'You work mainly with veterans,' he continues, and the knowledge that he's researched me does something strange to my gut.

It shouldn't. Most people research a doctor like me before making an appointment. There are myriad specialties amongst psychologists, countless ways to practise what we do. For Noah Moore to be here, he must know that I'm his best shot at help.

He's still researching me, though, in a way. Interviewing me before deciding if he wants to commit to a treatment protocol.

I think of the awards that line the walls of my office. They're just shiny statues, but to me they mean so much more. I can remember all my patients. The hurts in their eyes, the traumas of their souls. Those awards are the acknowledgement that I have helped some of them.

'I work with people who need me,' I say, returning my gaze to Noah's face. 'People who need help.'

'And you think I'm one of them?' There's fierce rejection in the very idea.

'You called me.'

He presses his lips together. 'This is a waste of fucking time.'

It takes more than a curse word to make me blush, though Noah Moore curses in a way that is uniquely interesting, drawing out the *U*.

I don't react as I want to. To be fair to myself, it's been a *long* time since I've felt anything for a guy and suddenly all of me is responding to all of him; my cells are reverberating on every level. 'You're free to leave.'

His anger is directed at me. Resentment too. It reminds me of the way he reacted minutes earlier when I told him no one was forcing him to be here and he simmered with that same angry rejection.

My mind ponders this as I sip my coffee. Our eyes are locked over the rim and my pulse ratchets up another notch. His eyes drop to my breasts and I feel an instantaneous zing of awareness. My nipples harden against the fabric of my bra and my stomach squeezes. I press my knees together under the table.

I'm used to this kind of attention. I've dealt with

it all my life. I'm on the short side, slim with breasts that are out of proportion to my small frame. They seemed to grow almost overnight when I was only twelve.

It's one of the reasons I wear dresses like this. Plain colour, dark, thick, demure. It falls to my knees and to my wrists, and the neckline is high. I'm not ashamed of my figure, but I don't want the nickname I had just out of university to catch on. 'The Sexy Shrink' is hardly the business pedigree I seek.

'I'm here now.' He shrugs as though he doesn't care, but I know otherwise. I know because it's my job to read people and I'm good at it, and I know because I have a sixth sense that's firing like crazy in my gut. 'Might as well let you sell yourself to me. Go on. Work your magic.'

I fight the urge to tell him there is no such thing as magic when it comes to trauma therapy. It takes hard work, long hours and dedication from both patient and physician. I'm willing to put in the hard yards, but is he?

I come back to the suspicion I have that he feels compelled to be meeting with me. *Obliged* might be a better word. Like he 'has' to go through with this appointment, not because he 'wants' to heal.

Usually, I would follow a more traditional form of approach to tease the answers out, but Noah Moore is not going to respond to traditional therapeutic means. It's why he insisted we meet here, in a coffee shop, rather than my office. I lace my fingers together, leaning forward slightly, elbows propped on the table. 'I get the feeling you're here against your will.'

'Yeah,' he grunts. 'Didn't you see the guy with the gun to my head when I walked in?' He laughs it off.

'You seem reluctant to accept my help,' I say softly. 'You keep stressing that this isn't an appointment, that we're just "talking". You refused to come to my office, because you feel safer in a neutral setting like this café. And yet while I've said you may leave, you're choosing to stay.'

There's a wariness that steals over him at having been called out. Good. Unsettling him is going to be crucial here. 'You think anyone could force me to do what I don't want?'

It's a good point. Noah Moore, even without the billions in the bank, is a man who would be impossible to intimidate. He is brawn, brains and beauty, all in one.

'You tell me.'

He expels a sigh. 'I contacted you, didn't I?'

'That doesn't mean someone wasn't holding a gun to your head.' I force another smile. 'Metaphorically speaking.'

He holds my eyes for a fraction too long and then reaches forward, wrapping his fingers around one of the water glasses the waitress brought and sipping from it. I wait while he swallows, impatience breeding frustration in my gut.

I'm not used to this degree of resistance. A little, sure. It comes with the territory. But generally there's some sense of apology for it. People know that my time is worth a lot of money. That usually encourages a compulsion to cooperate, even if only to a small degree.

'In a manner of speaking.'

It's an admission I don't expect and I can't suppress an outward display of surprise. My lips, painted a bright red, form an 'o'. I cover it as quickly as I can, but his grimace shows that he saw my response. Understands my surprise.

'Well, I'm glad.' Glad we are getting somewhere. 'In my experience, therapy works best when I have a willing participant on my hands.'

I swear I don't mean anything by it, but the speculation that grows on his handsome face shows he's analysing my words for a hidden meaning. For a sensual insinuation that should have stayed buried deep in the recesses of my brain.

Fortunately for me, he doesn't capitalise on the error, though he leans forward when he speaks so I catch a hint of his fragrance. Woody and alpine, masculine and strong. 'Are you saying you're not able to help me?'

A glimmer of disappointment pings in my chest cavity. Did I want him to volley back my unintentional double entendre? To tell me he'd be very willing to be in my hands?

He's looking at me, waiting for an answer. For almost the first time in my career, I'm struck mute. I run my eyes over his face, so handsome, and wonder at the secrets he's hiding. At the life he's lived that caused him to phone me. At the fact he's making me want to throw caution to the wind and make him mine.

'No,' I say finally. 'I think I can help you. If you want to be my patient.'

'I don't have time to be a patient,' he says, and it's so scathing that a shiver runs down my spine.

'Well, unfortunately, it takes time,' I point out firmly. 'There's no quick fix for whatever has led you to me.'

'You're confident saying that when you don't have the faintest idea why I organised this meeting?'

'Yes.' I glare at him. 'You know why, Noah?' God help me, the taste of his name on my lips is addictive. 'Because I do this all day, every day. People like you walk into my life, wearing your issues like a coat that only I can see.'

He narrows his eyes.

'It's in the set of your shoulders, the depths of your eyes. I see it.' I lean back and feel my heart pounding hard against my forearms. 'Trauma isn't something that can be drunk away. Nor is it something I can wave my magic wand and cure. The only way to get beyond it is to work through it. It's not a pleasant process, I won't lie to you. Sometimes the healing can feel worse than the original pain. But I can promise you that if you don't work through your problem you're going to come unstuck one day. I wonder if that hasn't already happened. Is that why you're here?'

'This is a load of bullshit.'

I can't help it. The woman might be hotter than

Hades, but she's spouting psychobabble crap out of that beautiful red mouth of hers and it makes my skin crawl.

I hate this shit. I've heard it all before. If it hadn't been for Gabe's ultimatum, I'd never have arranged to meet her. But I'd do just about anything for Gabe, even without the threat to stand me down from the company while I *'sort myself the hell out'*—his words. I don't want to see a shrink, and I have no intention of seeing Dr Scott-Leigh—hell, I don't want to see anyone. I'm going through the motions, that's all. But I didn't come here expecting her to get under my skin like she is. I didn't expect to find her utterly fascinating.

'I'm sorry you feel that way,' she murmurs, and I wonder how *she'd* feel if I were to slip my hands under her dress, finding the softness of her thighs, the heat between her legs.

I drink the water again, thinking I really should have chosen a bar instead of this busy central London café. I replace the water glass and prop my elbows on the table, enjoying the way her eyes flare a little wider as my body looms closer, before she tamps down on the response and is all businesslike professionalism again.

Is there a Mr Dr Scott-Leigh?

No wedding ring, and you'd bet her husband would be smart enough to make sure she wore one. With a body like hers, she's no doubt got a never-ending queue of men at her door. Hell, if she were mine, I'd chain her to my bed. At least until the novelty wore off.

My lips twist at the missed opportunity. Yes, I definitely should have suggested a bar after-hours. Somewhere I could actually do something about the fantasies I've had about her since she walked in, aching to dispel all professionalism and aloofness.

I heave out a sigh, returning my attention to her face. It's a face that is objectively beautiful. Huge blue eyes, a nose that can only be described as cute, with a neck that is elegant. Her hair is as fair as sunlight and it's plaited in a way that tells me she's trying to tame herself but, in contradiction to that, she's wearing little red earrings that I see now are Christmas gifts with glittering green ribbon.

She's what my nine-year-old self would have called *fancy*. All perfectly groomed and sweet-smelling, flawless and poised in a way that a ballerina would envy.

I know lots of women now, fancy and not. Fancy women tend to throw themselves at me, and it doesn't matter if their lingerie is high-end or from a supermarket, they're all just as eager to strip it off their bodies at the smallest encouragement.

They all scream with pleasure just the same.

She's watching me patiently, waiting for me to speak, and I can only guess it's a tactic taken from Therapy for Beginners. But it has little to no impact on me.

I watch back, my expression impassive, my lips curled with the derision I am famed for.

'Well.' She concedes defeat by speaking first. 'I suppose we can always talk about the weather.'

'Or we could talk about you.'

'Me?' I've surprised her. Again. Her lips open into a circle that is distractingly erotic. 'I'm not on the agenda. Sorry.'

Her manner tells me she's anything but apologetic.

'So I'm supposed to bare my soul and you give me nothing?'

Her smile is tight. She's pissed off. It's the first time I realise that I like riling her up; definitely not the last. 'Well, if you decide you want to undertake therapy, then I give you peace of mind in due course,' she murmurs.

But she's got no idea what ghosts run through me; what shadows fill my being. I am a wraith of my past's creation.

'Holly, I highly fucking doubt that.'

CHAPTER TWO

HER HAIR IS longer than I realised. And so much softer. Up close as I am, it smells like vanilla and honey.

I know it's a dream but, for the first time in a month, a woman has chased *her* from my mind and I am free from the cursed hauntings of my past. I clutch at the fine threads of this dream, refusing to let it slip from my mind.

'I love it when you kiss me,' Holly murmurs, her lips a perfect red. I reach for her, pulling her to me, my hands large against her fine frame, my fingers splayed wide on her hips.

Her body is pliant at my touch. Easy to control.

Surrendered completely to me, and what I can give her.

I yank her—hard—against my chest, enjoying the soft exhalation that brushes my jaw. Her breasts feel so much better than I imagined. They're firm and soft at the same time, so big and round. I lift a hand and palm one, my thumb brushing over her nipple, my fingers possessive and demanding.

She looks at me on a tidal wave of confusion and uncertainty. This is new and different and she doesn't know how to respond.

She doesn't need to worry.

I know enough for both of us.

I lift her easily—she's light and I'm strong—and wrap her legs around my waist. I don't know how I want her but, God, I know I need her. Her dress is floaty, it moves easily over her hips, granting me the access I need. Even though it's my dream and I should be able to control this shit, she's wearing underwear—a barrier I don't want.

Her hands wrap around my neck, drawing my head closer to hers, and she's kissing me, her tongue seeking mine, duelling with me, her eyes swept closed against the assault of this passion.

But I don't want to kiss her.

Kissing is romance and reward—fucking is not. Fucking is passion and need—a primal, physical act that is over when it ends.

I break my mouth free and stride across the room. I don't know where we are. Dreams are funny like that. I push her back against a wall and, with her weight supported by the wall and my hips, I rip her dress open at the front. She's not wearing a bra— thank you, dream gods—and I crush my mouth to her breast, rolling my tongue over her nipple until she whimpers, and then I move to the other, this time pressing it with my teeth so her back arches forward and her fingernails dig into my shoulders.

I'm naked now—in a dream, clothes are capable of simply disappearing—and I slide her panties aside with my fingers, my eyes mocking her, teasing her, as I nudge my cock to her entrance, hitching myself at her seam, feeling her moist heat before sliding deep inside her.

She groans, a sound that comes from the base of her throat, and I laugh.

'This is just the beginning, baby,' I promise.

And because I'm pursued by demons that seek to punish me, I wake up at that moment, sweat beading my brow and a cock that's harder than stone. I drop my hand to it, rubbing my fingers up and down my length, curving my palm over my thickness.

It's no good.

Having dream-fucked Holly, I need the real thing.

I reach for my phone and check the time. It's midnight. I've been asleep only forty minutes. For Christ's sake.

I scroll through my calendar, going back to Tuesday last week when I met Dr Scott-Leigh in that café.

Her contact details are in the appointment file. I click on her email address:

Holly,
I need to see you again. Tomorrow.

I consult my calendar once more—these sleepless nights are playing havoc with my short-term memory.

Four p.m. is my only free time.
NM

I drop the phone to my bed and push up. I dress quickly, or as quickly as I can when my dick is like a tent pole, and throw back a tumbler of straight vodka, then call one of my drivers—there are four on rotation.

Graeme is on the roster.

He's probably the least able to hide his disapproval of my lifestyle, and that gives me a perverse sense of amusement.

'Where to, sir?' he asks without meeting my eyes. Did I wake him? Tough. It's his job, after all.

'Mon More,' I say, naming a club in Putney. Julianne has haunted my dreams for a month and now Holly is taking over. The only thing I know is I can escape them both in a loud bar with free-flowing booze.

It's not like I've been thinking of him since our appointment. At least, not only of him. I've had a lot else on my mind. Like working out how I'm going to make a Virgin Mary costume for Ivy before her Christmas concert and when I'll have time to help her with the gingerbread house she's determined to give her grandmother this year.

No, I've been far too busy to think only of Noah Moore.

Except at night, when my head hits the pillow and I shut my eyes. Then, all I can see is his face, his beautiful, exquisite, tortured face, his haunted eyes and sexy mouth, his body that I want to throw myself at, to curl up against, to be held and comforted by. He makes me want to surrender to his touch, to be safe within his arms.

I'm smart enough to know how absurd that is, but if I can't have the real thing, I should at least be able to satisfy myself with the fantasy. Right?

I've had plenty on my plate this week but, when I arrive at my office this morning, fate seems to have conspired to throw Noah Moore at my feet.

His email detonates in my consciousness like a charge. It's barely civil and it's sure as hell not how appointments are made. I can't even say for sure how he got my email address—it's not on my business cards and I don't routinely welcome patients to communicate with me directly.

There has to be a divide between my work and my home life. That's the way this works best.

Not for Noah Moore, though. I'm surprised to find a wry smile has rubbed across my lips when I scan my calendar for availability and none of the usual clinical detachment chills my emotions.

My day is full, and yet if I were to swap my one o'clock for twelve o'clock and miss lunch, I could move my four o'clock forward and make time for Noah.

I swallow past the doubts.

I can't say why, but I am compelled to answer, and I am driven by a desperate need to see him again.

I send a quick reply:

Noah,
I can meet with you again, but it will have to be in my office. Four p.m. works. Don't be late—I have another appointment directly after.
Dr Scott-Leigh

I send it, pleased with the fact I've kept it so formal, pleased with the way my email doesn't, in any way, shape or form, convey how utterly devastatingly sexy I think he is.

I'm proud and pleased as I load up the news browser I always read before starting work and Beatrice strides in with a coffee and bagel.

'Morning, Holly,' she says with a smile and leaves again without waiting for a response.

I love this woman so much.

She knows how desperately I need my sacred ten minutes without interruptions and I so appreciate her giving me that. Only now my brain is *full* of interruptions. Questions about Noah, his habits, his problems, his intentions, his needs.

I want to know him and I want to help him.

And I can't be at my most effective, therapeutically, if other issues, like my raging desire and the fact I haven't slept with a guy in over five years, take over my brainpower.

I employ mindfulness, breathing in deeply, exhaling slowly, counting beats and blanking my mind until I feel more like myself again.

But it's a godawful day.

I feel like I'm operating at half my usual capacity.

I drag my brain through appointments, eat a muesli bar between my two and three o'clocks and then, after my three o'clock leaves, make a quick phone call to the hospital to check on a patient of mine.

When I disconnect the call, Beatrice buzzes through that Noah Moore has arrived.

My pulse leaps immediately, my heart thumps hard against my chest and my fingers begin to shake. I cast a quick glance at the compact I keep in my top drawer, run fingers over hair I have today left loose and stand to greet him.

I didn't know Noah Moore would book an appointment—it's not for him that I've worn this outfit but, the second he enters the room, his green eyes skim over me and I get a kick of satisfaction at the speculation I see in his eyes.

Holy hell.

What am I doing?

I have no business feeling all warm and tingly because he's staring at the way my leather skirt hugs my hips. It's high-waisted—it comes up to my belly button—and I'm wearing a gold cashmere sweater tucked into it. It's an outfit I would describe as perfectly professional but, the way his eyes light on my silhouette, I feel like a centrefold.

'Mr Moore.' My tone is cool. Good. Cool is good. 'Please, take a seat.'

He strides into the room, looking dishevelled in a way that is sexy but that I have every reason to believe is the result of a sleepless night.

He throws his large frame into one of the chairs,

his legs spread wide, his hands resting on his powerful thighs. Today he's wearing blue jeans and a long-sleeved top.

'Holly—' his lips flicker into a smile, but it's over in a millisecond '—nice to see you again.'

I compress my lips. Normally, patients would express gratitude at the fact I'd squeezed them in under short notice, but not Noah.

'Let's get started,' I clip. 'How are you?'

'Are you asking out of interest or as a doctor?'

My pulse ratchets up and I have to dig my fingernails into my palms to stop the guilty blush from creeping over my cheeks. 'As a doctor.' The words drip with ice.

His smile suggests he doesn't believe me. Crap.

'Then let me remind you; I haven't agreed to see you professionally.'

I frown. 'Haven't you? I would have thought that's just what you did when you asked for an appointment.'

'No.' It's cryptic. I leave it alone for now and reach for a pen. There will be time to discuss the semantics of how he wants to proceed.

'You were up late last night.' He arches a brow in silent enquiry, so I rush to explain. 'You emailed at midnight.'

He nods, dragging a hand through his hair, but says nothing. It's like pulling teeth!

'Are you always up so late?' I ask.

'Late? Midnight?'

I refuse to be embarrassed by him. 'Yes.'

'Yeah,' he grunts, and his eyes are wary. He's withdrawing from me, pulling back. Something about my line of questioning is hitting on an issue that is renewing his trauma.

It's nothing you would be able to tell, unless you had experience with this. Outwardly, Noah is every bit the charming, sexy bad boy he's renowned for.

I smile, lean back in my chair and drop the pen onto the notepad. 'It's cold today.'

A comment that surprises him. It makes him wary; his eyes skip to mine and a frown moves on his face. He doesn't say anything.

'Do you have plans for Christmas?'

'Christmas?' It's practically a sneer. 'Christmas is weeks away.'

I nod. 'It'll be here before you know it.' My eyes drift to the picture once more, a smiling Ivy, and I feel somewhat more centred.

'Do *you* have plans for Christmas?' he volleys back, his expression tight as he watches me with every fibre of his being.

I wouldn't normally answer—the question is too personal—and yet I hear myself say, a smile softening the words, 'Not really. Just a small family celebration this year.'

His eyes drop to my fingers. He's wondering what 'family' means to me. I don't elaborate on that score. That's common sense as well as training. Ivy is not a part of this world. She's mine—and she's all that is sweet and innocent.

'I make a pudding—my grandmother's recipe—

we sing carols. The usual. Do you have any Christmas traditions?'

He knows I'm relaxing him and yet perhaps he also knows he has to give me at least something to justify the fact I've moved my schedule around to see him today. 'Yeah. Getting hammered.'

I arch a brow.

'It's just another day for me, Doc.'

'No family?' I prompt.

I get the strangest sense that he wants to say something. That the temptation to open up is pressing against his back, pushing him forward, but then he just shakes his head sideways once. A curt dismissal.

It's normal for patients to clam up around me, but I don't generally take it personally. Intense frustration zips through me now and, against my usual therapeutic practices, I say, 'Noah, I really want to help you and I think you want that too, but you're giving me nothing to work with.'

He stares at me belligerently and I stand up, hoping that will dispel some of the frustrated energy that's firing through me. I move towards the window, looking out at London, and I don't know if I'm imagining it but heat warms my spine as though he's still watching me.

I habitually deal with soldiers who've come back from war zones—men and women who've witnessed and perpetrated unimaginable crimes. People who have done what no human should ever have to do, who have seen first-hand the bleakness and despair of utter destruction. I understand their hauntedness and I know how to help with it, generally. Every patient is different, but at least I'm operating from the same wheelhouse. Not now, not with Noah. I need to tease information out of him gently. But I do need to get *some* information. Without it, I'm flying blind.

'When did you decide to seek help?'

He expels a harsh breath that has me turning slowly to face him. I was right. He's watching me. Blood jolts through my system as though each cell has been subjected to an electrical shock.

'Noah.' I say the word quietly but with a firmness that shows I'm serious. 'I moved my day around for this. Are you wasting my time?'

He seems to withdraw from me even further. Not in the way many of my patients do, by becoming visibly upset or distant. Now he is looking at me as though he wants to eat me—and my tummy is in knots.

He stands and moves towards me. Every single fibre of my being is vibrating on high alert, but I don't withdraw. Maintaining control of the session is vital. He is right beside me, at least a foot taller than me, and close enough that if either of us were to sway forward slightly we would be touching. Crazy thought! Where did that come from?

He looks down at me, so dominant, so strong and somehow so broken.

I stare at him for a long time, waiting for him to speak, determined not to break first.

Finally, his throat bobs as he swallows. 'I don't

need therapy,' he says gruffly, as though I've dragged him here kicking and screaming.

'I see.' I nod, not wanting to mock his assertion, nor to question why he emailed at midnight if that's the case.

'I just…' He drags a hand through his hair and shakes his head. 'This is fucking ridiculous.'

'What is it?' I urge and, damn it, I step closer. Stupid, stupid move, because now there's barely a whisper between us and I can't surrender the strength of my position by pulling away. If I do, he'll know how he affects me, and that would be a disaster.

'I'm not sleeping.' He turns away from me and takes a step towards my desk, pressing his fingers against the wooden corner.

It is highly irregular for me to have people on this side of my office and I feel the invasion of Noah in every way. This is my space—my personal space. But the moment he's started to open up to me, I can't make him feel at fault. I move towards him and put a gentle yet professional hand on his elbow.

Tension is radiating from his bulky frame, as though this small admission of a perceived weakness has offended every iota of his hyper-masculinity. He flinches when I touch him and glares down at me.

Not with anger, though.

The desire that has me hostage is of a mutual kind. I feel him shift and it is all the confirmation I need that this crazy, dark lust surges through us both. My fingertips are still pressed lightly to his elbow. I nod towards the chair he'd been sitting in.

'Please, sit down.' It's a quiet murmur and for a moment I think he's not going to do as I say. He continues to stare at me and I find myself staring back, wondering what it would be like for those lips of his to drop to mine.

Temptation is thick in the air. I could push up onto the tips of my toes and kiss him... Would it really be so wrong? I step back just as he reaches for me, his fingers curling into my hair, wrapping it around his big masculine fist. 'Is this real?'

The question catches me utterly off guard. I take in a deep breath that barely reaches my lungs and stare at him with a sense of helplessness. I have a thing for bad boys, remember, yet I've never known anyone quite like Noah Moore.

I force myself to remember several things, and to remember them quickly. He is waging a battle against demons I don't yet comprehend; he has come to me for help.

And I don't do this.

I don't let men, no matter how sexy, make my pulse race and my knees knock.

That kind of thing was a million years ago for me.

'Is this real?'

The words are husky from his mouth and all my certainties and good intentions quiver inside me.

'What?'

Step away, step away! my brain is shouting at me, but I don't move. Instead, I swallow and his eyes drop to my mouth, then lower, to the column of my throat, watching the convulsive movement, before resuming their fascination with my lips.

Moist heat slicks between my legs and I clamp my lips together. My nipples press against the bra I'm wearing, little arrows darting through me from each hardened nub, radiating heat through my body. There is a fine tremble that passes over my spine.

'This. Your hair.' And his fist moves higher, towards my head, so his palm curves around my skull, his fingers still tight in the blonde lengths. He angles my head upwards and our eyes are locked. Our bodies are separated by inches and yet I feel the essence of him pulse into me, throbbing inside my gut. This is, hands down, the most intimacy I've ever felt with a man.

'Yes.' It's a word weakened by desire and my temptation to surrender to it completely. 'It's real.'

He nods but doesn't otherwise move. If I don't do something, anything, to grab control of this situation, I'm going to be in serious trouble.

'Noah.' I clear my throat and step away. For a second he doesn't relinquish his hold on my hair, and then he drops his hand to his side. His expression is knowing. As though he understands that I am now fleeing what we just shared.

'Please, sit down.' The words lack conviction and yet he complies, moving back to his seat and owning it with his body. I don't sit behind my desk, though. Instead, I cross to the other side of it and perch on the edge, crossing my legs at the ankle.

It's dangerous because I'm quite close to him, but

I feel we need to maintain some of the connection he just established.

'You're not sleeping?' I prompt softly.

'No, Doc.'

'Not at all?' I frown, reaching around behind me for my pad and pen.

He shrugs, like it doesn't matter. 'I sleep a bit. Ten minutes. Twenty.'

'Then what?' I write *10...20* in the corner of my paper.

'I wake up.' The words are droll, bordering on sarcastic. My cheeks warm, but I dip my head forward to write a note.

'Do you have dreams?'

The wry sarcasm fades from his features. He focuses on a point behind me. 'No.'

Liar. I don't challenge him, though. It's too soon and, for the moment, he's made some admissions, which is a huge thing for a guy like Noah. I need him to trust me, and that's going to be a tough sell with him.

I scrawl *no dreams* and underscore it, which is my way of reminding myself that I suspect it's not the truth. 'Have there been any changes in your life-style recently?'

'Besides seeing you?' he says thoughtfully, his eyes shifting back to mine, all confident, charismatic, sexy bad boy again.

My heart leaps.

'I mean changes that could affect your sleep.'

'Oh, you sure affected my sleep last night.' The

words are so far from what I expect that I lose my mask for a moment and show my surprise. I'm sure my face must pale visibly, that he must see the way I react. My stomach swoops and, briefly, I allow temptation to cloud my clarity.

But only briefly.

I'm a professional. I need to remember that.

'Perhaps we need to try something new,' I say, my smile an attempt at coolness that I suspect I don't pull off.

He lifts a brow, obviously teasing. 'I'm game if you are.'

CHAPTER THREE

'I SET ASIDE a full hour, but I can already tell there's
no sense keeping you here that long.' She pushes
off the edge of the desk and walks back towards the
window. The afternoon light shimmers across her,
backlighting her in a way that makes her look like
an angel. A very sexy angel.

'Sick of me already, Holly?'

Her eyebrows knit together and I can see her cogs
turning, analysing me. This is one of the many reasons I like to hook up with women who've got a
drink or three under their belt. None of this psycho
mind-reading bullshit.

And Holly Scott-Leigh is, I suspect, very good
at this.

'You don't want to be here. And yet you came.'

'I was curious about where you worked,' I say
lamely. Stupidly. She's too smart to fall for that kind
of bullshit.

'So…' She lifts a hand to her thick blonde hair and
scrapes it back from her brow. A sign of frustration?
The action pulls her sweater across her breasts, and

everything inside me jerks. She speaks as though I haven't. 'We're going to do five questions.'

'Five questions?' That's easy. Relief is palpable.

'But…' She lifts her finger, her lips twitching with barely suppressed amusement. 'You have to answer me honestly, and promptly. No faffing about trying to make something up and no dodging the questions.'

I can hear my blood throbbing in my ears like a fucking tsunami. There's a high-pitched noise too, like air from a balloon being pinched to release.

There was one summer I spent with a family who used to surf. They took me out with them, taught me how to ride a board. There is an art to keeping your balance; it's a constant seduction. Every tiny movement shifts your power and one wrong breath may mean you tumble into the ocean.

If I allow Holly to have this power over me, she will roll me into the sea.

I won't let that happen.

I stand, my eyes pinning her to the spot so I see the effect I have on her. She tries to cover it, but you can't hide desire. Not really. There are markers that I have seen often enough to recognise easily now. Her cheeks flush along the ridge of bone, her pupils swell to cover almost her whole eye and her breathing is rasped, her chest moving up and down, so that her round breasts push forward. Jesus, that shirt sweater thing looks soft. My fingertips itch to reach out and touch it. To scrunch it against her skin, to feel her through the fabric.

I stand just a couple of inches away from her and

she keeps staring up at me, her big red lips parted, her eyes whispering seduction even when I know she's doing her best to hold the professional line.

I wonder how long she'll keep that up.

'On one condition.'

Her frown is infinitesimal. Her eyes drop to my lips and my gut jerks, wanting to pull me forward, begging me to kiss her.

Nah, not to kiss her, that's far too sweet a word for what I want to do. I want to pull her lower lip between my teeth, I want to push her back against that window, I want to fucking own her.

'What's that, Mr Moore?'

It's an attempt to put us back on a professional footing. Her own surfboard is tipping.

I lift a finger, touching her cheek lightly. She flinches with surprise and her eyes lift to mine slowly. She's in the water; it's threatening to consume her whole. 'For every one of your questions, you answer one of mine. Same rules.'

Her breath is soft, warm. I feel it on my inner wrist. Imagining it elsewhere on my body, I throb with heat and need.

'I told you last week.' The words are uneven. 'I'm not on the agenda.'

It's an intentional reproof. My smile shows amusement at her attempt to put up barriers. 'Oh, I think you are, Holly.' But I drop my hand and step backwards. 'Do we have a deal?'

She swallows, her throat bobbing. She's torn.

Drowning and trying not to—drowning and asking me to save her all at once.

'I suppose it's fair,' she says after a beat.

Fuck, yeah, it's fair. If she expects me to pour out my heart, then she'd better believe I want my pound of flesh along with it.

She nods, as if to reaffirm to herself that she's going to go through with this. 'Shall I start?'

I ignore the twisting in my gut. I've agreed to this and I'm not afraid of much, least of all having a fucking conversation.

She is, though. She weighs her words carefully, studying me as she thinks. Her eyes are crazy beautiful. Huge and bright blue with a dark black rim around the iris and flecks of black close to the pupil. She has a tiny scar above one brow—like a line about half a centimetre long. I want to run my tongue along it—the certainty that one day I will fills me like cement.

'Did you have a favourite toy as a child?'

Of all the questions I expect, it's not this. I laugh—a dry sound that cracks from my throat.

'No. My turn. Did you think about me after I left last week?'

Her eyes widen and her throat jerks as she swallows. Her gaze darts to a space on the wall behind me. 'Of course I did,' she says, the words thready and soft. She darts her tongue out, licking her lower lip. 'You're my client.'

'No, I'm not. So far, I'm just some man you know.'

My smile is wry and I lean closer, my words mocking. 'And you know that's not what I meant.'

'That's the question you asked,' she volleys back, fire and spirit firing in her eyes. 'My turn. What's your favourite thing to do?'

I stare at her for a second, a sense of discontent rifling through me. A hobby? She wants to know what my hobby is? I drop my head close to hers, and when I whisper it's right in her ear, low and soft. 'Fuck beautiful women.'

I pull away so I can see her reaction. She's looking at me with something close to pity, though, and that fires me up. 'My turn.' I skim her face thoughtfully, then purposely drop my eyes to her rack. Jesus Christ, they're great breasts. 'When did you last get laid?'

Another swallow. 'Noah.' The word is half scold, half plea.

I shake my head, my eyes locking her to the spot and her intention. 'No lying.'

The room pulses heavily with silence.

'A long time ago.'

'That's not a precise answer,' I push, a thrill of something like triumph turning my blood to lava.

She expels a breath. An angry breath. 'Five years ago,' she snaps and then pulls herself together with effort.

'What's your mother's name?'

I don't bat an eyelid—not so much as a blink. 'Alison Parker.' She might have birthed me, but calling her a 'mother' is a step too far. I've spent thirty-six years wishing her name wasn't even in my mind, let alone her blood in my veins.

'Are you close to her?'

I shake my head. 'It's my turn, remember.'

A look of panic colours her spectacular eyes. She moves away to grab a glass of water from her desk. I follow her automatically and my eyes drop to the picture to the right of her. A little child, so exactly like Holly that it must surely be a relation, sits in a frame. 'Who's that?'

She looks at me and catches me looking at the frame. For a second I think she's not going to answer, or that she might lie, but then she shrugs. 'My daughter.' Her hand lifts betrayingly to a necklace she wears. A locket?

'Are you close to your mother?'

I was expecting this question. 'No.'

'You don't like her?'

I move my body closer—she braces her hands on the desk and looks up at me, and the air cracks like a whip as tension tightens between us.

'No.' Her expression flickers as she analyses this. 'Have you thought about me, other than professionally?'

Once more her eyes dart away from me. Such a giveaway gesture for a woman as smart as she is. I would have expected her to have a better poker face. 'I…' A very faint peach colour spreads over her cheeks.

'It's a yes or no question, Doc.' I brace my hands on the outside of hers, bending my body forward so that

I've effectively caged her on her desk. She closes her eyes and inhales deeply, drawing in a breath like she wants to draw me with it. When she speaks, it's with a courage I admire. A strength and determination—a fearlessness.

'Yes.'

I tighten all over and it takes every ounce of my willpower not to push her back on the desk and rip that leather skirt off, to make her mine.

'You weren't raised by your parents, were you?'

She's still got her eyes closed, but the question is no less cutting or incisive for that.

If she were looking at me, she might have seen how off-kilter it momentarily knocks me. But I recover quickly. She has asked the right question but phrased it wrong. *Who raised you?* might have been better. That would have forced me to document the myriad foster homes I was passed through, or to explain that no one really took the time to raise me—that I was left to raise myself.

'No.' She looks at me now and, with her eyes fixed on mine, I move so close that my lips are almost brushing hers. 'Do you want to fuck me?'

She gasps and, before she answers, I do it. I do what I've wanted to do since I first saw that perfect Cupid's bow. I put my mouth to hers, lift my hand to the back of her head, wrap my fingers in her hair and invade her with my tongue. She makes a moaning noise and then she's kissing me back, her tongue clashing with mine; one leg lifts and hooks around my waist, holding me locked to her, my cock pressed hard against her cunt. She tilts her head back to give me all the access I want and I fucking plunder her. I kiss her to punish her for making me talk about my fucking mother. I kiss her because I can't not.

And she kisses me back.

But she hasn't answered my question and I want her to. It's not enough to feel her wants—I want her to own them. To confess them to me. I have seen her courage, her spirit—but still I want more. I want to hear her be brave for me.

So I pull away but, before she can pretend she wasn't affected by what we shared, I thrust my cock against her, grinding my hips, and she moans, lifts her fingers to my chest and digs them in. She tilts her head back again.

Hell, if she hasn't been screwed in five years, I could probably make her come right now. To test my theory, I push against her again and she says my name, low and soft, huskily, a beg, a plea.

'Noah...' Just a whisper, but so heavy with need and desire. 'God, Noah...'

I laugh low in my throat and she looks at me with abject confusion, but then I drop my hand to her breast, finding her nipple and flicking it.

She shakes all over, her body trembling near mine. I can't tell you how much I want to finish this. To make her beg for me right here, right now. She's so close. I don't think she knows what day of the week it is.

Yeah, I want to fuck her, but here would be too

rushed. Such a waste of an opportunity to really make her ache for me…

'Do.' I pull her earlobe between my teeth and roll my tongue over it. She whimpers.

'You.' I scrunch her sweater in my fist and lift it out of her skirt, feeling its softness in my palm before running my hands over her naked side. She makes a guttural noise of pleasure.

'Want.' I push it higher still, until my fingertips touch the lace sides of her bra and then nudge beneath it so the ball of my thumb is on the underside of her sweet, rounded breast.

'Me.' Her leg that's wrapped around my waist jerks me closer, telling me not to keep her waiting. I laugh again, a sound of appreciation for a woman who knows what she wants.

'To.' I grip her ankle behind my back then run my hand along her calf. Holy shit, she feels so much better than I'd imagined. So soft and smooth and feminine. I pause in the hollow of her knee, watching her fevered face as her eyes darken and her cheeks glow. I run my fingers higher then, slowly, until I reach her inner thigh and she moans, once again digging her fingers into my shoulder and arching her back.

'Fuck…' I shove the elastic edge of her underpants aside and, with my eyes holding hers, mocking her for the fact she tried to pretend this wasn't happening between us, I nudge a finger inside her warm, throbbing heart. She's so goddamned wet I feel a drop of my own cum spill out, but I don't stop.

I push deeper inside her and she whimpers, her fingers now scratching into me.

'You?'

She blinks, glaring at me for a second, and then she nods, just a simple tiny movement that is the release I crave.

Fuck, I needed that. I move my finger around and her breathing gets hotter. I pull my other hand away, but with no intention of ignoring that delicious breast. I drop my mouth to it, taking her nipple into my mouth through the bra, and I use my free hand to jerk her skirt up higher and then one thumb rubs against her clit as my finger moves inside her.

She is mine within a minute.

She cries out so hard and loud that I have to give up her beautiful breast and claim her mouth instead, if only to silence her. I absorb her scream and cries as she orgasms around my finger. Her pleasure saturates the room, vibrating around us heavily—it's heavenly.

It's a start, but it's nowhere near enough…

'It needs to go higher, Mummy.'

'Up here?' I hook the ornament across and press it into the branch carefully.

'Nooo…' She sighs with exasperation that defies belief for a four-year-old. Ivy's mannerisms are captivating, except when they're frustrating. 'Way up there!'

I can still feel tingles in my body, unfamiliar and heavenly all at once, throbs of pleasure like little waves that rock me out of nowhere.

I blink and see the way he was *afterwards*. After he'd pulled his finger out of me and straightened my skirt with almost clinical detachment, stepping away from me and nodding, like I was an item on his 'to-do' list and he'd 'to-do-ed' the heck out of me.

'I'll come back tomorrow.' That was all. No 'What time suits?' or 'We should talk.' A directive rather than a question—a decision. A firm instruction.

And I'd nodded! What the hell had I been thinking? I should have told him no. That we couldn't see one another again.

I should have told him how wrong we'd been to do…*that*. Oh, God. My insides are knotted. I know that when I slip away from Ivy and take a bath, my underwear will be wet with proof of my desire, that my body has been changed by Noah's possession and he didn't so much as show me his chest.

I can't see him again. I must see him again. I'm so torn. I draw in a deep breath. I know I can't see him *professionally*.

Our relationship isn't formalised—he hasn't filled anything out. I haven't billed him. I sweep my eyes shut. That's a technicality and I know it. But if I spell it out to him, making sure he understands that I can no longer have him in my office, no longer treat him as a patient, does that leave me ethically free to see him in other ways? And am I really okay with that?

'Mummy!' Ivy stamps her foot. 'You're just staring into space!'

'Sorry,' I mumble, turning my attention back to the job at hand.

I loop the ornament on the second-highest branch and, apparently satisfied, Ivy nods before reaching into the box and carefully unwrapping the next one along. Ivy has always been very careful. Even as a one-year-old she would take care when doing anything. She has always eaten neatly, used a napkin to wipe her fingers, placed her shoes side by side at the front door. She is the definition of particular.

In other words, the opposite to me.

And her father, come to think of it.

I have always thought certain areas were black and white, but this is one with many, many shades of grey. Noah came to me for help and, though our relationship isn't that of patient and doctor, I worry about how this development might affect him. And, yes, I worry about how it will affect me.

'What's this one?' She wrinkles her nose—so like Aaron's—and passes me the ornament.

I force myself back to Ivy, the tree, and try to ignore the fuzzy worries on the periphery of my brain. 'Ah. I made this when I was ten years old.' I stare at the little decoration, the small foam ball that I painstakingly stuck fabric to, then dotted with sequins. I remember sitting on the floor of my parents' lounge, my knees covered in a blanket, my hair long around my shoulders, determined to make the decoration according to the instructions. 'It took quite a long time.'

'Really?' Ivy probably doesn't mean to sound so scathing and I can't help but laugh.

'Yes, dearest.' I push the ornament into the branches and wait for another decoration.

'Ebony James says it's too early to put up the tree,' she says, her eyes darting to mine and then flicking away, as if afraid of the sacrilegious assertion she's just repeated.

My smile is kind. 'Everyone has different traditions. Perhaps in Ebony James's house they put their tree up later.'

'Do most people put their tree up now?'

I shrug. 'They're up in shops, aren't they?'

Ivy nods but looks far from convinced.

'Why shouldn't we enjoy the tree for a month? Christmas only comes around once a year and it's such a waste not to enjoy it fully. Don't you think?'

'I suppose so.' Her smile is more genuine now.

She goes back to unboxing ornaments and I go back to hanging them, but my mind keeps threatening to drag me back to Noah, my desk, my office and that pleasure.

Decorating the tree is one of my favourite pastimes. We have a real tree, but of course it's too early to have a chopped tree, so ours is potted. I water it every few days to keep it fresh and then, after Christmas, once it's denuded of decorations once more, I put it on a trolley and push it back into our small courtyard garden. There it remains all year round, dormant and hibernating, waiting for its time to shine—literally—with the strings of lights we weave through its greenery.

I love doing this, and even more so now that Ivy is old enough to join in with me, but I'm barely in the moment.

By the time Ivy is in bed, and I have had dinner, I am itching to crawl between my sheets and surrender to the dreams of him that I know will follow.

I check my emails quickly first—a habit I've fallen into since having Ivy and needing to do some of my work from home—and his name is the first I see.

Noah Moore—Bright Spark Inc

I click into it faster than I can believe.

It's a short email. Just a few words. But they rob me of breath and make my knees sag.

I can smell you on my hand. Tomorrow I want to taste you.

CHAPTER FOUR

HIS EMAIL SPINS through my mind all day. I hear the words he'd written, voiced in his inimitable accent. Australian with a dash of arrogance and a bucket-load of don't-give-a-fuck. I guess having squillions of pounds could give someone that attitude, but I don't think that's the beginning and end of it.

I'd put money on Noah having been like this for a long time—before having money and commercial success. I think his arrogance is stitched into his being; every cell of his body is made up of the same.

But my lines of deduction are now very blurry. As a therapist, I would have the ability to look beneath that arrogance and see what he's trying to hide—to guess at what makes him tick. As a woman, I see only the arrogance and it's sexy as all hell. I don't want to push at it. I don't want to guess what's beneath him.

Professionally, that makes me redundant.

I make a soft groaning noise and dip my head forward, catching it in my hands.

'I'm heading off. You need anything before I go?' Beatrice steps into my office. 'Are you okay?'

I nod, masking my doubts with ease for her. It's only Noah who seems to have unstitched my defences, to have robbed me of my stock-in-trade ability to conceal my feelings and thoughts.

'I'm fine. Thank you, Bea.'

My smile feels wooden, but hers is natural, as though nothing is wrong. As though everything is fine. She leaves and a moment later I hear the clicking of the outer door.

It's Friday and that means I'm alone—no need to rush home. Ivy is spending the night with her grandmother—Aaron's mother, not mine. It's part of our agreement, one I didn't have to enter into but felt would be best for Ivy. Aaron might be an A-grade asswipe, but that doesn't mean his mother is. And it doesn't mean Ivy should lose all connection with that side of the family—just because I never want to see him again.

I can smell you on my hand. Tomorrow I want to taste you.

My stomach swoops and I fix my gaze to the screen, forcing myself to skim through my patient notes as though I'm not falling apart at the seams.

An hour later and I can't ignore the fact I'm disappointed.

Because he's my kryptonite. I barely know Noah, but there's something so indefinable about him. His cockiness and the haunted vulnerabilities I have glimpsed flash for a second before they are once again concealed beneath the surface. Far beneath the surface, out of my prying hands' way.

He makes me raw and exposed with just a look. Should I run a mile? Away from him? Or to him? Should I pursue this? Do I dare?

'You know, you frown when you're concentrating.'

Jesus Christ! My heart slams into my ribs and the hairs on the back of my neck stand on edge. Survival skills I had thought long since discarded leap to the fore, making my body tremble with its adrenal response, my eyes naturally darting to the door for an escape.

But it's not Aaron.

It's okay. I'm safe.

No, I'm not safe. I'm in more danger than I'd realised because Noah Moore is in the sanctuary of my office, staring at me like he has every right, and I am speechless.

'What are you doing here?' Slowly my heart finds a different rhythm. Still far faster than it should beat, but for a different reason.

He's wearing a *suit*.

A suit. All tailored and professional and smart-looking, but it's *Noah Moore* and he's as hot as ever. No, more so like this. The perfect contradiction.

He strolls towards me and places his hands on the edge of the desk, his body once more invading my personal space, his scent inviting me to breathe deeply. I do just that and see the quirk of his lips, like he knows what motivates me. It sobers me and I swallow, turning my gaze downwards.

'What do *you* think I'm doing here?' The words are drawled out slowly and they pour over my flesh like sun-warmed butter.

My heart skips a beat. 'I don't know,' I hear myself murmur, wondering at the fact I'm still able to speak at all. 'But, Noah, I have to talk to you. If you're here for therapy, I need to tell you that I absolutely cannot see you again. Professionally, I mean—' my cheeks flushing '—not after what happened. I'm a professional and I can't treat someone who's…who I've…'

'Yes?' he drawls.

'I just can't be your therapist, okay? I have to say that to you now, loud and clear. It's a line I'm not prepared to cross.'

'That's good. Because I don't want fucking therapy.'

There's a dark edge to the words. They are honest and plainly spoken. I cannot misunderstand him, and yet I ask: 'So what do you want?'

'You.'

There is only the sound of my own breathing. Fast and sharp. He is watching me, waiting for me to speak, and I can't. I fear I'm my own worst enemy. I cannot give in to this desire—*not again!* I don't do this kind of thing. Do I?

'Yesterday was a mistake.' I say the words bluntly, hoping to avoid his perception that there's any wriggle room. 'As you obviously know, it's been a long time since I was intimate with anyone and I…obviously…feel attracted to you.' Heat simmers in my blood; embarrassment clips at my heels.

'Why was it a mistake?'

I swallow. 'Where to begin?' I'm going for humour, but there's nothing lighthearted in the way he's looking at me. I stand up, reaching for my handbag, hiding the way my fingertips are shaking.

'You… Look.' I shake my head.

'Yes?' He's intense.

'You're *you*,' I say, shaking my head. 'Billionaire, famous, and I think you live in a very different world to me.' My smile is an attempt to soften the rejection.

'I'm not talking about marrying you,' he says with a slow, purposeful wink. 'I'm talking about you, me and all this chemistry…'

There's something like relief in the admission—that he feels as I do. That our chemistry is mutual.

'Chemistry isn't a good enough excuse for me,' I say, moving towards the door to my office as every single bone in my body wants me to throw myself at his chest.

My fingers curl around the doorknob and he's there, a hand pressing to the wood panelling on one side of me, then the other, caging me, so that when I turn I'm imprisoned by his beautiful body. He's so broad and tall, so strong and masculine. 'Let me tell you something, Holly.'

My name on his lips is pure, sensual heat. I swallow, not sure if I'm capable of speaking.

'You know what I think?'

I shake my head slightly. He catches my cheek in the palm of his hand, holding me still. His touch is like wildfire; it spreads flame through me.

'You're lonely. You want me. And I want you. So?'

There is truth in all those statements. Still, I can't bring myself to admit that.

'Noah.' His name is a moan. 'It's clear that we're attracted to one another. I'm not going to bother lying to you, or trying to hide it.'

His laugh is an arrogant agreement. 'I'm glad to hear you say that.'

'But you came to me for therapy…and I can't ignore that.'

His eyes narrow. 'You just told me you won't take me on as a patient.'

I nod. 'I meant that.'

'So help me in this way,' he demands.

My eyes sweep shut because it's exactly what I want.

'I need you to see someone else. I know a good doctor, Dr Chesser. I can make an appointment for you. I can help you in that way. Because I'm not going to be the reason you didn't get the therapy you need. Got it?'

Anger flashes in his face.

I lift a hand to his chest. 'I mean it, Noah.'

'I don't need fucking therapy.'

'That's your decision. But if you want me…then you'll agree to this. You'll agree to let Dr Chesser help you instead of me.'

His eyes lock on mine. I can see that he's waging a war, a battle that is ancient and primal and all-important. Finally, he leans closer and his breath glances across my cheek. 'And then you'll be mine?'

I nod slowly, a frisson of awareness travelling the length of my body. 'Yes.' And I mean it, from deep within my heart.

It's freezing cold when we emerge onto the street. My office is just around the corner from London Bridge. I've been here for the last three years; prior to that, I was in Mayfair. This is a far better commute, though—our home is a twenty-minute walk from the office and on days when Ivy is with her grandmother I prefer to walk. No matter the weather, I find it clears my mind. I walked this morning, though my mind isn't feeling particularly clear right now.

He is right beside me. Not touching, but I feel everything. His breath, his thoughts—I feel all of him.

'Here.' He reaches onto the back of a motorbike and pulls off a helmet. My chest thumps.

'This is yours?' I nod towards the bike. It's big, matte black and like nothing I've ever seen. It's like a stallion, all sleek and strong and somehow beautiful despite the fact I hate motorbikes. Their noise, their speed, their inherent danger.

'Nah. I just thought we'd steal it for the night.' He grins as he lifts the helmet onto my head.

All arguments are silenced as I am lost to the effect of his proximity. His fingers are surprisingly gentle as they graze my jaw, locking the helmet into place. And his concern for my safety is somehow pleasing, reassuring, like what we're about to do meets some criteria of a 'normal' relationship when there is *nothing* normal about this.

He turns back to the bike and climbs on, his haunches so powerful in his suit, his expression holding a silent challenge as he looks at me. 'Well? Aren't you going to climb on?'

The double entendre is intentional this time. My cheeks flame.

'On that?' I point at the rear end of the bike dubiously.

'Jesus. You're afraid of this too?'

'I'm not afraid of...' I close my lips and look around guiltily. 'Do you enjoy teasing me?'

'Yes. Get on the bike, Holly.'

My name on his lips kicks confidence into me. Thanking the heavens I wore pants today, I lift my leg over the side of the bike and settle myself behind him. There are little divots that are the natural resting place for my feet and so I place them there. My hands are another story.

Despite the fact I've twice now begged this man to fuck me, I am shy about holding him intimately.

He looks at me in the rear-vision mirror—he can't see my eyes through the helmet, but he wears none and his look is mocking. So much mocking from this man and it doesn't occur to me to mind.

'Hold on, Doc.'

I should ask him to call me something else but, now that I've spelled out the boundaries of our relationship, I have to admit that hearing him call me by my professional title is so damned hot.

I nod, figuring touching him is better than falling off the back of the bike and being roadkill.

I wrap my arms around his waist and wriggle forward so our bodies are melded together. His eyes burn into me and, despite the fact he can't see me, my soul sears at the eye contact; it melts at the physical contact. My body is on fire.

The engine throbs to life, a powerful reverberation beneath me, and I have to bite down on my lower lip to stop from groaning. My body is over-sensitised and every single nerve ending jumps in response to this stimulus.

He pulls out into the traffic and hunches down a little—I stay curved around his back, my head pressed to the side, watching London in a blur as we tear through the city.

Despite what Ebony James might think, London is already wearing her festive finery. Lights twinkle overhead and Christmas trees mark the public spaces. It's hard not to be caught up in the beauty of it as we pass—but I'm only partially aware of the sights. Same with wherever we're going.

Noah Moore between my legs feels amazing. I know this is crazy and out of character, but when did I last do anything like that?

I've never been into the casual sex thing. Aaron was my first boyfriend, my high school sweetheart. And before I knew what a controlling bastard he was, I'd lost my heart and my virginity to him.

Still, I've never been with anyone else. I don't know if I can make love to someone and then move on, if I can be Noah's drug of choice.

By the time he pulls up out the front of a bar—

and I have no idea where—my buzz is at risk of disappearing.

Despite that, I'm reluctant to walk away from him. Danger signals are everywhere and yet I loosen the helmet and place it on the handlebars, then step off the bike and put my hand in his, our fingers interlaced as though we are already intimate lovers, used to weaving our bodies together like this.

'Let's go, Doc.'

Pushing my doubts aside, I admit to myself that I want this with all of me. For once in my life, I'm going to do something selfish and stupid and to hell with the consequences. I suspect Noah Moore will be worth it.

CHAPTER FIVE

HE SHOULDERS THE door in—my stomach swoops because the small, meaningless gesture seems metaphorical. Like I've cracked open a wardrobe and I'm slipping into Narnia. One night, one decision and I already know my life will never be the same again.

The place is pumping. It's a Friday night, and though I prefer to be at home catching up on period dramas, apparently the rest of the world still does *this*.

I like it. No, I more than like it. I love it. I feel like an entirely different woman as I walk in beside Noah Moore. People turn to look at him, then me and, unlike my usually reserved self, I don't care. I like being seen with him. Confidence straightens my back.

It's probably almost loud enough to drown out my thoughts and doubts. He's known here. The woman behind the bar—Jesus, I thought I had big breasts—winks at him and now the jealousy is unmistakable. I go to pull my hand free, but his fingers squeeze mine. He looks down at me and, for a millisecond, it's like no one else exists. There is just the throb of heat between us, a bright, burning, existentialist need that I will have to face or conquer—and soon.

'Hungry?' It's so loud that he has to lean down and whisper into my ear. Just the feel of his breath on my skin spreads goosebumps across me. My tummy drops as though I've just crested over the high point of a roller coaster—I'm in freefall.

I nod, just a jerk of my head. It's all I'm capable of.

'What do you want?' His lips twitch, like he knows what I *really* want. And of course he does. He's forced me to admit that—to him, and myself.

'Whatever.' I shrug. It's definitely not my usual style. I'm more of an Italian-at-six kind of diner.

He grins and weaves through the people until we reach the bar, where he's immediately served by she-of-the-big-breasts-and-low-cut-top. He speaks quietly to her too, so I don't hear what he orders, and I think my tummy is too twisted into knots to manage food anyway.

His eyes pierce me then and he jerks his head to his left. I follow the direction of the gesture and see only more people. But Noah leads me that way, his fingers still tight on mine, guiding me through the throng of revellers and, behind them, to a table in the back. It's a high table with two stools.

'Something you reserved?' I ask as we sit down.

It's so loud I have to raise my voice and I'm still not sure he hears. That suspicion is confirmed a minute later when he shakes his head and then stands, coming to my side and propping his elbow on the table. Once again, I have the sense that I'm imprisoned by him, by his big body and strong arms. And I realise how much I like that feeling.

It is a dangerous impulse—remember? I like bad boys. And the sense of being protected is almost always a lie. Men like Noah break your heart. Men like Aaron nearly kill you. The only protection comes from within. I am my own strength now.

'You come here often?' I say instead, wishing I had a drink to swallow the sudden dryness in my throat. As if my thoughts could convert to deed, a waitress—not Big Breasts, someone else—saunters over and places an ice bucket with champagne in the middle of the table. Two glasses are hooked into it, but she also has a pint of beer. She pushes it towards Noah with yet another wink—is that how they communicate here?—then swishes her hips as she walks away.

I'm way happier than I should be when his eyes stay trained on my face instead of following her curvaceous departure.

He's staring at me, in fact, and the longer his eyes roam my face, the faster my pulse throbs in my body, the hotter my blood becomes. I don't look away; nor does he. When I swallow, in an attempt to bring moisture to my desert-dry mouth, his eyes drop—briefly—to my throat, and then my lips. My stomach twists.

'Do I have something on my face?' I arch a brow, trying to sound a little sarcastic when I desperately don't want him to stop looking at me.

But I should have known better than to stir Noah Moore. He reaches for my chin, gripping me lightly between his thumb and forefinger, holding me for examination. Holding me under the beam of his gaze, staring at me in a way that makes my skin goose all over. Staring at me like I am the only person in the room—no, the world. He moves closer, within the triangle of my legs. Our body heat is volcanic.

'Nah. Your face is pretty perfect.'

Pleasure pumps my heart.

He grins and drops his hand from my face—the absence of contact sears me—turning to lift the champagne flutes and bottle from the ice bucket. He pops the cork with ease, like a man who's done so often, and fills only one of the glasses before sliding it across the table to me.

In university, I used to drink vodka, lime and soda. And more than I should have. Now I don't drink often, and almost only drink champagne. Noah's chosen my favourite bottle. I lift the glass to my lips, savouring the first hint of bubbles as they pop against my flesh and breathing in its crisp, fruit-driven aroma.

He watches me with that intense way he has, as I take a sip and swallow, and heat is simmering through me. He's so close, just an inch or so from my knees. Doubts are somewhere deep in the back of my mind, but I cannot grasp them now. I don't want to grasp them. Instead, I smile at him and he smiles back. A slow, considered smile that makes me ache to know everything about him.

He draws a sip of his beer and then places his glass on the table, right beside my champagne flute. His hand drops to my knee. It's a casual touch, but it's possessive too, like he's staking his claim, and I like it. Oh, I like it so much.

'So, you have a daughter,' he prompts, his Australian accent sounding thicker here.

I nod, and my lips twist with a smile as I think of Ivy.

'How old?'

'She's four and a half. She'd want me to say the half—it's very important to her. She's already planning her fifth birthday extravaganza.' I'm babbling. His fingers have crept higher, to my hip, which brings his body right back to mine, so close.

'She looks a lot like you.'

'I know.'

'Who's the father?'

The question is surprising, and not. I mean, it's a natural thing to wonder about, isn't it? If I weren't wildly attracted to him, would it strike me as a strange thing to ask? Would I be hesitating like this?

Or is it just that I haven't spoken to anyone about Aaron for a really long time? Even within my family, he is a taboo subject. My parents' shame is a complex emotion—their shame at my divorce, at the situation I was in and at their inability to be there for me when I needed them.

'My ex,' I say.

Noah laughs. Just a short sound that mixes derision with amusement. *'Obviously.'* He drawls the word in his best, most mocking tone. Why do I find even that sexy?

Because I like bad guys. Shouldn't I have learned my lesson by now?

'When'd you break up?'

These are normal questions. And yet ice is taking over the flames within me, cooling me, reminding me of the fear that dogged my every step for many years. 'We…grew apart.' I reach for my champagne and take several sips, my eyes focused on a point over his shoulder.

'I call bullshit.'

He's right. I jerk my head in a small nod. 'We were together a long time. Right from school… We dated while I was at university and then when I opened my practice.' My eyes meet his for a moment and I'm comforted by whatever it is I see in their depths. He tops up my champagne and murmurs something I don't catch, but words I take as encouragement to continue.

To my surprise, I do just that. 'He's a musician,' I say, rolling my eyes at my innocent naivety. 'A guitarist.' As though that explains everything. 'Very, profoundly talented. But a tortured artistic soul.' I'm making light of the situation. My parents aren't the only ones with shame coursing through their veins.

He nods, his eyes drilling into me. 'What aren't you saying?'

I'm surprised. It must show on my face. I'm the one who reads people and yet he's summarised me with ease. And though this isn't a therapy session and he's not my patient, I add his perceptiveness to what I know about him. It is not uncommon in people who have experienced lengthy trauma—trauma like mine. I became adept at analysing every single flicker of emotion that passed over someone's face; I suppose that was my flight or fight instincts.

'Why do you think there's anything I'm not saying?'

He shrugs. 'Because it's the truth.'

'You think you know me so well?'

'Well? Am I wrong?'

Our eyes are locked; it is a battle of wills that is making my knees tremble. I reach for my champagne and realise he's hardly touched his beer.

'No,' I say, once I've had a sip. 'It's just not a subject I like to talk about.'

'There's an irony in that.' He grins.

'I'm a therapist,' I tack on. 'It's my job to ask the questions, not answer them.'

'Whereas you just want to fuck me?'

My cheeks burn at the directness of his question. 'I…'

'How long were you together?' He lobs the question back, his directness reminding me that he is a very successful businessman. That beneath the bad boy stubble and the loud, growling motorbike and the fact he swears and drinks like a sailor, he is smart and incisive, ruthless and intelligent.

'Six years.'

'And were you happy together?'

'What do you think?' I deflect. 'We split up.'

'That might mean he cheated or you did…'

'I didn't cheat,' I say firmly. 'And I don't think he did either.'

'So?' He shrugs. 'What happened?'

It's highly likely the glass and a half of champagne I've consumed on a near-empty stomach have loosened my tongue, or maybe it's the five years of not speaking to anyone except my lawyer and the judge, but I hear myself say, 'When I was four months pregnant with Ivy, he strangled me until I passed out.' I can't look at him. The shame that runs through me is hard to ignore. I trace invisible circles around the base of my champagne flute. 'I kept thinking he'd change, you know? It wasn't like he was abusive—that's what I used to tell myself. He was just stressed. His recording contract was dissolved, or he felt inferior to me because I earned five times what he did.' I shrug. The excuses sound so ridiculous to me now. 'And it was nothing—in the beginning. You know? Like he'd grab my arm too tight, but he was always so apologetic. And I'd known him and loved him for so long.' Tears clog the back of my throat. I thought I was done crying for him!

'Anyway. I kept waiting for things to calm down, for him to go back to "normal", but that became the new normal.'

'He beat you?' The question is asked softly, but I hear it loud and clear, despite the background noise of the busy bar.

Another waitress appears, placing a platter down

on the edge of the table. Neither of us look at her or it; I'm simply aware of it in the periphery of my vision.

'Beat me? Yeah, I guess you could call it that. He controlled me. Manipulated me. Pulled my hair. Broke my wrist. Locked me in our bedroom for two days straight and refused to let me eat or drink anything.' I lift my eyes to Noah's face now, finding the whip of strength that compelled me—finally—to leave Aaron. The look on his face robs me of breath.

There is such understanding there. Such a look of *empathy* that I feel I am speaking to someone who understands. 'I never thought that could happen to me. I'm strong and smart and I come from a close-knit family. They all adored Aaron. From the outside, we had the perfect life.' I grimace. 'Such a cliché.'

'Fucking bastard,' he says after a moment.

'Yeah. Anyway, once I was pregnant, I knew I couldn't take the risk any more. I'd let him treat me like a punchbag for years, but what if he did that to our baby? I'd tried to help him. I'm a therapist, for Christ's sake, surely I should have known what to say or do...'

'You can't help some people,' Noah says with authority, and I wonder if he's speaking about himself or someone he knows.

'I learned that lesson,' I admit.

'Do you ever see him?'

I shake my head. 'I have a restraining order. Not that I need it. He's in prison. A week after leaving me, he strangled a prostitute. Put her in a coma for six months.' I swallow. 'Attempted murder—fifteen years.'

'Jesus.' Noah doesn't touch me and he doesn't offer me platitudes, both of which I appreciate. I need to absorb the fact that I've just told someone my deepest secret. And that I'm still standing.

Well, sitting, technically.

He doesn't say anything for a really long time and I wonder if I've spooked him. There's a reason I usually keep this stuff to myself.

'I don't know why I told you that,' I say, shaking my head so that my hair fluffs against my cheeks. 'I don't generally...'

He lifts a single finger to my lips, holding it there to silence me.

'I asked.'

I swallow. I don't know why but the simple explanation is somehow important.

His finger lifts higher, running over my cheek, and I instinctively blink my eyes shut as he moves his finger higher, to the ridge of my brow. To the scar that is roughly six years old.

'His handiwork?'

I forget about the scar, most of the time. It is just a part of me now. One of the many bumps and indents that have formed on my body over time. Some from ageing, many from Aaron.

I nod slowly and Noah swears harshly under his breath. 'I want to kill the fucker.'

A frisson of something like danger rolls over my spine because I don't for a second doubt he means it. That he would—and could. His virile strength is a huge part of his appeal, but I want him to use that strength for pleasure, not pain.

As if sensing the surge of fear and adrenaline that rushes over me, he smiles, a smile that is sexy and charming and draws me back to the moment. I reach for my champagne and sip it, no longer self-conscious or nervous—no longer analysing the faults of my fate. I am simply surrendered to it.

'Sometimes you sound very Australian.'

He arches a brow, reading my comment for what it is: a distraction.

'I am Australian,' he says dismissively and surprises me then by leaning forward and pressing a kiss to my eyebrow, to the scar that marks my flesh.

My heart turns over in my chest and my danger sensors flare.

With a sixth sense that perhaps my emotional health depends on it, I smile thickly and continue, 'When did you move here?'

'To London?' He pulls back, reaching for his beer and sipping it before topping up my champagne. 'About five years ago.'

'To England,' I clarify.

I sense his desire to pull away from me, but he doesn't. I'm unbelievably pleased. 'A week after I turned eighteen.' His smile is a very masculine version of the Mona Lisa's, every inch as enigmatic and mysterious. I wonder at the secret memories he's holding on to, and why he keeps them wrapped to his chest.

'But not straight to London?'

'No.'

Closed answers. In a therapy session I would let him get away with it, being ever-careful not to spook him, to antagonise and alienate him. Here, in a packed bar, with his beautiful body between my legs and the temptation of a night together on the periphery of my mind, I make free to push him.

'Where did you go?'

He looks as though I'm the dentist and he's terrified of needles. Odd, when I think Noah Moore isn't afraid of much at all. 'Oxford.'

'Oxford? As in university?'

'Would that surprise you?'

I frown. It does, and I can't say why.

'My…business partner and I did a coding course there,' he says. 'It was just a summer school—not really affiliated with the university, just using the campus.'

'That's where you started Bright Spark?'

He nods again. 'At least, where we started on the path towards it. It was another few years before we launched.'

'And then it all happened very fast,' I say, noting the admiration that softens my words.

He dips his head forward in concession and I sip my champagne. Is that my second or third glass? I don't know, but it's delicious.

I am buzzing all over. In my abdomen and my soul, my mind and my mouth. I am a lightning storm and he is the ocean, drawing all of my electricity down, causing me to spark and flash.

I look at him and a bolt of awareness lights up, hard and fast. I shiver—a good shiver. One of anticipation and indulgence; one of reward.

I don't realise how affected by the champagne she is until she stands, looking for the ladies' room. She presses a hand against my chest to steady herself and my cock surges forward, thinking his moment is nigh.

Only, she sways and her eyes blink, like she's confused in some way. Shit. She's had almost the whole bottle and eaten very little. I've been demolishing the platters as we've talked, satiating one hunger before turning my attention to another.

Her eyes scan the bar, but her frown gathers, like she barely knows where she is.

'This way.' My voice is gruff. I put an arm around her waist, offering more support than guidance, and lead her to the restrooms at the back. I fight the urge to take her in myself—but wince as she walks down the hallway and has to hold the wall for support.

Five minutes pass. Six minutes. I'm on the brink of storming into the restroom myself when she comes out, looking a little more in control, though still resting her hand on the wall as she walks towards me.

Her smile is bright as she approaches. 'Let's go home.'

The words are slurred, but her meaning is clear.

My heart slams against my ribs as I imagine the doc in my home.

'Your place?' I prompt.

'No.' She shakes her head emphatically and then winces once more. She presses a finger to my chest. '*Your* place.' She runs her finger down the centre of my chest, all the way to my abdomen, lingering there as her eyes lock on mine and her teeth pull her full lower lip in.

I fight an urge to push her back against the wall. I fight many urges, in fact, in this moment. I'm as shocked as anyone could be to discover that I have some ancient decency within me that makes the idea of taking advantage of her violently abhorrent.

That makes me more concerned for her than I am aroused—which is really saying something as my body is like a fucking grenade about to go off.

'This way.' The words are unintentionally short, as though I'm angry with her, and I see hurt flash in her eyes.

She reads me like a damned book and I hate that. I smile—it's tight on my face, but I hope it placates her. At the entrance to the bar, I look outside. I can't see any photographers and this is hardly the kind of place that anyone of note frequents—one of the reasons I like to come here and unwind. Blow off steam. Be unknown. I prop Holly just inside the door and stride out, retrieving my bike helmet and then returning to her.

Her eyes are shut, but she's standing.

'Here.' It's a hoarse directive. I fasten the helmet

and then scrutinise her. 'Are you going to be able to hang on?'

'Yeah.' She nods. 'Let's go.'

I put an arm around her waist, guiding her from the bar, then seat myself on the bike. I keep a hand on her as she gets on behind me, relieved when I feel the press of her legs on my thighs, her arms around my waist, her head heavy against my back.

My place is only a ten-minute drive from the bar, but I practically hold my breath the whole time, needing to get her home, needing to get her off the back of my bike before she falls off.

She didn't seem at all affected by the champagne. She was talking, asking her fucking questions, eyeing me like she couldn't wait to get in my pants. And then she was…paralytic.

My face is a grimace as I pull the bike to a stop, the sludgy Thames issuing a steady, throbbing noise from its bowel as it bleeds a retreat to the sea.

'You okay?'

She's quiet for a moment before nodding, her eyes so beautifully, distractingly hooded that I have to bite back a curse. 'Yeah. I'm fine.'

She gets off the bike somewhat unsteadily, so I move fast, kicking the stand down and then covering the distance between us in one motion. She sways again and I swear under my breath, lifting her up over my shoulder and stalking towards my front door.

'Hey!' Her laugh is breathless. 'What are you doing?'

'Getting you inside before you fall down.'

'I'm fine,' she insists, slapping her hand to my back before sliding it lower, and lower, until her fingertips find the bottom of my suit jacket and pull it up. Jesus. I fumble with the key—this place is a hundred and fifty years old and the keys must be almost as ancient. Big and brass. That should be an advantage, but with all the blood rushing to my dick I'm finding it cumbersome as hell. Finally, I get the door open, right around the time Holly triumphs over my shirt-slash-pants scenario and finds the bare flesh of my back. Her fingers run over me with a curiosity that is sensual and distracting.

I flick the lights to my left and she swears softly. 'That's so bright.'

'You're still wearing a helmet.' I laugh roughly, carrying her into my apartment and dropping her onto the sofa. She falls elegantly—how can she do that when she's drunk as all hell and wearing a helmet?

Her fingers fumble with the straps to no avail and, suppressing a smile, I reach down and unclip it for her.

Shit. I'd forgotten her face. How distracting it is— how fascinating. I'd forgotten the fucking scar too. A surge of protective anger flashes through me so fast and shocks me to my core.

I'm not a protector.

Not even close.

At least, I've never felt that kind of instinct for

anyone other than Gabe—probably the only person who needs protecting even less than I do.

But I feel it now. I feel an inexplicable fury that anyone could damage Holly. And because I understand the way scars work, I know the formation of the external scars is nothing compared to what she must carry inside. A heart that is scratched all over from repeated lashings and torment, a soul that is part withered from neglect and terror.

I'm lost in this moment of contemplation and so don't realise that she's pushing up to stand. Not until her sweet body presses against mine, her eyes hooded by desire and drunkenness. 'I.' She lifts unsteady fingers to the buttons on her shirt and undoes the top one. 'Want.' She works quickly for someone who's so clearly affected by alcohol. I see the lace swirls of her bra. Shit. 'You.'

I swallow hard as she removes the shirt altogether, revealing creamy skin and breasts I could weep for. It's perfect. 'To.'

Her hands move to the button of her pants and I know that I need to put an end to this. That I need this woman, who is already scarred and hurting, to be better than I am.

'Fuck.' She says the word as she pushes her pants down over her hips, revealing a tiny white thong that matches her bra. My body is tighter than a spring.

She steps out of her pants and then reaches around, unclipping her bra, dropping it at my feet while keeping her eyes locked to mine. 'Me.'

Holy shit.

I take several steps backwards, not running away from what she said so much as needing to get a better view of her. My throat is drier than the Strzelecki Track; my abdomen tightens with an ancient, primal need to possess.

'Holly.' I hear the pleading tone in the way I say her name, my desperation so very obvious. She sways unsteadily as she steps towards me; it would be callous of me not to catch her. But fuck, I wasn't prepared for how her skin would feel beneath my palm. My hand drops, curving around her arse, feeling her sweet roundness, holding her against the answering hardness of my aching cock.

She moans, her sweet cherry-red lips parting as her eyes find mine. Her throat is exposed and I want to run my mouth over it, to taste every single inch of her—all of her.

'Please,' she whispers and pushes up on tiptoe, trying to kiss me, looking for more of me.

I have about half a second to make my decision and it is so far from being easy. Because I want to fuck her. I want to fuck her hard, to make her all mine, to make her beg and make her scream, but she's drunk and, as I said, I have discovered I am a better man than I knew. A fact that is borne out by the way I once more lift her, this time cradling her to my chest, holding her against me and taking her up the exposed stairs that dangle from wires in the ceiling, leading to the mezzanine bedroom. I am gentle when I place her on the bed. She reaches for me and I kiss her gently, tasting the champagne and need on the tip of her tongue. I press my body over hers and I swear I could come. There is something within her that calls to me and I am desperate to answer it.

But not now. Not like this.

CHAPTER SIX

'WHAT TIME IS IT?'

I lift my eyes to the clock in the kitchen. 'Three.'

'You're still not sleeping.' Gabe's disapproval is obvious. I grip my neck, massaging it hard as my eyes lift, without my permission, to the mezzanine. She is almost completely silent, but for the occasional rustling of bed linen as she turns her near-naked body in my bed.

For three hours I have grappled with the fact that I have Holly Scott-Leigh in my bed and that I am down here, staring at a pixelated screen rather than being up there with her. Holding her. Kissing her. Worshipping her body.

'I take it you didn't keep your appointment to see the therapist?'

It's useless. I stand, walking into the kitchen and grabbing a bottle of rum down from above the fridge. 'I wouldn't say that.'

There's a pause. 'Really?'

I can understand Gabe's surprise. I love him like a brother—hell, we *are* brothers, courtesy of the foster system that birthed us both—but I nearly flattened him when he gave me the ultimatum. When he told me I'd lost my grip and needed help.

'So you're going to see her?'

'I saw her this afternoon,' I say, pleased I can be so frankly honest with him. I don't add that she's flat-out refused to see me as a patient. That her sense of ethics has made that impossible. She's now just a woman I'm going to fuck—no, more than that, but I can't express that to Gabe.

I don't tell him that I've spent tonight with her. That I've felt her sweet, soft skin and tasted her delicious lips. That professionally I don't want a bar of Holly Scott-Leigh, but in my bed I want all of her; all that she's got to offer I'll take.

'Good.' I feel like a lying bastard when I hear the relief in Gabe's voice. 'I know how hard it was to lose Julianne…'

A familiar chasm in the region of my heart opens wide. My fingers shake a little as I half fill the tumbler, staring at the beautiful golden liquid. I lift it to my nose, inhaling its intoxicating aroma gratefully.

'I'm fine,' I lie. 'What's happening in New York?'

There's a longer than normal pause and then Gabe expels a breath. 'Nothing new.'

A frown tugs at my brows. I know Gabe better than anyone, and I know when he's lying. He *doesn't* lie. He's the most outrageously honest to a fault person I've ever met, even when being honest causes him to come off as an out-and-out bastard. He doesn't care. The truth is his thing.

'Gabe?'

'*Sì?*'

My lips twist at the way he slips into his native tongue. He had six years in Italy before his mother stole him away, dragging him to her native Australia before abandoning him into the foster system. I didn't know him until much later, but he's told me that he spoke not a word of English. That he spent the first year in Australia being bullied for his accent and called 'dumb' despite the fact he is, and always has been, incredibly intelligent and focused.

Now he spends much of his time in Italy, and sometimes that language is at the fore of his brain more than English. Particularly when he's stressed.

'What the fuck's going on?' I demand, cutting to the chase.

'*Niente.* It does not matter.'

'But something *is* wrong? Is it the Calypso?' Calypso is the code name for the smartphone we have under development. It's incredibly confidential—one team of thirty-seven engineers has been working on it for fourteen months—but it's obsessed Gabe and me much longer than that and we're close to launch.

'No. It's...nothing. You need to go to sleep.'

I grunt. 'Fat fucking chance.'

'Noah.' Gabe says my name quietly. 'If you don't think she can help, I will find you someone else. I am...concerned for you.'

I expel a harsh breath. I know he's worried. I've gone off the rails lately—even for me. I can see it from his perspective and I can see it's not fair to him.

I hate that I'm doing anything that might cause him pain but, Jesus, this all just happened a month ago and I'm still dealing with it. That's normal, right?

'Don't be.' Once again, I lift my eyes towards the mezzanine. 'I'm coping fine.'

What the hell is that? Why are there blades slicing across my brain? What is that beating of tiny little drums against my nerve endings, making my temples throb with an unbearable pain? Oh, my God, my throat is stinging and… Oh hell. I'm naked.

In a bed that I would put money on belonging to Noah Moore.

Oh, my God.

Did we…? I stare down at my body, my naked body, except I'm still wearing underpants, which surely means…what? What does it mean? I think back to the way he kissed me and touched me in my office, on my desk, and I have no certainty about what has happened here. How can I?

I turn bleary eyes towards the bedside—there is no clock there and I have no idea where my bag and phone are. The best I can do to estimate the time is look out of the window. I reach for the thin, soft blanket at the foot of the bed and wrap it around my shoulders like a cape, planting my feet over the side of the bed and standing gingerly for a moment while I wait for the tectonic plates of my brain to shift back into alignment.

I'm never drinking again.

I tiptoe across the room—I have no idea why I'm

being so stealthy—towards the window that's behind the bed.

London is still dark, the sky a velvet black, the moon a pearlescent glimmer hidden behind leaden clouds. I look back towards the bedroom, needing to take stock of my surroundings.

The bed is a mess, but that doesn't indicate that Noah was in it with me. I mean, I'm a flippy-floppy sleeper from way back. When Ivy was little, we used to co-sleep, but when she was two she asked to go into her own room because I woke her up so often. With the blanket wrapped firmly around my shoulders and desperately wishing I had some clothes I could put on instead, I take the first step down and then another. My head is throbbing.

No, it's cracking apart at the seams—emphatically, angrily.

I pause halfway down the stairs and study the apartment below.

It's less an apartment and more a loft, completely open and barely furnished.

A sofa—flashes of memory return, cemented by the sight of his motorbike helmet discarded carelessly on the floor beside it. A table. An armchair. There's no TV. No photographs or paintings on the walls, just one big whiteboard down the end with lots of writing on it, and another table in front of it that has several laptops all cabled together.

I have no idea where we are, what part of London, only that we're near the Thames. I can hear its lifeblood humming close by.

A noise calls my attention and I swivel my head—far too fast, *ouch*—towards it. Noah is emerging from around the corner, a glass of something that looks like alcohol in his hand. My stomach convulses at the very idea.

Please, please, *don't throw up.*

As if he hears my presence, his eyes lift to the mezzanine, landing on me almost instantly, and the tug of desire that swirls through me overtakes almost everything else. Almost, but not quite.

I hold the blanket tighter around me and resume my slow walk of shame, moving downstairs until I'm on the same level as Noah, albeit across the room.

He doesn't speak, but his face says everything. His face that is part-mocking, part-amusement and with a dash of concern.

'I...' What? What can I say to explain the way I wrote myself off? Hardly sophisticated. I wish I could remember what we did when we got back, but alas, my mind is an utter blank. 'What happened last night?'

It's still the same night, but he doesn't correct me. He throws back a glug of whatever he's drinking, keeping his eyes pinned to me.

'You don't remember?'

Oh, God. Did we sleep together? Did I waste my chance of being with Noah by being too drunk to remember it? Did he sleep with me when I was in that state?

'No.' I shake my head and then wince—he winces in response, apparently understanding my pain.

'Sit down, Holly, before you throw up.'

I glare at him, like this is all his fault. 'I'm fine,' I lie. 'Where are my clothes?'

He places his drink down on the table and prowls towards me, heat burning me with his proximity.

'I like you naked,' he says, his eyes dropping to the opening revealed by the blanket.

I can't meet his eyes. Instead, I stare at the floor, keeping my hands clasped around the blanket. 'Did we...? I can't remember.'

'Did we what?' He's enjoying my discomfort. Bastard.

'Did we sleep together?'

'I don't sleep, remember?'

And I realise that it's the middle of the night and he's wide awake, still wearing his suit, though he's shed the jacket and rolled his shirtsleeves up to his elbows, revealing tanned forearms that are works of art.

'Did we...have sex?'

'No, Holly.'

That jerks my eyes up to his, and I think it's relief that's swirling through me. But only because I have no memory of the night, not because I'm glad we didn't. I still want him in a way that robs me of air.

'We didn't?'

He shakes his head.

'Oh. Good.' I nod brusquely. 'Then why am I hardly wearing anything?'

He walks towards me, closing the gap completely, his fingers curling around the fabric of my blanket cape. He pulls at it and drops it to the ground easily, his eyes challenging me to say something. I don't. I don't know why, but being undressed in front of Noah doesn't feel as weird as I'd thought.

When his eyes drop hungrily to my body, as though he is starving and I am his feast, it feels pretty damned good.

'Because you…' He presses a finger to the space between my breasts and I inhale a tortured breath. 'Wanted…' His eyes hold mine as he draws a line outwards to my left nipple, running a circle around it that makes me moan softly. 'Me…' His hand runs lower, to the soft flesh on the underside of my breast. He cups me and then drops his head forward, taking my nipple in his mouth and torturing me with his beautiful tongue until my knees are so weak I feel like I might fall. I barely hear the 'to' as he says it right against me, against my desperate, tortured nerve endings, against my body that is quivering for him.

He lifts his mouth to mine then and kisses me far harder than I would have thought I could manage, given my pounding head and scratchy brain. He kisses me like we are lovers who have been parted a decade, a kiss that sears my flesh.

'Fuuuuck…'

He pushes the word into my mouth, rolling it around with his tongue before lifting his head an inch and staring into my eyes. His hand that held my breast has roamed to my butt and is pushing me against him so I feel the thickness of his arousal on my stomach. 'You.' The last word is a hoarse, whispered admission.

I am lost, floating in an ocean of indeterminate swell and destination, simply being pulled whichever way it wants me to go.

If I wanted him to fuck me, why didn't he? I know he wants this as much as I do... 'But...you didn't?'

'No.'

'Why not?'

'When I fuck you, Doc, you're going to be screaming my name, not slurring it.'

'I was *not* slurring,' I say defensively, though of course I can't actually remember that for sure.

'You were drunk.' He lifts a hand to my brow. 'How do you feel now?'

'Fine,' I say, not intending to tell him my head's about to blow apart. And you know why? Because I want him—and I don't want him to have an excuse for not sleeping with me. All this build-up, all the flirtation, all the seduction—I can't bear it if it doesn't go anywhere. In fact, I'm not going to let that happen. I'm going to reach out and grab him with both hands.

Having opened the floodgates to desire when I have sought to ignore its existence for five years, I am unwilling to ignore it a moment longer.

'I still want you to fuck me,' I say boldly and catch the speculation in his eyes, the look of interest.

'I know.'

'So?' I lift my hands to his chest, tentatively at first, lifting my fingers to his buttons and unbuttoning the top two. He watches me without a word as I move painstakingly down his shirt, separating it finally from the waistband of his trousers and revealing his broad, muscled chest. He has a tattoo on his left pectoral muscle, a muscle that is strong and firm. I lift a quivering fingertip to it and trace the letters: *MCMXCIX*

Roman numerals? I wish I could remember how to decode them, but it feels like for ever ago that I learned the symbolism, that I was taught to translate the *M*s and *C*s and *X*s and turn them into relatable digits.

'What is this?' I murmur, wishing I were brave enough to lean forward and kiss him, to taste his flesh, to kiss him gently, firmly, desperately.

'Numbers.'

I roll my eyes. 'Yeah, obviously. But what number?'

'Nineteen ninety-nine.'

He catches my wrist and pulls it away, but I lift my other one, running my hand over his chest and feeling every dip and swoop, every muscle and sinew. His skin is smooth to touch, roughened by hairs down the middle. I swallow, taking a step to his side, where I see more tattoos at the top of his shoulder and across the blade of his bone. Tattoos that are somehow frightening, yet I don't know why. One is of a wraithlike creature, eyes that are sunken and knees that look to be made of stone. I shiver when I look at it.

'What's this?'

His jaw clenches and I wonder if he's not going to answer. But then he speaks, slowly, his accent thick and a lingering aroma of alcohol on his breath that should make me queasy but doesn't.

'Malingee,' he says, the word inflected with sounds that are foreign and new.

'Malingee?' I repeat, hoping for the same accent and missing.

His smile shows that I haven't pronounced it correctly. 'It's an Aboriginal spirit.'

'Really? What's its significance?'

He looks at me then and my breath catches in my throat for his nearness and beauty overtake me. 'I like it.'

I nod slowly, tracing around his back. It is blanked of ink but ripples with muscles beneath sinew and flesh. I can hear my blood pounding in my ears, heavy and demanding, torrid and fast. I reach his other arm; there is a simple dark scrawl that runs over his round shoulder. My eyes meet his and perhaps he senses my doubt, for he lifts a brow and watches me, his own breath seemingly held.

I lean forward, emboldened by him, me, us, this. My tongue finds the swirling edge of the tattoo and tastes it and him; his saltiness makes my stomach roll with instant need. Suddenly, having sex with Noah Moore has become the most important thing in my world and I will do whatever I can to make that happen.

No longer do I hear a single doubt from within my mind; I am conviction and certainty. As if to underscore my commitment to this, I run my hands around his back and slip my fingers into the waistband of his pants, finding the inch of flesh at the top of his butt. I hear his sharp exhalation of breath, feel it rustle the hair at my temple.

My body no longer aches with the after-effects of overconsumption; I am alive with anticipation for what will be.

'I haven't slept with anyone since him,' I say, knowing Noah understands. 'I haven't slept with anyone *but* him. Ever.' I don't know why but my smile is apologetic, as though my lack of experience might offend him in some way. And indeed, I see the shift of emotions crossing his face, the charge of wariness that makes him tighten and stiffen.

'I don't want him to be my only lover,' I say honestly, shrugging my shoulders, forcing myself to hold his gaze. 'I don't want him to be that.'

'You want me to fuck you to erase him?'

'No,' I say quickly, surprised at the way that sounds, about how it cheapens Noah—who should mean nothing to me and doesn't. 'I mean yes, but not just because of that,' I say honestly. Uncertainty is creeping back inside me. 'I thought you wanted this too.'

He looks at me with a hint of the mockery that defined our first and second meetings, a look that makes my doubts surge and makes me feel like maybe he really doesn't want me at all.

Did I say something wrong? Do something wrong?

Heat tingles through me—regret is my bedfellow. I hate drinking to the point I am drunk. I never do it.

Aaron used to drink. Aaron used to be drunk, often.

I pull away from Noah, stepping backwards, wishing desperately I were fully clothed. 'I...' I lift a hand to my temple, pressing my fingers into it uncertainly. 'I'm sorry.'

He doesn't react. 'What for?'

Good question. Maybe I'm still a bit drunk, because I don't seem able to think clearly. Or maybe that's just the proximity to this guy, his naked chest, his... All of him. 'I guess just...drinking so much.'

He laughs, the sound filling the apartment. 'Doc, I don't care. You think I'm offended by that?'

I shake my head slowly, wishing I could regain the confidence of moments earlier.

'I should go.'

He's quiet and watchful. 'Is that what you want?' he says after several long beats have passed.

I don't know what I want. Rather, I do, but I don't know now if I *should* and my indecision is driving me crazy.

'Where's your daughter?'

'Huh?' I spin around, Ivy the last thing on my mind at that moment.

'I presume she's not home alone?' he prompts, skimming his eyes over my face thoughtfully.

'Oh...no.' I shake my head. 'She's...with Aaron's mother. Ivy stays with her every Friday night and most of Saturday. Sometimes Saturday nights too.

They're close…' I'm babbling. I don't realise until he crosses to me and lifts a finger, pressing it to my lips.

'So here's what's going to happen,' he says, speaking quietly. 'You're going to go back to my bed and sleep off the rest of your hangover. Naked, like this, so I can watch you if I want to, so I can see the way your breasts move as you breathe and your skin flushes as you dream of me. And then I'm going to wake you by kissing you here…' He touches my breast lightly and drags his finger down my body, lower and lower. 'And here.'

He touches the front of my underpants. 'And I'm going to kiss you here until you are falling apart and you are begging for me and then, Doc, I'm going to blow every other man from your mind. Sound like a plan?'

She is a restless sleeper, like me. When I do fucking sleep, which isn't often these days. She throws an arm over her head and her face scrunches up. I will myself not to wake her, not yet. I am testing myself—my strength and resolve—seeing if I can delay the inevitable. I am a man who enjoys instant gratification rather than delayed. I am a man who values instant pleasure.

And yet, with the Doc, I am savouring the anticipation of being with her, like I know the real thing won't live up to what I hope, what I need. Like I know she can't possibly feel and taste as good as she has so far.

But what if she does?

What if her body answers mine in every way? What if I feel a connection with her that is new and inherently dangerous for its impermanence? What if I get addicted to the way she feels and tastes and smells, to the small noises she makes in my arms. What if I become addicted to her smiles and her words, and her soft way of speaking?

Addiction is dangerous, so too the illusion of permanence, for nothing lasts for ever, and nor will this.

CHAPTER SEVEN

I DON'T KNOW what time it is when I wake. It is brighter; the sun has chased away the darkness, though the day is grey and gloomy. For a moment I forget where I am, stretching my arms over my head and expecting to connect with the familiar smooth wood of my bedhead and finding instead padded fabric.

A small frown as I consider this difference and then a noise, just a slight shift in body weight, and I look to the wall and see Noah. Noah Moore.

I'm in his apartment.

Memories of last night and earlier this morning shoot through me like flashes of lightning, spiking my blood.

He is reclining against the wall with a natural-born indolence, watching me. Staring at me. Devouring me with his eyes.

I sit up, the sheet tucked under my chin, my eyes doing their own hungry inspection of him. At some point since I last saw him, he has changed. Showered? His hair is damp. He's wearing a pair of jeans with the button undone, and nothing else.

My throat thickens with lust and hunger. 'Have you slept?'

He pushes off the wall but doesn't smile. He has two smiles—mocking and charming. I think I prefer the former for its honesty. The latter I suspect is simply a shield. A defensive mechanism developed to beguile and charm out of necessity rather than pleasure.

It is an insight that comes from nowhere and that cannot be explained nor substantiated.

'No.' For a second I forget what I've asked him, and what he's answering.

But then I see the hint of grey smudged across the skin beneath his eyes and something inside me flips over. 'You haven't slept at all?'

He shrugs, like it doesn't matter. 'I shut my eyes a few times.'

I trained as a psychologist but, beyond that, it's who I am. All thoughts of my own nakedness are forgotten. I drop the sheet and lean forward, concern etched on my face. 'You have to sleep,' I say urgently. 'It's important.'

He shrugs again. 'I will.'

'When?'

'When I do.' There's a hint of impatience zipping through the answer, but I refuse to be cowed.

'What is it?' I ask, bringing my knees up under my chin and looking at him seriously.

'Maybe it was the fact you were lying in my bed like this.' His smile is a ghost of a smile. 'Hard to sleep with a raging hard-on.'

I snatch a breath, holding it inside me, unable to exhale, unable to swallow. But I take the threads of our conversation and chase after them. 'When did you last sleep? For more than ten minutes,' I add before he can fob me off once more.

'Does it matter?' He strides towards the bed.

'Yes. There are loads of things that can happen if you're not sleeping properly. It's dangerous and...' He climbs in front of me and, as with last night—no, this morning, earlier—he presses a finger to my lips. I have no choice but to cease speaking.

'How do you feel?' His voice is gruff as he asks the question and my heart thumps.

'I'm serious, Noah. We need to talk about this.'

'Doc?'

I blink.

'I thought you said you didn't want to treat me.'

'I don't. I mean, not officially. But this is serious.'

'I really don't want you to be a therapist right now.'

I sink my teeth into my lower lip. 'No?'

'No.'

And he kisses me, hard, hard enough to press me back onto the bed, hard enough to make my head swim and my eyes close. His weight on top of me is the answer to a craving I didn't realise I felt. The feeling of him, pressing me against the mattress, makes all my nerves tingle.

'How do you feel?' He asks the question as his fingers slide into the waistband of my underpants, finding my thong and loosening it, pushing it down my thighs.

My arms lift and wrap around his neck, my fingers tangling in the thick dark hair at his nape.

'Doc?' He drags his mouth down to my breast, rolling his tongue over my nipple, drawing me into his mouth so that I arch my back and cry out all at once. I feel his smile against me and have no way of verifying that my feeling is correct because my eyes are squeezed shut, allowing the deluge of sensations to ransack my body.

'How do you feel?'

'Good,' I groan into the room, digging my fingernails into the sheets. How long has it been since a man has kissed me like this? Longer than five years. Five years since perfunctory, horrible, terrifying lovemaking with Aaron—so much longer since my body has been feted in this manner. He touches me as though I am made of porcelain and might break, and yet his kisses are savage and wild, thrilling me with their intensity and desperate need.

'No headache?'

'No!' And I no longer want him to treat me like porcelain. 'I'm fine!' I say the words loudly and push at his chest, wrapping my legs around him as I topple him backwards. On top of him, I have a thrill of something like power and pleasure and it dances through my system, fascinating my nerve endings.

I need him, need him so badly I cannot think straight. I find his jeans and push them down, just low enough to expose his dick. It's so hard and bloody huge that I have a momentary burst of doubt about what we're about to do. I try not to make comparisons to Aaron—it wouldn't be fair. No comparison to Noah seems fair, for any man.

I am so desperate for him, I ache to feel him between my legs, hot and strong inside me. He's disposed of my underwear and I hover over him, my fingers finding his cock and circling it tentatively at first and then more confidently as he groans. 'Fuuuuck…' The word is long and slow, the vowel extended, the tone dark.

'That's my plan.' I grin, lifting up and taking him inside me. Just his tip at first, and then he thrusts into me. It's been so long and he's so big that I feel almost as though it's my first time. I have forgotten how it feels to be so completely joined with someone. Have I ever felt this?

He holds my hips and anchors me so that I am on top while he is still somehow in control. He draws me down his length, my wetness slicking him, and then he holds me still while he thrusts into me, powerful and perfect. I am a bundle of feelings.

I tilt my head back, cresting along the wave of pleasure that his body offers, and when his hands run over my stomach, towards my breasts, his fingertips finding my nipples, I cry out—it's more pleasure than I have ever known. I am frightened and empowered all at once.

'It's so good,' I moan, lifting my hips now and trying to make him feel what I am, but he grips my hips tight and tumbles me back onto the bed, his eyes clashing with mine, daring me to argue.

His removal is an agony of extreme proportions.

He pulls away from me and I push up onto my elbows, prepared to chase him—prepared to chase him to the ends of the earth if necessary.

He strides to his bedside table and pulls something small and metallic out and it is the first time I recognise that I haven't even thought of a condom. I would have had sex with him; I would have welcomed his release if he had offered it, without hesitation.

It is frightening enough to draw me out of the moment. 'Oh, my God.'

'What?' He's worried for me. It colours his expression and a drum bangs somewhere near my heart. 'Are you hurt?'

'No, I just can't believe I didn't think of protection.'

His smile is my crack cocaine. 'I guess you really wanted this.' And he pushes back inside me, now with him on top, and it feels new and different all over again. Doubts have no space in the field of pleasure; I am simply a ball of nerve endings and they are delighting in his nearness.

I realise that he was holding back before; perhaps worried about the complications of being in me without a barrier. Now he thrusts hard, possessing me as though it is his path to happiness and joy, as though I am his anchor point.

The wave collects me and every thrust brings me higher upon it, taking me to its peak, rolling me in its crest and dumping me onto the next wave, dragging me higher and higher until I am so close to the stars I swear I could reach out and touch them. My fingers drag over the sheets, but I feel celestial magic within my grasp and then I hear a noise, a sharp, loud, agonised cry—it takes me a moment to realise it is the sound of my own ecstasy, wrapping around us both. It takes me a moment to realise that an orgasm is wrenching me apart, one delightful sob at a time.

And then he is with me, his fingers laced through mine, his body racked with the same grip of release, our cries combined, our breath fast, our bodies coated in sweat despite the coolness of the morning. He drops on top of me afterwards and I wrap my arms around him instinctively; my legs too. As though I am afraid he will withdraw and I will lose him—and this—even when I know that I must. That it is the natural conclusion to what we are and what we've done.

I can't think about that yet.

His breath is heavy and his body heavier still. I stay there, my arms wrapped around him, until he is unbearably heavy and then I shift a little, sliding sideways at the same moment I realise that he has fallen asleep. I wriggle out completely, my eyes searching his face, seeing the beauty in his sleep and recognising that it is, nonetheless, a tortured, unsettled repose. No rest for Noah. Not really.

What demons drive his tormented nights? What devils demand this fractured sleep of him? I want to know—not only because I want to help but because I *need* to understand. He is a puzzle that I suddenly, desperately ache to complete. He is an answer to a question I don't know how to pose.

I watch him sleep for a long time. At least ten minutes. I wait for him to wake, as he says he does, but his eyelids are flickering like moths near a flame and I suppose then that he is fast asleep. Knowing what a rare commodity this is for him, I dismiss the very idea of waking him.

Besides, I need space and time to process what I've done. To acknowledge this development and allow it into my being—to allow this to make up a part of my truth now.

I step out of the bed silently. There is nothing to remove from the mezzanine but myself. All my clothes and personal items remain where I left them, or where he left them—I'm still so foggy on the details of last night.

I creep down the stairs like a burglar post-heist, and it is only once I discover my shirt and trousers, neatly folded on the kitchen bench, that I realise I've left my underpants in his bed somewhere.

I look guiltily towards the mezzanine but think better of retrieving them. I plan to take a cab straight home—better that I don't wake him for a pair of briefs.

I dress quickly and, at the door, take one last look in the direction of where he's sleeping. I can hear his breathing, steady and rhythmic. I close my eyes, inhale and allow myself to imagine that I am still there with him, his arm perhaps casually thrown over my body, his hair flopping onto the pillow.

With a shake of my head to clear the seductive image, I take the irreversible step of leaving his home, of pulling the door shut firmly behind me. I am now on this side of Noah's world and he on the other.

We are worlds apart.

I wake as the door clicks shut, but I don't move. I know instinctively what the door signals and I fight every residual sensation of having been left. I feel every single closed door. And Holly is now a part of that.

I stretch my arms and roll over, keeping my eyes shut. Not in the futile pursuit of sleep so much as an attempt to replay what we've just shared. I can smell her in my bed; I can hear her in my bed. Her fervent, vocal pleasure. Her surprise at the orgasm.

It was painfully obvious that she hadn't felt like that before and I am glad for my sake, and sorry for hers.

Good sex is a gift; everyone should expérience it. Is there anything that is more natural and more important in life than the body's ability to pleasure another?

I see her face again as she fell apart, her eyes rolled back in her head, her mouth clamped shut, her nipples hard beads thrust forward, her skin goosed all over…and an animalistic surge of power throbs through me.

I did that to her.

And I'm going to do it again.

I don't know if I expected to hear from him. I know he knows how to email me. I know he has my number. And as Sunday bleeds into Monday, which gives way to Tuesday, I have to face the fact that perhaps he is choosing not to contact me.

I have always been analytical, perhaps too much so, and in the last three days I have found myself going over every single detail of our time together, reliving his words, touch, mood. I wonder at the way we came together, at the euphoric sense of heaven that overtook me, and the way I stole out of his home.

By Thursday, I am contemplating calling him. Worrying for him. Wondering if he is okay. It is absurd and stupid and I have learned not to let a man weaken me—I am not who I was five, six, seven years ago.

If Noah doesn't want to call me, if all he wanted was one night with me, then it is better to learn that truth now than in a year's time. Right?

I tell myself I am grateful that it only got this far, and I congratulate myself for the escape from possible disaster. I focus on what is right in front of me, and what matters. I concentrate on Christmas and Ivy and the fact she's asked me about her father for the first time in her life—this is a day I have dreaded. I have no ready-made answer to respond to her question. I don't know how to discuss Aaron with her.

Old-fashioned platitudes, like *We both love you very much, but we were better living apart*, don't seem to apply here, seeing as he tried to kill me when I was pregnant with her.

Instead, I focus on the fact her father is a beautiful musician and put on one of his CDs for her to

listen to, even though it sends shivers of panic riot-
ing through my body.

I hate his music.

I hate him.

On Friday afternoon, it has been a week since I
saw Noah Moore. My heart drops at the thought that
it's simply the first of many weeks I must tick off in
this fashion. I know from experience that it will get
easier—that I will become more adept at sidestep-
ping this ache of need.

Besides, I took a step out of my comfort zone and
I'm glad for that. I'm glad to have slept with him.
I walked into it with my eyes wide open and I got
what I wanted.

As if on cue, heat floods my body and my nipples
tingle with remembered pleasure. I smile.

It was an incredible night. Morning. Whatever.

I tidy my desk, sort my files, answer emails and,
near seven o'clock, I go to close my computer down.
Out of nowhere, in my mind I see Noah. I see him
as he was—so beautiful, so strong, so handsome, so
mysterious. I remember the tattoo on his shoulder,
the one that frightened me and weakened my knees
and stirred my gut all at once.

What had he called it?

Malingee?

I can't do justice to the way he pronounced it, but
it was something like that.

I open a browser and type *Malernguy* into the
computer. I get a Danish computer company. That's

not right. I try three more variations on spelling before I hit on something that sounds close enough.

Malingee: an Australian Aboriginal spirit, both nocturnal and malignant, that terrified humans. While it didn't seek to engage them, it would ruthlessly slay any who crossed its path, using its stone dagger to kill. A terrifying spectre.

A frisson starts at the base of my skull, tingling and pulsing and running down my spine like wildfire, spreading unease and doubts anew.

Why would Noah have this tattoo on his shoulder?

Dozens of new questions open up inside me. There is so much about him I don't know—so much I will never know, if last week was the end for us.

The thought is like a detonation and it fires me to stand. I shut my computer down and grab my bag, locking up my office.

I am reminded then of closing Noah's door as I left his apartment—and I wish I could go back in time and stay, as I had contemplated. I wish I hadn't left.

I want him—all the more because I have felt him move inside me and the reality outstripped every single one of my fantasies.

Once, surely, just wasn't enough.

CHAPTER EIGHT

I SEE HER the moment she steps out onto the street, her hair pulled into a bun that I instantly imagine loosening with my fingers, pulling free and tangling around her shoulders. She's wearing a cream trench coat belted at the waist and, from this distance, it looks like dark pants that hug her slim legs. Legs that have wrapped around me; legs that I haven't yet tasted—remiss of me. I have been fantasising about running my tongue down her calves, finding all her sweetest spots and tormenting her with them.

Her head is bent; she doesn't see me. I wonder where she's going?

Has she been thinking of me?

She hasn't called. She hasn't emailed. Did I expect her to? Has she been waiting to hear from me? I don't chase women. I don't chase anyone. But damn it if I didn't want to turn up at Holly's office Monday evening and drag her back to my bed. Ditto Tuesday, Wednesday, Thursday and, finally, here I am. Telling myself that having waited a week I have proved to myself that she is as disposable as everyone else in my life.

A familiar sense of distance calms my pulse. It doesn't matter what she's been thinking or wanting; I don't care.

This isn't about anything except the present—and the present we can give each other. I have no expectations of her and she sure as hell doesn't of me, or she would have tried to contact me.

That's perfect. There's no need for my chest to be feeling like this—Holly Scott-Leigh *is* different to my usual lovers, but she's the same in many ways. I can manage her, this, us, whatever the hell I'm doing.

And I did sleep better after she'd left. For the first time since Julianne died, I was able to get several hours of sleep in a row. Perhaps Holly did that. Maybe fucking her worked magic on parts of me distinct from my cock.

She looks towards me as she crosses the street, but it is a cursory inspection, only to make sure she is safe to go, and she doesn't look towards me long enough to recognise me. She drops her head down and surges forward. As she reaches the footpath, I step off my bike.

A thrill of anticipation is unmistakable, and when I step forward the thrill trebles in intensity.

She has been abused and she is wary—perhaps it's a wariness she'll always feel? The idea of that rubs me completely the wrong way, but I shelve my reaction to better observe hers. She looks at me, her expression confused and hurt and then angry and, finally, cold, colder than ice, as she lifts an elegant brow and crosses her arms.

'Noah.' My name is a dismissal, not a hello.

She's pissed with me.

Fascinating.

'Holly.' I grin, enjoying the way my cavalier response needles her. I told you, I like needling her and the more I do it, the more I realise that.

She doesn't know what to say. She's looking at me as though she's trying to find words and I offer none; I simply watch the play of emotions as they constrict her face.

'What are you doing here?' she asks finally. Unmistakably cold now.

'What do you think?' I reach behind me for a helmet and hold it out to her. She makes no effort to take it. Something like iron wraps around my chest.

'A booty call?' She is outraged at that, angling her face away from me, showing only her cold profile.

'Are you okay?' The question is surprising to me. I think it's the first time I've evinced concern for anyone's emotional state, besides Gabe's perhaps. I'm not into dating; I don't do it often. If I see a woman, it's a light, casual affair. A few nights. A bit of fun.

I don't ask them if they're 'okay'. I don't hold my breath while waiting for the answer, as I am now, desperately needing to hear that she is.

'Fine.' The crisp answer shows she doesn't care that it's a first for me. She draws in a breath and turns back to face me; I feel as though I've been slammed in the chest with a stack of knives. She's so beautiful and somehow I'd forgotten, even in the thirty seconds since she spun her face away from me. 'Anyway—'

I hear the finality in the word '—I was just about to head home.'

I narrow my eyes and nod. 'I'll give you a lift.'

'Noah…'

A car goes by, Christmas carols playing loudly, and she waits until it has passed.

'I don't know what you want from me.' It's simple and complicated. Terrifying and empowering.

The problem is, I don't know what I want from her either. Besides the fact that she's an addiction that's spilled into my bloodstream, I know only that I need her now. Here. Not here, because she deserves better than that, but the first place we can get to with a modicum of privacy.

'Don't you?' It's a gruff reply that has her tilting her head forward.

There's a look of defiance in her eyes. Surrender too. 'I guess it's exactly what I want from you.'

We didn't have the 'your place or mine' conversation, but I'm glad he's taking us back to his apartment. I was drunk when he brought me here before, but in the morning I realised we were in Bermondsey and his home was actually a converted wharf building right on the river. Completely hollowed out at some point, leaving the open-plan design he obviously prefers.

It's not far from my office and he rides quickly—as eager as I am, obviously, to renew our bodies' acquaintance with one another. And I am *so* desperate for that, but other things are knotting through me.

Noah Moore is a mystery and the part of me that likes to find order in chaos needs to understand him. Despite the fact he isn't my patient, and never can be, the therapist I trained to become and have spent years working as *needs* to dig through his issues, to understand what brought him to me in the first instance. It's a compulsion.

I need more than just to understand him, though; I need him.

He pulls his bike up in front of the building and I step off before he does, removing my helmet, not giving him a reason to touch me—yet.

I wait by his front door and he takes only a moment to join me, unlocking it and pushing it inwards, staying on the outside, his arm outstretched to allow me entry. I move past him but, once inside, all the memories of last week slam into me and I am sucked back in time.

'Are you hungry?' He is maintaining a distance that is interesting.

'Yeah.' I think I might be, though it's hard to read beyond the desire that's swarming me.

I follow him into the kitchen, where he disappears into the fridge—it's a huge fridge, two, actually, side by side. I wonder at the kind of entertaining he does to necessitate that.

He pulls out a couple of cardboard boxes, each the size of a laptop, and places them on the bench, then reaches in for a bottle of wine. He pours me a glass and grabs a beer for himself.

'So, did you rationalise what we did last week?'

I think about lying to him, but don't. 'You want me. I want you. It's a simple equation. Apparently desire outweighs common sense.'

He nods. 'I like that. Mathematical sex.'

'Sure.' I bite down on my lip. 'I never thought I'd do anything like this.'

'Why not?' he asks curiously.

'Isn't that obvious?'

'Obviously,' he teases. 'Not.'

I force myself to meet his eyes. 'My whole life is dedicated to helping people.' I swallow. 'You came to me for help. And I can't be that person. But, beyond that, what if I do something that hurts you...?'

'Do you think I'm that fragile?' he prompts with disbelief.

I shrug my shoulders. 'Why did you come to see me? Why do you think you need therapy?'

He is instantly wary, just like in our first session. He tries to cover it, out of deference to what we've shared, but I see it. I see the wall he throws up between us.

'Don't hide from me,' I say softly. 'Tell me.'

His jaw clenches and a muscle moves at the base of his throat. 'Tell you what?'

'Why you came to me!' I shouldn't be annoyed—in my office I wouldn't be. With my patients I can control my emotions completely, but Noah isn't my patient. And here, with him so close and my body flaming with liquid heat, I am just a woman, not a doctor; I'm a woman who is full of desire and little else right now.

'I've told you. I'm not sleeping.'

'And have you ruled out any physiological cause for that?' I push, watching as he steps away from me and grabs his beer, throwing back at least half of it in one long draught.

'Such as?' He has slipped into a combative mind-set. He looks at me as though I am his enemy and I don't want that—I am pushing him too hard and I know it won't achieve results. Not with anyone and least of all Noah Moore.

There's more than one way to skin a cat, though. I've always hated that expression! Perhaps I can circumnavigate Noah's situation and find his pains all on my own.

With an effort I smile, but it is fake. A forgery. An imitation of what I think a smile should be. 'Alcohol in the evening can actually disturb your sleep. Perhaps that's it?'

We both know it isn't. He smiles and, just like mine, it rings with falseness.

'Could be.' He takes another sip from his beer, though, his eyes holding mine over the rim and there is a challenge in them. *Back off.* He doesn't want me to have my therapist hat on. I promised him I wouldn't, didn't I? Wasn't that the trade-off I made, to sleep with him?

But I can't *not*. It's hard to draw the line between what I do for a living and how I live my life. Particularly with people I care about.

Yes, I care about Noah Moore, and not just because we've slept together. I care about all of him, including his health, his happiness. I want to help him, but not as a therapist. As…what? As the woman he's sleeping with? That's normal, isn't it?

'What's for dinner?' I prompt, desperate to return our mood to its previous lightness. He hesitates only a moment before reaching for the cardboard boxes and flipping the lids. One is filled with oysters and scampi, the other with sushi.

I adore all three and my tummy gives a little groan of appreciation. Now when he smiles, it is genuine.

'What would you like?'

'Um…oysters.'

He lifts a brow, but neither of us says what we're thinking—the rumoured effects of oysters as an aphrodisiac. I've never found that to be the case anyway; then again, until meeting Noah Moore, I had thought myself to be somewhat disinterested in sex. I reach for my wine. Before he takes a plate from the cupboard, he washes his hands at the sink. It's a normal gesture, just a small one, but it seems almost incongruous. He dries his fingers slowly and then turns to face me.

He catches me watching him and smiles. My heart lurches.

'Have you ever been to Rivière?' I ask the first thing that pops into my head.

'The oyster bar?'

'Yeah.' I nod. 'It's one of my favourite places. I used to go there all the time when I was younger, and get a half-dozen oysters and have a glass of champagne.'

'Before you had your child?'

'Ivy,' I supply.

His smile lifts to me. 'Ivy?'

I nod.

'Like Holly and Ivy.'

Used to being teased about my love of Christmas by all and sundry, I'm more sensitive than perhaps I should be. 'Yes.'

'Like the Christmas carol?'

'Like the Christmas carol,' I confirm with a defiant nod.

'That's pretty fucking cute.'

My pulse throbs. 'Really?'

'Sure.' He takes a plate down and begins to arrange oysters onto it for me. 'Lemon?'

I nod.

'So I take it your asshole of an ex didn't mind you going to your oyster dates solo?'

'He didn't know.'

'Really?' Noah passes me a plate and then begins to arrange his own. I stay sitting on the countertop and he perches his arse opposite, watching me as he swallows his first oyster. It's strangely erotic to see it go down his throat. I look away.

'I used to leave work early on Friday,' I say. 'I'd go there and have a quiet hour all to myself.'

'With the oysters,' he says, the jocular comment undermined by the ice-cold determination in his eyes.

'Right, with the oysters.'

'You said you met him in high school?'

Do I want to speak about Aaron? Not really. Yet I find myself nodding. 'He's two years older than me. You know what it's like when you're a kid—there's something so…cool…about older guys.' I roll my eyes. Before he can ask another question, I reach for an oyster. It is ice-cold and so salty that I moan as I eat it.

'Jesus. Maybe that's why they're supposed to be sexy.'

I laugh self-consciously. 'What about you? Any sexy school girlfriends in your past? Big, romantic love affairs?'

'Nah.' Another word that makes him sound so Australian.

'Nah?' I try to imitate it and fail. He grins.

I like his grin.

'Nah. Nope. Nada.' He takes another oyster and eats it. I look away, sip my wine. My face is warm.

'Nothing?'

'Nothing,' he says with a shrug.

'You mean you've literally never been in a relationship?'

'You going to psychoanalyse that?'

I reach for another oyster, buying time. 'I can't switch off my brain just because you don't want to talk about your past.'

He arches a brow. 'So what do you read into it, then?'

'I thought we agreed I wasn't going to do this.'

'I'm just curious,' he prompts.

'Well—' I choose my words with attention '—I suppose I'd say that it's…interesting.'

'Why?'

'It's unusual,' I continue. 'To be your age and not have someone in your past.'

'I haven't been living a monk's life,' he points out.

'Things you probably don't need to discuss with me.' It's unexpectedly haughty.

He laughs, a sound that runs like smooth caramel over my back. 'Jealous?'

I don't answer. I am—it's no doubt very apparent. My silence seems to sober him.

As if realising that he's crossed a line I don't like very much, he sighs. 'I'm a busy man, Holly. Gabe and I have been like hamsters on a wheel since things took off. Ten years later, I look around and I'm thirty-six. I haven't exactly had time for anyone else in my life.'

'So you're saying you want a relationship, to get married, grow old with someone, but you just haven't had time to find the right person?'

'Better than marrying an abusive shit like you did.'

Silence follows his statement. I'm hurt, of course, and the depth of that emotion is unexpected. But I have slipped back into my therapeutic headspace and I am used to having patients throw insults and cross reprimands at me—usually, it is a sign that I am close to finding a wound they don't want reopened.

'I'm…sorry.' Noah frowns. 'That was fucking rude.'

I laugh, because only Noah could apologise for rudeness and include a curse with it. 'Yeah, but you're right.' I smile reassuringly, not wanting him to think I'm upset. Not wanting him to shut down. 'I'd do anything to not...'

I freeze, surprised at the admission I'd been about to make. It goes against the determination I have to see the positives in my relationship with Aaron.

'Yes?' he prompts, finishing off his oysters and moving back towards me.

'I mean, I'd do it all again in a heartbeat to get Ivy, but it was...a dark phase of my life.'

He lifts a brow. 'Is that therapy-speak for it sucked balls?'

I laugh. 'Something like that.' He watches me as I sip my wine; his eyes on my face make my skin flush. 'What about family?'

He doesn't welcome the question. He visibly bristles and his shoulders tense. 'What about them?'

'Well—' I shrug my shoulders '—you have one, I presume?'

'Everyone has family, right?' He moves towards me, placing a hand possessively on my thigh. 'Did you miss me this week?'

The question is out of left field. He's trying to change the subject and I let him, but I make a mental note, determined to return to this later, determined to find out *something* about him that he doesn't necessarily want to share.

'Did you think about me?' I'm wearing a silk

blouse and he undoes it slowly, his eyes hooked onto mine. My breath is forced, my pulse frantic.

'I…'

His smile is just a mocking twist of his lips. 'No lies, Doc.'

'Of course I thought about you,' I say, knowing on some level that he needs to hear that. He is tough and appears confident, but I sense his insecurities and this is one of them. There is no sense in obfuscating. I don't want to be the kind of woman who sleeps with someone like Noah and doesn't think about him, anyway.

For this reason I don't ask the question back. I know he thought about me. I don't need to surrender to my insecurities and beg him to admit it.

But, without prompting, he says, 'I wanted you so fucking bad.'

'When?'

'Every day.' He pushes the shirt down and I lift my arms out, mesmerised by him, distracted by him, owned by him.

'I thought about these.' He cups my breasts, pushing them out from under the bra before reaching around to unhook it. 'A lot.'

'Did you?' A whisper. I don't need to speak, though, my body is speaking for me. I push myself forward, nudging my breasts closer to him, needing him to touch me, to kiss me.

His smile shows that he knows. 'I thought about the way I touched you in your office, and how ready you were for me. How wet and sweet. How quick to come.'

A gargled whimper dies in my throat. I'm all that again, already. Oysters and wine are forgotten.

'Noah…'

He runs his mouth along my jaw, not touching me, just close enough that I feel the warmth of his breath. I shiver. He pushes his lips against my throat and kisses me, sucks on me, and a whirl of feeling starts in my gut. His touch is like flame; my body burns in response.

When he finally drops his mouth to an aching, hard nipple and sucks it deep in his mouth, I am beyond rational thought. I make a bubbling cry and wrap my legs around his waist, just like on that first day in my office, holding him close to me.

I feel his hard cock through his clothes and mine and I grind myself against him, needing to feel him inside me, but for the moment making do with this. Feeling his firm length against my pulsing heart is heaven.

'Are you wet now?' he asks, the words breathed against my flesh, reverberating through me.

I nod, though I think his question is rhetorical.

'Let's see.' His fingers find the waistband of my pants, loosening them, and I wiggle my bottom so he can slide them down lower. I am naked in his kitchen and it doesn't even occur to me to be embarrassed or to think it's weird. It's not. It's perfect.

The only sound is my breath, loud and rasping, as

though I've run a marathon when, in fact, it is anticipation, not exhaustion, that fires the sound.

'Noah.' A whimper, a need.

He knows. 'Lie back.'

I don't, not straight away, so he grabs my knees
and pulls on them a little, sliding my butt forward.
I drop back onto my elbows; the kitchen counter is
marble and ice-cold beneath me.

I don't have time to process that discomfort,
though, because suddenly his mouth is on me. On
my seam, his tongue running across me, his hands
holding my legs wide.

I have *never* been kissed there.

'You're kidding.'

I must have said that aloud—I didn't mean to.
But, seriously, I have never been kissed there and
I've never even really been interested in it. I mean,
it seems almost gross. Or it did. Noah's mouth on
me is the best thing I've ever felt—just about. I am
breathing harder and faster, louder, arching my back
on the marble slab, reaching for him, for something,
for sanity, but there is nothing.

Just me and my abandonment to this beautiful
rightness.

'You taste so fucking good,' he groans, and the
words tip me over, spreading through me like a whip
of desire.

I curl my toes around the scalloped edge of the
bench and cry out as I come, hard, fast, impossibly
inevitable.

It is like being doused in warm water, so beautiful

and perfect and relaxing despite the fevered racing of my heart. I need to take stock, to feel this, to let it permeate my being, but Noah doesn't allow that. He grabs for me, pulling my hips, and I don't realise he's undone his trousers until he's lifted me around his waist, away from the bench. We don't go far; he pushes me against the fridge, my back used to cold surfaces and not minding the shock of that when answering heat is promised.

And it is.

He thrusts into me, hard, and his mouth reclaims a nipple, and my body zips with feelings, still processing my first orgasm, as he drives me towards another. I hear something, a voice, keening over and over, and realise it is me. I'm crying out in a fevered state, the words shaking with intensity.

His hands on my hips are splayed and his possession of me feels so unbelievably natural that I don't stop to think about the fact that he's possessing me so completely, that I have fallen under his spell and would do anything he asked of me. Anything. I am addicted to this and him.

The pain I've endured this week, the wondering, the loneliness—these things don't matter. It is just Noah, and now.

And, for now, this is enough.

CHAPTER NINE

HER BODY IS sheened in perspiration and her cheeks are pink. Her eyes moist—not with tears but with heightened pleasure. I stand above her, watching her, my arms crossed, the thrill of power unmistakable.

I have done this to her. And I am pretty sure it's the first time she's ever known this kind of drugging desire. A thrill spreads through me.

Her ex was a bastard; I shouldn't feel any kind of competition with him. I have seen his marks on her body now. Little marks, small scars, but I know without asking how she came to wear them.

He isn't worthy of competing with, and yet the knowledge that I have given her so much pleasure, that he certainly didn't, does something inside me.

Then again, at what cost?

Holly Scott-Leigh is dangerous for me—there is risk here, with her. She has entered my bloodstream and I don't even bother trying to pretend otherwise. She's not like any other woman I've ever known. If I make her feel new different pleasures, she does exactly the same to me.

Losing myself in her body has become my latest addiction, and not just because it seems to give me a reprieve from my dark thoughts—if only for a while.

Her chest, and those beautiful breasts, are shifting with each of her breaths, slowing down now, and I wonder if she is tired? If she would like to sleep?

I swallow past a throat that is constricted by pleasure and reach into my bed, lifting her. I've lost count of how many times she's come. In the kitchen downstairs, on the bench, against my fridge, and then in my bed, when I used my fingers to drive her to the edge... I scoop her against my chest and her eyes lock onto mine.

Something shifts in my chest. Desire, surely, rampant and uncontainable. I look straight ahead, needing her as an addict needs their next fix.

My en suite bathroom is big—the kind of place I could never have imagined, growing up as I did. It's at least twice the size of most bedrooms I knew as a kid and it's covered in marble tiles. A spa bath is at its centre and to the side, with frosted windows that overlook the Thames, there is a shower. I like to shower. I like the feel of water on my skin and I have an overhead nozzle as well as one from either wall.

Holly lifts a brow with amusement. 'You don't think this is kind of overkill?'

It's impossible for someone like her to understand. You grow up with nothing and it does things to you. Trust me, I know about this stuff.

'You haven't felt the shower.' I grin, making light of it, not wanting to open the door to my reasons for living as I do. My bathroom is a palace and the rest of my home is like a loft—there's nothing luxurious nor expensive, nothing particularly personal, anywhere in this place. As though I'm expecting to pick up a rucksack at any point and walk right out that door. Like I've done so many times. I guess old habits really do die hard.

'I don't know if my feelings can take anything else wonderful tonight…' she says, teasing me, reaching out and curling her fingers in my hair in a gesture of such simple intimacy that my heart stalls with ice and rejection immediately.

Intimacy—other than physical—is a lie. A lie people tell themselves, a benign lie, but one with the power to rip your soul out.

'Let's test that theory.'

I designed a home app that runs this place—I can control everything from my watch or phone, or from within my car, where I have an audio transceiver hooked up. I programmed the shower with seventeen settings. I go for number five now. All the jets turn on and the water is warm, just warm.

I don't put Holly down, though. Instead, I lower her onto my cock—my ever-hard cock, right now, thanks to her—and she moans as I do so, her body covered in water, her hair slicked back, her eyes almost panicked when they meet mine. As though she can't quite believe how good it is between us. How much she wants me.

She tips her head back, her eyes on the ceiling, a cascade of water dousing her.

I'm not wearing a condom. I just want to feel her like that first time, when she climbed on top of me and took me without a single thought for anything other than assuaging her needs, for slaking this desire.

'I'm on the Pill,' she says, the words higher in pitch, which I now know means she's close. Her words drill into me. Is she saying what I think she is? 'Are you...' Her eyes drop to mine for a moment and, despite the pink in her cheeks, the tautness of her nipples, she seems to find sanity for a moment. 'I mean, I presume you're...safe?'

As it happens, I had to get a full raft of tests a couple of weeks ago—my life insurance is worth enough to buy a country and they like to keep an eye on me. I suppose I'm one of their higher risk clients.

She nods. 'I don't want you to use a condom.' She tilts her head back again and the way she said that, what she's giving me, is just about the biggest turn-on I can imagine.

I make a primal sound of assent and pull her away from me. She's so small, I seem to have forgotten she has free will and I'm moving her according to my own desires. One look at her face, though, and I see that she doesn't mind. That she wants this. That she feels all the good feels right here with me.

I spin her around, facing her towards the windows that overlook the river, bracing her hands on the window ledge.

'It's a nice view, but I kind of liked what we were doing,' she says.

I don't answer. Not verbally. I push into her from behind and her legs spread wider for me, her body tilting forward so I have complete access to everything I want and need. *This!* This is how I need to feel her.

I cup her breasts possessively as I push into her and my mouth drops to her shoulder, my teeth pressing against her flesh. She whimpers, her body throbbing around me already. But I'm not going to give her time to absorb each orgasm; I'm going to deluge her with them. I drop one hand to her clit, finding the sensitive cluster of nerves and teasing them with my fingers as my cock moves hard within her. I torment her nipple, rolling it between my thumb and forefinger, plucking it, pulling it until she's crying out and I am addicted to the sound of that, her raspy, broken moans of surrender.

I know what Holly has been through and from the moment she told me I have felt protective towards her, have thought I should treat her with kid gloves. But what I want, and what I am realising she wants, is for me to simply fuck her, hard.

I do that now, pushing into her as deep as she'll take me, and the harder I move the more she cries out, begging me over and over, 'Please, Noah, please.'

My name on her lips is heaven. I will never stop, so long as she keeps calling to me like that. 'No— ahhhhh…' She pushes backwards, giving me better access, and I grip her hips with both my hands, holding her hard against me as I slam into her. Her body shakes and quivers and her voice is a primal, feral cry that reverberates around the bathroom as she comes.

I hold her still, steadying her, reassuring her, and my dick throbs inside her as Holly's warm, wet muscles squeeze me tight, whispering at me to join her, to find my own ecstatic release. But I don't want this to end yet. I am high on what I can do to her, what she can do to me.

I am high on this feeling.

It takes all my willpower, but I stay hard inside her, refusing to give in to the waves of euphoria that are running through me.

She stays as she is, staring out of the window, or perhaps not seeing, I don't know. She is shaking all over, her body physically changed by what we just did. I remember then that I didn't want to give her time to recover.

I run my hand around to her beautiful pussy, brushing against the base of my cock in my quest to touch her. I rub my fingers against her and she moans; I feel her muscles clench anew, wrapping around my cock. Hell, I feel my own ministrations as I massage her into another climax and grit my teeth together, holding off, wanting her to come again, needing her to.

'What are you doing to me?' she whimpers, right before she explodes and now I hold her breasts tight, cupping her with both hands, thinking they are the most perfect breasts I've ever felt. Thinking she is perfect.

It's a stray thought and I dismiss it, but then Holly

does what I could never have expected. She pulls away from me, a moan of emptiness escapes her as she removes my cock. She turns around to face me and she looks just what she is—a woman who has been fucked. Thoroughly.

I wonder what she'll say or do. My dick is hard and huge between us and her eyes drop to it. I see her swallow as she takes in my length, perhaps wondering how the hell I fit inside her in the first place.

And then, slowly, fatalistically, she drops to her knees, right in front of me, her hair a wet pelt against her head, her eyes locked to mine.

Is she going to do what I think? What I am now hoping against hope?

Her lips, always painted a bright red, have been kissed free of cosmetics and are simply pale pink, full and perfect. My fingers find their way to her hair, stroking it gently at first.

Then she opens her mouth and takes my tip— just my tip—inside, encircling me with her tongue, testing herself and me, and I find my fingers curling tighter, fisting around her hair, and I'm trying not to hold her still and push myself farther forward. It should be at her pace; she's tentative and I gather this is new for her too, that she hasn't done this often, maybe never. Power is an aphrodisiac.

I want to roll my hips and claim her mouth; I want to feel the back of her throat, hitch myself in deep and far. I don't, but I do hold her hair tightly, as though it alone will save me. I am drowning in this—in her.

And then, out of nowhere, she moves her mouth along my shaft, and my tip hits the softness at the back of her mouth. I cry out, a hoarse sound that might be her name or might be a curse, and I throw my head back for a second, letting my body feel everything. But only for a second because I want to watch her. Her on her knees, her hair drenched by the shower, her body pale and creamy except for the pale pink patches I've left with my stubble and my touch.

She draws back, rocking on her knees a little, and then swallows me again, making a little sucking noise that is hotter than I can say.

My breath hitches in my throat and she pulls away, looking up at me, removing her mouth. 'Show me what you want,' she says.

'You're doing it,' I promise throatily.

'No—' And she knows me so well, knows what I want. 'Show me.' She lifts a finger to my hands that are curled in her hair, her eyes challenging me. 'I'm not made of glass,' she whispers.

God, she's in my head. She hears my thoughts. It terrifies me. But she's right. I am treating her more gently than I want to, and she doesn't want that.

'Show me,' she says again.

'Because you haven't done this before?' I ask, needing to hear it. Getting off on the admission.

She shakes her head. 'Never.'

Fuck. I'm done for. I'm fucking done for.

The darkness within me consumes me then, the need to possess her and own her and fill her up with me takes over. Almost against my will, my hands push her head forward, bringing her back to my cock. A thread of concern runs through me and I hear myself say, 'Tell me if I'm too much for you...'

'You're definitely too much for me,' she says, a small laugh on her face that is taken away when I throb into her. I push her head all the way forward; my cock fills her mouth and I jerk my hips back and forth, fucking her lips, my fingers digging into her scalp. Her eyes hold mine and then, as I move her, she drops a hand between her legs and touches herself.

It's the most erotic thing I've ever done.

Her mouth is so moist and I'm so far back, her tongue flattened by me. I know I need to look after her, and I pull back out to let her recover before taking her mouth once more.

She makes a moaning noise and I see that she's climaxing again, her body quivering.

And I can hold off no longer. 'I'm coming,' I grunt, letting go of her hair, giving her a chance to pull away, but she catches my wrist and lifts it back, her eyes warring with mine.

Fuck.

I hold her right against me, so deep her lips encircle the base of my cock, and I thrust twice more into her mouth, releasing myself with a guttural oath, giving her my seed and holding her there while I shake with the power of my release.

I am weakened and strengthened by this. I reach down for her, grabbing her under her arms and lifting her, her wet body sliding along mine as I cradle her against me. I step out of the shower, using the voice command to turn it off. I have a stack of freshly laundered towels on the bench—not my work, obviously, so much as the cleaners who come and look after this place—and I wrap one around her as best I can, without relinquishing our bodies' contact. Her eyes are heavy, dropping shut as though weighted with cement.

But as we reach the bed and I lay her down gently she smiles at me, her lips curving upwards and her eyes holding mine. There is a silent question we each pose the other: *Are you okay?* She smiles and I return it.

We're better than okay.

She is asleep almost the second her head hits the pillow. I towel her dry gently, squeezing water out of her hair so that she doesn't feel uncomfortable, and then I pull a sheet up around her.

She smiles in her sleep and rolls onto her side, facing the emptiness of the bed. I look at her for a moment and think of going downstairs, of having a Scotch or a coffee or a fucking sandwich. But instead I peel back the sheet and lie in bed beside her, staring at her, watching her sleep, envying the ease with which she's found peace.

I watch her and, the next thing I know, she is watching me and it's morning.

The sun is reaching in through the windows, though it is wintry and weak.

'Hi.' She smiles at me and my gut twists, like

her hands have reached inside me and toyed with my organs.

'Hi.' My voice is gruff.

'You slept.' She reaches a finger out and touches my lip, tracing it in a way that tickles.

I frown. She's right. I *did* sleep, and the whole night through. When was the last time that happened? Before she died. But I don't want to think about Julianne now.

I don't want to think about the way I treated her. About the impossibility of making amends, changing my actions, mending her heart.

Holly has this thing she does, when she's trying to work out what to say to me. She bites on her lip and pinches her eyes together, just a little, just enough to make me know she's worried she's going to offend me or push me away.

It gives me enough time to prepare for whatever is coming. How long has she been watching me? And what has she been thinking about? An unfamiliar—no, not unfamiliar—a long-forgotten vulnerability creeps along my spine. A sense of being exposed and weak.

I swallow. Ignoring the feeling. Telling myself it doesn't apply here.

'Why don't you talk about your family?'

Jesus. I wasn't prepared for *that*. We were talking about this last night, though. In the kitchen. Before. Before everything.

'Why do we have to?'

Her frown is infinitesimal…and instantly unpalatable. I don't want to make Holly frown. I want to make her smile and laugh, to make her face contort with pleasure in a way that is evidence of her mind being blown.

'We don't *have* to. I'm just curious…'

Of course she is. A normal woman would be curious by now and Holly is no normal woman. 'It's *family*,' I say with a roll of my eyes. It's an act I've perfected over the years. A pretence that I'm long-suffering, like everyone else. Like I have a raft of aunts and uncles and siblings and cousins who drive me crazy instead of the paralyzing loneliness I have known almost my entire life. 'Do you want to talk about *your* family?'

She frowns. 'My family is…nothing special.'

I sense a reprieve, and also curiosity sparks inside me. Both push me to ask, 'They must be to have made you.'

The compliment shivers across her flesh, goosebumps spreading before my eyes. Power thrills in my gut. 'Tell me about them.' I drag the sheet down, exposing her nakedness to me, my gesture possessive and unapologetically so.

'I thought you didn't want to talk about family.'

'My family.' Or lack thereof.

She rolls her eyes. 'That's not fair.'

'Isn't it?' I grin, my fingers finding the curve of her hip and drawing invisible circles there, running figures of eight over her silky flesh until she exhales softly.

'My parents are very conservative, both in the

armed forces. My mother has an administrative role—it's how they met. My brothers signed up as soon as they were eighteen. I don't think my dad's ever forgiven me for not doing the same.'

'He must be proud of what you do.'

'He hates shrinks,' she says with a shrug.

'Why?'

'Does he need a reason?'

'In my experience, there's usually a reason.'

'Like with you?' she prompts.

'Nice try, Doc, but I asked first.'

She rolls her eyes, such a sexy gesture that I want to pin her back against the bed and kiss her until she whimpers. My dick jerks.

'Let's just say there's a reason I specialise in PTSD. Particularly with returned military personnel.'

'Your dad?'

'My dad *and* my older brother. But I was already practising by the time Logan came back from Iraq.' She sighs. 'My dad was in the first Gulf War. He was…changed by it. Irrevocably. Not so you'd notice if you didn't know him well. It was just…little things around the house. A temper that would come out of nowhere, whereas he'd never been like that. Paralysing panic attacks that made it impossible for him to go out, and a weird anger whenever Mum tried to organise normal stuff, like family holidays.'

'How old were you?'

'Young. Seven…eight. I saw the way he'd changed and I wanted to fix him.'

'And did you?'

'Not me, but he did get help.' Her lips form a lop-sided smile.

'And now you help other people.'

She looks at me meaningfully for a long moment. 'Yeah, if they'll let me.'

CHAPTER TEN

'YOU TOLD ME you're not close to your mother.'

Noah looks like I'm digging into his flesh with a knife. He is recalcitrant, closed off and apparently kicking himself for agreeing to this. But he *did* agree to it. I reach for a slice of cheese and taste it, waiting with the appearance of patience for him to speak.

Finally, his voice gruff, he says, 'I did.'

'And that you weren't raised by your parents. So, who did you grow up with?'

A muscle flexes in his jaw as he grinds his teeth. He doesn't want to have this conversation, but I'm done waiting for him to open up to me. This is for both our sakes. This is important.

'Noah?' I lean forward, pressing my hand over his. 'I want to help you. Not as a doctor but as a…' I search for a word that encompasses all that we are. 'A friend.' It's manifestly unsuitable, but it's the best I can do.

His eyes hold mine and there is hopelessness and pain in them, like he wants, so badly, to believe me.

I ache for him then, and I swear I will make him whole again, no matter what.

'I was a foster kid,' he says slowly, standing, walking towards the enormous windows that overlook the Thames. His back is to me and I allow that; perhaps he finds it easier to speak without looking at me. That's not unusual. His shoulders are tense, his back ramrod-straight. 'From when I was three.'

So little!

'But my mum still had visitation rights—I saw her every second week. When she wasn't high or stoned or pissed.'

He says the words as though it's a joke, but I hear the pain scored deep in his voice.

'Do you…remember your life? Before foster care?'

'No.' I suspect it's a lie, but I don't want to push the point now.

'And what about your foster family?'

'Foster family?' He angles his head so I see his profile. 'I lived in seventeen homes, Holly. I didn't have a *family*. I had a revolving door of bedrooms and people and new schools and new rules.'

It starts to make sense to me now, and my heart throbs in sympathy for the little boy he was. 'Which foster home did you spend the most time at?'

There is a pause, and I don't know if it's significant or if he simply can't recall. 'The Morrows,' he says after a moment. 'Julianne and Paul.'

There is no malice in his tone. 'You liked them?'

He shrugs. 'It was a long time ago. I was with them when I was eight years old.'

'And what happened?'

'What do you mean?' He's impatient now.

'Why did you leave them?'

'They left me,' he says matter-of-factly. 'Paul got transferred interstate. A big job in Melbourne and my biological mother wouldn't give permission for me to leave the state. I had to stay in Sydney.'

I nod. 'I imagine the foster system is similar to here—your mother's wishes had to be respected.'

'My mother was a drugged-out whore,' he says bitterly. 'Her wishes should have been irrelevant.'

'You wanted to go with the Morrows,' I surmise.

'At the time,' he says coldly, 'I didn't want to have to move into a new home, a new school, find new friends. I wanted to stay with the Morrows because it was easier.'

'But you would have had to meet new friends and go to a new school if you'd gone to Melbourne,' I point out logically.

'I was eight. I didn't think it through like that.' There's rich frustration in his tone now.

'So they left,' I say quietly. 'That must have been hard for you.'

'Not really,' he says, and again I feel he is lying. Hiding something. 'I was used to it by then. They were my seventh family already.'

'So many,' I say with a shake of my head. 'Did you keep in contact with them?'

'No.' A terse word. I make a mental note to ask him about this again later. Another time.

'Do you keep in contact with any of them?'

'Any of who?' Belligerence is back.

'The people you knew through foster care?'

'Yes.'

Closed book. 'Such as?' I prompt.

'Gabe.' The word is very quiet; at first I almost don't catch it. And it's not immediately meaningful to me. But then I recall something I've read about Noah at some point, and I recall his business partner is a man named Gabriele Arantini.

'Your business partner?' I prompt.

'Friend, business partner, foster brother. Take your pick.' He turns to face me and his face is pale. There is a hint of perspiration on his brow.

His response is classic for someone with PTSD; I've pushed him too far. I still don't know what exactly provokes this reaction in him, but somewhere within these questions is the key.

'You know,' I say thoughtfully, tilting my head to the side, 'Ivy would love to stay another night with her grandmother. Why don't I organise it and you and I can do something...fun?'

'Fun?'

He repeats the word, his eyes clouded, still pained by his recollections. I must remove that hurt for him. Now with a sticking plaster, and in time with conversation and understanding.

'Yes. Dinner? Movie? You know. Fun.'

He says nothing for a moment and I wonder if

he wants to be alone. If perhaps I'm moving him too fast.

But then his eyes lock onto mine. 'I have a better idea.'

Noah's better idea is something I would never have predicted. Standing at City Airport, staring at a sleek white jet with the Bright Sparks logo on the tail, I have the sense that I'm falling down a rabbit hole with no end in sight. How far does it go? When will I land?

He grips my hand, intertwining our fingers in that intimate way, and grins at me as we walk towards the jet, leaving his driver and his limo—so he *doesn't* always use the racehorse bike—on the tarmac.

'I suppose you think this is all very impressive,' I say with a small laugh, being purposely ironic.

'I already know you're impressed by me.' He winks and reaches up to my cheek with his spare hand, touching me lightly.

My heart squeezes. I turn back to the jet. It's small, as in not like a passenger jet, but when we step inside and are greeted by two women in smart navy blue uniforms, I see it's bigger than I realised. There are seats at the front, bigger than first class, in rows of two. Behind them, there's a large table and, beyond that, some sofas and armchairs all angled towards a movie screen.

'Jesus.' I blink as I study the obvious glamour and luxury. 'This is how you travel?'

He shrugs. 'Something wrong?'

'Are you kidding? It's amazing. I just don't want to go back to the real world afterwards.' It's a throw-away comment, but it could so easily apply to our personal relationship as well as his aeroplane. 'It's beautiful,' I say, to cover up any misunderstanding.

He shrugs. 'You get used to it.'

It's not yet lunchtime and the prospect of the twenty-four hours ahead fills me with excitement.

'You're smiling,' he says, his eyes latched on to my face.

I nod. 'I was just thinking how nice it is to be doing something like this. Something just for me. It's been a long time since I've...had fun. It's...kind of nice.'

'Nice?' He arches a brow, but his smile is broad, like I've said something that's making his heart glow too.

'Better than nice.' He leads us to the sofas and waits for me to settle down. There's a seat belt low down in the cushions; I slip it around my waist.

'You've done it tough the last few years?'

I shake my head. 'Not as tough as most. I'm lucky to have such good support with Ivy. And she's an incredible kid. Smart and funny, and sweet, and so easy. She's always been a good sleeper, great eater, well behaved. But, yeah, there have been times when it's been hard. I mean, just having someone to laugh with about her silly games, or whinge to when I'm exhausted and she's not listening, or have a glass of wine with and watch a movie, someone to rub my feet when I'm tired.' I lift my shoulders. 'But I love my job and it keeps me busy and, other than wishing, sometimes, that Ivy had a dad in her life, I don't regret the way I'm doing it.'

He is quiet for a moment, letting my words sink in. 'I'll bet you're a great mum.'

'I'm the best mum I can be. Some days great, other days not so much. But that's parenthood.' I eye him thoughtfully. 'What about you and kids?'

He grimaces exaggeratedly. 'As in having kids of my own?' Another grimace. 'No, thanks.'

He's making light of the question, so I laugh, just a small laugh, but something the exact opposite of amusement courses through me. I tell myself it's just surprise—surprise he can be so adamant about not wanting children when the experience is so rewarding. If *I* can say that—when I've borne a child to a person I hate, when I've raised that child on my own—then surely anyone can.

'You don't like kids?'

'From a distance? If I can't hear them or smell them? I like them okay.'

I roll my eyes. 'They're not that bad.'

'Sure. They're just not for me.' He's grinning, like he doesn't realise the significance of this conversation. Like he doesn't comprehend that it is an admission that immediately restricts our relationship. I mean, it was probably already limited by who we are, but I don't know. There's something so different about Noah and the way I feel with him that, without overthinking this, I would have said it was impossible to define what we are and where this will end up.

But an unnegotiable aversion to kids is a deal-breaker. I mean, I have one. But I'd like to have another one day. Holly would be a great sister and I've always clung to the hope that some day in the future I'd have what I so badly coveted as a single mother. A real family.

A loud family.

A family who talked and laughed and shared ideas and went on holidays together.

'Excuse me, Mr Moore?' A stewardess approaches us with an efficient click of her shoes. 'Can I get you a drink before take-off?' Her smile encompasses us both.

Noah flicks a glance at his watch. 'Yeah. A beer. Holly? Champagne?'

I shake my head. 'Just a water, thank you.'

He nods. 'And something to eat. I'm starving.'

'Of course, sir.'

She departs quickly, leaving us alone. There is a whirr, though, as the engines fire to life.

I push aside my misgivings with regard to Noah's desire not to have children. After all, this is all new and different for both of us. I'm not naïve enough to think I can change his mind, but I do feel like there might be a hundred reasons for this thing to run out of steam. Maybe we'll just wake up and decide we don't want each other any more. Maybe this is just an itch I'm scratching. I mean, five years, come on.

I smile brightly at him, refusing to let my tendency to analyse the heck out of everything tarnish this wonderful break from normality. When was the last time I did anything even remotely like this? The answer to that is simple.

Never.

'So, Mr Moore,' I purr. 'Where are we going?'

'That, Miss Scott-Leigh, awaits to be seen.'

The stewardess appears with a tray. She places our drinks down, then reaches between us to arrange a little armrest-cum-table. She places a bowl of fries and a fruit platter on it, then smiles brusquely and walks away.

'Is this how you like to wine and dine women, Noah?' I watch him thoughtfully, pleased that I can ask such a sensible question without sounding jealous or possessive.

'I don't wine and dine women,' he responds seriously.

'Then what do you call this?' I gesture to the food.

'Lunch.' He grins, reaching for a chip. I watch him eat it, not realising that I'm frowning. He scans my face, though, and I make an effort to relax.

'Well, I'm starving,' I say, just to fill the silence.

'You had an active night,' he points out, his voice deep.

My cheeks flush pink.

'And you're fucking adorable when you blush like that.'

'I didn't know I blushed until I met you,' I say seriously.

He laughs. 'I'm glad I can bring your blood to the boil.'

'In more ways than one.'

His phone rings and he lifts it out of his pocket, frowning. 'I have to take this.' He unbuckles his seat belt, standing and moving away from me.

Despite the fact he's on his phone and standing in the middle of the plane, we begin to taxi. Apparently the rules are vastly different for private planes versus commercial, or perhaps Noah Moore was just born to disobey rules.

I think about the conversation we had this morning—about the information he reluctantly gave me. His upbringing was far from conventional, and that would have a huge effect on his development.

As children, we need to feel safe and secure, to have a healthy attachment to someone or something. It governs all our relationships for the rest of our lives—the ability to form natural relationships, relationships that rely on trust and respect. It's a problem with a lot of kids who come from abusive homes or, yes, end up in foster care.

As children we are taught that, no matter what we do, our parents will still love us.

Noah never had that.

Noah doesn't do relationships, even now, except his friendship with Gabe Arantini. The roadblocks that were put in place during his childhood continue to shape his personality, his ability to attach.

But there's something more.

His sleeping issues suggest a deeper trauma—a trauma that has re-emerged in recent weeks. I'm not treating him; he's not my patient. And yet I know

I will find out what's happened to him, because I can't not.

Because I care.

I care about his problems and I'm terrified that I'm starting to care about *him*. All of him.

We are in Paris. Of all the places I thought Noah would bring me, Paris wasn't on the list. And I don't know why. Maybe because it's so classically romantic and he's insisted that he doesn't 'wine and dine' women, and this ancient city is quintessentially romantic, especially at this time of year. Right now, it has fairy lights sparkling and Christmas wreaths hanging from the ornate lamp posts and snow drifting down on the glorious buildings.

I am in love with Paris. It's a new love affair, just a couple of hours old, but it feels like the best place on earth to me.

When he slips the key into the lock of the penthouse suite of the Ciel Étoilé and pushes the door open, I am instantly hit by the view. The Eiffel Tower is perfectly framed by enormous windows, hung on either side by burgundy velvet curtains. The whole apartment is more sumptuous than I knew hotels could ever be. Gorgeous white leather sofas, a grand piano, hallways that are tiled in marble, a Christmas tree decorated with sumptuous gold baubles, and a Juliet balcony that has views towards the Seine.

'Wow.'

'You like?' he asks, unbuttoning the top of his shirt to reveal the column of his neck.

'It's beautiful, Noah.' I smile at him, and then something catches my eye through an open door. I move towards it on autopilot, aware he's following just behind me.

The bed is huge. King-size, covered in cream bed linen and enormous European pillows. There's another floor-to-ceiling window scenario in here, offering yet another breathtaking view of this glorious city. But that's not what caught my eye. A dress is draped over the bed—a stunning dress, designer for sure. I frown, moving towards it. My first thought is there's been a mistake. I run my fingers over it and look to Noah. He's casually reclined against the door jamb, watching me, a small smile curving his lips.

A knowing smile.

'Is that…?' I ask him, confused.

'A dress.'

I frown. 'For…me?'

His nod is slow.

'Noah…' I lift it up and hold it against my body, moving towards the mirror. It's a beautiful dark blue with spaghetti straps and a demure neckline, but at the back it scoops right down—I imagine that when I wear it, it will show almost my whole spine. The skirt falls to my knees. It is soft and silky.

'It's…beautiful,' I say, my breath hitching in my throat. It's so far removed from the kind of clothes I usually wear—my mum clothes or my work clothes—and a thrill of pleasure runs through me at that. All of this is unusual for me—wonderfully so.

He walks into the room then and looks at the dressing table. He opens a drawer and pulls out a box. A velvet box, about the size of a small sheet of paper. He walks towards me, holding it flat in his hand. 'And for this beautiful neck...' He watches me intently as he opens the box.

I don't look at it, though. I'm frowning at him, my heart racing. He doesn't wine and dine women and yet there's no other way to say how I'm feeling. I am spoiled and I am adored and I am happy.

'I saw this and thought of you.' His voice is thick with emotion—emotions I can't comprehend.

I look down then and I can't help the sound of confusion that escapes my throat. It's a huge pink gemstone, so sparkly it's almost blinding, and it's surrounded by crisp white diamonds.

'What is this?'

'A necklace.'

I can't help but roll my eyes. 'I see that. Why?'

'Because—' he lifts it out of the box, his fingers distracting as they find the dainty chain and hold it '—I want you to have it.' He comes to stand behind me so that he can clasp it behind my neck. The gemstone falls to the base of my throat, resting in the hollow there. It's heavy and cool. I turn towards the mirror, lowering the dress now to stare at the image I make.

The necklace is distracting in its size and beauty. 'Is it a...a pink diamond?'

I'm guessing. I have no knowledge of jewellery. My mother never wears anything but her wedding ring, and it's not something I've ever bought my-self. Nothing more than costume jewellery, anyway.

'It's Poudretteite,' he says, though I barely catch the word. 'Very rare.' His eyes meet mine in the mir-ror and my heart stutters. 'This gem once belonged to Marie Antoinette.'

'Noah—' I say his name softly '—it's too much. Way too much. This must have cost a fortune.'

He shrugs. 'I have a fortune.'

Like it's nothing. Unimportant. Irrelevant. It's strangely disconcerting when I'm sure he meant to assuage my concerns.

'Well,' I say quietly, 'you didn't have to do that.'

'I wanted to,' he reiterates. 'You deserve beauti-ful things, Holly. I want you to wear this tonight and then, when we get back here, I want to take you to bed wearing only the necklace.'

CHAPTER ELEVEN

'I couldn't eat another thing.'

His eyes find mine, laughing and scorching, reminding me of the way I took him into my mouth.

'I'm sorry to hear it,' he drawls, his accent thick, his words seductive.

I grin. We are sitting beside one another, looking out of the window at the street beyond. I lean over a little so that my breath warms his cheek. 'At least, not for a while.'

His eyes meet mine and I see anticipation heat them. Beneath the table, his hand curls over my thigh, his fingers resting there as though that is natural and normal.

And it feels it; it feels wonderful.

We are in a tiny bistro somewhere in the Latin Quarter. We passed the Sorbonne as we came to dinner, our taxi moving quickly, with scant regard for my desire to take everything in. Then again, perhaps if he'd slowed down, I would have been overwhelmed. Not just by the beauty of Paris in the lead up to Christmas, all twinkling and magical, but by the feelings throbbing between Noah and me. By the way my heart, mind and body all seem to be bursting with something warm and huge, something I can't define but that I am greedy to feel more of.

We've feasted on baked Camembert, scampi, steak and frites, oysters; we've sipped wine and shared a crème brûlée for dessert. I am full, satisfied and fuzzy around the edges in the nicest possible way. His hand on my thigh is the cherry on top of a night that is already one of the best of my life.

I place my hand over his, lacing our fingers, no longer feeling it to be an odd intimacy. I've known him for weeks, slept with him, and I glimpse in him something that I didn't even know was missing in my life. I feel a strange completeness when we are together. If you'd asked me a month ago if my life was missing anything, I would have denied it. I've worked hard to build a great life for Ivy and me. I never considered letting anyone else into the fold. How could I risk it after what Aaron was? How could I trust my judgement?

Strange then that I know Noah is keeping so much of himself closed off from me and yet I still feel like I could trust him with my life. Some things, some instincts, go beyond what is said. This is a feeling, and I like it.

'Do you come here often?' I rub the pad of my thumb over his hand gently. His eyes fall to our fingers, his expression inscrutable.

'We have an office here.' He nods. 'And a factory in the south. Gabe and I split the responsibilities.'

He hasn't spoken of his friend much. I go gently, careful not to scare him off. 'Do you do basically the same thing in the company?'

Noah's smile is rich with amusement. 'No.' I wait for him to expand and he does, taking a sip of his beer before continuing. 'I'm the coding side. I love programming. I don't do it so much now, except for fun—'

'Like the shower you talk to?' I tease.

He nods. 'Exactly. Gabe was never into computers. He's the business side. He got our first bank loan that floated the company, that allowed us to launch; he runs all that stuff. I've got no interest in that.'

'What is it about programming you like?' I wrinkle my nose and he leans over and places a light kiss on its tip. My heart twists.

'Everything.' There is an intensity in the word.

'Elaborate.'

He laughs. 'Are you ordering me, Doc?'

'Yep.' I smile to soften the command. 'I'm curious. It's very foreign to me. I wouldn't know where to start.'

He shifts his body weight and his hand on my thigh moves higher. Sparks of desire shift inside my gut. 'I used to do it to get into my own head,' he says, the words almost dragged from him. His eyes are stormy, filled with past pains. I hold my breath, aching for him and needing him to tell me more. 'I was twelve when I first started. I got a book from the library and devoured it, cover to cover. I was in a boys' home at the time,' he says, so casually, as though that's not devastating in and of itself. 'And they had good facilities.' He laughs awkwardly. *'At the time,* I thought they were good facilities. Now I see it was just a couple of old PCs, but for me, being able to load them up and practise what I'd read was what saved me.'

He has a faraway look in his eyes, like he's in the past. There is a haunting pain. Holly who is his lover wants to kiss it away. Holly who is a professional therapist wants to dig into the wound and expose it, knowing it gets worse before it can ever get better.

'Saved you from what?' I ask, hoping to strike a middle ground by smiling brightly.

He expels a sigh. 'You're going to drill me until I bare my soul, huh?'

But it's said almost with wry humour, and so I reply in kind. 'You betcha. But I'll make it up to you later.' My wink is a promise we both know we'll fulfil. Heat simmers in my blood; I ignore it. My brain is demanding more of me. I want to know him. I want to understand him.

'I was heading for a different kind of future,' he says stiffly. 'The boys' home was like a last chance for kids like me. Most of the guys I was in with had juvie records. I was there because no one else would take me. I'd been in and out of foster homes—sixteen times. I'd developed some…not good habits.'

My heart squeezes for him. 'You were just a kid.'

'A kid who torched cars, stole from my families, got into fights over nothing. I was always bigger than everyone else. Stronger. I was glad for that.'

'You're not violent, though,' I say.

'How do you know?' His eyes pin me to my seat.

I speak slowly, calming a heart that is racing. 'Because I've known violence. I've seen it, remember? I know the lure of it, the control of it, the temptation it holds for those who respond to it. You might have lashed out because you were angry and scared, because you didn't know how to handle your emotions differently. That's not the same thing.'

His eyes widen at my comment. I see something strange in his face. Relief? As though I have said exactly what he needs to hear?

'Did you ever get a rush from hitting someone? Did you ever crave that?'

'Fuck, no. Jesus, Holly. Never.' It's like he's remembered where we are and who he's talking to. He lifts his hand from my thigh, cupping my cheek, locking us together. 'I would *never* hit anyone, ever. I would never hurt you. I'm not that kid I was. And I'm not Aaron.'

Something like tears clog my throat. I haven't cried in a really long time. I can't believe I feel that emotion now! But his assurance pulls at something deep inside me. Something that aches to be told I am safe.

'You're so right,' he says, moving closer. It's just us in the restaurant—or that's the way it feels. 'I didn't *want* to be like that. It felt, sometimes, like the only way I could be heard.'

'What happened? After the boys' home?'

He frowns.

'You told me you had seventeen homes. And just now you said sixteen. So? Where did you go next?'

'You're astute,' he says, the words almost panicked.

'I pay attention. It's my job.'

His eyes skim my face thoughtfully. 'I was taken in by a couple who had four grown children still living at home. It's where I met Gabe.'

'He's one of their kids?'

'He was fostered by them. They needed *"strong young men"*.' He says those words differently, like he's impersonating someone. 'To help around the house. We were basically slaves.' The words are said with derision. 'Gabe had been there years before I came along.'

'Were you happy there?'

He is thoughtful for a moment. 'I was safe there. They fed us. The house was clean. Gabe and I shared a room, but it was big, and they were worried enough about appearances to buy us new shoes each season and dress us good. It was one of the better homes I was taken in by.'

In all ways but one, Holly thought sadly, her heart breaking for both Gabe and Noah. To have never known love, to have never known the security and peace of mind it offers…

'I didn't like him at first.' Noah's smile is loaded with memories. 'He's a good guy. Always has been. Smart. Loyal. Intelligent. He drove me crazy. But, once I got to know him, I understood he was just like me. He'd learned to cope with the foster system by flying under the radar. I coped by railing against it. We were apples and oranges.'

'And peas in a pod,' I say, striving to lighten the mood.

He nods. 'Yeah.' But he's lost in thought. I watch him, the flicker of emotions on his face, each transition seeming to carry weight and meaning. 'He's the reason I came to you. It was his idea.'

And the crumbs he'd dropped in our first meeting come back to me. 'He wanted you to get therapy.'

He shrugs, like it doesn't matter.

'Why? Why did he decide you need help now?'

'You know why,' he says with a shrug, pulling away from me, putting distance between us.

'Because you're not sleeping. But he must know more. He must know there's something at the root of it. Something that has hurt you. Something new.'

'He's not a fucking psychic, Holly. I sought therapy because Gabe begged me to. Because I'd do anything not to worry him. I've done enough of that in my time. Besides, it was no hardship to come to you, believe me.' His eyes linger on my face for a moment before dropping to the necklace at my throat and then the swell of my cleavage.

A torrent of emotions swirls through me, frustration chief amongst them. 'I don't believe you,' I say softly. 'I think you were terrified of therapy. I think you still are. I think your idea of hell would be submitting to me for a full hour, letting me pull you apart, piece by piece.'

'I don't know. If you were naked...'

'You make jokes to keep me at a distance.'

He doesn't say anything.

'You throw up barriers every opportunity you get. You clam up when I ask you too much about your past. You are sitting on feelings and emotions that are like ticking bombs inside you. You're not violent, but you are hurting. I'd guess that something happened recently, something that hurt you. And it reopened all the wounds of your childhood. Things you thought you'd dealt with. Feelings you didn't even know you still carried. Until you process that, you're not going to sleep. You're not going to be able to breathe properly until you find a way to comprehend what you're feeling.'

'This is bullshit,' he snaps, but he puts a hand over mine, almost apologetically. 'I know it's your job and your reputation is impressive, but you're wrong here, Holly.'

'No, I'm not.' There's sadness in my tone, because I grieve for him and for myself. He will never have a meaningful relationship until he faces these demons. There will only ever be sex for us. Sex, Paris and a beautiful necklace.

'Fine. What do I have to do, Doc? What's your prescription?'

'Like I told you the day we met, there's no easy fix. No one-size-fits-all counselling approach. You have to face whatever you're running from.'

His eyes give nothing away when they meet mine. 'And what are you running from?' he prompts, turning the tables on me with ease.

'Me?' My lips tug downwards as I frown thoughtfully. 'What do you mean?'

'I mean—' his hand grazes my thigh beneath the table; the intimacy is very welcome '—your dickhead ex has been in jail a long time. Why haven't you been with anyone else?'

My heart rolls over. 'I've been busy. Raising Ivy. Running my practice. It's not an easy juggle.'

'And you're proud of yourself,' he prompts, hearing the lines I haven't spoken.

'Yes.' My chin juts forward. 'There have been times in the last few years when I could have surrendered to a feeling of hopelessness. Of grief and shame. There have been times when each day has seemed insurmountable and I've wanted to curl up into a ball and refuse to go outside, to refuse to parent, to refuse to be anyone to anything because it's all so damned hard. There have been times when I have berated and blamed myself and been so *angry* with the choices I made. But none of this was my fault. I fell in love with the wrong man. That's all. And I loved him even when most people would have been long gone. I loved him until that love threatened the only person I loved more. Ivy saved my life, you know.'

'*You* saved your life,' he says seriously. 'She might have been the catalyst, but the hard work was all you.'

I half smile in acknowledgement. 'Had it not been for her, I probably wouldn't still be here.'

A muscle jerks in his cheek. He's pushing his teeth

together. 'So you never met anyone else that made you want to get back out there?'

I feel a dangerous lure in this conversation. A tug towards swirling undercurrents of an ever-darkening ocean; a riptide that will suck us under before we realise it. Because neither of us is ready to discuss what we are, what we're doing, and defining this so prematurely might be disastrous.

'No.' I shut the conversation down with a bright smile. 'Shall we go for a walk?'

He looks at me for a long moment and then lifts his hand in silent agreement, signalling for the bill. It is brought swiftly but, before Noah can brandish his credit card, I've pulled mine from my bag.

'You got the flight and the hotel, not to mention the necklace and the dress. Let me get dinner.'

His eyes show surprise; he covers it quickly, removing my credit card from the small silver tray and sliding it towards me. His own credit card replaces it—a type I haven't seen before. It's matt black with a gold stripe at the top and his name is written in white cursive letters. 'I thought you wanted to be wined and dined.' The statement is droll and my tummy flip-flops.

A waiter removes the card and we are alone once more.

'I thought you didn't do that,' I volley back.

'So did I.'

It is snowing when we emerge onto the near-deserted streets of Paris. Just a few people walking in the distance and a swirl of white in the air that ruffles my hair. I reach for Noah's hand, lacing our fingers together, and my pulse pounds through my body.

How perfect this moment is!

'Thank you for dinner,' I say, looking up at him. My breath catches in my throat. He's so handsome, so rugged and primal and masculine and hot. It takes effort to remember to put one foot in front of the other.

'No problem.' He is distracted, but when he looks at me he smiles. 'What are you doing for Christmas?'

It's such a normal question. I wonder what he was like a few weeks ago. Before whatever happened to reignite childhood traumas. Still, essentially, the same man, sure, but more socially functional. More able to perform as people expected. Without this huge chip on his broad, muscled shoulder.

'My parents, brothers and Aaron's mum will come over. Ivy is at an age where she wants to help with everything, so we'll cook together.' I lift my shoulders in a shrug. 'What about you?'

'Will it be a big traditional lunch?' he asks, ignoring my own question.

'Yeah.' I smile but squeeze his hand because I want to know about him too. 'Turkey, stuffing, potatoes, greens, pudding, mince pies—*everything*. You?'

'Sounds delicious.' He drops my hand but only so he can put an arm around my shoulders and hold me to him. I breathe in his masculine fragrance and something in the region of my heart pings.

I know all the dangers here and yet I feel myself sinking. I feel my heart cutting itself in two, leaping into another person's body, offering half of itself to a man who will undoubtedly break it. Not because he's an awful bastard like Aaron but because he won't be able to help himself.

'Do you spend Christmas with Gabe?'

'We both hate Christmas,' he says. 'We have an unspoken agreement not to speak of it.'

'Wait. What?'

'We hate it.' His eyes shift to mine and they are swirling with emotions that are dark and resentful. His eyes warn me not to push this.

I don't listen. 'How can anyone hate Christmas?'

'How can anyone love it? It has no significance to me. I'm not spiritual, religious. It's not my holiday.'

I can't imagine feeling as he does and yet I understand. With what he's told me about his upbringing, I imagine Christmas was a time of great sadness. 'Did you ever have a good Christmas? With presents and food and something that made you happy?'

His fingers stroking my shoulder pause, stilling as I speak. Then, as if he doesn't want to, he says slowly, 'Yes. Once.'

I am fascinated. 'When?'

He clears his throat, tilts his head away from me. We continue walking through the snow with no destination in mind. We are moving nearer to the Eiffel Tower.

'Years ago.' A rebuff.

I won't let him put me off, though. 'How many years ago?' The words are patient yet firm.

'I was eight,' he says.

Eight. My head jerks to his. 'The Morrows?'

His answering smile is tight. Pained. The feeling that I am close to finding what has upset him settles around me. There is something in his manner that speaks of fresh hurt, not old ones. I must uncover it. And I will. But slowly, gently.

Cautiously.

'How did you…?'

'You told me about them,' I say quietly. 'Remember?'

He nods, but it's as though he's trapped, imprisoned, and he doesn't want to be.

'What did you do with them that Christmas?' It's a question designed to relax him. To take him back to a more pleasant time.

But Noah isn't like anyone I've ever spoken to; he's not my patient and he doesn't act like a man who wants help. 'It was twenty-eight years ago. Before you were born. I barely remember.'

'Liar,' I say, half joking. 'Did they give you a present?'

He is stiff at my side and then he lifts a hand and points at the Eiffel Tower. It is midnight and it's sparkling like the stars from heaven have drifted across it. It's a subject change I don't want to allow, but it's breathtakingly beautiful.

And, as if he needs extra insurance, a guarantee that the matter is closed, he spins my body in the circle of his arms and kisses me—kisses me to silence me and distract me and remind me of how much we need *this*, both of us for different reasons.

'Spend Christmas with me.' I breathe the invitation into his mouth, my tongue whispering it to his.

He stiffens again, frozen, still, rejecting.

It only serves to heighten my determination. I pull away from him slightly. It was an impulsive suggestion, but now that it's out there I realise how *right* it is.

'I mean it, Noah. Why not come over?'

'Jesus, Holly, you don't ever give up. I've told you, I don't want to fucking celebrate Christmas, okay?'

CHAPTER TWELVE

I DON'T WANT to hurt Holly but Christ, if she won't back off, that's what's going to happen. Not physically—never, ever physically—the very idea of her being wounded wounds me. But her emotions are far too invested in this, and I don't want her emotions.

Emotions are untrustworthy and dangerous.

But when she frowns, blinks as if she's misheard me, my gut rolls and I think maybe her emotional wounds wound me as well.

'I'm sorry.' I mutter the apology, shoving my hands into my pockets and turning to stare at the Eiffel Tower. 'But I think us spending Christmas together would be a bad idea.'

To her credit, she rallies. Holly's not like anyone I've ever known. She is sensible and confident even in the face of outright rejection. 'Why? Why is it a bad idea?'

'Because, Holly! I just told you, I hate Christmas, and you're like a fucking elf. I bet you've got a big tree up and decorations and presents all wrapped with matching paper...'

I don't look at her, but I know I'm right. I don't need confirmation.

'You have a daughter! Have you even thought about what it would mean to her to wake up and see the man you're sleeping with on Christmas morning?'

Her cheeks flush and her jaw drops; I can tell that she hasn't. Worse, I can see that she's anguished by that realisation. I soften my voice, but it is no less intense for that.

'And because I don't need you to take pity on me. To include me in a family celebration because you feel sad about how I'm spending my day.'

'And how will you spend your day?'

'I don't know. It's a few weeks away. I guess I'll shower, eat, work, drink.'

She makes a noise of disapproval.

'And then, if I'm really good, maybe Santa will send you over at night.' I turn to face her then, my eyes holding a warning, hers ignoring it.

'To sleep with you.'

'Not to sleep with you.' I lift a finger to the thick lapel of her coat, pushing it aside so I can touch the soft skin of her décolletage. 'To fuck you.'

She blinks up at me and again I feel her hurt rolling over me. 'You're trying to push me away,' she says simply. 'That's what you do when you start to feel something for someone, isn't it?'

'For fuck's sake. Do we have to do this?'

'You want my help? Then yes.'

'I *don't* want your help!' My voice is raised and I lower it with effort. 'I never did. I don't need help.'

'Gabe apparently disagrees.'

My eyes narrow. 'Don't bring him into this like you know him. You don't know anything about him, or me, or why he wants to force me into bullshit therapy. No offence,' I tack on—the most useless phrase in history because obviously I've offended her.

'If you think therapy's so bullshit,' she says, defiance in her eyes, 'then submit to it and see.'

My breath burns in my lungs. 'What?'

'It's simple. If therapy is bullshit, as you claim, then go and see the guy I've found. He's good. He'll help you.'

It incenses me. 'No.'

'Why not?'

'It's just...not necessary.'

'So? You lose an hour.'

'I'm not going to go and tell some man my inner secrets, okay?'

'Then see me,' she says, and I see wariness in her expression. 'Let me help you, Noah. Give me one hour to work on you. If it's just a load of *crap*, as you seem to think, you've only lost time—and not much. But if you're wrong, that hour could change your life. For the better.'

'You're the one who said you can't be my therapist,' I point out, knowing I'm clutching at straws.

'And I still think that. I still think you should see someone else.'

'Then what are you saying?'

'That the most important thing to me is helping you.' She pauses, her eyes skimming my face.

'I wouldn't really be your therapist. It would just be you and me, just like we are now, but we'd be in my office.'

I don't say anything because I don't know what to say.

But she looks at me with her big eyes and a hopeful expression. Inwardly I groan.

'Come on,' she says softly. 'Please?'

It's stupid, and yet I've hurt her and I don't want to have, and so I find myself nodding. Smiling. A smile that is tight and wrong, angry and resentful.

'Fine.' I lean down and press a kiss to her nose. 'I'm not afraid of you.'

I'm nervous. Despite the fact I've been doing this a really long time, I've never felt like a therapy session is as high-stakes as this. Even a weird one-off therapy session with the man I'm sleeping with. I know how important this is, though. If I can't help him, then we have no future, and I realise that this isn't a temporary thing for me. I want more. I want all of Noah, and I want him for all time.

'Please have a seat.' I gesture towards the chair opposite my desk, the seat he occupied the second time we met. Everything feels different now. Off-kilter.

He's wearing black jeans and a white long-sleeved tee shirt that makes the tan of his skin pop. He seems relaxed and calm, but I know it's a veneer, because I know him.

'Sure. Why don't you come join me?' He gestures

to his lap. To his powerful thighs. Thighs that have straddled me, pinned me to walls, wedged my legs apart. My mouth goes dry.

His smile shows that he knows it. He stands, slowly, purposefully, moving towards me, coming around to my side of the desk. He stands above me, then bends forward, dropping his hands to the arm-rests of my chair, imprisoning me.

'Don't I at least get a kiss?'

It's been three days since we got back from Paris and to say I've been craving his touch is an under-statement. I've been busy as all hell—I finally or-ganised Ivy's nativity costume and the pudding has been made—but, no matter how much I have on in my days, all I want is to see Noah. To hear his voice. To touch him. For him to touch me.

It takes an intense amount of willpower to shake my head now. 'You're my patient today.'

'Not your lover?' He lifts a hand to my shirt, his fingers finding an erect nipple through the lace of my bra and the silk of my shirt.

I shiver involuntarily. 'Not now.'

But I groan and my legs spread, so he moves for-wards into the triangle I've created. 'God, Noah—' my eyes meet his '—I've never felt like this.'

There's a look of satisfaction on his face. A look of triumph that is primal and masculine and thrilling.

'Like what?' he prompts, crouching down in front of me and sliding his hands along my thighs. He finds my underpants and I groan again as he drags them lower.

I want to talk to him. We have an hour and time is precious. But he pulls my pants down my legs and I bite down on my lip to stop from moaning.

As if he understands, he lifts a finger to his own lips, urging me to be silent.

I need to stop this. He's doing this to waste time—to avoid therapy. But God, I need him.

'Don't think this gets you out of our session,' I say.

His eyes mock me as he takes my hands in his and pulls me to standing. My underpants are discarded on the floor at my feet. He takes my seat, unbuttoning his jeans as he does so, pushing his cock out of his boxers.

Hell.

'Sit on my lap,' he demands, the words throaty, his expression dark.

'I…'

'I'll pretend to be Santa if that helps.'

It's so ridiculous I laugh, but my eyes drop to his dick and its throbbing arousal. I lick my lower lip so that now it's Noah who moans. 'Now, Holly.'

I nod, my need as primal and demanding as his. I hike my skirt around my hips and position myself over him, clenching my lips together as I take him inside me, needing not to scream even when a roar bursts through my insides.

His fingers dig into my hips as I drop over his length. I am on top but he's in control, lifting me and pulling me down, moving me as I need to be moved. Flames spike in my blood. I am dying and immortal all at once. I dig my nails into his shoulders and bite down on my lip, hard. He thrusts harder and I come apart, silently but with an intensity that terrifies me.

He watches me and the look of primal possession on his features robs me of breath.

But I'm not a possession and Noah doesn't own me.

Before he has enjoyed his own release, I stand, my legs wobbly but my expression determined.

'Thanks. I needed that.'

Surprise whips across his features.

'Get back here.' The growl is demanding and seriously hot.

I eye him thoughtfully, my hand on my hip, my breath not at all steady.

'Not yet,' I say softly. 'Not until we've done this.'

His cock jerks, drawing my eyes downwards for a moment. There's triumph in Noah's face. Like he understands that I want more of him, that I'm forcing myself to be strong when I desperately want to just give in and take what he's offering.

But I'll never get him back in my office. Not willingly. This is my one shot to help.

'Answer my questions and you can have me.'

He shakes his head. 'All night.'

I frown. 'It's a Wednesday.'

He nods slowly. 'I don't care.'

And I feel his burning need. Not for me sexually, but for me personally in the aftermath of whatever will happen here.

I think of Ivy and my heart turns over. I can arrange a sleepover for her with Diane easily enough.

And I *do* want to see this through with Noah…

'Let's see how…compliant…you are first.' And, unable to suppress the regret from my voice, I say, 'Zip up, Noah. Let's get down to business.'

'I thought we were.'

I shake my head, repressing a smile. 'You can stay in my chair if that helps.' I can't sit down. My blood is zipping; my insides are quivering. I stalk towards the window and look out at the view. The sky is grey today, reminding me a little of the morning we left Paris. Snow had turned to sludge on the ground, stained brown by feet and time.

'Tell me about the tattoo.'

'Tattoo?' He almost laughs. 'Which tattoo?'

'Nineteen ninety-nine.'

His eyes narrow. 'What about it?'

'What does it mean?'

'Why do you think it means anything?'

I roll my eyes. 'You just got a random number burned into your skin?'

'Inked, not burned.'

'Whatever. What's the deal?'

He presses his lips together and I force myself to stare at him, not his cock, which is still exposed to my view and hard as anything.

'It's the year I met Gabe,' he admits finally.

I feel like I've cracked a hard nut. Success fires through my blood. It's small. Inconsequential.

'He has one too.'

Any other time, I might have disarmed him with

a quip about friendship bracelets, but not this time. Not now. I nod seriously and change tack.

'Let's talk about your childhood.'

He stands and I watch him for a moment, but he's simply zipping his jeans up. He doesn't sit down again, though. He comes to stand opposite me, his shoulder pressed against the window jamb, his eyes resting on the same view as mine.

'What do you want to know?'

I hear the terror and displeasure in his voice, but he's here. Answering me.

'Were you ever hit?'

'No.'

'Abused physically in any way?'

'No.'

'Sexually?'

'No.'

'Were you happy?'

A slight pause. 'No.'

'Were you afraid?'

'Sometimes.'

'Did you have friends?'

'No.'

'Did you read books?'

'No.'

'What were you afraid of?'

Another pause. 'The dark.'

'Really? Anything else?'

A muscle throbs in his jaw. 'The bogeyman?'

He's not being serious. Fine.

'Tell me about the Morrows.'

Just like that, his eyes whip to mine. Anguish. Anger.

'Why?'

'Because I want to know about them.'

'They were a nice couple. Full stop.'

'What did they do with you?'

'Nothing.'

'On weekends, for example. How did you spend them?'

His eyes assume a faraway look. 'I can't remember.'

'Don't lie to me,' I say, barely able to keep the frustration from my voice.

'I'm not lying to you.'

'Did you play sports with them?'

'No.'

'Watch television together?'

His eyes are haunted. 'We rode bikes,' he says thickly, the words dragged from him, hurting him, aching in his mouth. 'Julianne taught me. She was so patient.' He shakes his head. 'I'd never known patience. I didn't know it was called that then. It was more just an absence of criticism when I didn't do something wrong.' He lifts his broad, powerful shoulders.

'How long did it take you to learn?'

His eyes clash with mine, then look away again. 'A while. I'd never had a bike before.'

'And she bought you one?'

He nods. A slight dip of his head in concession. 'It was red. With a black stripe down one side. And a horn that sounded like a dying frog.' His laugh is brittle. 'Once I got the hang of it, I'd ride it all afternoon, around and around in circles until my legs hurt. And even then I wouldn't want to come in, but eventually Julianne would make me.'

'How long were you with them?'

He looks at me, anger unmistakable now. 'Is this really necessary, Holly?'

'Don't you think?'

'No. I don't. Everyone has a childhood. A past.'

'Yes, but not everyone's past torments their present. How long did you live with them?'

'Almost a year.'

'And after them you went…'

'Somewhere else,' he says, like it doesn't matter.

'Where?'

He glares at me. It is a battle of wills and we are both too stubborn to back down. 'The Adams family. Two parents, three fosters.'

'Were you happy there?'

'No.'

'Why not?'

'They were assholes, Holly.'

'In what way?'

'If you want me to define the faults of every single foster home I lived in, we'll be here all night.'

'I'm game if you are.'

'This is bullshit,' he says wearily, dragging a hand through his hair. 'You want to help me and I'm telling you there's nothing fucking wrong.'

But there is, and I think I know. I'm trying to prod

around the edges of his life, but he's making it difficult. 'How did Julianne tell you they were leaving?'

His head whips around to face mine as though I've asked him to jump out of the window.

'What?'

'When Paul was transferred, how did she tell you?'

His throat bobs, like he's swallowing hard. 'She just told me. I don't remember.'

'Did you wonder why he didn't turn the job down? I mean, once they knew you couldn't go?'

'It was a much better opportunity. They needed the money.'

'More than they needed you,' I say softly. 'They wanted money, not you.'

His expression is closed off. 'No. It wasn't like that.'

'Yes, it was. They could have stayed in Sydney with you, but they ran away. They left you. Like everyone leaves you. Because you're not worth staying for. Right?'

He opens his mouth to say something—something that I suspect would have been a curse-laden tirade, but then he clams up, eyeing me warily.

'You're not worth loving,' I push on, hating saying these words but needing him to admit his wounds, to find them, hold them and weave through them.

'They left—' he grinds the words out '—because they had to. My biological mother, fucking bitch that she was, is the only reason they didn't keep me.'

'No, that's not true, Noah. Lots of people get offered jobs interstate and decide not to go.'

'Fine.' He shrugs, like it doesn't matter. He's so good at this—this pain is one he has obviously ignored for a very long time. 'They didn't want me. That was nothing new. It wasn't the first nor the last time I'd been kicked out of a home.'

'But it was the only time it hurt,' I say. 'It was the only time you let yourself fall in love with your foster parents.'

'Jesus, Holly. What do you know?'

'I know that the day they left you something happened deep inside you that you still can't change. You were heartbroken and ever since then you've kept your heart locked up in case you're rejected again. I know you were set on a destructive path until you found programming and Gabe. That you found it easier to screw things up and be unlovable before anyone could reject you.'

His eyes narrow. 'Thank you so much for the elucidating character sketch.'

I feel like the ground is tipping beneath my feet. It occurs to me that helping him like this might be ruining everything we share, but *not* helping him isn't an option. I want him to be better. To be happy. To be capable of accepting love, to open his heart to trust and relationships.

'Did Julianne stay in contact with you?'

'She wasn't allowed,' he says, his expression rock-hard. 'The foster system is very "protective" of its kids. Once I moved on, I was assigned to a new guardian. She wasn't allowed to have my details.'

'So you never heard from her again?'

A muscle jerks in his cheek, but he is quiet. Quiet for so long that I contemplate a new line of questioning. 'When I turned eighteen,' he says quietly, 'she was able to get my contact information from the foster system then.'

My heart warms. This woman cares for him. Loves him. To have contacted him after so long shows she never forgot him. 'What did she say?'

'Does it matter?' There is a bleak pain in his voice.

'I think it does.'

His jaw tightens. 'She said she thought about me every day since they left. That she wondered about me and hoped and prayed that I was happy. That I was with someone who loved me as much as she did. She said she wanted to see me again.'

Tears clog my throat, but I can't give in to them. I am trying to be professional, and to treat him as I would any other patient. 'How did that make you feel?'

I expect him to say *happy* or *relieved.* Instead, I get 'Fucking livid.'

'Livid?'

'Yeah, Doc. I mean, for fuck's sake, I didn't want to see her. She was in my past.'

'You were still angry with her. For leaving you.'

'No! I just didn't want to know her.'

'When did you last hear from her?'

He scowls at me. 'Two months ago.'

'What did she say?'

'I don't want to do this.'

'I know.'

'I mean it, Holly. I'm done. This is shit.'

He stalks towards my desk, bracing his hands on its edge. I know I'm close. So close to whatever has brought him here, whatever brought us together.

'Are you afraid?'

'No!' He whips around angrily and his face is pure emotion. Handsome but scarred by the wounds he carries. 'I'm not fucking afraid. I'm bored. Sick of this. Over it.' His nostrils flare as he draws in a deep breath, so deep his chest puffs with it. 'Two months ago she wrote to me to say she had cancer. That she needed me to know how much she loved me and how goddamned proud she was of what I'd achieved.' His chest falls as he exhales. 'Two weeks after that, she died.' He pauses, his eyes spearing mine like blades. 'There you go: the answer you've been looking for this whole fucking time. She died, I went to the funeral and since then I haven't been able to sleep. Ta-da! It's no deeply held secret—it's life, and it's *my* life, and I want you to butt the hell out of it.'

I've had patients shout at me before, but only one man I loved has ever done so. I have endured so much worse from Aaron, but it never hurt like this. I brace my back against the wall because I'm not sure I can stand any more.

'You think you know what makes me tick?' he

says, moving closer towards me, his body a contortion of rage. I am not afraid, not like I would be if this was Aaron. I am afraid *for him*, for the emotions that are coursing through him. For the pain he feels and how it controls him.

'I'm trying to,' I say softly. 'I want to.' A muscle near my heart throbs and I know then what I need to admit to him and myself. 'I want to love you, Noah. I want you to let me love you. I know that's not going to be easy for you, but I'm falling in love with you and I need you to be brave enough to own that. I want to help you deal with this so we can be together. Properly.'

He stares at me like I've started speaking a foreign language. 'Are you fucking kidding me?' he whispers, haunted and cross.

'Fight your instinct to push me away. Isn't that what bothers you? That you pushed away Julianne? That you pushed away her love when you wanted it so badly?'

'You don't know shit about me, Doc.' He stalks towards me, close but not touching me. 'You think this is love? This is sex. I like fucking you. I decided I'd fuck you the first moment I saw you to prove that I could. That's who I am and that's what this is. You think I have issues with love? Maybe you're right. But they're nothing compared to your issues. You have a sick need—you *want* to love someone who's going to hurt you. You were hurt by your parents—you could never win their approval. You weren't what they wanted. So you look for that hurt now—you found it in Aaron and you're looking for it again in me. You know this is a disaster waiting to happen—we both do—but at least I'm smart enough to walk away before it explodes. *Fucking* bloody love!'

I am shivering and hurting and shocked in equal measure. 'Noah…' I lift a hand to his chest. His heart is beating slowly, like he's not even bothered by what he's just said. But I take a punt. 'You're angry. Maybe I've pushed you too hard. Let's…just…let this go for now.'

'You don't get it,' he says condescendingly. 'That's what I'm doing. I'm letting it go. I'm letting you go.'

'Wait a second.' I shake my head, trying to see things clearly with a heart that's breaking. 'You're doing what you always do. You're pushing me away before I can push you away. I'm not going to hurt you, Noah.'

'Oh, for God's sake, Holly. I don't think you're going to hurt me. You don't hold that power over me. I don't love you.'

I pull in a breath, shocked. Hurting. Aching.

'I'm not single because I'm damaged or running from love. I'm single because I want to be. I like being on my own. I like fucking a variety of women. You must know that about me. Surely you've heard the rumours? Well, Doc, they're all true.'

My heart shreds. I stay standing, somehow.

He straightens and turns away from me.

He's pushing me away, that's all. But he's doing a damned good job of it.

No one's ever loved Noah enough to fight for

him through his bullshit. But I'm going to. 'You're angry,' I say calmly, even when my insides are on fire. 'You're trying to hurt me because I've hurt you. I understand.'

He laughs. 'Your optimism is a marvel.' He grabs his leather jacket from the back of the chair. 'How can I put this more simply? I'm walking out that door and I don't want you to follow me. I don't want you to call me. I don't want to see you again. You and your so-called love can go fuck themselves.'

He doesn't even slam the door when he leaves. I stay, staring at the door, exactly where I was, pressed against the wall, my body trembling, my heart cracking, my mind spinning. What the fuck?

That did *not* go as I planned. I walk towards my desk... My underpants are still where they were dropped. I bend down to pick them up and a single tear falls onto my wrist.

I am almost certain that I'm right. That he's just pushing me away however he can, terrified by what he's revealed and what I've offered him. Terrified of losing him.

I reach for my phone. My fingers are trembling, but I type a quick message to Diane, asking her to keep Ivy for the night.

Something's come up with a client, sorry.

I'd love to have her! We're learning The Night Before Christmas.

I smile at that, slipping my phone into my handbag. I have three patients to get through before I can go to Noah, but I'm going to fix this for him, for us, because I love him, and I'm going to show him that love means fighting. Love is lasting. Love is permanent and he is worthy of all of those things.

CHAPTER THIRTEEN

SHE'S WEARING THE same perfume as Holly. It smells like chocolate and flowers. It's why I approach her, because I catch a hint of the fragrance as I pass the bar on my way back from the john and the smell draws me in, like a man who needs an urgent fix of a drug he can't have, so he settles for something—anything—to ease the pain.

This woman is nothing like Holly, though. This woman has a body like a fashion model, all skin and bone, draped in a black leather dress. Her hair is black, pulled into a silky ponytail. Once upon a time, I would have fantasised about wrapping my fingers around the ponytail and pulling her head back, kissing her lips, taking her against the bar.

Instead, I take the seat next to her and order two Scotches. 'Join me.'

It's a gruff command. She doesn't seem to mind. Her eyes are brown; I'm glad they're not blue. Holly's eyes are like ice.

Out of nowhere, I see them as they'd been that afternoon. I was right, in Paris. I feel Holly's pains as if they were my own. Her emotional hurts haunt me.

But fuck her.

What did she expect?

Making me talk about Julianne and whether or not she could have kept me? Should have stayed in Sydney? Then telling me she, Holly, loved me? Jesus. I've known her only a few weeks. It's just sex!

And sex is something I'm good at, I remind myself, wishing I felt a stirring of desire for the very beautiful woman I'm sitting next to. I don't, though, but I've done this enough times to fake it.

'Nice…dress,' I say, dropping my eyes to her cleavage.

When I look at her face, her lips are parted and then she smiles at me. Her fingers run across the dipped neckline and she leans forward, purring, 'You should see what's underneath.'

'I'd like that, sweetheart. Have a drink with me first, though.'

I slide the Scotch across to her and throw my own back, signalling the barman for another. It's busy for a Wednesday night. I guess that's this fucking Christmas time of the year, though.

'You drink like you're trying to forget,' she says smoothly, a hand creeping over to my thigh.

'Do I?'

She tilts her head to the side, her feline eyes appraising me. 'There are other ways to forget. Better ways.'

She's right. Holly used me to fuck Aaron out of her body and now I see the logic of that. Of being able to devalue what you had with someone by having exactly that with someone else.

'What's your name?' I ask the woman.

'Do we need to swap names?'

My chest lifts with relief. What a pleasure it is to talk to a woman who doesn't want to psychoanalyse everything I say and do. I tell myself this is good. This is healthy. It's an added bonus that she doesn't recognise me. I'm not exactly famous, but I find I get recognised often enough to dislike it.

'I'll tell you what I want, sweetheart. I want to get drunk. And then we're going to…'

The words die on my lips. I see Holly. Not here, just in my mind. But I see her as she'd been that first night: in my bed, so beautiful, so willing, so gentle, so kind.

I see her as she'd be if she knew I was planning to fuck this other woman. I see her hurt and my heart cranks in my chest.

Fuck it.

Holly was an aberration. A break from my usual rules. That doesn't mean I'm bound to her for ever. I don't owe her anything, just like she doesn't owe me anything. She could be with someone else and I wouldn't care.

That's a lie. The very idea fills me with bile. The thought of another man's hands on her body makes me want to vomit.

But that's wrong. Because Holly deserves a nice man. A nice man who won't hurt her. A nice man who smiles when she says she loves him, and buys her roses as a sign of his love. All that romantic shit I don't have any time for.

'Yes?' the woman opposite asks, running her palm higher so her fingertips graze my cock. I fight an impulse to dash her hand away.

I've been in this bar for the better part of the night. I have no concept of what time it is. But another Scotch doesn't feel like the answer.

'Let's go,' I say, standing up, reaching for her hand and holding it as though it is the talisman that will save me from the nightmare I've woken up in. 'Now.'

The air is frigid against me as we step out of the cab. My place is just down the street a little way. Whatever-Her-Name-Is is slightly uneven on high heels and with a shitload of alcohol in her system. Drunk messy sex is going to get Holly and her fucking therapy session out of my head.

This is the therapy I need!

'So,' the woman purrs, snuggling up beside me, so I wrap an arm around her waist, holding her there, refusing to compare her slim, hard figure to Holly's beautiful, soft undulations. 'You're rich.'

I laugh. 'Am I?'

'You have, like, two thousand pounds in your wallet and you live here,' she says, shrugging her shoulders.

She must have seen my cash when I paid for the cab. And, as for where I live, I suppose it is a sign of wealth. I look towards the steps; it is dark, but a light from just down the street highlights the outline of a figure on my steps, hunched over.

A tramp?

I am already reaching for my wallet, happy to throw a few hundred quid his way, when the figure straightens and I stop walking, my heart jerking frantically inside me.

Holly.

She is as surprised as I am, her face pale, her eyes frantic, her lips parted.

She was waiting for me and instead she got us. Me and a woman whose name I don't know, who is practically drooling at the thought of being in my bed.

What we are about to do is impossible to misinterpret. So I don't bother insulting Holly's intelligence by pretending. By apologising. I meant what I said in her office. We're done.

'Noah.' The word is tortured from her, a groan that reaches inside me and snaps what little self-control I have left. I turn to the woman beside me, the woman who doesn't even want to know my name, and smile.

'Go inside, sweetheart. I'll be in soon.'

'Don't keep me waiting,' she murmurs, standing up on tiptoe and nipping my earlobe.

Holly gasps as though she's been stabbed. My gut responds accordingly.

I unlock my door and hold it inwards while Skinny Model Girl teeters in. I pull the door shut afterwards, giving Holly my full attention.

'What are you doing?' she whispers, her knuckles white as she grips the railing behind her.

'Isn't that obvious?'

Her eyes are huge. 'You don't… You don't want to do this, Noah.'

'Oh, believe me, I do.' And maybe it's seeing Holly, maybe it's a reaction to the panic inside me, but my cock is hard. I grab Holly's hand and palm her across my front.

Tears sparkle in her eyes. Fuck. Not tears. I can't handle that, and nor can I handle her.

'What do you want?' I ask bleakly, my buzz disappearing. I am stone-cold sober now.

'I… Noah…' She swallows, lost for words. She hadn't prepared for this. 'I can't do this while she's here.'

'Do what?' I demand. 'I told you today, we're done. I meant it. This is who I am, Holly. This guy. Not the man you think you can make me.'

'I don't want to change you…'

'You just want to "heal" me,' I say.

'Is that so wrong?' she whispers.

'Yes. I don't need to be healed. Now kindly fuck off.'

She draws in a harsh breath, but determination is stoked anew in her gaze. 'No.'

'Well, I hate to break it to you, Holly, but I've got plans and, unless you're into threesomes, you're not invited.'

More tears. 'You're such a bastard,' she says.

'Yes. But that's your thing, right?'

'Apparently.' Her face is pinched. 'Fine. Go and… and fuck her. See if I care.'

'You don't care, Holly, not really. That's the whole damned point.'

I stare at her for a long second and then turn away,

my blood gushing through my body and my chest feeling like it's been split in half.

When I go inside, I lean against the door, my back pressed to it for several moments while I come to terms with what's just happened.

That afternoon I had Holly in her office and she was so sassy and confident, bribing me with sex for therapy, and I loved seeing that she knows how many cards she holds with me. For using them to her advantage. I loved her confidence.

And then it all unravelled.

The night I thought we'd share had become this.

I feel like I'm halfway down a river, there's a waterfall at the end and the current is going too fast to turn back. I am at the whim of the tide and it's definitely turned against me.

I can't breathe. I stare at the front door, and it's as though my body has been tortured, or silenced, as though I am withering from the inside.

I squeeze my eyes shut, trying to breathe, trying to think.

Noah is going to have sex with that woman. And I'm what? Going to let him? I can't. I have to do something.

But what?

Barge in there? Pull him off her? What good is fidelity if it's achieved through such measures? I grip the railing and move down the steps slowly, my body feeling bruised all over.

I knew he was broken when I first met him; I saw the pain in his eyes and still I went and fell in love with him. Maybe Noah's right. Maybe that's my thing. Maybe I like men who are closed off. Maybe I'm addicted to healing and fixing.

I reach the bottom of the steps and turn to face the door. No. It's more than that. Aaron wasn't broken when we fell in love. At least, not in any of the ways I could have recognised. His wounds were buried deep inside him.

And I love Noah despite his hurts, not because of them. I love him anyway. I love all of him, body and soul, mind and magic, and that means accepting him as he is.

But this? How can I possibly accept this?

I swear under my breath, wrapping my arms around myself. There is a bar somewhere nearby and it's playing Christmas music. I move in that direction without thinking, my feet going one in front of the other. The crooning sound of Diana Krall is instantly familiar to me. 'What Are You Doing New Year's Eve?' makes my stomach drop.

Because I know that whatever I'm doing, it won't be with Noah.

My life suddenly drags before my eyes—everything I've been, everything I've done and now this. The absence of him.

I've acknowledged that I love him, but it's only now, right here, that I understand what that really means. It's a complete infiltration of my life. He has found a space in my being, in my home life, despite the fact he's never been there, in my family life, even though he's never met Ivy. I have *imagined* him there, I have *foreseen* a time when he would be with me all the time, by my side.

I dash at hot tears that are clinging to my lashes. What a foolish, idiotic woman I've been!

To let him so deep into my soul when he's insisted all along that he doesn't want that.

Hurt morphs to fury, carrying me farther down the pavement, away from the bar. I step out onto the road without looking and might have been hit by a black taxi cab had it not blared its horn loudly and swerved to avoid me.

My heart beats a frantic tattoo in my chest, and I support my weight against a thick tree trunk. I stare at the road and, beyond it, the Thames, and I curse. I curse Noah, I curse Gabe, I curse Julianne, and everything that conspired to bring him into my life. How dare he do this to me.

How dare he think we were ever just about sex. Fuck him!

I glare back in the direction from which I've come and I begin to walk that way, my back straight, my eyes unwavering from Noah's door. He thinks he can do this to me? No way.

He's going to hear exactly what I think of this decision—to hell with his pains and hurts. This is about me now.

The girl from the bar has helped herself to a drink and is looking around my place.

I'm bored of her. I want her to go. I feel invaded and angry that she's here.

But I don't want to admit that, even to myself.

'So, sweetheart. What do you do?'

'Do?' She lifts a brow. 'You mean sexually?'

I laugh, but it's a sound of despair. Frustration. Confusion. What's happening? Is this a dream? Can I shake myself awake from it? I look down at my hands. They're real enough. Shaking slightly.

'I mean professionally.'

'Oh. I'm a model.'

'Of course you are.' I can't help—and don't bother trying to hide—the derision that curls my words.

'I'll take that as a compliment.' Her fingers find the straps of her dress, toying with them.

My body doesn't respond. Not even a little bit.

'What do you do?'

'Software development,' I say, somewhat disingenuously. It's been a long time since I've coded for more than fun.

'That explains all this.' She waves a hand around.

I don't want to sleep with her. I want to get rid of her. Holly's eyes are in my mind again. Filled with tears. Her lips parted. Her face pale.

Fuckety-fuck.

'Look, sweetheart, you're very attractive, but you're not really my type.'

Her eyes narrow. 'You don't like models?' she prompts, sashaying towards me, her skinny hips jerking from side to side. I would have gone for her a month ago. Three weeks ago. Pre-Holly I'd be stripping that dress from her body and pulling her against me.

'I've never been with a model.'

She pauses in front of me, locking her hands behind my back. Still my body doesn't respond. I am impatient to be alone now. 'And I don't intend to be now.'

She lifts up on her toes, dragging her lips against my cheek. I step back.

'I think you should go.'

'What the hell? You invited me back here.'

'I changed my mind.'

'Well,' she snaps, but steps away from me, 'you could at least let me finish my drink.'

She throws it back in one go. I remember Holly on that first night, when a few glasses of champagne knocked her sideways, and my gut clenches.

I call the model a cab, and when I hear it beep out the front I open the door, intending to make sure she at least gets safely inside, feeling somewhat responsible for her fully drunk state.

Holly is standing at the bottom of the steps when I open the door. Our eyes lock and my body squirms, my heart throbs, my blood stills.

Holly.

She looks away almost instantly, her arms crossed. She's bundled up in a huge coat, wrapped tight against the weather. She's pale, her face pinched, her eyes firing into mine.

I press my lips together, walking Model to the waiting cab and holding the door open for her. She smiles at me as she slips in and I slam the door shut with more force than intended.

Holly.

I turn back to my steps and walk towards her, my expression guarded.

'What are you still doing here?'

She opens her mouth to speak, but she can't. She's gaping like a fish out of water and then she shakes her head, digging her fingertips into her chest and staring at me like she's drowning and only I can save her.

'I… I don't know. I just… I'm so angry at you! I had to tell you…' But she doesn't sound angry. She sounds like someone who's deflating slowly before my eyes.

'And I guess… I guess I had to know. I had to know, without a doubt, that you'd… I had to know that you'd slept with her,' she says thickly, gripping the railing again, needing its stability.

Thinking I'd fucked the model is killing Holly and I don't want to do that, not even a little bit. I'm angry with her and she's angry with me, and I know I can't see her again, but I don't want her to hurt because of me. Not because of this. There are enough things I've genuinely screwed up without adding a phantom lay into the mix.

'I didn't sleep with her.'

She nods. 'Fucked her, I should have said.'

'I didn't do that either.'

'I don't believe you.'

'I'm not lying.'

Her eyes narrow. But she shakes her head. 'It doesn't matter.'

'Doesn't it?'

'No. If I hadn't been here, would you have slept with her?'

I open my mouth to deny it but can't. 'Yes. Probably.'

She sweeps her eyes closed, the pain on her face unmistakable. 'God, Noah. You're seriously messed up.'

'No shit.' And suddenly I want Holly. I want Holly so damned bad. I need her. I take a step towards her, but she shakes her head, lifting a hand to hold me at bay.

'Don't. Don't you dare touch me.'

Had my intent been so obvious?

'You don't get to touch me,' she says, as though the idea is repugnant to her when I know otherwise.

'Why are you here?'

'Because I love you.' She says the words as though they offend her. 'I can't be with you, Noah, and God, you make me madder than hell.' I see then that she's been crying and my chest heaves. I ache for her. 'Maybe you were right about everything in my office today.' It's just a whisper, an admission that I am desperate to rebut. 'But that doesn't mean I don't care about you.'

It's the last thing I expect her to say.

'It doesn't mean I don't still want to help you.'

'Come inside,' I say gruffly, but she shakes her head.

'No. I don't... I don't ever want to go into your house again.' She swallows, her beautiful throat bobbing with the action. 'But I'm going to make an appointment for you with Dr Chesser.'

'No.' I'm emphatic. 'No more doctors.'

'He's great at what he does. You won't be able to pull your crap with him.'

'I said *no*.' The words are forceful. 'If you're not going to come inside, Holly, then go home. This conversation is over.'

I give her a second to agree, to join me, and when she doesn't I storm into my home and shut the door. As before, I lean against it, waiting for my breathing to return to normal, waiting to feel like myself.

I don't. I don't know how long passes with me standing like that, but eventually I straighten. I wrench the door inwards, wondering if she's still there, not knowing what I'll say if she is.

She's not, but a carrier bag is on the top step. I hadn't noticed it before.

I reach for it automatically. It has the Rivière logo on it. I peer inside. A dozen oysters and a small bottle of champagne, as well as a little box. My heart races as I open it. There's a single ornament inside. A turtle dove made of silver, with a red velvet ribbon and a bell at its base. It twinkles as I shove it back in the bag and then my fingers curl around a piece of card. A business card, as it turns out. Her name is on the front, and on the back...

This isn't over, Noah.

She obviously wrote it before tonight. Before this.

And maybe she believed it when she wrote it. But I'd sure shown her. She walked away from me like everyone else—but only after I made it impossible for her not to.

I had Christmas lunch around the corner from her house.

I had Christmas lunch surrounded by happy families, couples, people drinking and eating turkey, ham and pudding, and now I am here, half-cut, staring at her door with a belligerent rage. A rage at how beautiful her house is. At how picture-perfect, like all those houses I coveted as a child. A big, fluffy green wreath on her door, made of holly and ivy, and more strung down the steps that lead to it.

The windows are glowing now, the light from within warm, and my heart achingly cold, like the rest of me.

I nurse the bottle of beer against my gut, leaning on a fence across the street from Holly's perfect house, biding my time.

It underscores how bad I am for her. How wrong. Wrong in *every* way. Holly is beautiful, smart, with a daughter just like her. Holly has suffered enough. Holly has a great job and a beautiful home and she deserves to be with someone who will slide into this lovely life of hers. Who'll sit by her side and eat roast turkey and sing carols and laugh with her.

My stomach has a stitch deep in its lining. It's not me. That will never be me.

Eventually, another couple leaves and I'm sure this must be the last of them. I stare at her house, waiting to catch a glimpse of Holly, just a glimpse.

She is my kryptonite and I am hers. She talks of love, but that's not how it's meant to be, is it? Love is meant to strengthen people, not weaken them, and Holly has unpicked me to the end.

Or is it the absence of Holly?

My needing Holly?

I grimace and cross the street unsteadily, waiting on her doorstep to see if I hear noises within but catching only the faint rasp of Christmas carols.

I lift my hand, thumping it loudly on the door, then step back, arms crossed, waiting.

She answers quickly enough, but it feels like an eternity. Her surprise is obvious.

'Noah?' She grips the door jamb. 'What are you doing here?'

'You invited me. Remember?'

Her eyes narrow and a pulse point jerks at her throat. 'I invited you to Christmas lunch. It's almost eight o'clock.' She shakes her head. 'And that was a long time ago.'

It wasn't. Just over a week. But a lot's happened in that time.

'I don't want Christmas lunch,' I say simply. 'I want you.'

Her eyes sweep closed and she swallows. I feel her weakness. I feel her swaying towards me.

'I… This is my *home*. My *daughter* is asleep upstairs…'

'I'll be quiet,' I say, and now I push past her, into her house. It is so picture-postcard perfect that I almost groan. Everything is cosy and pretty and normal and so very fucking Holly that I feel like I'm at my wits' end. I spin around as she closes the door, latching it in place.

It is a home. The kind of home I've only known once before—at the Morrows'. Love and happiness is visible in every corner; every knick-knack is chosen for its rightness and significance to Holly.

'Noah.' Her brow is drawn lower, her expression wary. 'You said you didn't want to see me again.'

'True.' I shrug, like it doesn't matter, when it matters so damned much. The idea of not seeing Holly again fills me with a strange drowning sensation.

I step towards her; she holds her ground.

'I thought I meant it. But I've been thinking about that session in your office.' Her eyes lift hopefully to mine, as though I'm here to fucking talk, to let her 'fix' me in the ways she thinks most valid. With therapy.

I need to dispel that notion. I wrap an arm around her back and pull her towards me, holding her tight against my body, pushing my arousal forward so she feels it for herself.

'I've been thinking how we need to finish what we started.'

And I step forward, pushing her back against the wall, supporting her body there while I kiss her, hard, desperately, hungrily. I taste her tears in the kiss and still I don't stop.

She is my kryptonite.

'Noah.' She says my name into my mouth. 'You're drunk.'

'So what? Who cares? I want to fuck you, Holly. Drunk, sober—what does it matter?'

She sobs, her hands pressing against my chest. 'No.'

'No?' I hadn't expected this, and I don't know what to do with it. No means no, always, without exception, and yet I know Holly and I know what she wants. Or do I? Maybe she doesn't want me as much as I want her. Isn't that what I've been fearing all this time?

'This isn't the answer,' she says, her fingers relaxing, dropping to the bottom of my shirt, finding my skin, running over it hungrily.

'Maybe not, but it's something.'

Her eyes hold mine and a shiver runs the length of my spine.

'It's another mistake,' she says quietly, and now she pushes at me—pushes me away. 'We're not having sex.'

My cock jerks hard in my pants, its rampant needs unwilling to be quashed.

But Holly is strong—stronger than I've ever known myself to be. She offers me a smile, but it's tight and it's sad. 'You can stay and have coffee, sober up, before you go. You can stay and talk to me about the Morrows and the boys' home and Gabe Arantini. You can stay and sleep this off—in the guest room—but you don't get to touch me any more.'

'I thought you loved me,' I respond sarcastically, even as her words are doing weird shit to my gut.

'I do love you,' she admits softly. 'But I can't sleep with you.'

'That's not love, then.'

She responds with a calmness that is somehow terrifying. 'Believe me, Noah, it is. If I loved you less, I'd sleep with you now, but we both know it's just letting you run from what you really need to sort out. I won't be a party to your denial any longer. I never should have been.'

'You're saying you regret this? What we did?'

She bites down on her lip, stares at me, and then she nods. 'Yes, Noah. I regret it. But we can't change the past. You and I both know that through personal experience.'

Of all the things we've said and done to each other these last few weeks, her admission now is what breaks me apart fully. Her desire to undo everything we've shared, her fervent wish to go back in time and not sleep with me. Maybe to not even meet me.

I stare at her for a long minute and then turn away.

'I was wrong to come. Forget I was here.'

'Noah—' she follows me '—you can't go home like this. Have a coffee…'

'I don't want a fucking coffee.'

I slam the door behind me and don't look back.

'You said this was urgent?'

God, he is so like Noah my heart stutters in my chest. I know they're not related by blood, yet there is something in them that is instantly familiar. In looks, they are similar, both bigger than the average man, strong-looking, with a raw sort of animalism tangible. Gabe Arantini is wearing a suit, though, and a top-quality watch. He looks every bit the expensive banker, and he speaks with an accent that is tinged with Italian and Australian.

He's looking at me with barely concealed impatience, and I know it's impatience to hear what I have to say, not to be away from me. Because he cares about Noah. And I am happy—so happy Noah has someone in his life who will fly internationally on the day after Christmas because a woman he's never met called him.

'Yes. Please, take a seat.'

'I'm fine standing.'

So like Noah, a tired smile slides across my face. 'As you wish. This won't take long.'

My penance is the smallest part of my concerns. Confessing to what I did weighs on me like a ton of bricks, yet it is just the beginning of what I need to tell Gabe.

'I don't want to talk about what Noah has told me. I consider that confidential.'

Gabe crosses his arms over his chest, staring at me as if he can see into my mind with just that look. 'But I can imagine.'

'Yes. You know him better than anyone.' It hurts to admit that. I thought I knew him, but if I did, then I wouldn't have pushed him so hard he'd run away. I wouldn't have hurt him like I did. 'Gabe,' I say slowly, knowing perhaps I should employ formality, refer to him as Mr Arantini, but I can't. This man I have heard so much about I now feel I know him too.

'*Sì?*'

He's worried. I must do this better. Faster.

'There's no easy way to say this.' I stand up, needing to be more on a level with the handsome tycoon. 'Noah and I…became involved. Personally involved.'

He stares at me for a long moment, angry colour slashing his cheeks. 'You're a *psychologist*,' he snaps, gesturing to the wall that is adorned with my degrees and awards.

'I know.' I shake my head with frustration, knowing there's no point explaining the shade of grey that our relationship inhabited, knowing that it won't matter to Gabe that I'd outright refused to see Noah as a patient, just so I could sleep with him. That's a pretty unprofessional thing to do anyway. 'It shouldn't have happened.'

'You think?' His sarcasm is scathing. 'I sent him to you because you help people! People like him! You were supposed to talk to him, not go to his bed.'

It strikes the error of my decision into my heart, more firmly than before. Because he's right. I chose my own sexual satisfaction over Noah's welfare. I'm so ashamed. 'I know, believe me, how much I've messed up. I know how much I've let him down.'

'So what? You're dumping him on me? You don't want to deal with this mess, so I have to?'

It's not far from the truth. 'I *can't* deal with the mess. I've tried. I…love him, Gabe.' Admitting it to someone else helps. 'And Noah being Noah, he's determined to push me away. He's so angry with me. And he's… It's all wrong. I… I have my own reasons for needing it to be over. But yes, I'm worried about him, and I know you care about him, and that you'll speak to him and stay with him until he gets help.'

'Another doctor who'll seduce him?' he snarls.

'It wasn't like that, believe me,' I say, but wearily, because it doesn't matter who seduced whom, nor how we defined and justified our situation. 'I know a doctor who will be perfect for Noah, but he… I suspect he's on a downwards spiral. I think he's going to need to be dragged, kicking and screaming, into therapy.'

'And whose fault is that?' The words are said with haughty derision.

'Mine. I know that. Believe me, Gabe, you're wasting your energy trying to make me feel bad about this. I couldn't feel worse than I do.'

'Oh, I doubt that.' He glares at me for several seconds and then crosses his arms. 'He deserved better than this.'

CHAPTER FOURTEEN

'FUCK OFF!' I SHOUT the words, but the sound makes my head bang. Screw this hangover. Where am I? I lift my head up and stare across the room. I'm on my sofa. Wearing jeans and nothing else. I push up to sitting as the banging at the door continues.

What time is it?

I stand. A wave of nausea surges through me. I grip the sofa back.

The banging continues.

The clock on the wall tells me it's almost four o'clock. What time did I go to bed? Was I alone?

Holly.

My chest squeezes and I taste her tears in my mouth. I remember going to her home and practically demanding she fuck me. Jesus Christ. As if on cue, I see the discarded beer bottles littering my home.

Is it Holly at my door? Has she come to see me?

I stumble forward, lurching as fast as I can go in my probably still drunk state, and wrench the door open.

'Cristo.'

Gabe's lips compress. I haven't seen him in a couple of months, since Julianne died.

'You look like shit.'

'Thanks.' I step back, not bothering to invite him in. There's no need. Gabe knows he has a standing invitation to my home.

'So it's true. You're just going to drink yourself into oblivion? That's your plan?'

'It was Christmas,' I say defensively, my head splitting in two. 'I have it on good authority it's okay to over-imbibe.'

'You don't celebrate Christmas.'

'I did this year.'

'Alone?' He is looking at me with sympathy. I don't want it.

'So?'

His eyes lift to the mezzanine bedroom. 'You got hammered here, by yourself?'

'What's wrong with that?' It's not as though Gabe leads the life of a saint.

A muscle jerks in his jaw. 'You *know* what's wrong with that. What the hell is going on with you?'

I am so angry in that moment. So angry—angry enough to shove Gabe out my door.

'Nothing's wrong.'

'I saw your girlfriend,' he says scathingly, and because I don't think of Holly in that way it takes me a second to understand his meaning—and to unpack the consequences.

'Holly?'

'Yes, Holly. How many doctors are you sleeping with?'

Jesus. 'She told you about us?'

'*Sì.*'

Immediately I see it from Gabe's perspective. Gabe with his black and white morality. Everything is right and wrong with him; there is no middle ground. It won't matter to him that Holly refused to take me on as a patient. All Gabe will see is that he found me a doctor, the best doctor for men like me, and she screwed me.

'It's not her fault,' I hear myself say, my head ripping itself apart. Fine beads of sweat have broken out on my forehead. I collapse onto the sofa, lying back and throwing a forearm over my eyes.

'She chose to sleep with you, did she not? After you went to her for therapy?'

'I wanted her,' I say. Annoyed to be talking about this with Gabe. Annoyed to be talking about Holly as though she's erred in any way. 'You know how persuasive I can be.'

'She's a psychologist. She should have known better.'

'She did. I didn't consult her professionally. From the first moment I saw her, it was just about sex.' Saying that hollows me out completely. About sex? Holly? It was so much more than that, but I can't define how and why.

'Jesus, man. You can sleep with anyone you want. Why the doctor I found to help you?'

'I told you, I wanted her…'

Gabe grimaces, grinding his teeth together. 'She should have known better.'

'She did! She knew it was wrong…'

'But still acted on her feelings,' Gabe says scathingly. 'Anyway. I don't give a shit about your sex life. I care about your head. What's going on with you, man?'

'Nothing.' I'm sullen. Angry. Hungover as hell.

'Liar.' Gabe spins away from me, stalking to the other side of the room. 'You need help. I can't help you. She can't help you. No one can until you decide you want that.'

He stalks to the door of my apartment, staring at me angrily. 'You owe it to yourself, and me, to see the guy she suggested. Until you sort your shit out, don't bother coming in to work.'

I stand up, my head spinning, ready to fight him, ready to fight anyone.

'Don't.' Gabe lifts a finger. 'Don't give in to that impulse. You know I'm right.'

But he doesn't leave. He stares at me for a moment, long and hard, and then he walks back to me and wraps me in a hug. I can't remember the last time we did this. It's been years. But he hugs me and a strange lurching grief spasms in my chest.

I pull away from him, shoving my hands into my pockets.

'How was she?'

He doesn't immediately answer. 'You can't think of her. There'll be plenty of women once you get yourself sorted.'

'How was she?' I repeat more emphatically.

He sighs. 'I don't know her well enough to say. She was quiet. Obviously concerned for you.'

That fills me with guilt. I'm pretty sure I don't deserve Holly's concern.

'Sleeping with a patient is seriously deplorable. Talk about questionable ethics.'

'It was very mutual,' I say wearily. Defensively.

I blink and see Holly. Holly in all her guises. Loving. Laughing. High on the drugging need of sex. Crying. My gut twists.

'I really fucked up.' My statement is bleak.

My blood is screeching through my body, begging me to do something, enraging me, enlivening me and, yes, enlightening me. Holly loves me. She loves me and she fought for me. She isn't pushing me away, even now, after all I've done. She called Gabe.

My stomach is on a bad acid trip, lurching and squeezing. I grip the back of the sofa and swear. 'I fucked up.'

'Noah—' Gabe sighs '—you need help. You don't know which way is up right now.' He pauses, dragging a hand through his hair, his eyes full of emotion. 'We both carry the scars of our childhood. I understand you, Noah, because I've been there. We are birds of a feather, my friend.'

'Yeah?' I stare right back at him. 'Then how come you never go off the rails? How come you seem fine with everything?'

Gabe's eyes lance me; something in the coldness in his gaze makes *me* worried about *him*. 'Because

I don't have a heart like yours, Noah. You feel everything deeply. You need help to process your feelings, whereas I have none.'

I laugh because it's such an absurd thing to say, that he must, surely, be joking.

'I do feel deeply,' I mutter after a while, and I look at Gabe, completely lost, and uncertain as to what to do. 'I fell in love with her. With Holly. I thought… I don't know. She was different from the start, but I didn't realise…' It is a strange thing to recognise love, an emotion that should be filled with hope, and to simultaneously understand how utterly hopeless it is.

There is no going back from the errors I've made. I love Holly because she is smart, strong and fearless—qualities that will stop her from ever forgiving me for how I've acted.

It is four weeks since I last saw Noah. Four weeks.

I know that doesn't sound like long—a lot can happen in four weeks. But my God. I have felt every second that has made up each long, barren day. I have never known such a soul-deep hurt as this.

I've worked hard. I've spent extra time with Ivy, holding her close, knowing that it will be her and me for the rest of my life. How can I love again? How will I ever?

I walk slowly, barely feeling the January chill that is thick in the air. Ivy is staying over with Diane, and I'm glad. On these nights, these rare nights when I am on my own, I can accept my grief, and I do.

I plan to soak in the bath and then watch a depressing movie. *Schindler's List* or *The Piano*. Something that will allow me to cry all these tears, to hang my grief on something inherently sad.

I unlock my door without looking down the street, pushing it shut and sliding the chain in place.

Our breakfast bowls are still on the table. On the mornings when I have to go to work and Ivy has school, we are often rushed like this. I dump my handbag to the floor, stretch my back and then scoop up the bowls, carrying them through to the kitchen. The fridge is covered with Ivy's artwork—pictures of her, me, the cat she desperately wants and sometimes pretends we have.

My smile tastes metallic on my lips. I open the fridge door and retrieve a bottle of sparkling water, cracking it and drinking several sips before placing it on the counter.

I'm almost out of food and, though I'm barely hungry, I know I should take advantage of the fact Ivy's not here to go to the supermarket.

It's the last thing I feel like doing. Then again, that's true of everything now.

I stack the dishwasher and then retrieve my handbag, pulling it over my shoulder and wrenching the door inwards.

The last thing I expect to see is Noah Moore, handsome as hell a dark grey suit with a crisp white shirt, his expression sombre, his body tight.

My handbag slips from my shoulder, falling to the floor, but otherwise I don't move.

'Holly.' He says my name softly, as though I'm an animal about to bolt. I must look like I feel. So full of emotions that I'm terrified.

'Don't shut the door.' The statement is throaty, and I realise I'm clutching the wood with that exact intention. 'I just…need a minute.'

I shake my head, my eyes filling with tears. 'No.'

He nods, as if he understands. But how can he? How can he realise how impossible I'm finding it to function? How can he know that his being here is undoing four weeks of hard, hard work?

'I'm sorry it's been a month.'

A month? It feels like so much longer.

'I'm sorry about what I said in your office. I'm sorry about the night at my place. I'm just so sorry.'

I squeeze my eyes shut, shaking my head, locking him out. But I can't do that, not completely. 'How are you?' He touches me. Just a light touch against my cheek, but I pull away.

'Don't.' It's a gasp. A gasp of fear, because I am so close to wrapping my arms around his waist.

He nods, a muscle jerking in his jaw. 'I didn't mean to.' He jams his hands into his pockets, as if to physically keep himself away from me. 'Will you give me five minutes?'

Five minutes? I've given him my whole life, whether he knows it or not. 'Fine.' But my grip tightens on the door. 'But out here.'

I can't say why, but it's important to me to keep him out of my house, as if symbolically that will stop further incursions into my heart.

'Okay.' He nods, and I'm relieved. Relieved he doesn't push this. 'You were right about me.'

My heart tingles. 'In what way?'

'About Julianne. About you. About why I wasn't sleeping.' He hesitates, his eyes locked to mine. 'I've been seeing Dr Chesser. He's helping me.'

I sob, a sob that comes out of nowhere. 'I'm so glad.'

Something sparks between us and he moves closer, just a fraction of an inch. 'It's hard work, like you said. I still fucking hate therapy, Holly.'

'I told you, there's no magic cure…'

'Damn right,' he grunts, but his lips are soft, as though he wants to smile, or cry, I don't know.

'I haven't had a drink in a month,' he continues.

I close my eyes because I don't know what to say, and looking at him is hurting me.

'I didn't want to need you, I didn't want to need anyone. But, fuck it, I can't live like that. Not any more. Not now I've met you. I want you in my life, Holly.'

My heart is being blown up like a balloon. It hurts so much.

'And I know I'm messed up and that I've messed this up. I know I need to work out my own shit, but I'm asking… I'm here today, asking if you'll wait for me. If you'll wait for me while I become the man you deserve. I don't want to lose you, and I know you should go, that you have to think of yourself, and Ivy, but God, Holly, I don't want to lose you and I know I can be what you need.'

It takes all my willpower not to show how much his words mean to me. Because he's right. He's messed this up. 'You're not the only one with baggage, Noah. I have every reason to stay away from you. I don't want to be with another man who makes me miserable.'

'Your happiness is my life's mission,' he says with such honesty that my heart lurches.

Trust is a force at my back, but I'm stronger than I used to be and I ignore the emotion. 'I'm glad you're getting help. I really am. I want you to be happy and well. But I don't for one second think I can trust you again.'

'Then let me show you.'

I open my eyes, looking at him, trying to understand, and I'm shaking my head.

'I'm not talking about what we were,' he says softly. 'I know we'll never be that again. I can't undo how I was. I wish, I wish beyond any words I can offer, that I had listened to you. That I'd got help at the beginning. But I'm doing it now, and I'm doing it because it's important, and I want to not feel like this. And because I want a future with you, and I know I'm going to have to work my arse off to deserve you.'

I bite down on my lip and taste tears; I hadn't realised I'd let them fall.

'I just… I'll never forget the sight of you with her.' I shiver and push away from the door so I can support my back on the wall just inside. 'I'll never forget the things you said. And I know it's because you're messed up and you needed to push me away, but… Don't you get it, Noah? You were my pleasure. You were everything I'd been waiting for and I loved you so hard and I gave you my whole heart, all of it.'

'And I didn't even act like I cared,' he admits thickly, coming inside so he can cup my cheeks. 'I cared. Believe me, Holly, I cared. I loved you then and I love you now, and I'm going to prove it to you.'

He presses a kiss to my forehead, his eyes holding mine with an intensity that can't fail to make my chest throb, and then he smiles.

'I'll be seeing you.'

I watch him go with a frown and yet a lightness is living in me for the first time in a month. Hope is beating its tired, broken wings…

A week later Noah is waiting for me outside my office when I leave. I wasn't expecting him and the sight of him in jeans and a leather jacket bowls me over.

I stand still, staring at him as he crosses the street, my heart in my throat.

'I came to walk you home,' he says, lifting his hands in a gesture of surrender. 'We don't have to talk. I won't ask to come in. I just…want to be in your airspace for a bit. Is that…okay?'

And hope beats again, little wings seeking light.

'It doesn't mean anything,' I say coldly, locking my gaze straight ahead, refusing to look into eyes that have always enchanted me.

'I know.'

We walk in silence. At the bottom of my steps I turn to him and he's just watching me, as though trying to memorise everything.

I don't smile. I turn away from him and walk inside. I dream of him that night and for the first time in a long time I don't wake up feeling like a devastating cyclone has rushed over me.

He is waiting for me the next week, this time on the same side of the street as my office. We walk as before, with no conversation, no contact. But I feel him beside me, I hear his breathing and his heart calls to mine. When we reach my home, I leave him on the footpath without a goodbye.

For four more weeks we do this. But on the fifth week he has something. A gift in a bag. I frown but take it from him.

'I don't want presents from you.' I think of the necklace he gave me in Paris that I've stuffed into a shoebox in the bottom of my wardrobe.

'It was your birthday on Tuesday,' he says softly.

My eyes jerk to his and my breath escapes in a ragged noise.

'I wanted to call, to see you, but I wasn't sure...' His uncertainty breaks something inside me, but it's a good breaking. It's like the bursting of something tight and painful.

'What is it?' I lift the bag.

'Have a look.'

I peek inside, but whatever he's chosen is wrapped

in tissue paper. I open it carefully, the precious ornament the most beautiful thing I've ever seen. It's the most delicate glass, and it's been etched with a nativity scene, the intricacy incredible. It hangs from a red velvet ribbon and a dainty bell is inside.

'Do you like it?' The question is soft.

I nod. 'It's beautiful.'

'They're very rare. Gabe…collects them.' His smile is wry. 'I had this one made for you.'

My chest heaves. 'Thank you.' I wrap it and place it gently into the bag. We walk, side by side, in silence. But at the steps, I turn to him.

'I'll see you next week?'

Triumph glows in those beautiful eyes. 'You can count on it.'

I start to count on it. On him. Every week he is waiting for me without fail.

Sometimes he brings hot chocolates for us to drink on the walk, other times small gifts. Never anything extravagant. A book he thinks I'd like. A scarf he saw and knew I'd love. Occasionally, he goes overseas for business, but he's always back by Friday, and when he's been somewhere exotic he brings me something from that country. Bookmarks from Japan, magnets from Australia and then a set of princess merchandise from Disney for Ivy.

It is four months before I ask him to come inside, and even then only for a cup of tea.

I curl my fingers around the mug and look across my dining table at this man I have loved since we first met and I smile. A natural smile. A smile without reservation, a smile that is stretched by my hopes and the certainties that have slowly been re-forming.

'How is therapy?'

His eyes hold mine and I don't see even a hint of hesitation. 'I still go every week.'

My heart turns over.

'I still haven't had a drink, Holly.'

I swallow and look over his shoulder, not knowing what to say to that. He understands. He doesn't want to pressure me.

'I love you,' he says simply and then stands, pushing his tea aside. He comes to my side of the table. 'And I'm not going anywhere.' He brushes a kiss against my hair and then lets himself out.

I sit there for a long time, staring at his mug, his empty seat. Strange that I think of that seat as his even though he's occupied it for only a brief period of time. Perhaps I long ago allocated it for his use, when I was painting fantasies in my mind about what my future would look like.

Five more weeks of walking home together and sharing a quiet cup of tea, and then I hear myself say as he stands to leave, 'Can you come next Thursday instead?'

His eyes meet mine, a silent enquiry in their depths.

'Are you busy Friday?'

There is pain in the question. Pain, like he thinks

maybe I'm seeing someone else. I can't bear to hurt him. I shake my head.

'It's just…' I suck in a deep breath. 'Ivy will be here,' I say. 'I thought we could have dinner.'

His smile is everything I have ever wanted in life. It is bright and beautiful, bold and so full of every single shred of joy that surges inside me. He nods. 'Thursday.'

He's nervous as we walk home, and I remember then that he doesn't want children. That this is a stumbling block distinct from all others. I ask him about it, and he looks at me slowly. 'Dr Chesser has helped me understand that I'm afraid of becoming a father. Because I never had one. I don't know if I'd be any good…that's all. It's not that I don't want that…'

I let him leave the sentence unfinished because I understand.

And by the end of the night I know what he perhaps doesn't. He will be an excellent father, one day.

We continue to walk home together on Thursdays but also on Fridays, and three Fridays after he first met Ivy I ask him to stay for dinner—with me. Not just a hot drink. The weather is warm now and we have a salad in my courtyard.

He leaves after he's stacked the dishwasher, and my heart drops. I contemplate asking him to spend the night, but something—a shyness born out of how new all this is—holds me silent. The old rules don't apply. It's as though we haven't been together yet.

* * *

Two weeks later, I find my courage. 'I want you to stay,' I say simply.

His eyes shine with triumph and gladness, but he shakes his head. 'Not yet.'

I don't know what he's waiting for.

A month later is Ivy's birthday, and Noah is at the party. He is an important part of it, for Ivy now adores him as much as I do. He sings 'Happy Birthday' loudly, and I know then how much I love him.

Autumn nights morph into winter and we no longer see each other only twice a week. He comes over most nights for dinner, sometimes a movie. Sometimes he picks Ivy up from school when I have to work late, and stays with her until I'm back.

He is with me every day, but in a way that exists outside of our relationship. I feel like I have been holding the world on my shoulders for a very long time, and now someone is doing it with me.

Christmas approaches, and I remember this time last year, when I first met Noah. I remember the way sexuality formed so much of our relationship and now our love is full of so much more. Though God, if we don't make love soon, I am going to combust, because I still want him as though he is the salvation to all my ills.

Ivy performs in her school concert; this year she's a Wise Man. Noah comes with me, sits beside me, laughs with me and holds my hand. When I get tears of pride over Ivy's performance, he lifts my hand to his lips and kisses my inner wrist. My heart soars.

It is Christmas Eve and Noah is with us. I didn't invite him, but it makes no sense that he'd be anywhere else. My family come too; they are all familiar with Noah by now. And while they don't understand our relationship, they like him. Even Aaron's mum seems to find him charming. I serve turkey with all the trimmings, and Ivy has made custard for dessert. It's late when everyone leaves.

Noah doesn't.

It's a long time since we met, and a long time since my heart was ripped apart. A long time since hurt and pain dogged my steps and life seemed like an impossible journey.

I'm happy.

I shower, butterflies in my stomach, because I know that tonight is special. I know that he's staying over, and that tomorrow it will be Christmas, and that beautiful morning will be all the more special because he'll be with me. With Ivy. With us.

When I emerge into the lounge, everything is spotless. Noah has done the dishes, tidied the table and put out some mince pies. There is a little gift bag beside them.

'Just a small trinket,' he says with a shrug.

'Oh, Noah.' My heart churns. 'Shouldn't I save it for tomorrow?'

He shakes his head. 'There's more for tomorrow.'

And I look towards the tree and draw in a shocked breath. He's right! The tree is groaning under the weight of gifts.

'They're mostly for Ivy,' he admits with a self-conscious grimace. 'I hope that's okay.'

God. He's so perfect. I nod and close the distance between us. The bag is simple white and inside there's a small box. I open it, my confusion growing when I see a ring inside. A ring with an enormous sparkling diamond in the centre and several more surrounding it.

I turn to Noah to ask him what it means, but he answers me silently, for he's knelt to the floor and his expression is loaded with feeling.

There is no long, flowery speech. What can he possibly say that will mean more than these last eleven months? He has shown me every week, every day, every minute we've been together that he loves me.

'Will you marry me?'

He need say no more.

I nod. 'Yes.'

Our hearts, though, are full and they communicate for us, and when he stands and kisses me everything we've been, everything we are, explodes around us. I cry, but they're happy tears. The Christmas tree shines, my ring sparkles and hope no longer beats its wings only within my chest: it is everywhere around us, and I know we deserve that.

* * * * *

SECRET
PLEASURE

TARYN LEIGH TAYLOR

MILLS & BOON

For Tina—this book would not be without you.
Thank you from the bottom of my heart.

And for Crystal—alpha consultant, proof-reader,
sanity-restorer, best friend. I don't know how you do
it all, but I sure am glad you do. I hope this one lives
up to pineapple-shorted expectations.

CHAPTER ONE

"LADIES AND GENTLEMEN, put your hands together for the one and only Lola Mariposa!"

The rush of that moment, the split second before anything happened, hit like a freight train. Nervousness, excitement, fear, anticipation, all toppling over one another, crowding her chest, grappling for dominance.

The curtains whooshed open. The spotlight beat down. She could feel their gazes on her.

It thrilled her to her core.

The music started, the old song sounding a little tinny and scratchy in the top-of-the-line speakers, and just like that, Kaylee Whitfield disappeared completely into her braver, sassier, sultrier alter ego.

The blond wig, blue contacts, and stage makeup helped, of course, but there was something magical that happened when she was out on the stage. Anonymous. Free.

She sat at the prop vanity set, her back to the club, pretending to brush her hair and apply blush. Then the incomparable Ella Fitzgerald launched into the first verse of *"Bei Mir Bist du Schön"* and Kaylee threw a coy glance over her shoulder, careful to keep her sight line just over their heads as she placed her index finger between her ruby-red lips. In a practiced move, she tugged her black satin glove off with her teeth before twirling it over her head and tossing it aside.

She never made eye contact while she was onstage. Because her performances weren't for the crowd.

No, this moment in the spotlight was all about her.

She let the silk dressing gown slip off one shoulder before pulling it back up. Someone in the back gave a catcall, and Kaylee's sultry grin grew more so.

Being onstage was a physical expression for the rebelliousness she'd been swallowing down since she was old enough to realize her mother's terse rebukes of *"You're embarrassing yourself"* actually meant Kaylee was embarrassing her mother, her family, and the esteemed Whitfield name, and that some Draconian punishment awaited her when they arrived home. As a result, Kaylee had learned early on how to blend in, to not cause a scene. She was a master at dousing her wants and desires under an impenetrable veneer of propriety and good manners.

But once a week, burlesque saved her, set her free.

She loved its costumes and pageantry.

She loved its tongue-in-cheek showmanship.

And most of all she loved how in control it made her feel.

There was power in the art of the tease, in bringing people to the brink before retreating, only to do it again. She drew power from leaving them wanting more.

She tugged off the other glove in the same fashion before pretending to do a final check of her makeup in the vanity mirror and standing up.

As planned, she twirled one end of the sash holding the dressing gown closed and did her slinkiest walk toward the front of the stage. What was completely unplanned, though, was when her coquettish sweep of the crowd—carefully aimed just above their heads, of course—collided with a pair of green eyes that stopped her dead.

Not that she could see their color from the stage. But despite the distance and the dim light of the club, she knew they were rich jade, darker around the edges, and unlike any eyes she'd seen before…or since. That they squinted when he concentrated. That they sparkled when he teased. That they cut when he was angry.

Aidan.

It had been ten years since she'd last seen him. Five since he and her brother had unceremoniously ended all contact. Still, she'd know Aidan Beckett anywhere.

Something suspiciously like desire bloomed in her abdomen, reminding her of hormone-addled summers spent pretending to read books by the pool so she could furtively admire Aidan's sun-kissed chest and the way rivulets of water clung to his back muscles as he and her brother, Max, showed off for the omnipresent bevy of interchangeable, age-appropriate, bikini-clad girls giggling and preening nearby.

If he'd been sitting like everyone else watching the show, she never would have seen him. But instead, he was leaning against the wooden pillar at the edge of the seating area, with a bottle of beer in his hand, looking bigger and broader and more delicious than he had when he'd visited during college breaks. Manlier. Like he knew what he was doing.

In fact, he was so devastatingly gorgeous in jeans, a black T-shirt, and a black motorcycle jacket that she couldn't look away.

With a deep breath and a swivel of her hips, she reminded herself that in addition to being a decade older, she was wearing a damn good disguise. And even if she weren't, there was no way he'd ever associate the sexy, sensual Lola Mariposa with the awkward teenage incarnation of Kaylee Whitfield.

Then Aidan shifted and his tongue darted out to moisten his lips, the way it had all those years ago, right before he'd leaned in and kissed Natasha Campbell, unaware that a young, puberty-addled Kaylee had been jealously spying on the two of them from behind her mother's prized rosebushes.

And just like that, lust and vindication shoved fear of discovery out of the way.

Because if he'd recognized the woman onstage as Max's shy little sister for even a second, there was no way he'd be staring at her with such undisguised hunger.

And Kaylee intended to do everything in her power to make sure he stayed hungry.

She shed the dressing gown with no fanfare, catching her routine up to the beats of music she'd let slip by, reveling in Aidan's undivided interest.

His attention crackled across her skin like an electrical current. A rash of goose bumps followed the same path as she expertly controlled his gaze—rolled a bare shoulder, swept her fingers along the sweetheart neckline of her black satin-and-lace corset, cocked a hip before tracing the edge of her matching panties. She shot him a mischievous smile before bending at the waist as she ran her hands the length of the leg closest to him, from the top of her garter belt down her black thigh-high it held in place. She paused at the bottom so she could undo the strap of one three-inch metallic-edged black T-strap heel, and then the other one.

Free of her shoes, she settled into the rest of her routine, letting her body dip and sway with the music, daring him not to want her.

Even her favorite part of the routine, when she put all the hours of ballet class her mother had forced on her to taboo use and used her perfect *développé* as an opportunity to unhook her garter belt before perching her toes on the stool and tugging the seamed stocking down and all the way off, was dedicated to Aidan tonight.

She spun so she was sitting on the stool and extended the other leg so she could remove that stocking, too, being sure to aim her flirtatious looks in his direction.

Her routine was all vintage bump and grind, from the music to the victory rolls in her faux blond hair, but there was nothing old-fashioned about the way her body was responding to having his eyes on her. She loved being onstage, but it had never turned her on like this before.

Kaylee put her back to the audience so they could

watch her loosen the laces of her corset, every cell in
her body acutely attuned to Aidan.

When she turned to face front, her body subcon-
sciously angled toward him as she began undoing the
hook-and-eye closures that ran the length of the bustier.
After unfastening all of them under his careful watch,
she held the stiff garment to her body, drawing out the
big reveal, and her nipples tightened almost painfully
as she imagined how differently her evening might
have ended if, instead of a club full of people, this
had been a private show for Aidan. Heat pooled at the
apex of her thighs, and she bit her lip against the erotic
thought of their bodies pressed together.

When her corset hit the floor, Kaylee was clad in
nothing but sequined pasties and ruffled panties, but
in all her performances, she'd never once felt so deliciously naked or so desperately wanted. She barely
heard the applause and whistles. There was only her
and Aidan and his stark look of desire as she executed
an impressive shoulder shimmy and struck her final
pose as the music ended.

She was breathing faster than normal, not from exer-
tion but from the sensual thrill of stripping for the beautiful boy she'd wanted with her whole heart back then
and the sexy man she wanted with her whole body now.

He lifted his chin and raised his beer bottle in trib-
ute, and the intimacy of the moment in a club full of
people stole her breath altogether.

Then the curtain rushed closed and swallowed him
from sight.

CHAPTER TWO

JEE-ZUS.

Aidan Beckett took a long swallow of his beer.

He didn't know how the fuck it had happened, but he was half-hard for the leggy blonde with the tiny butterfly tattooed on her ribs who'd just seduced him in a room full of people.

He'd never seen a burlesque show before. It was different from strippers. The women had a spark to them. No dead eyes and rote movements. There was joy on the stage. Cheekiness. Playfulness that made you feel like you and the performer were sharing some sort of inside joke, even if you couldn't quite figure out what it was.

He'd been scanning the bar, half cursing his PI for sending him here on a wild-goose chase, half following the dance moves of some redhead in sparkly lingerie shimmying around and mugging prettily about diamonds being a girl's best friend.

Then the audience had erupted in appreciative cheers, and he'd glanced at his watch as the emcee of the evening introduced the next performer.

That's when *she'd* appeared.

Lola Mariposa.

There'd been something…electric about her, something that transcended the mile-long legs. The way she danced. Hell, the way she'd looked at him. Before they'd made eye contact, he would have sworn she didn't even care that she had an audience. She looked like she had a secret she wasn't about to share.

She might be dancing, like the performers before her. She might be saucily removing most of her clothes, like the performers before her. But unlike like the performers before her, there was something aloof about her, a definite "you should be so lucky" vibe, and he'd liked it.

But then, Aidan had *always* liked a challenge.

When their eyes had locked, something had pulsed between them.

Attraction.

Desire.

She'd ensnared him and she knew it. Reveled in it. It was one of the sexiest damn things he'd ever seen.

The kick of lust had caught him off guard. He'd been in a dark place lately. Too dark a place to put the effort into seducing someone. So he'd been making do, tiring himself out at the gym and in the boxing ring, and rubbing one out when the need arose. But for the first time in a long time, his hand seemed like a poor substitution for a down-and-dirty fuck.

The burlesque dancer had made him realize how much he'd missed sex—the give and take, the heat and friction, that release. She'd unwrapped her body and his libido at the same time.

He pushed away from the rough beam at his back and set his half-empty beer bottle on the tray of a passing waitress.

If it was any other night, he might have sought Lola out. Explored that pulse of want that had crackled between them. But tonight, he had business to attend to.

He'd come to the club looking for someone, but the minute he'd pulled his bike into the parking lot, he'd known the intel was shit.

Little Kaylee Jayne Whitfield, apple of her mother's watchful eye, wouldn't set foot in a burlesque club on the edge of downtown LA. But the PI he'd hired to track her down was the best, and he said he'd seen her car here on Friday nights for the last month.

No silver Audis had graced the parking lot when Aidan had arrived tonight. But his curiosity had him walking inside for Booze and Burlesque Friday anyway. He'd dropped Kaylee's name, and a fifty-dollar bill, but the bartender hadn't heard of her. A quick survey of the patronage hadn't panned out any better.

He needed to have a word with his intel guy.

Aidan pulled his phone out of his leather jacket and headed for the side door of the club. Ignoring the Emergency Exit Only warning stuck to the door in peeling red letters, he pushed through into the parking lot, wedging one of his riding gloves between the door and the jamb. He'd go back in and do a final sweep of the club before he called it a night.

"What's up, Aidan?"

"That's what I want to know. You're sure this is

where you saw the car? Because it's not the kind of place a Whitfield would normally frequent."

He remembered a young Kaylee, her dark, shiny hair twisted in a bun, her mother forever dragging her to ballet class or violin lessons. This place was *definitely* not her style. Too seedy for matriarch Sylvia, not fucking seedy enough for patriarch Charles. There'd been a time when he could have talked Max out of his country-club ways and into a night of debauched fun at a place like this—but that felt like a lifetime ago.

Aidan shook off the inconvenient memory and focused on the phone call.

"I told you predictive stuff wasn't a hundred percent. But yeah, it was her car. She's been showing up at that address on Friday nights like clockwork."

Aidan raked his fingers through his shaggy hair, shoving it back from his forehead. "I'll do one more lap, but if I can't find her, we're going to need a plan B."

"Well, she's pretty consistent with her time at the gym, but I'm leaning toward the coffee shop. Her regular haunt starts construction on Monday, and with a coffee habit like hers, I think she'll find a new place for her caffeine fix. I'm running numbers on her most likely deviation now."

Damn. This was getting too complicated.

That's exactly why plan A was for him to "accidentally" run into Kaylee tonight, play the "old friends" card, and hope his ongoing feud with her brother wouldn't deter her from accepting his offer to take her to dinner tomorrow. From there, installing the malware on her phone and downloading a copy of the app should be easy. According to his sources, she was one of five people that Max had trusted to test the prototype version of SecurePay, the digital cryptocurrency app that was poised to take Whitfield Industries to the next level.

Actually, plan A had been to buy the damn SecurePay app legally and have his guys pull it apart to find the string of code he needed to prove Max had violated the exclusivity clause in his contract with John Beckett. Unfortunately, thanks to a security breach, the launch of Whitfield Industries' flagship tech had been scrapped at the last minute. So now if Aidan wanted to gain the rights to his father's legacy, he'd have to improvise.

"Let me know what you come up with."

"Will do."

He hung up and glanced over at his bike, pulling a hand down his face.

Jesus, he hated this covert bullshit.

You have a problem with someone, you tell them to their fucking face.

Like you're doing right now? his conscience asked.

Aidan frowned.

He had no choice. *Right now* was when the stars had aligned.

Charles Whitfield had been indicted for blackmailing a key member of the SecurePay team, Emma something-or-other, and Aidan was damn sure it wasn't the first time. Because five years ago, the same day he'd died, Aidan's dad had signed away all rights to the code that represented the pinnacle of his life's work, a move so out of character that coercion was the only explanation that made any sense.

No way in hell was he going to let Max rule from on high, poised to make billions by commandeering tech that existed only because of John Beckett's genius. Besides, he thought darkly, there was a certain poetic justice to using the only Whitfield who meant anything to Max—the shy, studious girl who'd stared at Aidan with hearts in her eyes, the intense, focused woman who currently served as her brother's PR consigliere—to take him down.

Yes. Kaylee was the nuclear option—the quickest, most brutal way to ruin Whitfield Industries the way Whitfield Industries had ruined his father.

And Aidan wasn't in the mood to wait.

"Damn it."

Kaylee pulled her hand from her bag to find it covered in liquid foundation. Her jeans were coated in beige, her white T-shirt splotched with it. So much for a fast getaway. She'd been hoping to change and sneak out as quickly as possible. Fooling Aidan from a distance was one thing, but she didn't want to tempt fate by running into him again.

She laughed at herself as she flipped the light switch in the tiny backstage bathroom with her elbow. As if Aidan would be looking for her at all. Unlike her, he'd spent the majority of their youth completely unaware of her status as a member of the opposite sex. She stuck her makeupy hands beneath the tap, washing the mess from her skin.

She remembered the first time she'd seen him. He'd stolen her breath, throwing her long-held beliefs that boys were gross and cooties were a fate worse than death right out the proverbial window. A golden boy with shaggy hair and a leather jacket. He'd been fifteen to her eleven, and she'd thought he was the coolest guy she'd ever met. So different than Max's other friends. There was something rough about him, more dangerous than the country-club jerks she'd grown up with. But the best thing about Aidan was that he never ignored her. And sometimes, when Max was busy doing something for their parents, Aidan would talk to her, tell her stories full of adventure—races he'd won, fights he'd started, the trips he planned to take.

Her crush had only intensified with puberty, and by the time she was fourteen, she was counting down the days until Max and Aidan came home from university on break. By then, his boyish promise had been realized, and Aidan had grown into his cocky swagger. He didn't just have the attitude anymore but a muscled body that could back it up. Kaylee had been mesmerized.

By that point, Max was a cool, distant stranger, but Aidan still made time to greet her, tell her a story, flirt a little. At least she'd thought it was flirting, until one fateful evening when she'd come home from studying at the library to find Max was having a get-together. Kaylee had witnessed firsthand what real flirting was like when she'd covertly watched Aidan and their neighbor Natasha wrapped in each other's arms, indulging in the kind of kissing that Kaylee had only

seen in movies. She'd fled from the passionate scene
with a heavy heart, made heavier when she'd heard that
Aidan had gone on to seduce the pretty blonde right
out of her bikini. Or at least that was the story as Natasha had told it later that summer.

Her hero worship of her brother's best friend had
taken a big hit after that, and to punish Aidan for the
transgression of not waiting for her, Kaylee had done
her teenage best to treat him with polite disdain. Trouble was, he hadn't even noticed.

And she'd realized for the first time that her crush
had been one-sided. It had broken her infatuated little heart.

By the time she was sixteen, they were nothing more
than polite acquaintances, discussing things no deeper
than how school was going and summer plans. But he
was still the most beautiful man she'd ever seen.

Tonight, though. Tonight, Aidan had looked at her
like he'd looked at Natasha all those years ago. With
heat. With lust.

And it had felt incredibly good to inspire something
other than pleasantness in him. Even if he had no idea
she was the one doing it. *She* knew it, and she would
let the rush of it wash over her for a long time.

After shutting off the taps, she dried her hands with
some paper towels and headed back to the dressing
area. One of the other girls loaned her a simple black
jersey skirt, and she donned it before stuffing herself
back into her corset.

She'd sneak out the side door and wait outside until
her Uber arrived to take her home. Of all the nights not

to drive herself. But last Friday, one of the other performers had let her know some creep had been checking out her Audi, and Kaylee had decided it might be safer to get a ride this week. A woman couldn't be too careful.

She skirted along the billiards area, glad that most of the attention remained on the stage, and Ginger Merlot's performance, where it belonged.

She was almost at the side door, almost all the way to freedom, but she couldn't resist a final backward glance at the man who'd made tonight one to remember. The pillar would probably block most of him, but she tried to discern the sleeve of his jacket from the post anyway. The creaky metal door to her right swung open and the sound stole her attention a split second before she slammed into someone. Someone big and solid. Someone wearing a leather jacket. Someone whose strong hands steadied her, warm against her arms.

She recognized the scent of him on a primal level.

His proximity did funny things to her pulse.

She couldn't look away.

Neither of them said anything.

It took her a moment to realize he was still holding her, that she should pull back. But as she looked up at the man who'd starred in many of her girlish fantasies, she couldn't quite bring herself to do it. Because the rush of hormones and lust, the thrill of being so close to him and having him looking at her that way—like he felt some of the maelstrom of desire churning in her belly—was heady…like a wet dream come true.

And suddenly she wanted that dream. Wanted it desperately.

The seductive siren song of rebellion wound its way through her bloodstream.

What would it hurt?

He obviously hadn't connected her alter ego with her real self. And there was no reason he should.

It was a great wig. She had her contacts in.

Why shouldn't they both have what they wanted?

And he wanted her. She could feel it in the flex of his hands on her skin the second before he let go of her. Could see it in the flare of his eyes, the tightening of his jaw.

And she definitely wanted him. Always had. But there was nothing girlish about it anymore. It was a triple-X, adult-content-warning kind of want.

Kaylee was high on the rush of a live performance, of their public flirtation, so why shouldn't it be Aidan instead of her detachable showerhead that made her come tonight?

She licked her lips, and his eyes dropped to her mouth.

Slowly, he dragged them back up her face. And the wicked, dangerous gleam she saw there made her wet. She didn't want propriety or duty or sweetness from him.

She wanted passion.

She wanted him to want her.

The air grew thick and heavy between them. She could feel her pulse everywhere, as though her skin was beating with it. She didn't see him reach for her hand, didn't remember reaching for his, but suddenly there was skin to skin contact as their palms slid together, and the warm roughness of his hand around hers sent an arrow of lust right through her core. The next thing she knew, he'd turned and was tugging her along in his wake. She had to run to keep up with his long strides. Aidan spared a quick look around the bar before he pushed through a door marked Employees Only, and she followed him inside.

Because in that moment, Kaylee would have followed him anywhere.

CHAPTER THREE

THE STORAGE ROOM was dark and smelled faintly of chemicals. After a moment, Aidan found a light switch, and a single yellow bulb buzzed to life, revealing a small room filled with cleaning supplies and paper products lined up on four shelving units.

Kaylee didn't have time to notice anything else, though, because Aidan grabbed her hips and pushed her back against the door, and then finally, he was kissing her. His lips crashed down on hers, his tongue driving into her mouth with a hungry urgency that shocked and delighted her. He tasted a little bit like beer and a lot like sex, and she couldn't help a groan of satisfied pleasure at the culmination of her longest-held fantasy. Kissing Aidan Beckett.

Take that, Natasha Campbell.

Kaylee buried her fingers in his thick hair, raking her nails over his scalp, running her fingertips along his neck and across his shoulders before she pushed his jacket down his arms and he let go of her long enough for it to fall to the floor with a satisfying thump.

Then his hands were back on her hips, and he'd spun

around, walking her backward until she collided with a shelving unit.

He stared down at her, and Kaylee shivered at his hungry look. He shifted closer, cradling her jaw as he lifted her face to resume their kiss. His fingers flirted with the edge of her hair, and some part of her recognized the danger even as his mouth tried to drag her into an abyss of pleasure.

Kaylee had to distract him, keep him away from the wig. She covered his hands with hers, pulled them down her neck and over her collarbone to the top of her corset. Aidan pulled back, but the moment of worry that he'd figured out this wasn't her hair dissipated as he stared down at her, ran a finger over the swell of her cleavage, the look on his face almost reverent. Kaylee watched as he set about unhooking the closures of her bustier, his long, blunt fingers surprisingly deft on the tiny fasteners. She was mesmerized by the look of concentration on his face as he worked diligently on his task. Just him and her, and an understanding born of heavy breathing and no words.

Her corset joined his jacket on the concrete floor, and she bit her lip to keep from mewling with frustrated pleasure as he cupped her breast, running his thumb across the sparkly black pasty that kept her nipple from basking in the attention it craved.

He was so goddamn gorgeous. The years had been kind to him, darkening his golden hair, turning his features more rugged, widening his shoulders and sculpting his body. He was all man now, and proving her younger self wrong, for teenage Kaylee hadn't believed there was a way to improve on the perfection of him.

And now he was hers to kiss, to touch, and she didn't want to miss anything.

She reached for the hem of his T-shirt, pushed it up his chest. Aidan was quick on the uptake, pulling it the rest of the way off. Kaylee couldn't help her sigh. His chest was a masterpiece, all ridges and planes, a smattering of hair across well-defined pecs, and abs that deserved to be immortalized on the cover of a fitness magazine. And then, just for good measure, there was a six-inch scar along his ribs to mar all that perfection and make him look even sexier. Even more dangerous.

She couldn't remember wanting anyone so badly.

Leaning forward, she kissed her way along the ridges of his stomach as she tugged her ruffled panties down her thighs. They fell to the ground, and she licked her way back up to his clavicle.

The rough sound of his voice as he swore raised goose bumps across her chest.

She reached for the button on his jeans, undid it, and then gave his zipper a firm tug, reveling in the inadvertent brushes of her fingers against the evidence of his desire.

At some point he'd retrieved a condom from somewhere, and she tugged her borrowed skirt up her legs in preparation as he pulled himself free of his underwear. Jesus, he was beautiful. Long and thick. Kaylee watched in fascination as he fisted his cock, stroking the length of it twice before rolling on the condom with his other hand.

She was so turned on, desperate for him to ease the ache he'd built inside her. Everything went still for a moment, and then they were all over each other, and he was hoisting her up, the edge of the cold metal shelf pressing into her bare ass. Kaylee grabbed the shelf above her head as an anchor.

The thrill of wanting to touch him but not being able to heightened her pleasure as he buried his lips against her neck and pushed deep inside her. She was so wet, so primed for this, the culmination of this incredible night, and the hot, sweet friction didn't disappoint. He growled with pleasure, nipping the sensitive skin of her neck before laving it with his tongue.

Oh God. This illicit tryst made her feel so damn sexy, like being onstage but more potent. More visceral. To be lusted after by this man she'd wanted for so long was everything. She locked her ankles together at the small of his back, glorying in his panting thrusts, loving everything about the moment. The clean, spicy smell of him, the rasp of his beard abrading her skin, the sound of his ragged breathing.

Aidan was fucking her in a dive-bar supply closet.

Aidan was fucking her like he meant it.

Aidan.

It was too much. Too much sensation. Too many feelings.

The tingling in her abdomen said she was close, even though it was way too soon.

Desperate to touch him, she let go of the shelf above her head and grabbed his face. His beard prickled the palms of her hands as she buried her fingers in his hair and dragged his lips to hers, gasping against his mouth as she came.

The orgasm hit her like a tidal wave, gathering force as it rolled through her before crashing in a burst of pleasure that put everything she'd ever accomplished with her showerhead to shame.

This was not what she was used to—staid, missionary sex with a long-term partner.

This was passion unleashed. Elemental.

This was a decade of wanting made real.

When he'd grabbed her hand and tugged her into a supply closet, Aidan had been expecting a quick, utilitarian fuck against the wall. He sure as hell hadn't expected her to melt all over him after a couple of strokes, but she'd definitely come, gasping against his mouth before she'd kissed him into oblivion.

Sexy as fuck.

And yeah, it had been a while for him, sure, but that didn't explain the way she was blowing his mind right now. There was something about this woman, something different that he didn't understand at all.

He slid his hands up her torso until his thumbs made contact with the soft, sweat-slick undersides of her breasts, and he wondered what shade of pink her nipples might be under the sparkly pasties. Not knowing just made him want her more. He flexed the fingers of his left hand on her rib cage as though he might be able to feel the butterfly etched into her skin.

He was so goddamn close, but he wasn't ready to lose this mindless pleasure quite yet, wasn't ready for this to be over. And then, to his surprise, she tightened her legs around his waist and started undulating her hips. The way she was grinding and twisting herself against him and the sudden restlessness of her body, the soft noises she made in her throat, signaled she was going for round two.

Jesus. She was going to come again, and the realization made him so hot that it took everything in him to hold off the heat and desperation that was building in his balls, the unstoppable rocking of his hips.

He focused on the bite of her nails on his skin, doing his best to read the rhythm of her movements, granting her wordless requests as she brought herself to the brink again, falling over the edge with a sweet cry, and this time, he couldn't help but follow.

His thighs shook as he twisted his hips as high inside her as he could get before he gave in to the inevitable, riding the contractions of her muscles to a climax that rocked through him with such force he had to grab the shelving unit to steady himself.

She was kissing him as she unlocked her ankles and slid down his body, a decadent, satiated kiss that felt like *thank you* and *you're welcome* at the same time. When Aidan had recovered enough to open his eyes, it was to find her staring up at him, sexy and triumphant.

Which he understood. He felt like a fucking conqueror just then.

Aidan leaned down and kissed her again, lingering over her mouth before he pulled away. She smiled to herself as she tugged the skirt back down her thighs and reached for her discarded clothing. Aidan took care of the condom and zipped himself back into place before donning his T-shirt.

On a whim, he grabbed his leather jacket from the ground, pulling his phone and gloves from the pocket before he draped it over her bare shoulders. Startled, she looked up from fastening her corset, and something…familiar flashed through his chest, but he couldn't quite place it. There'd been a flash of vulnerability, a glimpse of the woman behind the vixen, but he couldn't get the pieces to fit.

"Take the jacket," he told her, his voice sounding gruff, even to his own ears. It was too big on her, obviously, and there was no reason he should like seeing her in it, but he did. The realization made him uneasy.

He didn't like the sudden shift in his chest. Meaning being assigned to what was nothing more than some great fucking in a supply closet. A momentary and mutual escape into pleasure. It was just a jacket, he assured himself as he turned away from her and pulled the door open a crack to check if the coast was clear.

It was, and he let her duck under his arm and slip through, awareness prickling all over his skin as she pressed into him more than necessary on her way out. Those electric-blue eyes snagged with his for a split second, a final farewell, and then she was gone.

Aidan closed the door behind her and wrestled his body, so recently sated, back under control before he, too, ducked out of the supply closet. He didn't look for her again, just pushed out the side door, revved up his motorcycle, and took the long way home.

CHAPTER FOUR

AIDAN WONDERED IF Lola performed on Saturday nights.

Which was a pretty fucked up thing to wonder.

Unfortunately, there wasn't much else to distract him from thoughts of her as he sat alone in a booth in a shitty pub, waiting for a smug prick. Classic rock and the crack of pool being played in the back corner had nothing on his X-rated memories. He tried to blame his single-mindedness on the fact that he'd broken his sex fast, reminded himself how good it could be and that this…*infatuation* was just the result of being horny.

Except he wasn't just looking for a willing partner, because if he had been, any number of the flirtatious glances he'd received when he'd walked in would have enticed him.

He wasn't thinking about sex.

He was thinking about sex with her.

His abs knotted at the memory, drawing tight beneath his T-shirt. Sure, some of it could be chalked up to newness, to the risk of being caught, but that wasn't the part that still had him by the balls. There was something deeper, something so…trusting about the way she'd looked at him, taken his hand, followed him.

It was almost as though—

"Christ. Remind me not to let you pick future meeting locations. This place isn't 'under the radar.' It's 'waiting to be condemned.'"

Aidan's head shot up at the verbal attack. Liam Kearney, Cybercore's CEO, had managed to surprise him. And that wasn't good. He couldn't afford to be distracted by a hot body and a butterfly tattoo right now. He stood and shook the man's hand once, quick and hard, and if he'd gripped too tightly, it was only because his adversary had done the same.

Kearney ran an assessing gaze down Aidan's brown leather jacket and jeans. "So nice of you to dress up for the occasion."

The two of them slid into the booth across from one another.

"Yeah, *I'm* the one who looks like a fucking moron here." Aidan rested an arm along the top of the beat-up pleather bench. Like he was going to take shit from some prick who wore a three-piece suit to a dive bar. He pulled an envelope containing their agreed-upon price out of his pocket and tossed it onto the table in front of Kearney. "Funny how your distaste for my clothes never keeps you from taking my money."

Liam bared his teeth. It wasn't quite a smile. "Of course I'll take your money. You think Tom Ford suits come cheap? Besides, one of us should look good."

Aidan caught the waitress's eye, and with a tip of his chin she started toward them.

By the time he turned back to Kearney, the envelope was tucked away. Discreet. The prick had style; that was for damn sure. "You want a drink?"

Liam glanced at their surroundings and gave a disdainful shake of his head. "I've got a date with a supermodel in a couple of hours, so it's in my best interest to avoid contracting hantavirus between now and then."

Their server sidled up to the table. "What can I get you, hot stuff?"

"Scotch. Neat."

"And for your handsome friend?"

"He's not my friend. And he's not staying."

She sent Kearney a flirty once-over. "Too bad."

The man placed a hand over his pocket square, which he probably wore to remind himself where his heart would be if he had one. "Sadly, I have a previous engagement."

"Sucks to be me." She cocked her hip, bracing the edge of her tray on the curve of her waist. "So, if you're not friends and this one's got 'brooding bad boy' on lock," she said, thumbing in Aidan's direction, "what's that make you? His flashy, high-paid lawyer?"

Liam reached into his suit jacket and extracted his wallet. "If you're asking if I think I can get you off, the answer is *yes*."

She giggled as he tugged a couple of bills free and held them up between his fingers.

"Why don't you bring my client here a double in a clean glass? And keep the change."

She plucked the money from his hand with a wink. "You got it, counselor."

When she was gone, Liam exchanged his wallet for a shiny silver cell phone, which he slid across the scarred wood of the table.

"This is a prototype version, but we've had good success in the first round of testing. You'll have complete control of the target's phone—location, microphone, camera, texts, whatever you want. Just open the program and get within a foot of your target's phone to install it. Once you're in, download at will. You can remove it remotely."

Aidan whistled long and low. "You've outdone yourself, Kearney."

"What can I say? As the enemy of my enemy, you're practically my friend. That's why I took the liberty of preloading this bad boy with all your stuff. Contacts, photos, apps. It's all there."

Son of a bitch.

"Is this where I thank you for hacking my phone?"

Liam's smile was smug. "This is where you thank me for using my powers for good. I left your passwords the same."

"Nobody likes a show-off."

Which was precisely why Aidan was keeping it to himself that during a recent trip to Asia, he'd acquired a knockoff version of The Shield, Cybercore's upcoming entry into the digital-cryptocurrency ring. At least until he proved both SecurePay and The Shield were based on his father's code. He doubted Liam Kearney would be quite so arrogant when Aidan shut down both products with one fell swoop. But for now, Kearney was still useful to him.

As if on cue, the waitress sent a flirty little finger wave in their direction while she waited for the bartender to pour Aidan's scotch. Kearney returned it. "Funny. That hasn't been my experience."

Aidan squelched the urge to roll his eyes. "Don't you have somewhere to be?"

Liam nodded but made no move to leave. "I don't suppose I need to make clear to you that this tech is not intended for tracking private citizens without their knowledge. Cybercore cannot condone such usage. And if said activity is discovered by law-enforcement agencies, the company will disavow any knowledge of top-secret tech under development for government use being employed in such a manner. We will then prosecute any perpetrator thereof for the theft and misuse of our intellectual property to the fullest extent of the law."

Aidan pointed to his chest and raised his eyebrows in a *Who, me?* gesture. "Don't see any reason that you'd need to."

"I didn't think so." Liam got to his feet. "Pleasure doing business with you, Aidan. We appreciate you choosing Cybercore for all your tech-related needs."

Aidan waited until Kearney had left the bar before he hit the button on the side of the phone and watched the starting graphics flash across the high-res screen.

Although he didn't know precisely what had Cybercore and Whitfield Industries at loggerheads—the feud seemed deeper and more personal than your typical business rivalry—using Max Whitfield's biggest competitor for this scheme was a surprisingly satisfying *fuck you* to the man he'd once considered his closest friend. The man he'd trusted. The man who'd let him down.

Once again, Aidan was pulled out of a recollection, this time by the thunk of a glass on the table in front of him. He needed to pull his head out of his ass and pay attention.

"So how about you, hot stuff?"

He ran a hand over his close-cropped beard as he shifted his attention to the waitress.

She smiled invitingly. "You got plans?"

Aidan lifted his drink in response. "Just a quiet night with my date here."

She shot him a practiced pout. "Well, if you change your mind, you know where I am."

Aidan took a swallow of subpar scotch and watched her walk away.

He'd known something was off with his dad. John Beckett loved technology—tinkering, solving problems, cracking code. A high-paying tech job with Whitfield Industries should have been a dream come true for his father, but instead, with each passing year, John had seemed less excited to go to work. Their phone calls and visits had become punctuated with disillusionment, references to how John felt trapped. Words like *coercion* and *blackmail* started to pepper rants about how his genius wasn't appreciated, and in the next moment, John was stoic, resigned, saying it was no more than he deserved.

At first, the episodes were few and far between. By the end, his father had grown moodier, more taciturn.

Like he'd been after Aidan's mother had died…right before he'd started drinking heavily.

Aidan had known it was getting worse, but instead of flying home from his latest adventure and taking care of things himself, he'd called Max. The one person in the world he'd trusted. The guy who'd always had his back. He'd told his friend all his suspicions, that Charles Whitfield had blackmailed his father somehow, that something was wrong.

Max had assured him he'd take care of things.

Two weeks later, Charles had taken early retirement, Max was the new CEO of Whitfield Industries, and John Beckett was dead.

Aidan had been in Spain when he got the news.

Single car accident. Driving under the influence. Dead on impact.

He hadn't even known his father was back on the bottle.

He should have known. Should have cut his time in Pamplona short. A good son would have.

Regaining control of his father's code and keeping it out of the hands of the family who'd ruined John's life was the least he could do. Too little too late, maybe, but an apology to his father all the same.

Aidan finished his drink in two long swallows and wiped his mouth with the back of his hand. It was time to get to the bottom of what had happened to his father.

He set down the glass and picked up the phone, tucking it away in his pocket as he got to his feet.

CHAPTER FIVE

KAYLEE TAPPED THE toe of her Louboutin on the tiled floor. Her usual coffee shop was under renovation this week—a fact she'd forgotten until she'd seen the sign on the door directing her to this location and thanking her for her understanding.

Judging by the length of this line, she wasn't the only displaced coffee patron looking for a fix. She pulled her phone from her purse to check the time. She had about twelve more minutes to spare before she needed to be in her car and on the road. Otherwise she'd be late for work. Max might be an ocean away, but knowing him, he'd tasked his executive assistant, Sherri, with sending him daily reports about the office. Kaylee considered it a matter of pride not to give her exacting older brother anything to call her out for when he got back. The world didn't stop turning because he was gone, and Whitfield Industries wouldn't stop, either. She might have quit before he left, but it was her name on the building, too.

The memory stung. She'd let her emotions get the better of her that day. Last week, out of the blue, Max had announced a security breach, scrapped Whitfield's project, turned their father in to the Feds, and then told her he was flying to Dubrovnik, leaving Kaylee to pick up all the pieces as PR director, daughter, and interim CEO. Something inside her had snapped, shocked that he would just dump all of that on her with no warning, and she'd given him her two weeks' notice in a fit of pride. Truthfully, she was hurt that Max didn't respect her enough to keep her apprised of the life-altering decisions he'd made.

But now that things were somewhat under control again, she was regretting her resignation. The six days since Max had taken off had reminded her exactly what she loved about PR—the challenge and the rush of making people think and do what she wanted them to. It was something she'd never really pulled off in her personal life, but she excelled at it in her professional life. Despite everything, she was damn good at her job, and that was because deep down, family drama aside, she loved it.

As if she'd conjured him, the phone in her hand buzzed, flashing Max's photo and number across her screen. With a frown, she declined his call. Again. She was too busy and too pissed off to talk to him yet.

But underneath the skin-deep layer of mad, there was concern she just couldn't quite purge. It was there in her bones. No matter how much her family infuriated her, she couldn't help but care about them. And the entire situation was just so unlike Max.

No. No emotions.

Being good at PR meant being calm and collected,

and if there was one thing that Kaylee excelled at, it was swallowing her feelings. She supposed she could thank her mother's lifelong obsession with perfection for that.

"A lady remains poised and calm no matter the situation at hand."

Besides, screw him, she decided with a certain measure of detached equanimity. She was an adult with a caffeine addiction, and she'd get to work when she got to work, whether he had his assistant tattling on her or not. Max didn't deserve this loyal streak she couldn't quite banish. He hadn't thought twice about walking out on her in the middle of the biggest PR crisis to hit the company since she'd started working there.

She glanced at her phone again. Seven minutes until she should hit the road.

But caffeine wasn't optional today. She hadn't slept well all weekend, haunted by hot, furtive dreams of Aidan's hands on her, of him thrusting deep and driving her out of her mind.

God. She hadn't known sex could be like that. She wasn't sure if it was the naughtiness of semipublic sex, the danger of being caught, or Aidan himself. Maybe it was the magical combination of all three.

The memories brought a secret smile to her lips, even in the midst of the busy coffee shop. Made her square her shoulders. Made her stomach muscles clench with a shot of hot lust. Sex was good for the soul. And good sex, well, that was even better. She seemed to be oozing sensual satisfaction. She'd been hit on three times in the last two days.

"Well, well, well…"

Make that four times in three days, she thought at the sound of the deep voice close behind her. She prepared to deal firmly and disinterestedly with the ever-classy *What do we have here?* and its accompanying leer, but when she turned, her mind short-circuited and her mouth refused to open.

Which was okay because the man behind her didn't even say, *What do we have here?*

Nope. He said, "If it isn't little Kaylee Jayne Whitfield all grown up," and she had no firm-but-disinterested answer to that, especially not when he was smiling that rebel smile at her—at *her*—the sexy one that flipped up the right side of his sinful mouth.

"Aidan!" She took an awkward step back on her high heel, bobbled on the slick tile. And he reached out to steady her, like he had Friday night when they'd bumped into each other, but not before her phone crashed to the floor.

The sickening clatter left no doubt that it hadn't survived its run-in with the tiles, but she could barely bring herself to care—not when Aidan had his hands on her again. God he was beautiful.

Get it together, Kaylee.

She pulled free, crouching to retrieve her phone at the same time he did. He beat her to it by virtue of his longer arms.

His handsome face grew serious—almost annoyed—as he picked up the phone and looked at it.

"Bad news," he told her, turning it so she could see the shattered screen. "I'm sorry for your loss."

"Ouch." She did her best to smile as he handed her the useless phone, but his fingers brushed hers, and her skin tingled to life. Which was really inconvenient. She didn't need all her nerve endings sparking up an electrical storm right now. She needed to focus on acting like a grown-ass woman instead of a gangly teenager with braces and heart eyes for her older brother's adventurous best friend.

She stood quickly, needing space and cursing the cruel irony that would see all of her mysterious sex-goddess vibes destroyed by the man who'd gifted her with them in the first place. She dipped her head, let her hair shield her face, felt herself getting smaller, trying to escape notice. She couldn't have him ruining her incredible secret night by recognizing her as the woman from the supply closet. She wished she had the darkness of the club at her disposal now. Or at the very least, the magic, confidence-giving power of her sparkly pasties.

Then he stood, still close enough that she could smell him—man and fresh air and leather and motorbike, all warmed by his bronzed skin.

"Stand up straight, KJ," he teased, his voice soft and low as he quoted her mother, tacking on the nickname that only he had ever called her. It reminded her of their past, when he'd sometimes felt like her only ally. A tiny smile curved her lips despite herself as she lifted her face to make eye contact.

But the chaste sweetness of the moment morphed into heat as she looked up at him.

He might not recognize her from the club, but her

body recognized every inch of his big frame. Her nipples beaded instantly, and she was glad she was wearing a padded bra beneath her ivory blouse.

Her childish crush on him had been based on nothing but his kindness and her journey into puberty. But what was happening now was built on torrid, sexy memories that raced along her skin. Her belly pulsed back and forth like the shoulder blades of a jungle cat preparing to pounce. And she wanted to pounce. Her whole body purred at the idea of being in his arms again.

Could he feel the sizzle that had taken up residence beneath her skin, or was the heat only flowing one way?

He leaned close so she could feel the warmth of his breath on her cheek, and her heart stuttered an SOS, even as her chin notched up involuntarily to bring their lips into alignment. "Line's moving."

She released the exhalation stuck in her chest in a disappointed sigh as she stepped up to the counter. "I'll have a vanilla latte, please."

"Can I get a name for the cup?"

"Kaylee," she started to say, but before she got to the second syllable, Aidan stepped close behind her, and the dazzled barista stared distractedly over Kaylee's shoulder.

"You can add a black coffee to that."

Aidan handed her a couple of bills before Kaylee managed to retrieve her wallet.

"Oh! You don't have to pay." Kaylee dug into her purse. "I can…"

Aidan's fingertips brushed her wrist to still her hand, and her voice trailed off. Her pulse fluttered madly beneath her skin. "Your money's no good here, right…" He spared a glance at the smitten barista's name tag before adding, "Tanis?"

The girl nodded dreamily. Kaylee was pretty sure Aidan could have said, *This is a stickup—empty the till into this bag or I'll kill everyone in here,* and still gotten the same reaction. Seeing it reminded her that she wasn't a teenager anymore and went a long way toward making her feel more like herself. She tucked a wayward strand of dark hair behind her ear. "Thanks."

"Least I can do. It's been a while."

Two frustratingly horny days, her body reminded her. "Um, almost ten years, I guess?"

It wasn't a guess. She knew. Aside from Lola Mariposa, in the storage room, with Aidan's candlestick, she'd been seventeen the last time she saw him, freshly graduated and all packed and on her way to study at Oxford. Her crush on him had cooled by that point— no sense in pining over someone who would never see you as anything more than a kid sister—but that hadn't kept her from reveling in the goodbye they'd shared.

"You got this, KJ," he'd said in a way that made her believe him. And then Aidan had hugged her. The only hug she'd received. Max hadn't. Her mom and dad hadn't. And for a scared seventeen-year-old leaving her home for the first time, that hug had buoyed her courage, as though being wrapped in his arms had transferred some of his strength to her, some of his wanderlust.

It was a moment that had meant the world.

It was nice thinking someone believed in her.

"So what have you been up to?" he asked.

"University, grown-up job, the usual stuff," she averred. She didn't want to bring up anything that might ruin their easy camaraderie. Besides, she wasn't exactly sure how Aidan and her brother had turned into mortal enemies. It was safer to steer the conversation away from her PR position at the company named after her family and run by her brother.

Aidan shot her a look that said he had other ideas. "Nope. Not buying it, Ms. Public Relations. This is a no-spin zone, so stop being modest and tell me about how you're putting that fancy Oxford education to use nowadays."

The realization that he remembered her major and her alma mater combined with the interest on his handsome face edged the lust in her belly with a sweetness she hadn't expected. Maybe that was why she still didn't mention Whitfield Industries by name, just left it hanging like a guillotine blade, hoping it wouldn't sever this thread of…*something* that was pulsing between them.

"Mostly I write media releases and deal with questions from the press. And every now and then a scandal breaks out and things get interesting." The words fell out of her mouth without her meaning them to, and the sharp pain of the current situation knifed through her gut. That Max had worn a wire, turned their father in for blackmailing Emma Mathison, the head of R and D for SecurePay. That Charles was currently wearing an ankle bracelet, under house arrest after ponying up the five-million-dollars bail. That she'd been completely in the dark about her own father until it had all gone down...

"How about you? What have you been doing with yourself for the last decade?"

He grinned, and her heart stuttered at the flash of straight, white teeth. "Before or after I got gored running with the bulls in Spain?"

She couldn't help but smile back. She'd always loved Aidan's stories. He was the reason she'd begged her mother to let her study abroad. Actually, getting as far away from Sylvia Whitfield's nitpicking as possible was the reason she'd done that, but Aidan's stories had given her the courage to persevere, to board the plane when her mother had unexpectedly relented and let her go. "Liar."

Her mouth went dry as he reached down and lifted the hem of his T-shirt up his side, revealing that jagged scar across his rib cage. The one her fingers had traced during their time in the storage closet. The one her fingers wanted to touch now. Oh God. It must have hurt and everything, but *damn*. Like the man needed to be any sexier.

The two ladies chattering at a nearby table stopped to take in the deliciously masculine sight of Aidan showing off his wound.

Oblivious, he dropped the white cotton. "Twenty stitches."

"I have a vanilla latte for Karly and a coffee for Hot Guy," called the barista, and Aidan quirked a conspiratorial eyebrow, startling a smile from her. It might not be the heat that had sparked between him and Lola, but it was nice to see him as herself, too.

They grabbed their coffees from the counter. The grande cup looked small in his hand.

"Got time to sit with me for a bit?"

She wanted to. Wanted to indulge the desire simmering in her belly. But she had a meeting that she couldn't blow off, and the prudent part of her—the part that knew the longer she tempted fate, the more likely it was that Aidan might connect her with her alter ego—warned her to get out immediately, before her secret came back to bite her.

With an apologetic smile at the handsomest man to ever flash her at a Starbucks, Kaylee put herself out of her misery. "I'm sorry, Aidan. I really need to get to work, but it was great seeing you."

She reached into her purse to grab her keys. Despite her very smart decision to leave, her whole body shivered when he reached out and touched her hand to stop her. She swallowed against the resurgence of lust as she looked at him. "Then see me again."

"What?"

"Lounge 360. Nine o'clock. I'll buy you a drink."

She really shouldn't. Max would hate that. Her *mother* would hate that.

"I'll be there."

Shit.

He shouldn't have talked to her. Liam's tech was good enough to install without making contact. That had been the goddamn plan.

She'd been completely oblivious to him when he'd taken his place in line behind her, but he hadn't been able to keep his mouth shut.

In his head, she was this gangly, shy teenage girl with braces who stared at him like he'd hung the moon when she thought he wasn't watching. At four years his junior, she'd been mostly off his radar when Max would invite him over.

When she was on his radar, it was just because she'd always seemed so...lonely. He'd felt sorry for her. Sylvia Whitfield had been on her constantly and about everything—*Kaylee, stand up straight; Kaylee, your hair is a mess; Kaylee, stop being so noisy.*

And Max had been weird about his little sister, keeping a very conscious distance, though he'd never explained his reasons.

But she wasn't an awkward girl anymore. And some perverse part of Aidan had been too curious to content himself with the brief glimpse of her profile he'd gotten in the parking lot while he'd waited to see if she'd show up like his intel guy had predicted.

He'd wanted to see the woman she'd become, and so he'd broken his own damn rule and talked to her.

Stunning. That had been his first thought when she'd turned to face him. Then her hazel eyes had flared with surprise and recognition as they scanned his face, and her skin had flushed in a way that made the hair on the back of his neck stand up. Her full lips, slicked shiny with gloss, had popped open in an unconsciously provocative O that had hooked him in the gut right before she stepped back in surprise. He hadn't expected the jolt of familiarity, hell, of *attraction*, that had arced up his arm as he'd steadied her.

He spared a brief moment to wonder if she'd felt it, too, or if it was just the surprise of seeing him again after so many years that had sent her phone tumbling to the ground, smashing both the screen and his plan to install the spyware and get the hell out.

That's what he got for thinking with his dick, which obviously didn't care that she was part of the enemy camp. Though to be fair, neither did his brain, judging by his offer to take her out for drinks tonight. Fucking *drinks* with Kaylee Whitfield.

Now all he could do was hope that she'd replace her phone before they met up again, or this whole day would be a complete waste.

CHAPTER SIX

KAYLEE ARRIVED AT the office eleven hours and forty-six minutes before she was going to meet Aidan for drinks. Which was fourteen minutes late for the daily briefing with Soteria Security, where she was playing the role of Max's factotum.

"I'm sorry to keep you both waiting. Slight issue with my phone." Not exactly a lie, she decided, setting it shattered-screen up on the boardroom table. She placed her coffee beside it and took a seat.

"Damn." Jesse Hastings winced. "I hate to see good tech suffer."

Kaylee had no doubt that, as a certified tech geek and one half of the crack cybersecurity team Whitfield Industries kept on retainer, Jesse felt her pain.

"Me, too, but not as much as I hate having to sacrifice my lunch hour to replace good tech."

"Here. Take this one."

Kaylee did a double take as Wes Brennan, the quieter, more serious half of Soteria Security, pulled a top-of-the-line phone out of his suit pocket and held it up.

"Seriously, Wes?"

"Yeah, seriously, Wes?" Jesse shook his head and turned to Kaylee. "I just gave him that phone this morning. After spending hours configuring the safety features to his exacting standards."

"My old phone is fine. I did some upgrades to it last week that I wanted to test anyway, so I haven't even activated this one." Wes gave his patented low-key shrug and pointed at her broken phone. "Hand it over. I'll change out your SIM card."

Kaylee passed it across the table.

"You ever feel massively underappreciated by your boss?" Jesse asked with a sigh.

Her brother's stern face flashed through her mind. "You have no idea," Kaylee assured him, and they shared a knowing eye roll.

"I saw that," Wes said drily, making quick work of the phone. The second he turned it on, the calls, texts, and emails rolled in with a cacophony of buzzes and dings. With a raised eyebrow, Wes switched the phone to Silent and handed it back across the table.

Kaylee glanced at it warily and set it facedown. "Okay, what do you have for me, gentlemen?"

After the security briefing—Wes and Jesse were still no closer to figuring out who had installed the malware on Emma Mathison's computer that had led to the postponement of SecurePay and the domino of scandals that had followed—she'd spent the rest of the day plowing through the quotidian concerns of running a multimillion-dollar business.

She'd known Max worked hard, but she hadn't quite realized that every day for him was as busy as being in the middle of a PR crisis was for her. It was eye-opening to see firsthand the difference between how her father had run the business—an unapproachable figurehead who doled out more blame than praise—and the more interactive style her older brother had adopted. He was available without micromanaging, and as a result, there was a level of respect for him among his employees that was quite a revelation to Kaylee. She hadn't realized how much she'd let their frigid relationship as siblings color her view of Max as a boss.

His long work hours made infinitely more sense to her now. She'd had to force herself to leave the office at eight o'clock, giving up food just so she could steal half an hour to change and freshen up before meeting Aidan.

The bar he'd suggested was classier and more upscale than she'd been expecting, with chandeliers, gleaming wood, and dim lighting. Floor-to-ceiling windows gave the circular room a three-hundred-and-sixty-degree view of the city.

It was a sexy, grown-up place to have a drink.

She pressed her hand to her abdomen to quiet the sudden zigzag of nerves.

When she'd been getting ready, some annoying flare of feminine pride had reared its jealous head at the memory of the polite nothingness she'd seen in his eyes at the coffee shop. It bugged her that while she'd been drowning in lust, he'd been completely oblivious to her status as a female of the species. Little Kaylee Jayne. Completely beneath his notice.

As a result, she'd applied her makeup with a little more flair—slightly winged liner, faux lashes, and she'd painted her lips with the same red lipstick she wore onstage. Then she'd donned the sexiest dress she owned. Well, not including her Lola costumes, but she never included those. They belonged to her blonde, blue-eyed alter ego. It was the sexiest Kaylee dress she owned. A black shift that skimmed her curves without clinging anywhere, but she hoped it was reminiscent enough of the black skirt she'd been wearing that night to give him a little déjà vu—déjà screw?

It was madness. Her goal at the coffee shop had been to escape recognition, and tonight she was doing everything in her power to jog his memory.

What if he noticed? What if he didn't?

Honestly, Kaylee. Stop fidgeting.

Her mother's voice was loud in her head. Not even a decade of living on her own, it seemed, could banish Sylvia Whitfield's scolding. And it was always loudest when Kaylee was nervous.

"Can I get a shot of tequila, please?"

Partly for some liquid courage, partly to remind her mom's ghostly nagging that it had no dominion here.

Drinks with Aidan Beckett.

Well, sort of.

It wasn't like this was a *date* or anything. Still, it was as close as she'd ever get.

The bartender obliged her, and she let the liquid courage burn a path down her throat. The warmth in her stomach centered her back in her body, got her out of her head.

I can do this, she told herself. *We're just two peo-*

*ple catching up. And sure, he doesn't know we man-
handled each other against a shelf full of cleaning
products, but that's no reason to think things will
be weird between us. He didn't recognize me this
morning. Not even a little bit. Not even a glimmer.
I was the only one drowning in a bunch of sexy en-
dorphins. He was cool and above it all. Like always.
The golden boy. Supremely unaffected while women
swooned around him.*

Kaylee set the shot glass on the bar with more force
than necessary.

"Actually, I'll take another one."

With a smile, the bartender grabbed the Cuervo and
gave her a refill.

"Make it two."

The deep voice startled her from her inner mono-
logue, and she blinked at the man in front of her.

He was handsome, in the smooth, generic way of a
manufactured pop star. Brown hair, toothpaste-com-
mercial grin, killer suit. Kaylee made herself return
his smile.

Warm-up flirting. Something, along with the tequila, to calm her nerves.

"I'm Rick."

"Kaylee."

He raised his shot glass. "To sharing a drink with
a beautiful woman."

It was a sweet toast, she reminded herself when the
compliment elicited absolutely nothing from her. She
clinked her glass to his before downing the contents.

"Starting without me?"

Electricity prickled through her, straightening her spine.

Even his voice was sexy as sin. And in that moment, Kaylee understood why none of her previous relationships had worked out. She needed this, the illicit zing that came from flouting the rules. She got off on hidden pleasures, on keeping secrets. And her schoolgirl crush on Aidan had been her first secret thrill. It was disconcerting, she realized as she turned to face him, that it was still going strong a decade later.

Aidan was dressed in a cream-colored Henley and another black leather jacket—this one was slim fit with quilted sleeves and a mandarin collar—which he'd paired with black jeans and boots.

He didn't look blandly handsome; he looked dangerously sexy. She salivated a little at the sight of him. "Hey."

He tipped his chin in greeting but barely spared her a glance before stepping past her. "We'll take another round." His gaze flicked from the bartender to Kaylee and back to the bartender, making it clear which *we* he was referring to.

The barkeep refilled Kaylee's shot glass before grabbing a clean one for his new customer. Aidan waited until he started pouring before he added, "And another one for my friend here."

Rick shook his head. "Nah, it's cool, man."

"I insist. Consider it my way of thanking you for keeping my girl company until I got here."

Kaylee's fifteen-year-old self went into full-squee mode at the idea of Aidan considering her his *anything*, but her adult self squashed the flare of giddy hope. Male posturing did not a declaration make.

Rick's testosterone obviously rose to the implied challenge, and without breaking eye contact, he rapped his shot glass on the bar so the bartender could fill it.

Aidan raised his tequila. "To new friends," he said, before the three of them drank.

To awkwardness probably would have been a better toast, Kaylee figured, setting her empty glass on the dark wood beside Aidan's and wiping her mouth.

He turned to look at her, and she was almost certain her pulse spiked in direct correlation with the quirk of his brow. "What are you drinking?"

"Uh…" Caught slightly off guard by the abrupt shift in the air that came from Aidan's possessive display, she turned her attention to the man behind the bar. "I'll try the house red."

"I'll take a Macallan 18. Neat." Aidan pulled his wallet from his back pocket and threw two hundred-dollar bills on the dark wood. The bartender delivered their drinks in record time, obviously hoping that if he impressed Aidan with his efficiency, he wouldn't have to make any change. His gamble paid off. Aidan grabbed his drink and handed Kaylee hers.

Both the bartender and Aidan turned expectantly to the other member of this little tableau.

"Sorry, man. I didn't catch your name." The taunt had the other man straightening to his full height, about four inches short of Aidan's six foot two.

"It's Rick."

Aidan reached for her, his hand coming to rest on

the small of her back, and her wine sloshed perilously close to the rim of her glass as Kaylee's knees grew woozy at the unexpected familiarity of the touch.

"Well, if you'll excuse us, Rick, our table is ready."

And with that, Aidan escorted her past her would-be suitor and to a prime spot, closest to the window.

Game, set, and match.

Not that she could imagine Aidan playing anything as civilized as tennis, but she had no idea what cavemen used to say when they bonked each other over the head and declared victory.

Kaylee savored the drama of the exit, and even though she was mostly sure he only held out her chair for Rick's benefit, it was still something to have Aidan Beckett being so chivalrous to her.

She sipped her wine and watched as he took the seat across from her. God, the man could sit in a chair. When she was young, she was so in awe of that—his confidence, the way he wasn't afraid to take up space in the world. She admired it because all she'd wanted back then was to shrink, to hide from her mother's judgmental gaze.

Polite society dictated she say something innocuously charming now. Compliment him on his choice of venue. Ignore the thing that she most wanted to know in favor of something bland and acceptable.

The rebellious streak that was the bane of her mother's existence reared up, as it usually did, and instead of opening with polite small talk, Kaylee got straight to the point.

"So, what was with the Mr. Macho routine back there?"

Aidan shook his head, doing a credible job of looking like he had no idea what she was talking about.

"I was in the middle of a nice conversation. That could have been a love connection," Kaylee lied.

"What, that guy?" Aidan scoffed. "He's not your type."

Right as he may be, his certainty pricked the edge of her temper, but she watered it down with self-deprecation. *A lady never feels too much in public.* "Oh really? And what put him out of my grasp? Was he too handsome? Too charming? Or maybe he was too—"

"Boring."

Kaylee tipped her head and raised an eyebrow at that pronouncement, watching as he brought his glass to his lips. The muscles in his throat worked as he swallowed, and just like that, the visceral want that plagued her when he was near tingled along her nerve endings.

When she was a teenager, it had been a vague restlessness—the hollow ache of not quite understanding what her body was asking for. Now she knew precisely what she wanted from him, exactly how Aidan's touch could make her burn.

She looked at her wine. "Well, we can't all run with the bulls, Mr. Pamplona."

"Hey." He shifted forward in his seat, bracing his elbows on the edge of the table and hunching forward over his drink. He ran his thumb hypnotically up and down the tumbler. He had sexy hands. Big. Strong.

Capable. A couple of scars and some calluses to keep them from being too perfect. The flaws only made them more appealing.

She could still feel them running over her body if she really concentrated. Which she had. In the shower before she'd gotten ready for tonight. She'd thought it would be a good idea to take the edge off. Instead, it had her feeling primed for action. She shifted in her chair. A bit of a backfire on that plan.

Aidan tapped her knee with his under the table, and with a sigh, she relented. When she flicked her gaze from his hands to his face, he was closer than she expected, and his earnest expression did weird things to her pulse.

"He didn't make a single move when I stole you out from under his nose. And you deserve better than that."

To combat the heat spilling through her chest at the sentiment, she let out a desperate-sounding laugh. "I'm pretty sure not wanting to get his ass handed to him by the big, intimidating guy in the biker jacket just proves that he's also really smart."

Aidan leaned back in his chair at that, a smug grin lifting the corner of his sinful lips.

"What?"

He shook his head. "Nothing." He let a beat slip by, eyes lit with a wicked gleam. "And thank you."

Kaylee took a sip of her merlot and tried not to rise to the bait, but she couldn't help herself. "For what?"

"For your confidence that I could take him."

Not that it was much of a contest. Aidan could probably take any guy in here.

"But you're wrong about him being smart. If he was, he'd be sitting here instead of me."

The compliment warmed places inside of Kaylee that were already overheating, and she reached for her wine. The sip she took did nothing to cool her, so she took another.

"Well, on the upside for him, it looks like his night turned out okay without me." She lifted her chin in the direction of Rick, who was laughing with a pretty blonde in a green dress.

Aidan hooked his arm over the back of his chair and turned to follow her sight line. After a moment of observation, he turned back to her, shaking his head. "What's happening over there is a lie staged completely for your benefit."

She shot him a skeptical frown. "How could you possibly know that?"

"Because he keeps glancing over here to see if you're watching. He took the path of least resistance and now he knows he made a mistake. That's what happens when you don't fight for what you want. The what-ifs haunt you."

Kaylee swirled the wine in her glass and idly wondered if he was still talking about Rick. "Do you have what-ifs that haunt you, Aidan?"

The question stilled him, furrowed his brow. She leaned forward, bracing an elbow on the table. "Things you want?" she pressed, her voice husky, knowing she was pushing her luck but unable to stop herself.

His eyes snapped to hers, something dangerous in their depths. Something hot. She squeezed her thighs together at the flare of heat that had sparked between them.

"Things you're willing to fight for?"

He wouldn't have to fight too hard for her right now—that was for sure. If the table wasn't in her way, she'd already be straddling his lap.

Almost as though he heard the dirty direction her thoughts had taken, he shut it down. Two blinks and he was back to the usual unaffected neutrality with which he'd always looked at her. She was Max's little sister again.

"I'm not talking about me. I'm talking about you shooting drinks with guys who don't deserve you."

She forced a smile through the disappointment. "So the moral of your story is 'Don't trust guys in suits.'"

His expression turned serious as their gazes locked. "The moral of my story is Don't Trust Anyone."

"Except for you," she teased, hoping to lighten the mood a little. Restore some of the friendly intimacy they'd shared tonight.

Aidan took a swig of his drink, shaking his head as he set the tumbler back on the table. "Not even me. People are inherently selfish, KJ. When it comes down to it, they'll pick themselves over you every time. You need to look out for yourself."

His voice sounded almost…bleak.

"That sounds like a lonely way to live."

"You think I'm lonely?" he asked, cocking an eyebrow and leaning back in his chair.

As if to reinforce his implication, she could see at least a half-dozen women eyeing him up like they would be happy to relieve him of that particular condition.

"Having anonymous sex with strangers in back rooms doesn't mean you're not lonely."

Aidan stiffened, and Kaylee winced at the blunder. Shit. She set her wine back on the table. Why had she said that? She was entering dangerous territory. Okay, maybe her pride was a little hurt that he hadn't put it together, but wasn't that what she wanted? To keep her secret? That was what made their rendezvous so hot. That it was clandestine. And it was better to keep it that way, she reminded herself.

Despite that, she remembered the stage, the power of performing, the want in Aidan's eyes, the feel of his body driving deep into hers. And with a deep breath, she set it aside.

She'd gotten her fantasy night. Now they were back to normal.

Well, not quite.

"You've changed," she noted. The charming boy she remembered had been quick to smile, quick to flirt. This Aidan was harder. Still easy with his movements, but stingier with them, too. It seemed to Kaylee that he only moved, only spoke, economically.

He didn't deny it. Just stared contemplatively at her in that way that made her want to roll her shoulders to alleviate the resulting buzz under her skin. She needed a distraction.

"Tell me about Pamplona."

His lips quirked with a hint of a surprised smile. "You don't want to hear about that."

The teasing words were a ghost from the past, part of the little game they played.

"I want to hear everything," she recited back, and she could tell by his hesitation that he was recalling the same memories.

He loosened up as he told her about his adventures, and a familiar ease had settled over the two of them when he got to the part about the Spanish emergency room and the beautiful nurse—Aidan's stories always had a beautiful villain for her to seethe with jealousy over. By the time she was seventeen, she'd begun to think he oversold whatever leading lady featured in his adventurous tale just to see her frown.

The storytelling he was doing now was automatic, the verbal equivalent of changing into sweatpants. As natural to him as breathing. Light. It used to be enough, but it wasn't anymore.

No matter how much she tried to talk herself out of it, she wanted the heat. Now that she knew what it was like to have Aidan want her, to be the focus of his attention, to see those jade green eyes darken with need, she craved it.

To think she'd spent the entire morning worried he'd figure out who she was, and now, two hours into this farce of a "date," she was offended he hadn't connected her with their kinda-public tryst. It was stupid, but she was jealous of herself. Of the hard truth that Aidan couldn't even fathom that Kaylee Jayne Whitfield had the power to bring him to his knees.

Asshole.

She finished her wine with an unladylike swig that would have scandalized her mother.

A gorgeous, gorgeous asshole with a killer smile and some serious prowess in the bedroom. Well, the supply closet anyway.

Man, she felt good all of a sudden. Loose. Like she was floating a little. "I'm going to powder my nose," she lied, needing to pee so badly that she didn't even grab her purse to perpetuate the fabrication women had been using for decades to excuse themselves. "Don't go anywhere."

CHAPTER SEVEN

AIDAN KEPT AN eye on her retreating form as he dug into her sparkly purse with quick efficiency. Since the tables were close, he took no chances, setting their phones side by side so that they touched when he hit the button that would load the malware. Kearney wasn't kidding about the easy install. When it was complete, he tucked her phone away, leaving everything as he'd found it.

He drowned the flare of guilt with the final sip of premium whiskey in his glass. He shouldn't have told her about Pamplona. That had been...purely sentimental, and he wasn't that anymore. He'd known it was completely ridiculous when he'd morphed the proficient, elderly woman who'd taken care of him into a nubile Spanish goddess just to make Kaylee frown at him in that cute way she used to. She hadn't disappointed.

The first time he'd mentioned a pretty girl in one of his stories, she'd been real, and Aidan had realized it was an easy way to keep Kaylee's crush on him in check. The way she used to look at him sometimes, like he was all good things, had vacillated between humbling and fucking uncomfortable. She'd cast him as a hero, and everything in him rejected the mantle and the expectations that came with it. He hadn't deserved her devotion back then, and he sure as hell didn't deserve it now.

He caught sight of Rick across the bar, still flirting with some other woman who didn't hold a candle to Kaylee, and his right hand fisted with the urge to throw a punch. Expelling a deep breath, he forced his muscles to unclench. It bothered him that he cared.

What had happened at the bar earlier was no big deal. He's been protecting a friend from a creep. It meant nothing.

His conscience chose that moment to remember the heat that had arced between them when her hazel eyes had grown stormy and her voice had turned husky, asking him about things he wanted. Igniting a lust in his veins that made him want to shove the table aside and haul her into his arms.

Christ.

He was all turned around. Being back in LA had him on edge. He couldn't wait to conclude his *business* and get the hell out of here, to wherever caught his fancy next.

Aidan wasn't prepared for the nostalgia Kaylee brought out in him. It made him realize that he'd been alone for a long time. It made him wonder what he'd been missing out on.

And that was a dangerous path. One that had him thinking dangerous things. About Kaylee.

Who had been like a sister to him. The Whitfields

were like family. Well, they used to be. Now they were the enemy, and he'd do well not to forget that again.

When Kaylee came back she stumbled, bracing herself with a hand on his shoulder. He had the distinct impression of warmth in that moment of contact, a warmth that didn't fade as much as it should have when she let go.

"Sorry." She giggled, dropping into the chair with less grace than she had the first time she'd sat.

He noticed the flush in her cheeks.

The glassiness in her eyes.

A quick mental tally told him she'd had two shots and a glass of red since he'd arrived an hour and a half ago. Not wasted, he decided, but depending on when she'd last eaten, definitely feeling no pain. He should have taken her to dinner instead. Shit.

He had the disquieting thought that Max would be pissed if he knew Aidan had gotten Kaylee drunk, and then chastised himself for thinking it. Max was none of his concern.

Kaylee, on the other hand…

"You okay there, kiddo?"

"I feel so amazing," she told him expansively, "that I am going to let that *kiddo* slide."

He had to bite back a smile at that. "In that case, I think it's time I took you home."

Her pretty face lit up. "I've never been on a motorcycle before."

Aidan got to his feet, and Kaylee followed suit, though more slowly and more deliberately.

"Well, you're not going on one tonight, either."

She gave him her best puppy-dog eyes.

"I'm not scraping you off the pavement," he told her, reaching over to grab her forgotten purse from the table and pushing it into her hands. "Max and I have enough problems already."

"Max wouldn't care." Bitterness crept into the words, dulling her inebriated dreaminess from the moment before. "Well, I mean, it might be inconvenient for him because then he'd have to hire another PR director. But I guess he has to anyway now that I quit. I only did it so he'd ask me to stay, but he didn't. He didn't even care."

Aidan stared at her as they made their way out of the bar and into the elevator. Was that really what she thought? That she meant nothing to her brother? Defense of his former friend welled up on his tongue, but Aidan squelched it with a sudden frown.

Fuck Max. His life and the people in it were none of Aidan's concern. Let the bastard fend for himself.

Aidan jammed the lobby button with more force than necessary.

"And if there's one thing Max hates," Kaylee rambled on, blissfully unaware of Aidan's mental strife, "it's to be inconvenienced." She laughed in the way people did when they'd said too much. "My death would definitely annoy him."

Kaylee went silent for a moment, and he felt her glancing uncertainly at him, though he kept his gaze stubbornly forward.

"You wouldn't understand because Max likes you." A cute little frown crumpled her forehead. "Well, not anymore," she said bluntly. "But he used to. What happened with you two anyway?"

This was not the time or the place to discuss it. And she definitely wasn't the person. You didn't explain the battle plan to the grenade. Especially when you still had no idea how much she knew.

Thankfully, the doors slid open, and he grabbed her elbow, partly to steady her and partly to hurry her through the lobby and outside. The evening air was warm but stagnant. Tonight, it reeked of big city—concrete and exhaust and a hint of urine. "Which way is your car?"

She stepped away from him, turning in a slow half circle as she oriented herself.

Two guys walking past took a good long look at her, and Aidan frowned, mostly at them but partially at the sudden protective streak that had him stripping off his jacket and holding it out to her. "Put this on."

Her dress was the kind of sexy that snuck up on you. The classy kind that left something to a man's imagination instead of showing him exactly what he was in for. And though he had no problem with being shown what he was in for—his Friday night with Lola had been epic—there was definitely something in the tease of filling in the blanks. Despite his earlier resolve not to, he liked it a little too much.

Her dreamy smile hit him right in the gut.

Yeah, right. *Protective.* Such a load of bullshit, but he clung to it because the alternative was... There was no acceptable alternative.

"You're not gonna have any jackets left," she mumbled nonsensically, pulling it on and snuggling into it.

Aidan set his jaw against the charming scene. "You got keys somewhere, KJ?"

She shoved the sparkly purse at his chest and he took it as they headed toward the silver Audi she'd left in a nearby pay lot.

Once he had her loaded into the passenger seat and buckled in, he joined her inside the car, though he had to shove her seat back as far as it would go and change every mirror setting.

"You drive stick?"

"Is that an invitation?" She ruined the sultry question with a hiccup, but Aidan's body didn't seem to care.

"Please tell me you remember where you live?" he asked gruffly, trying to resurrect the polite distance he'd managed for most of the night.

She guided him to her fancy building, and the key fob gained them entry to the underground garage. He cut the engine, and silence descended upon them. He looked over to find her eyes closed, her long lashes casting shadows on her cheeks, her mouth curved provocatively at the corner, like she was in the middle of a very good dream.

Self-preservation had him unbuckling his seat belt and getting out of the Audi. He slammed the driver's door with more force than necessary, with every intention of waking her up, because he didn't trust himself to touch her right now, not even to shake her awake.

He circled the back of the car and pulled open the passenger-side door.

"Okay. Let's get you upstairs."

"I'm too tired. I'll just sleep here," she countered, snuggling into the black leather seat.

"What kind of gentleman would I be if I left you sleeping in your car?" he asked sardonically. With an aggrieved frown, she shoved her hand toward him, and against his better judgment, he accepted it.

"You've spent your whole life telling me you're not a gentleman at all," she countered when she was finally standing in front of him. She was tall, he realized, and her high heels made her even more so.

He'd barely have to dip his head to kiss her right now, to bring their mouths into perfect alignment. He leaned forward.

"Aidan?" His name sounded breathy on her lips, and lust coiled deep in his belly.

"Yeah?"

"I think I forgot my purse."

He exhaled at the near miss as she spun away from him.

Aidan didn't mean to stare at that round, pert ass as she dived back into the car, bracing a knee on the seat so she could retrieve her clutch. His mouth went dry. No panty lines.

"Got it!" Her voice was triumphant as she backed out of the Audi, tugging her dress down her shapely thighs as she fixed him with a victorious smile. "Man. We should have shared some appetizers at the bar. I'm starving," she announced, pushing past him. Her unsteady footsteps echoed in the concrete cavern as she headed toward the elevator.

He swallowed as he shut the door and locked her car with the press of a button, taking a moment to re-adjust himself before he followed along in her wake.

Nope. He was definitely not a gentleman.

CHAPTER EIGHT

THEY MANAGED THE trip to the elevator pretty seamlessly, though in her inebriated state, Kaylee kept misjudging how much space she was taking up. Every time she brushed against him, which was often, his libido and his brain went to war. Any relief he felt when they finally stepped onto her floor was ruined by his inability to concentrate on anything but the sway of her hips as he followed her to her place. She leaned heavily on the wall as he unlocked the door.

He stepped back. "After you."

With some effort, she disassociated herself from the wall, haphazardly shedding her shoes and his jacket as she meandered into the space.

Aidan followed her in. It was a nice place. Of course. Ritzy, subdued furniture that bespoke old money. Tidy, elegant, no hint as to what lay beneath the surface.

So very much like its owner.

Aidan stepped into the high-end kitchen. "Where are the glasses?"

His question stalled Kaylee's forward progress, and she wandered back to join him, pointing at the cupboard to his right. He grabbed the tallest one he could find and shoved it under the tap before holding it out to her. "Drink this."

"I'm not thirsty."

"Drink it anyway," he suggested, doing his best to ignore the danger of her proximity. All this time, she'd been stuck in his memory as a winsome teen who used to beg him for stories when she worked up the nerve to speak to him. So much time had passed between then and now. So many things had changed.

Kaylee took the glass, placating him with a half-hearted swallow before she set it beside the sink.

She'd changed, too. But he'd do well not to notice that.

"You'll thank me tomorrow."

Something dangerous lit in her eyes. His body braced for the impact, all his muscles drawing tight.

"I'd rather thank you tonight."

Aidan gave a silent curse. Damned if he didn't want to let her.

Had since she'd turned around in the bar, looking fresh and beautiful and so goddamned sexy that he couldn't think straight. The buzz between them was unlike anything Aidan had ever experienced, as hazardous as a downed power line.

"Want to know a secret?"

He wanted to know all her secrets. What made her moan. What turned her on.

Goddamn it. He'd been so horny since he'd broken his unintentional sexual fast and lapsed into hedonism with that burlesque dancer. But he was not going to slake his reignited libido with Kaylee Whitfield.

"I've always had a crush on you."

The sweetness of her confession gave him a moment to get ahold of himself, subdue his raging hormones. "That's not a secret, KJ."

But the feeling had never been mutual.

At least not until tonight.

"That's not what you're supposed to say!" Her affronted frown was cute as hell.

He relaxed a little as they fell into old roles, him cajoling, her exasperated. "What was I supposed to say?"

"Something gallant. Or something sweet. Basically, anything but that."

"Duly noted. Now, let's get you to bed." He instantly regretted his choice of words as something dark and sexy supercharged the air between them, turning his innocent words into a lascivious proposition.

"You're a fast learner. That was better already."

She stepped closer, dragged her fingers down his chest. He caught her wrist, stilling her hand. Her gaze dropped to his lips, and he could feel her pulse kick up.

That thrum between them filled his head.

"Do you want me?" she asked.

His eyebrows snapped together. This was definitely not the Kaylee he remembered. "What?"

This time when she lowered her gaze, she didn't stop until she got to his zipper. "Do I make you hard?"

His body responded against his will, and she smiled the kind of smile that could drop a guy to his knees. "Because I want you."

"You're drunk." He tried to shut her down. "You don't know what you're asking for."

"You wanna bet on that?" She caught her bottom lip between her teeth and gave him a look that was all liquid sex and mysterious woman. "I know *exactly* what I'm asking for."

Something about the way she said it made him believe her. Made him want to give it to her, too.

"And you know what else I bet? I bet you fuck like a stallion."

"Jesus, Kaylee." He dropped her hand, took a step back. She was more potent than he'd thought. More dangerous than he'd given her credit for.

"What? I can say *fuck* if I want to. I'm an adult woman."

"You're not acting like it." It was a feeble defense, but Aidan committed, injecting his tone with acid as he tried to get his brain out of his pants and back where it belonged.

She wasn't embarrassed as much as put out, if her pout was any indication. "You sound like my mother."

That startled a laugh from him. Par for the course tonight, he figured. Past and present had collided in the most disorienting way. He pulled a hand over his face, down his beard. "Christ, I really do."

Her answering smile was wobbly. He was objectively struck in that moment by how beautiful she was. The promise had been there in her teens, but the result was like a kick to the chest.

"How is Sylvia these days?"

"The Dragon Lady still rules with an iron fist. Wait." She shook her head, and the force made her sway. She braced a steadying hand on the counter. "Why are we talking about my mother right now? You're not getting out of this that easily."

Beautiful and stubborn as fuck.

He was trying to avenge his father, to tear down the family that had ruined his. She was the enemy, he reminded himself. Max's baby sister. He wasn't supposed to want her. And he sure as shit wasn't supposed to like her.

She zeroed in on his face, searching for what he didn't know.

"Max's kid sister."

His head snapped up. "What?"

"That's all you see, isn't it?"

She looked…disappointed in him, but for the life of him, he couldn't figure out why. Something about the way she'd phrased the question didn't sit right in his chest.

"That's all you are to me."

She stepped close, this time leaving no space between them. Testing the statement. Testing his resolve.

More seductive than anyone who'd been onstage Friday night. The vulnerability of it.

Nothing coy. Nothing but Kaylee looking up at him like she thought he was something special. It was fucking terrifying.

"Prove it." Her hands snaked up his chest, over his shoulders, brushed the nape of his neck. "Kiss me."

She felt good pressed against him. Too good. Like they fit together.

It took everything he had to pull her arms down.

"Not tonight." *Not ever*, his conscience reminded him.

The hurt in her eyes was too much for him to take, but her troubled expression cleared a moment later. "I'm going to change your mind, Aidan."

"No, you're not. Now, come on." He slipped his arm under her knees and picked her up, even though she was perfectly capable of walking. She snuggled into his chest, and just for a moment, Aidan let himself enjoy the feel of her in his arms.

He carried her out of the kitchen and into her bedroom. It took him too long to set her down, and it took her too long to step out of his arms.

The room was girly—a chandelier hung over her bed, which had a curvy upholstered headboard and way too many pillows, but the mattress was big. Probably a king. And he really needed to not concentrate on the bed right now.

Unfortunately, turning his attention back to her did nothing to alleviate thoughts of her bed, only now, he was imagining her naked, licking her lips exactly the way she was doing right now...

He was relieved when she turned away from him, but she ruined it quickly enough with a glance over her shoulder.

"Can you help me?" She caught her dark hair in her hand and twisted it up to reveal the graceful line of her neck. "With my dress?"

Shit.

Aidan swallowed as he reached for her zipper.

This couldn't happen while she was drunk.

The thought stopped him short. *What the actual hell?*

This couldn't happen while she was sober, either.

This couldn't happen at all.

But even knowing that, his cock wouldn't obey his brain, responding instead to the soft rasp of the zipper as he tugged it down and the slow reveal as the material gaped, baring the soft skin of her back inch by glorious inch. He wanted to run his fingertips along the delicate ridge of her spine. Unhook her lacy purple bra. Push the dress off her shoulders.

Lay her down on the bed and fuck her until they were both too weak to move.

Christ, he needed to get out of there.

"I'm going to get your water while you get changed." His voice was rough with desire, and he hated himself for it as he turned and left the bedroom.

But his conscience wasn't done with him yet. The far wall of her living room, he noticed, was dominated by a massive set of shelves packed with books.

When she was a teenager, Kaylee's nose had been constantly in a novel. The reminder of the quiet, studious girl she'd been unleashed a torrent of guilt in his belly. He was here to ruin her brother for his cowardice, and she was destined to be collateral damage at best and the reason for Max's downfall at worst. Aidan swore under his breath. Just because he'd had a soft spot for her back in the day didn't mean he was going to let it derail his plans. The eagerness on her face when she managed to get him alone for a few minutes, begging him to tell her about his latest adventure. He'd always indulged her, trying to make up for Max's intentional coldness.

Aidan used to wonder how Kaylee had grown up to

be so sweet and curious when her mother spent most of her time beating her down, harping on everything from her clothes to her posture to her book obsession.

It always broke his heart a little, watching her desperation to please Max, who never betrayed for an instant how much he loved and respected his little sister.

At the time, Aidan had thought it ludicrous, but it hadn't taken long to see that Max knew what he was talking about. Charles Whitfield aimed his verbal abuse at Max, and while he didn't exactly dote on his daughter, he treated Kaylee with a superficial affection that she lapped up—next to the way Sylvia Whitfield treated her, it must have felt like unconditional love.

He'd always respected that about Max. The way he'd done what needed doing to protect his family.

If Aidan had known it was going to come back and bite him in the ass, he might not have. He'd confided in Max about his concerns over his dad, but when push came to shove, Max had been a Whitfield through and through. He'd sold John Beckett out to his own father. A man Max didn't respect—hell, a man he barely even liked—and in doing so, he'd shattered what was left of Aidan's family. And Aidan intended to return the favor.

As he grabbed Kaylee's water, his conscience reared up, but he pushed it down. There was no room for sentiment and definitely no room for lust. The two of them couldn't be together. She was simply an in to Max's world. Nothing more.

When he returned, Kaylee was slung out on her stomach, one knee drawn up toward her chest, spectacular ass on display in a sexy little purple thong, snuffling drunkenly and fast asleep.

Thank Christ.

Aidan set the glass on her bedside table, beside the stack of books piled on it. But when he turned to leave, he caught sight of a mark on her skin, just beneath the lacy band of her bra, and everything in him went still.

It took a second for his mind to piece together where he'd last seen the tiny, graceful lines that made up the delicate butterfly perched on her rib cage.

In a starkly lit storage room.

In a midrange bar.

On a woman who'd made him crazy, driven him to unparalleled sexual heights.

Well, *fuck*.

CHAPTER NINE

THE JACKHAMMERING IN her head let Kaylee know she was in trouble even before she opened her eyes. There were a couple of other clues, of course. Her mouth tasted like death, throwing up sounded like a viable way to spend her morning, and her mind was replaying an embarrassing highlight reel of her night with Aidan. She whimpered, cradling her head.

She'd practically thrown herself at him, and he hadn't even been tempted. She stumbled out of bed and headed straight for the en suite to brush her teeth and down a couple of aspirin.

She caught sight of the makeup sliding down her face. *Ugh.*

She was a mess.

Kaylee did her best to clean the smudged eye makeup while she replayed her time with Aidan. It would figure that she finally got her chance with him, her chance to be herself—have him see her as the woman she was now, not the girl she'd been then—and she'd ended up acting like a fifteen-year-old at a house party, doing nothing to dispel her kid-sister mantle.

It was mortifying.

With an inner groan, Kaylee made her way to the kitchen. She was at the counter and reaching to grab a mug from the cupboard by the time her muddled brain noticed the coffee was already brewed, which made no sense.

"We need to talk."

Kaylee whirled around, hand to her chest. "Jesus, Aidan. You scared me."

Her heart thundered in her ears, and she forced herself to take a couple of deep breaths. She didn't know where he'd appeared from, but he was wearing the same clothes, including the jacket he'd loaned her. And unlike her, he looked just as amazing as he had last night.

The realization made her self-conscious in her bra-and-sweatpants combo, and she wished desperately she'd taken a moment to brush her hair before she'd begun her migration to the kitchen.

"You stayed here all night?" She turned her back on him, using the moment to calm her racing heart as she poured herself a mugful of coffee.

Her pulse was hammering in her skull, but she couldn't tell if that was because of the hangover or because of Aidan. What was he still doing here? Surely getting her home safely marked the end of any duty he felt to keep her from doing something stupid. Like driving drunk. Or going home with Rick.

What did it mean that he'd stayed? The question sent a frisson down her spine. As Aidan approached, the air got thicker, making it tough to breathe.

She took a sip of caffeine to steady her nerves, but her hand was trembling so hard that she set it back on the counter before she turned to face him.

Her breasts were heavy, aching at his nearness. God he was beautiful. Big. Starkly male. Imposing. And given the sharp edge in his eyes, angry.

"Did you have something you wanted to tell me?"

He stepped closer, cutting the distance between them to a couple of feet. It should be intimidating, but the leashed danger of him sparked something primal in her, and it made her want to reach out and touch the flames, not quite convinced such beauty could be a threat.

As if sensing her fascination, he stepped closer again, crowding her, and belatedly she realized that the danger was real. Logic told her to step back and maintain some semblance of safety. Something else urged her to step forward and take her chances in the storm.

"I don't know what you're talking about."

He frowned. "Don't you?"

The accusatory tone put her on edge as she racked her brain for what possible grievance he might have already tried and convicted her for. He stepped closer still, and her muddled thoughts got even more so. Against her will, she inhaled more deeply the heady scent of coffee and angry male.

"I'm sorry about last night. If the pounding in my head is anything to go by, I'm way too old to be getting drunk on a weeknight. That tequila hit harder than I expected."

"I don't give a shit about the tequila." His words were edged with steel.

"You don't?" Her forehead crinkled with confusion. "Then what—"

"This," he bit out as he pulled her to him. Her breasts brushed his chest, and he ran a palm up the left side of her torso, igniting the lust that had begun simmering deep in her belly the moment she'd realized he was still in her apartment.

Did he feel it too? The pull of attraction? The realization that he hadn't made a move while she was drunk but that he'd stayed all night anyway made her heart beat faster. The blood rushing in her ears had nothing to do with her overindulgence and everything to do with the man in front of her. The man she'd wanted for so long. The man who finally wanted her back.

She stood frozen, waiting for whatever came next—for him to press his mouth against hers, or sweep his hand up to cradle her breast, or pin her against the counter with his hips. But he didn't do any of those things.

He just stood there looking down at her, their bodies close but not close enough. Their breathing had synced, and nothing moved except for the slight pressure of his hand along the side of her rib cage. The pressure increased steadily, growing slightly uncomfortable before she realized his thumb was digging into her skin, right below the lacy edge of her bra, right where her...

Oh shit.

Her eyes widened with realization. The goddamn

butterfly tattoo throbbed beneath his thumb, and she cursed her stupidity.

Aidan's frown deepened at her confession, the one she knew was written all over her face. But the pressure on her tattoo eased, and when he spoke his voice sounded more off balance than enraged. "What the fuck, Kaylee?"

Can you help me with my dress?

The memory made her woozy. It had seemed a brilliantly flirtatious play last night, inhibitions dampened by tequila and Aidan and desire.

Now she saw it for what it was. A huge mistake.

She'd never thought for a second something so tiny would give her away, never considered that he'd noticed the show of teenage rebellion. Ironic, considering she'd been scrupulous about hiding it when she was a kid lest her mother see it and ground her for life.

Hell, Sylvia Whitfield *still* didn't know about it.

She didn't answer, but she didn't need to. He knew.

He knew what she'd done, and he wasn't happy. The accusation in his gaze cut deep.

"It was you."

It took her a moment to realize he was stroking the pad of his thumb back and forth across the winged talisman inked on her skin, shooting tiny sparks along her nerve endings and erasing the pain he'd inflicted a moment ago.

The sweetness of the gesture had lulled her into complacency, and his next swing made her stagger because she hadn't braced for it.

"Did Max put you up to this? Is he trying to figure out why I'm back?"

She'd never been punched before, but she imagined the lurching disorientation his words inspired must be what it was like to be coldcocked.

She was never going to be free of her brother. Aidan was never going to be free of her brother. The two men hadn't spoken in five years, yet they couldn't have been more linked.

"Why would Max have anything to do with my sex life?" Her voice was flat. Cold. An attempt to extricate herself from the box she occupied in Aidan's mind, the few times he bothered to think of her at all. The blunt question seemed to shake Aidan, and he stepped back, jerking his hand away as though he'd finally realized he was touching her.

As expected, talk of Max had leeched all the gray out of their tête-à-tête, and Aidan's hard gaze told her that he was firmly back in the land of black and white.

"It should never have happened."

The dismissal of their liaison, of the hottest experience of her life, piqued her anger.

"You wanted it as much as I did."

He raked a hand through his hair. The look on his face, like a wild animal trapped in a cage, was humiliating. "I had no idea who you were!"

The truth slashed at her.

"Maybe not, but you felt it, too. I know it's never been like that for you with anyone else. I could feel it in the way you touched me."

Aidan crossed his arms, trying to keep her out. "It was anonymous sex. It didn't mean anything."

Kaylee knew this was it, her one shot to take what she wanted. "It wasn't supposed to mean anything, but now that you know it was me, you know the truth. And it scares the shit out of you."

"If I'd known, if I'd even suspected it was you in that club, it never would have happened."

"But it did happen. Because I wanted you. I still want you." Something flared in his eyes, and Kaylee pressed her advantage. "And you want me. All you have to do is give in."

"You think you're a seductress now? Because we fucked in a supply closet? This doesn't end well, Kaylee. That's why it should never have started. You're messing with things you don't understand."

"Maybe I understand better than you think."

"If you did, you would never have resurrected whatever feelings you think you have for me. I don't return them. I never have."

"You didn't then. You couldn't. I was just a kid. But I'm not a kid anymore, Aidan. There's nothing stopping this now."

"Oh no? Then why didn't you tell me it was you?"

"I just…"

"You knew I would have sent you on your way. So you kept your mouth shut. Because you're a liar. Just like Max. Just like Charles. You're a Whitfield through and through. You take what you want when you want it, the rest of the world be damned."

It hurt. Of course it hurt. But the precision of the attack was so out of character from a man who'd always been so kind. He was angry, but she suspected it was more with himself than with her, so she kept pushing.

"Is that what I did? You weren't into what was happening? I thought it was just going to be sex. That you'd never find out. But then the way you looked at me when you put your jacket around my shoulders?"

He stiffened, like she'd accused him of something heinous.

"You looked at me like you saw me, like you knew something was different, and I…"

"You what? Thought if you tricked me into screwing you in a supply closet we'd fall in love and live happily ever after? Grow the fuck up."

And with that he stalked out of her apartment, out of her life, slamming the door behind him.

Kaylee watched him go. His words burning into her chest, even as her fury had her breathing hard. Asshole. He could deny it all he wanted, try to pretend nothing momentous had happened when their bodies touched, but she knew the truth. He'd wanted her in that supply closet. And he wanted her now, even knowing who she was.

CHAPTER TEN

SHE'S A FUCKING LIAR.

Aidan landed a one-two combination on the heavy bag he'd installed when he'd renovated his dad's old workshop into a living space.

The words had lost most of their heat days ago, but he made himself turn them over and over in his brain anyway. It was like a shield, something to remind himself that she was a Whitfield, that he should hate her.

The sound of Kaylee's laughter filled the room, mocking him, and he glanced over at his phone. He should turn it off. He'd already accessed the SecurePay prototype and sent it off to his tech guy so it could be analyzed against Cybercore's competing product.

But damn, she had a great laugh. Rich and throaty. And though he had no idea who this Jesse guy was, Aidan definitely didn't think he was as funny as Kaylee was giving him credit for. He was listening in on her daily briefing with Soteria Security, but judging by his erection, you'd think he'd called a goddamn phone-sex line.

For the past three days, he'd been listening to Kaylee run Whitfield Industries in her brother's absence. And doing a hell of a job of it. She was decisive but fair, supportive but exacting. Nothing like the girl he remembered who used to shrink whenever anyone so much as glanced at her. No, at work Kaylee was in charge. In control. Like she had been on that stage.

Jesus.

He was still having a tough time accepting that the sexy siren in the supply closet and little Kaylee Jayne Whitfield were one and the same.

And the fact that he hadn't put that together on his own made him want to punch things. A person. A wall. He wasn't choosy. Luckily, he was old enough to know better, so he kept his fists directed at the heavy bag.

But no matter how many punches he threw, he couldn't shake the way she'd looked in her kitchen that morning—hungover and beautiful and so effortlessly sexy. The sweetness of her had been in direct contrast to all the dirty things he craved from her as she stood there in her purple bra, staring up at him as his thumb stroked her ribs.

Kaylee.

He tried to name the toxicity oozing through his chest and was surprised to find it resembled betrayal.

But not the kind where he despised her for duping him as much as the kind where he resented her because he'd missed out. He'd had Kaylee in the supply closet, but he hadn't enjoyed it the way he should have because he'd thought she was someone else.

Even knowing, it was hard to believe she was the hot, sexy woman who'd melted all over him at the bur-

lesque club. Hell, maybe she was right to keep her identity from him. Maybe Max's little sister was all he'd
ever see her as.

He knew it was a lie the second he thought it.

Because she'd gotten him plenty hard with her
clumsy, drunken kitchen seduction, and he'd known
exactly who he was dealing with then. He was hard
right now reliving the details of that night in the storage room, imagining it over and over without the blond
wig and blue contacts.

Jab, jab, cross.

His boxing gloves made satisfying thuds against the
sand-filled leather.

It should never have happened. But after realizing
how attracted he was to Kaylee at the coffee shop, at
the lounge, he wasn't so sure anymore that, had she
revealed her identity in the supply closet, he would
have stopped.

A bead of sweat dripped along his temple, and he
pulled off one of his gloves and grabbed the hem of
his white tank to wipe it away.

He'd been a world-class asshole to her and stormed
out of her kitchen. She didn't deserve to be dragged
into the middle of his issues with Max. But that's what
he'd done. Used her. Put her between them.

He listened as Kaylee wrapped up the meeting, but
as she and Jesse and the other guy—Wes, maybe?—
were discussing what time they would meet on Monday, Aidan lost the signal and static crackled through
the phone speaker. It had happened a couple of times
before. When the signal was strong, Kearney's tech

was the real deal. There were moments that the sound was so crisp he could hear the whisper of Kaylee's sigh, and in the next second it would cut out completely or hum with white noise. Obviously the self-proclaimed tech god still had some bugs to work out.

And he was going to relish letting Kearney know his spyware wasn't all that, Aidan thought with a grim smile. He pulled off his other glove and walked over to the phone so he could stop the app. He dropped his boxing gloves on the end table and unwound his hand wraps with a disgusted sigh.

Usually, hitting the heavy bag cleared his head. But where Kaylee was concerned, not even boxing was doing the trick anymore.

Aidan dragged a hand through his sweaty hair.

Neither were cold showers, he thought wryly, reaching down to readjust himself.

He'd had a perma-erection for the last four days, despite having jacked off so much that he was giving his puberty record a run for it its money.

He pulled off his tank top and headed for the shower. His dick slapped his stomach when he shed his sweatpants and boxer briefs. With a disgusted sigh, he stepped under the warm spray of the shower and tried to remember the last time a woman had affected him so viscerally. He was no closer to finding an answer by the time he'd finished washing his hair.

Aidan grabbed the soap, lathering it between his palms. She'd gotten into his blood, he realized, running sudsy palms across his chest, trying his damnedest not to let thoughts of Kaylee pull his hands south.

But as he followed the sluice of water down to his abs, all the while remembering the bite of her nails over his back, the rasp of her breath on his neck, how it felt to be buried so deep inside her that coming became more vital than oxygen, Aidan realized he was going to lose that battle.

She was impossible to forget.

Or at least that was his excuse when he gave in and wrapped his hand around his aching cock.

His knees softened at the contact, and Aidan braced his free hand on the slate-colored shower tiles, tipping his head back and closing his eyes. He stood statue still, letting the rain-head shower wash over him as he stroked himself. And it was good, fuck yeah it was good, but he realized in that moment that his hand wasn't going to give him what he needed, what he craved.

Because right now, he was experiencing Schrödinger's Supply Closet. He'd both fucked Kaylee and not fucked Kaylee, and the paradox was killing him. Because whether he had or he hadn't, she'd come twice with the sweetest cries he'd ever heard.

His hand stilled even as the memory made him harder.

There was only one way he was getting free of sexual purgatory, and it wasn't courtesy of his goddamn hand.

Aidan shut off the shower and toweled dry. Naked, he headed for his room, grabbing his phone on the way past the table. He opened Kearney's spy app and tossed the device on his bed so he could tug on a pair of jeans.

The app beeped as the tracker came to life, and he glanced at the screen. Kaylee was on the move. He froze as she arrived at her destination. He didn't need to look up the address. He remembered all too well—hence all the masturbatory records he'd set over the past week.

Pulling on a T-shirt, Aidan grabbed the keys to his bike and his leather jacket—the one Kaylee had worn home from drinks—and headed for the club.

CHAPTER ELEVEN

KAYLEE FELT HIM.

It didn't matter that the club was particularly packed tonight or that he stood off to the side doing a credible job of blending into the shadows despite his size. The electrifying jolt of his attention was undeniable, just like it had been a week ago. Kaylee reciprocated by making her bumps bumpier and her grinds grindier. Because this time there were no secrets between them. This time he knew it was her.

There was only one reason for him to show up here tonight, and she wasn't going to waste it.

After her performance, Kaylee didn't bother with her street clothes. Instead of returning the black jersey skirt she'd borrowed last Friday, as had been her intention, she tugged it on. Then she laced herself back into her corset as quickly as she could.

As expected, he was waiting near the battered exit door. There was an extended moment of staring at one another, a reenactment of that moment before he'd tugged her into the supply closet, but this time with no subterfuge. Aidan's pupils were large in the dim light, ringed with jade, and Kaylee felt their focus so intensely it made her shiver. A slight frown marred his forehead as his eyes searched her face. Like he was looking beyond the blond wig, past the blue contacts, behind the red lipstick.

Looking for Kaylee.

He squinted, and she met his gaze, giving him time to catalog her face, to reconcile her features with Lola's, a glimpse behind the curtain so he could figure out how he'd been fooled last time. How time and makeup and expectation had conspired to keep him from seeing the truth.

And after he'd put all the pieces together, there was a flare of heat in those unforgettable eyes of his and their reenactment of the night that changed everything for her continued as he grabbed her hand. His palm was warm and wide and calloused, just as it had been before, but it felt different this time. Because this time, Aidan was holding *her* hand, not the hand of some nameless burlesque dancer he'd picked up in a club.

And this time, instead of dragging her off for a quick fuck in the supply closet, he pushed through the exit door and into the parking lot.

His bike gleamed under the streetlight, two helmets propped on the leather seat. Wordlessly, he handed her one. She put it on, and even with the wig it was too large. Then, as was becoming their custom, he pulled off his jacket and draped it over her shoulders.

She shoved her arms through the too-long sleeves, watching his white T-shirt pull taut over his muscles as he donned the other helmet.

It was a distinct pleasure watching Aidan. The way his body moved. She'd spent so much of her time back in the day slung out in a lounge chair, pretending to read as she covertly dissected his every move. But there was something luxurious in being able to watch him openly, to dedicate her full attention to the sinuous slide of muscle beneath cotton without worrying about getting caught.

The sight of him as he mounted the bike with a deft grace only heightened the tough, manly picture he made as the motorcycle roared to life.

A thrill shot through her as he turned his head in invitation. With distinctly less grace than he'd shown, she crawled behind him and onto the growling black-and-silver beast.

Aidan revved the engine and Kaylee let the vibrations tingle through her. She fixed the moment in her mind as she wrapped her arms around him and they took off.

It was her dirtiest dreams come true, Aidan between her legs, his jeans abrading her bare thighs in a way that drove her mad. She pressed her breasts against his back, sighing at the delicious pressure as she tightened her hold, speed measured by the wind on her skin.

The ridges of his abs were evident through the soft white cotton of his T-shirt, and Kaylee ran her nails over them, loving how they tightened beneath her fingers and how he punched the speed of the bike in response.

She'd been waiting for this her whole life. For Aidan to want her.

And despite what he might think, this wasn't about fairy tales or girlish wishes.

Aidan made her feel alive. And she craved him for it.

She wasn't looking for forever. She was looking for right now. That wicked thrill she got from misbehaving. From knowing her family wouldn't approve. It was her catnip. She couldn't resist the excitement of it.

Aidan took a hard right, and Kaylee looked around, curious about the unfamiliar neighborhood that was a fascinating blend of commercial and residential. Older warehouses and a lot of auto-body shops and parts stores randomly butted up against old single-story, flat-roofed houses with a distinctly '70s vibe. After a few more turns, Aidan slowed the bike and approached a two-story structure that, judging by the faded paint and two big garage doors on the front, used to be some sort of repair shop.

The garage door on the left began its ascent, and Aidan drove inside and cut the engine. The motorized hum of the door closing behind them accompanied Kaylee's dismount from the bike, her body still vibrating from the ride as she removed the helmet and drank in the odd building.

This side was definitely a garage, with massive silver tool chests lining the wall to her left and another motorcycle—vintage looking, from the '50s or '60s maybe—tucked off to the side. But to the right there was a living room, with an area rug on the concrete floor.

There was a heavy bag hanging from the ceiling, as well as a weight bench and a couple of other pieces that functioned as a gym area.

The back half of the bottom floor housed a kitchen full of stainless steel and exposed brick, and a room with a large window. When this place had been a functioning auto shop that room must have been the office. Beside that was a set of stairs that led to whatever occupied the second level.

It was kind of a loft, kind of a work space, very industrial and, in a weird way, seemed to embody the man beside her, straddling the line between rough and civilized.

Aidan grabbed the helmet from her and set it beside his on the seat of the bike.

With a speculative smile, she wandered out of the workshop area toward the living room setup to their right. She felt more than heard Aidan follow her as she dropped her bag on the couch and stopped in front of the coffee table.

There was a large steel sculpture on it, fire morphing into a herd of running horses. The detail was incredible, the flames blending seamlessly into the manes of the fleeing animals. She reached out to touch the fire, so intricately wrought she half expected it to burn her, but instead the smooth, cold surface leeched heat from the pad of her finger.

Max had something like it on his desk—less intricate, but similar—a horse with a mane of flames.

She glanced over her shoulder, intending to ask about it, but rather than standing on the edge of the area rug where she'd expected him to be, Aidan had taken a seat in the armchair, knees wide apart. His left hand was on his thigh, his right elbow on the armrest as he ran a hand over his beard, watching her with a look of such contemplation that it sucked the breath from her lungs.

Kaylee turned fully to face him. With shaking hands, she ran her fingers up the zippered edges of the front of his jacket before dropping it from her shoulders. She paused for a moment, working the art of the tease, enjoying the tingles that ran along her nerve endings as Aidan's eyes raked over her body. It was… thrilling, the taut, hungry look on his face, knowing that *she'd* put it there. Take that, Lola.

She let gravity and the weight of the leather drag the jacket the rest of the way down her arms before pulling it off and tossing it onto the couch.

Her breath came faster as she watched him look at her, trace her body with his gaze. He flexed the hand on his thigh, and the realization that he was imagining touching her made her wet. Just like that. Ready for him.

She'd thought that night in the supply closet had been potent, but it was nothing compared to this.

They hadn't spoken in days, but Aidan knew exactly how to break their word fast with deadly, sensual precision.

"Take it off." His voice was low, gruff, but it exploded in the silence, ricocheted through her chest.

Kaylee reached for the hooks of her corset.

"Not that."

She looked up.

"The wig."

The words stopped her heart.

Heat washed through her body. With shaking hands, she tugged off the blond wig and her wig cap together. Aidan's jaw flexed as her dark hair uncoiled, stoking the performer in her. She tossed the wig onto the couch and shook her head a few times so that her hair spilled over her shoulders.

He shifted in the chair, and power prickled across her skin. He might be giving the orders, but he was as much under her spell as she was under his, and she loved it.

She raised her hands to the top hook and paused, quirking an eyebrow in question.

Aidan swallowed, the muscles in his throat working even as his tongue darted out to moisten his lips. He was so intensely masculine, and having his total focus on her was heady in the extreme.

He gave a curt nod of permission, and Kaylee's body turned liquid and wanting as she began the familiar process of unhooking the corset. But if the action was familiar, the desire was not.

In the club during one of her shows, there was an anonymity to the sexy striptease, a coyness and irreverence that gave her near nudity a bawdy sense of fun. Now every move was purposeful and serious and dizzyingly sexy.

As the last hook came loose, excitement rippled over her skin. There was something so intense about the momentous step of taking her clothes off for this man. Of him knowing her identity, of them having sex as themselves.

A shyness she wasn't used to reared up as she gripped the sides of the corset and prepared to remove it.

This was him.

This was her.

Without her Lola persona, she was suddenly and uncomfortably aware of her body.

"Kaylee." His voice was a pleading growl that infused her with courage.

That first night in the club, she'd thought she'd wanted to dance for him, a private striptease to seduce him, show him how different she was from his memories of her as a shy, awkward teenager. But now that the moment was upon them, she found it wasn't what she craved at all.

She wanted Aidan to want her tonight. Just her. Not the stage show.

He'd pulled her out of the club.

He'd told her to take off the wig.

Those facts gave her the courage, and just like that, she dropped the corset. No showmanship, just honesty.

And sparkly pasties.

His breath came out as a curse, ratcheting up her excitement.

Aidan shifted in the chair, leaning forward. "Come here."

Kaylee obeyed, walking toward him in her heels. The jersey skirt rode up her thighs with each step.

She wanted to touch every inch of him before this

night was over, but she forced herself to draw out the anticipation, stopping in front of him and waiting until he managed to pull his attention up her body to meet her eyes.

"Well?" She laced the question with challenge. "You got me here. Now what are you going to do with me?"

His face darkened with leashed passion and he dragged rough fingers down her belly with such gentleness that her heart clenched. When he encountered the waistband of her skirt, he began inching the black jersey down her hips, his fingertips skating down her thighs until he reached her knees and gravity took care of the rest.

Then Aidan flattened his hands on her skin, releasing an electrical storm as he ran his palms up the backs of her legs, over the curve of her ass, to her lower back. His thumbs stroked the sides of her torso just below her waist, and through it all, he didn't break eye contact.

It was perfect. Soft. Dreamy. A sweet moment of restraint before the wave of lust crested and swallowed them both.

Aidan's hands tightened, his fingers digging into her flesh, and she felt him fight it, trying to hold on to that calm, peaceful moment before the storm of desire swept them both away. He pulled her closer, just a step, so her shins were touching the rough fabric of the chair between his spread legs and his forehead rested against her abdomen.

She pushed her fingers into his hair, cradling his head there.

His breath raced across her skin, leaving a trail of goose bumps that disappeared under the shocking heat of his tongue before reemerging with a vengeance.

He pressed his lips to her skin, dragging them up her stomach before kissing a path between her breasts. Kaylee braced her hands on his shoulders as he wrapped his arms around her, pulling her onto the chair with him as he leaned back.

Bracing a knee on either side of his hips, she straddled him and slid her hands up his neck to cup his jaw, to hold him still as she lowered her head and captured his mouth.

She'd told him that he fucked like a stallion, but he kissed like a damn poet, perfect rhythm, every stroke of his tongue and nip of his teeth wringing so much feeling from her that he could probably bring her to orgasm just from making out. Tonight, though, she wasn't patient enough to test that hypothesis.

She lowered her hips, pressing herself more fully against his erection.

He broke the kiss with a curse, but she had only a second to lament the loss of his hands on her body before he reached over his shoulder, grabbing a fistful of white cotton and tugging his T-shirt up and off, revealing acres of warm, golden skin.

"Aidan," she breathed, needing to say his name just to prove to herself that this was happening, that it wasn't a dream. Her fingers ached to touch him, to restore order to his shirt-mussed hair, to trace the dips and swells of his chest.

But there would be time for that later. First, she needed to get herself naked so she could feel him everywhere.

She cupped her breast with her left hand, the action immediately capturing Aidan's attention even before she tugged the skin taut with her thumb. He leaned back in the chair to watch, and his hips lifted, grinding against hers as she wedged her fingernail beneath the edge of the pasty and peeled it from her skin.

She watched the rise and fall of his chest as she repeated the same steps with the other pasty.

He ran his calloused palms up her back, pulling her toward him, and Kaylee braced her hand on the chair as he captured her nipple with his mouth, nipping and sucking until she was writhing against him.

"Do you need these?" He hooked a thumb between her hip and her panties, tugging the lace away from her skin.

"What?"

"Are they important for your act?"

"Not really. I—"

He ripped one side with surprising adeptness, then the other.

"I'll buy you new ones," he promised darkly, tugging the ruined lace from beneath her and tossing it on the floor.

Aidan wrapped his arms around her and pulled her hips flush with his, and she gasped at the rough friction of his jeans against her clit.

Oh *gawd*. And she'd thought she'd been keyed up that night in the bar. This was a hundred times more potent, though, because this time when he looked at her, he wasn't seeing Lola.

Aidan stood up, taking her with him. She wrapped her legs around him and braced herself for the ride.

CHAPTER TWELVE

She was driving him fucking crazy.

He needed to get her up to his room so he could have her the way he wanted to, laid out like a feast on his bed. But she kept distracting him, slowing his progress toward the stairs.

Her hands were busy, reaching between them, unbuckling his belt, unbuttoning his jeans.

Then her eager fingers breached the elastic of his boxer briefs and came in contact with his pulsing cock. Almost stumbling with the mind-numbing pleasure of it, he shoved against the nearest pillar so he could pull himself together.

Both of them groaned at the increase in pressure.

"Here's good. Please. I need you inside me."

He wanted to relent, to sink into her over and over until the desire raging through him was sated. It took everything in him to shake his head, to still the mindless rocking of his hips. "No," he ground out, though if she didn't stop stroking his cock like that, they weren't going to make it to the bedroom like he'd intended.

He dragged a ragged breath into his lungs and

pushed her legs down from around his waist. When her feet touched the floor, he stilled her hand with his.

He braced his other palm on the pillar beside her head, trying to make his brain work, trying to make her understand before he fucked this up. Already her mouth had gone slack, and her muscles tensed, preparing to withdraw. He'd do anything to erase the hurt and confusion seeping into the dreamy, hazy lust of a moment before. "I missed out on you the first time, KJ. I'm not rushing this. Not again."

Her eyes widened, and swirling in their depths was relief and desire and something else he couldn't name that almost knocked him to his knees. And for the first time in the history of ever, a woman letting go of his cock got him even harder. He grabbed her hand, and once again the heat of anticipation built between them while he tugged her up the metal staircase that led to his bedroom. Only this time, he knew exactly who was behind him.

He needed to get his fucking jeans off so badly that she was almost running to keep up with him by the time they'd made it up the stairs and crossed the threshold to his bedroom. He toed his boots off, pushing jeans, underwear, and socks off in one move. Then he stood there, naked, torn between savoring the view of her crawling onto his bed and grabbing a condom from the end table.

Condom first.

He ripped the package open, stifling his groan at the contact and pressure as he rolled it on. He was so fucking hard for her, so desperate it hurt. And now she was on her knees on his bed and he wasn't sure he was going to be able to make it last like he wanted.

"Aidan?"

She bit her bottom lip as he joined her on the mattress, on his knees, stopping scant inches from her, not quite trusting himself to touch her and listen to her question at the same time. "Yeah?"

That mouth was going to be his downfall, no doubt about it. "We've got all night to do this as many ways as you want, so please put us both out of our misery and fuck me now. No one's ever literally ripped my panties off before, and I'm so hot for you I can't stand it. We can go slow next time."

His arm was around her waist before she finished talking, and he hauled her up against his body, the warm, wet heat of her aligned with his throbbing cock.

Her whimper undid him as she undulated her hips, working her clit up and down his erection, taking her pleasure as she wrapped her arms around him and her nails bit into his back. He wished to fuck he hadn't put the condom on yet because the sweet slide of her pussy along his length was so damn good and he didn't want to think he was missing even a fraction of it.

He buried his free hand in her hair and pulled her head to the side so he could lick her neck, mark her with his teeth.

"Come for me this way. Grinding on my cock."

She shook her head, even though her hips continued to rock. Her fingers dug into his skin. "I need you inside me."

"After," he insisted. "I want to watch you get yourself off first."

Kaylee gave in to his demand with a moan he felt under his skin. She sped her rhythm, and he lifted his hips to meet hers on each downward slide, increasing the force of the friction until she was biting her lip, clutching his shoulders.

Then she cried out and came apart for him, and it was frantic and messy and goddamn perfect.

"Jesus, KJ. I want to fuck you so bad," he growled, biting her bottom lip as she reached between them, grabbing his dick, positioning herself over him.

"Do it," she whispered, and then he was sliding home, and it was so much better than he remembered from the storage room. Hotter. Sweeter.

Time slowed, and what he'd expected to be a frenzied mating of mouths and tongues and bodies turned way more profound. He wanted to kiss her, but he couldn't stop staring at her, watching her.

Her face was so expressive, her desire so raw. He was on edge just bearing witness to her passion.

He laid her on the bed, her ankles hooked over his shoulders, and the sexy little catch in her breath increased his pace.

This should have felt wrong, but it didn't. It felt so fucking right that he thought his heart might pound all the way out of his chest. She was gorgeous, pink lips parted, dazed with pleasure, and he wished she wasn't wearing those damn blue contacts, because he didn't want any part of her hidden from him right now.

She reached up, put her palm on the back of his neck, fisted her hand in his hair.

Pleasure crackled over his skin like a gathering electrical storm, but something darker and more profound was building low in his gut, and the dual sensations drove his hips forward with more purpose. And still, with so much sensation set to break over him, he clamped his jaw tight. He wasn't going under without her, so he took his cues from her soft sighs of pleasure, the way her orthodontist-perfected teeth caught her bottom lip.

And then, despite the fake blue of her contacts, she met his gaze with a look so real, so full of wonderment as she gave in to the friction, her body tightening under his, clenching his cock. She was fucking beautiful, his KJ, and he tried to hold out, to still the rock of his hips, to let her have this moment all to herself, but then her orgasm hit full force, and the sound of his name on her lips as she came pulled him into the vortex with her, leaving him helpless to do anything but follow her into oblivion.

CHAPTER THIRTEEN

THERE WERE FEW things better than lying in bed next to a naked, drowsy woman.

"I don't even know what you do for a living. That's kind of weird, right?"

Check that. A naked, *curious* woman.

But her question made him pause.

It reminded him that despite knowing each other for so long, they were virtual strangers. In a lot of ways, he didn't know her at all, and that was a bit disconcerting.

"I invest in good ideas."

"Sorry, what?"

"People in the tech industry come to me when they have big ideas and no seed money. I help them fund their projects."

She pushed up on an elbow so she could look down at him. "*You're* an angel investor?"

"That so hard to believe?"

She glanced pointedly at him, and he watched her expressive eyes—God, he hated those fucking contacts—as she took stock of him.

"Let's see…rock-star hair, hard-muscled body, and

a devilishly wicked grin." She shook her head. "You don't look much like any investor I've ever seen. And the *angel* part seems highly unlikely," she teased, leaning over for a slow, deep kiss.

He'd barely recovered from his earlier orgasm, and still the taste of her lips and cleverness of her tongue stoked the need in his belly.

He shifted on the mattress, hooking a hand beneath his head to stare at her. Sated from good sex and with a gorgeous woman stoking his ego, he grinned with pure male satisfaction. "I consider both of those compliments."

Her lips curved in a smile that made him want to kiss her again. "That's how I meant them." Kaylee traced a finger along his chest. "So how did you get into that?"

"I like watching people innovate."

She nodded, and her dark hair whispered across the sensitized skin of his chest. "Because of your dad?"

"Yeah, I guess so. He was never happier than when he was building something, whether it was a computer or a string of code. That statue downstairs? The horses with the flaming manes? He built his own 3-D printer and made that out of a drawing I did in high school."

"That's amazing. Max always spoke very highly of your dad."

Aidan nodded. Max and John Beckett had always shared a connection. They both loved to take things apart, figure out how they worked. Aidan had learned a long time ago that it didn't much matter how things worked, as long as they did. He'd stopped looking too closely at things after his mother's diagnosis. Knowing the particulars didn't change the outcome.

"Yeah. He was a good guy, my dad." Aidan ignored the guilt that accompanied thoughts of his father. Especially here, where his legacy loomed large. He forced his muscles to relax when Kaylee shot him a questioning glance. "Mostly," he added. That made his earlier statement less of a lie, he decided. Five years after his father's death and covering for the man was still like breathing to Aidan.

"Hey, you okay?"

The concern on her face humbled him. Apparently, he'd lost some of his skills at hiding his true feelings. "I'm good. It's my first time back here since he died. I thought the renos would make it feel different. But my old man's still here."

Kaylee glanced around the room. "What is this place?"

"It was my dad's first workshop. It was just a garage back then. Full of ripped-apart computers. He used to let me come hang out here when I was little. Before my mom got sick."

She angled her head on his shoulder so she could look at him, ran her palm soothingly along the planes of his chest.

He skated his fingers down the length of her arm, pulling her closer.

"After she got sick, this is where he came to drink."

Her hand stilled. "What was she like?"

Shit.

Things were too fucking deep for this soon after an orgasm.

"She was a cardiothoracic surgeon."

"Wow."

"Yeah. Pretty cool job. But it meant she wasn't home much. My dad and I spent a lot of time together. And I guess things were relatively normal. Until she was diagnosed when I was twelve. She was dead before my thirteenth birthday. By the time I turned fourteen, my father was a full-blown alcoholic. He'd pretty much given up on everything by then."

Aidan shoved down the bitterness that still surfaced whenever he remembered taking care of his father as though they'd undergone some sort of role reversal during their grief.

"My mom's dying wish was that no matter what, I got the best education, and she made me and my dad promise the money she left us would fund my education. And he did his best to make that happen, enrolled me in the fanciest school he could find."

And still, here he was, naked and spilling his guts.

She smiled at that, and Aidan was glad he was masking the underlying anger in the memory. Finding out that, between booze and gambling, his dad had blown through a lot of the education fund his mother had set up for him.

"I didn't bring anyone here, because my dad was hitting the bottle pretty hard back then. But Max wanted to see the place, so we snuck in once when I thought my dad was at work, and he and your brother really hit it off, geeking out on tech stuff. After that we came here a lot."

"You didn't geek out with them?"

"I didn't feel left out, if that's what you mean. Truth was, I liked the time we spent at your place better. I thought Max had it all. Fancy house, two parents, annoying little sister."

She gave him a playful swat.

"Enough money that he didn't have to worry about anything. I wanted what he had. I wanted to be like him. Your dad was this formidable guy who seemed so in charge of everything. I admired that."

"Yeah, well. Appearances can be deceiving."

He ran his fingers along the back of the hand she'd splayed on his chest, tracing the delicate ridge of her knuckles.

"They can. And I learned that lesson well enough. But at the time, my father was in a downward spiral. He lost his job because of the drinking and the gambling. Between that and the medical bills, we didn't have as much money left over as he'd hoped. I did my best to take care of him. And then your dad gave him a job. We used what was left of my mom's money to send him to rehab, and he managed to help me pay for college. He really got his life together. For a while, things were good."

She'd still been away at university at the time, but she knew about the accident that had ended his father's life, of course. "And then they weren't."

He nodded at the assessment, appreciating her tact. "I wish I'd...been around more. There are a lot of things I wish I'd told him."

"I'm sure he knew," she assured him, obviously assuming he meant heartwarming things, like how much he loved and respected John Beckett. Aidan didn't bother to correct her. He preferred to keep his anger and resentment toward his father, toward the choices he'd made, buried as deeply as possible.

"I wish I could have met him."

God, she was sweet. "He would have liked you."

"How do you know?"

"Because I like you."

The compliment earned him a lazy kiss that didn't last nearly long enough.

"Anyway, long story short I fixed this place up after he died, turned it into a living space so I'd have a place to stay when I'm in town."

"But you're not in town much anymore?" she asked, and he didn't like where the question was taking them. Because this was leading into a question about Max. And him. And he didn't want to fuck up this thing he and Kaylee had going by getting into nitty-gritty details. Time for a subject change.

He picked up her hand, kissed her fingers.

"Your turn to spill. Last time I saw you, you were a ballerina. What changed?"

Kaylee shook her head. "I was never a ballerina, much to Sylvia's dismay. But when I was in college, a group of friends dragged me to this burlesque workshop one weekend and I was enamored."

There was a spark in her when she talked about it, Aidan noticed, still tracing a finger across her knuckles.

"It makes me feel in control of things. I pick the music, I pick the costume. It's a way to be creative and a way to direct people's attention however I want to. I can seduce them, tease them."

"Sounds a lot like PR."

She laughed at the observation. "I never really thought of it like that, but I guess it is." She shrugged, propping her head up with her hand, and stared down at him. "It makes me feel sexy. I like having secrets. I always have. Knowing I'm doing something I shouldn't be, something my mother would disapprove of, is a turn-on."

An angel trying her hand at rebellion. It kind of worked for her. It definitely worked for him.

"Oh yeah?"

She nodded.

"Well, I know for a fact that your mom would hate it if you kissed me right now."

Something sultry sparked at the implied dare, and she leaned down and pressed her mouth to his. Her nipples were tight beads when they pressed into his chest, and his body reacted to the stimulus with gut-clenching speed.

"And she'd really hate it if you put your hands on me."

Her smile was dangerous to his equilibrium. "You think?"

Aidan nodded, stifling a groan as she tugged her fingers free of his and slid them across his chest. She teased his nipple before retreating so she could trace his sternum, down to his abs, lower, until they flirted with the Egyptian cotton that bisected his hips and did little to hide the effect she was having on him.

"What would she think if I did this?" she asked, shoving her hand under the sheet and palming the growing length of him. Her fingers were driving him crazy, and Aidan squeezed his eyes shut at the pleasure.

"Stern disapproval," he ground out, even as she circled her thumb over the head of his cock. "No doubt about it." God, he was desperate for her again. Just like that.

"Well, if she's going to disapprove anyway, we might as well give her something to disapprove of," she purred as she slid down his body, and Aidan half swore, half laughed as she bypassed further teasing and swallowed him deep.

It was soul destroying to have her mouth on him like this and the pain-edged pleasure of it built fast and hard. She alternated between licking and sucking until sensation turned sharp, undeniable, and he couldn't keep his hips still.

"Jesus, Kaylee." He reached down. Fisted his hand in her hair. To what end, he didn't know. "You're gonna make me come."

She obviously took his words as a challenge, and Aidan groaned as she massaged his balls and sped the bob of her head.

"I can't… You need to stop or I…"

He fucking lost it under the onslaught, his hips jerking as his climax pounded through him.

CHAPTER FOURTEEN

KAYLEE STRETCHED LANGUOROUSLY, a slight smile curving her lips as the scent of coffee and the sounds of someone moving around in the kitchen woke her from sleep.

Someone wickedly sexy who'd kept her up all night driving her body to the edge of pleasure and beyond.

It had been the most incredible sex of her life, and she allowed herself a moment to savor her sore muscles and the erotic memories of the man who'd made them that way before she finally pushed off the covers and swung her legs over the side of Aidan's bed.

Cool air rushed across her bare skin. The bag containing the change of clothes she always took with her to the club was downstairs, abandoned at some point between the thrilling motorcycle ride that had brought her here and the halcyon glow of lust and need that had blurred last night into this morning.

Her corset and pasties and the underwear he'd ripped off her—her stomach clenched at the delicious memory—were downstairs, too.

Left with no other option, Kaylee grabbed the gray

T-shirt draped over the arm of the chair in the corner of the room and pulled it over her head. It smelled like Aidan, and she inhaled deeply as she padded across the floor. In the upstairs bathroom, she took a moment to smooth her sleep-tousled hair and remove her disposable colored contacts before staring at herself in the mirror.

Some tiny part of her, the part that had written Kaylee Beckett in various notebooks, was expecting to see a different person in the reflection. But she was still her, Kaylee Jayne Whitfield. Perhaps her smile held a sensual smugness now, but overall, nothing had changed, and she was relieved to see it. Because that meant there was nothing magical about what had happened last night. That girlish dreams and womanly desires could collide in several earth-shaking orgasms without requiring overanalyzing or second-guessing.

She'd had a sexy secret liaison with a wild, handsome man, and now life could go back to normal.

Kaylee headed back into the bedroom and caught sight of the clock next to the bed. She was due at the country club for her weekly brunch with her mother in an hour and a half, and she still had to get back to her car and then home to change. Apparently life would be going back to normal more quickly than she'd hoped.

She hurried down the metal stairs.

Clad in nothing but low-slung jeans, Aidan Beckett was a sight to behold. Add the fact that he was holding a mug of coffee in her direction, and she'd never seen a more perfect sight in her life. Kaylee accepted it gratefully, indulging in a sip of caffeinated heaven. She couldn't help a little moan of contentment.

"This coffee is everything."

"You think that's good, you should try my world-famous omelet. You want one egg or two?"

Kaylee shook her head, taking a gulp of incredible java before setting her mug on the counter. "None. I can't stay." She stole a raspberry from the bowl to his right and popped it in her mouth.

Her answer made him frown. "What's the rush?" He grabbed her hand and tugged her between his body and the edge of the counter, pinning her there with his hips.

"I have to go change before I meet my mother for brunch," Kaylee told him, but despite her words, her hands migrated up his bare chest to twine around his neck. Her fingers toyed with the ends of his hair.

"Why? You look great."

Kaylee glanced down at herself and laughed. Her mother would go apoplectic if she showed up at the club wearing anything as plebeian as a T-shirt, let alone *just* a T-shirt. "Sylvia Whitfield, though she has not yet seen me, disagrees vehemently with your assessment."

"I love it when you use big words." He grabbed her hips and hoisted her up onto the granite countertop, stepping between her legs.

"Oh yeah?"

He nodded, running his hands up her torso. "Apparently women with extensive vocabularies really turn me on."

Kaylee gave a playful moue, injecting a little Marilyn Monroe into her voice. *"Dodecahedron."*

Aidan shot her that sexy smirk of his, lifting his eyebrows. "Mmm. That's the stuff," he teased, leaning forward and burying his face in her neck. Her head lolled back, granting him unfettered access, and her exhalation was shaky as he dragged his lips along the underside of her jaw.

"Sesquipedalian," she whispered.

"Yes, baby. Just like that."

She wanted to laugh, but the hot swipe of his tongue over her thudding pulse undid her, and despite the ticking clock of her looming brunch, Kaylee's arms tightened around his neck, pulling him closer.

"Antidisestablishmentarianism."

Aidan groaned as he finally gave her his mouth, and she sighed at the perfection of the endless, drugging kiss. Soft but with an edge of desperation, one that begged her to stay and see what happened next.

It took everything Kaylee had to pull back. "Hold that thought, for now I must embark on my peregrination." She planted a final kiss on his lips, one that lasted several beats longer than she meant it to, and hopped down from the counter.

"Mean," he chastised, and Kaylee giggled when Aidan's big palm landed on her ass with a loud smack.

How he could be so sexy and so fun at the same time was a mystery to her. She realized suddenly that he'd always been a bright spot in her life. Max never teased her or commiserated with her. Her mother made the things she loved, like dance and music, feel like a heavily regimented burden. Her father casually doled out scraps of attention between bouts of ignoring her completely.

But Aidan had always made time for a quick greeting to let her know she wasn't invisible. Whether it was a teasing wink, a sympathizing eye roll, or a story to distract her, he always seemed to know just how bring a smile to her face. It was one of the reasons she'd looked forward to his visits, hormones aside.

"Hey, you want backup?"

The softly worded offer snapped Kaylee's spine straight, and she turned to find him leaning a hip against the counter, his arms crossed over his beautiful bronze chest. She searched his face for some sign that he was still kidding around.

His gaze was steady. Scrupulous. Serious.

Something quaked through her body, but unlike a few moments earlier, this wasn't lust; it was fear. She tried to imagine her and Aidan arriving at the country club on his bike. Him sitting across from her mother in his jeans and T-shirt, looking defiant and bored and so sexy it made it hard to breathe.

The Dragon Lady wouldn't care that his bank account could back up his membership. That he'd grown from a troubled boy to a self-assured man. All she cared about were the optics. She'd be eating with the son of a former Whitfield Industries employee, one who'd never had fancy letters behind his name, like CFO or even VP. It was why she'd barely tolerated Max and Aidan's friendship back in the day. And why she would ruin Kaylee and Aidan's relationship now.

No. Not a relationship. Sex. A tryst. He wasn't her boyfriend.

"What? That's not… You don't have to do that." Her voice was strained. Everything in her rebelled at the idea. "You don't want to have brunch with my mom."

"That—" Aidan looked like he was going to deny it for a second, but sanity prevailed "—is true."

Kaylee's laugh lodged in her throat when he added, "But I want to have brunch with you."

The words made her ribs feel too tight for her lungs, for the hard beat of her heart—prison bars for the emotion trying to push out of her chest.

What the hell was he doing?

They'd just shared a perfect night, made even more incredible by not having to pretend to be Lola this time. And it was everything she'd hoped it would be. Why did he want to ruin their clandestine affair by taking it public?

She smiled, hoping it looked more natural than it felt. "Then let's do that sometime when we don't have a chaperone."

"Yeah. Okay." He nodded, but the air felt infinitesimally colder. "Some other time."

Despite Aidan's agreement, there was a tightness to his jaw and a stiffness to his shoulders as he turned away from her that made her doubt his sincerity. That he wanted to come with her made her anxious. That he was angry she wasn't going to let him made her wary.

"Aidan…"

"I get it. You don't want her to know."

"It's not that."

"Then what's the problem?" he asked, turning to face her.

Kaylee exhaled, trying to find the words to explain the phenomenon that had been leeching her joy since childhood. The reason she wasn't ready to share him yet. Not with the world at large and most especially not with her mother.

"My family ruins everything I care about. They pick it apart and judge it and tell me the reason that what I want is fanciful or silly or impractical. And I don't want… I'm not ready to have them dissect whatever it is that we're doing. I don't want their opinions on us. I just want it to be you and me for as long as this lasts. I just want it to be ours."

It wasn't the answer he was expecting.

Aidan refused to acknowledge that his earlier annoyance had loosened its grip on his chest. He should be irritated that she wanted to sneak around like goddamn teenagers. He was too old for games. So was she, for that matter. But he'd always been a sucker for KJ. He couldn't remember a time when he didn't care about her, when there was nothing he wouldn't do to put the sparkle back in those pretty hazel eyes.

"So don't go." Seemed simple enough to him.

Her whole body deflated on a sigh. "I have to."

"Why?"

Kaylee looked genuinely stymied for a minute, like she'd never considered the question. He could see the unguarded flash of possibility that sparked before she tamped it down and smothered it. "Because my mother and I always brunch on Saturdays. And today is the first day she's going back to the club since my dad... since what happened."

Aidan kept his face neutral, pushing down the satisfaction he got from imagining Charles Whitfield wearing an ankle monitor.

"Rebel a little." He walked forward until their bodies collided, until she rolled her eyes at him and a tiny smile curved her lips as he backed her into the edge of his dining room table—one of his father's stainless-steel workbenches that he'd had cut down and converted during the renovation.

"It'll do you good."

Before she could protest, he picked her up and set her on the cool metal.

"You just want to get laid," she teased. "And for the record, I'm excellent at rebelling. I've been doing it since I came out of the womb."

He reached down and fisted his hands in the hem of the soft gray material that covered her body. "Name one rebellious thing you've done in your entire life," he challenged.

"My tattoo." Her answer was muffled behind fabric as he dragged his T-shirt up and off her. And there she was, she and her attempt at rebellion, bared to his gaze.

A tiny butterfly that had caused a tsunami in his life.

Chaos theory made manifest. An unexpected series of events that had started the first night he'd seen her and led them to this moment.

Kaylee was perched naked on the edge of his table, looking like his fantasies, dark hair spilling over her shoulders and flirting with the tops of gorgeous breasts that were full and high and begging for his mouth.

He wanted to look at her, but he needed to touch her more. Aidan reached out and dragged his fingers across the tiny winged tattoo, reveling in the rash of goose bumps that flooded her skin in the wake of his touch.

She closed her eyes and bit her lip and his whole body throbbed with need.

"When'd you get it?"

Her eyelashes fluttered open, revealing an intricate pattern of brown and gold and green that eclipsed the flashier fake blue contacts—less showy, maybe, but more interesting, more captivating. He could get lost in those eyes.

"On my sixteenth birthday. Right after my mom said she thought tattoos on women were vulgar. She still doesn't know I have it."

Her voice was soft. Low. Laced with sex. He could feel it in his balls.

He placed a hand on either side of her jaw and buried his fingers in her hair as he angled her face up. "You're not a rebel." Aidan leaned forward and caught her bottom lip between his teeth. The sharp intake of her breath tightened his body. "Rebelling is about doing what you want to do and not giving a damn about the consequences. You're just good at keeping secrets," he challenged against her lips. "It's not the same thing."

He captured her protest with his mouth, kissing her deep and wet until she kissed him back. Until her body went pliant. Until she pushed her breasts forward in search of contact and sighed into his mouth.

Then he pulled his hands from her hair. Stepped back from her. It was the hardest fucking thing he'd ever done. His body clamored in protest, and her look of wounded confusion made it worse.

"Why a butterfly?" he asked, fisting his hands, resisting the temptation to move forward, to drag her against him and forget everything but how good it felt to be buried inside her as she clung to him and whispered sexy words against his skin. Because he had something to say, and if he gave in to impulsive lust, he might never get it out.

CHAPTER FIFTEEN

KAYLEE DIDN'T WANT to talk about her tattoo anymore.

Or be told she wasn't a rebel.

She didn't know why the hell the topic was so important to Aidan, either. The sizeable bulge in his jeans let her know that she wasn't the only one interested in putting his dining room table to X-rated use. Still, something reared up inside her, demanding she defend herself.

"Because my childhood felt like a prison, schedules and straight lines. And I wanted to remind myself that one day I would fly wherever I wanted to. I'd break out of that chrysalis and take to the skies. Live the life I always wanted. Do my own thing. This butterfly is why my stage name is Mariposa. This butterfly reminds me who I want to be."

Aidan nodded like he was absorbing that. "You ever heard the story about how they tether elephants?"

Kaylee frowned at the non sequitur.

"They put a post in the ground when the elephant is little, and they chain her to it. And no matter how much she pulls, she can't get free."

Kaylee shivered as an eerie dread flooded her skin. She didn't like this story.

"But then the elephant grows up, and pretty soon she's strong enough that she could pull that post right out of the ground with one good yank. Thing is, by that point she's used to her boundaries. She doesn't realize that it's not the chain holding her where she is. It's that she doesn't even try to escape anymore."

Everything in Kaylee went still. Got small. It was hard to swallow. "What are you trying to say?" she asked, her voice tight.

"I'm saying maybe you're not a butterfly. Maybe you're an elephant."

Aidan's words were matter-of-fact, with no particular emphasis, but they punctured like broken glass, jagged and misshapen, leaving her chest raw and gaping. She was already naked, but he'd just stripped her bare.

"Fuck you, Aidan." She made a move to shove herself off the table, but he was there caging her in, his palms flat against the table beside her hips.

"You say you're sick of your family taking advantage of you, of giving everything and getting nothing back." There was heat in his voice now. "So don't let them. Don't go for brunch with her. Spend the day with me instead."

"Why? Because you're horny and you want to christen your dining room table?" she spat, using her anger as a shield to keep his words from piercing her skin.

With a curse, he stepped back and ran a hand through his hair with obvious frustration. "Because she doesn't own you, KJ. Because she makes you miserable and you don't owe her anything."

"She's my mother."

"So?"

Why was he being such a dick?

"You know what? I don't have time for this right now. I have to see if I can catch an Uber to the club and I'm going to be late as it is." She twisted around to grab his T-shirt from the table.

"Don't fucking move." The words were hot, ringing out like a gunshot.

Kaylee froze. She hated that her body betrayed her, obeying without her brain's consent. Hated that his imperious tone sent a thrill through her, that it made her wet.

Her chin notched up as she turned back to him, her nakedness forgotten in the flash of rage. "Who the hell do you think you are? You don't get to tell me what to do."

He'd seemed furious a second ago, but it wasn't that now. Something shifted in his expression and she blinked at the dark, dangerous energy that crackled between them. No, not anger. Not exactly. Her body buzzed with it like she'd just been granted superpowers from a downed electrical wire. Like there was lightning in her veins.

His breathing turned harsh. Too fast. Hypnotic. Her palms itched to feel the rise and fall of it, to feel the heat of his skin and the hard muscle beneath. He stood close, but not close enough. She could probably skate her fingertips along his abs if she leaned forward, reached for him.

She didn't.

There was something feral about the sudden tilt of his lips, and she had the odd feeling that she'd somehow impressed him. That he was proud of her for yelling back. Warmth spread through her limbs.

"What do you want?"

"What?" The rapid shifts in conversation had her a little off balance.

"Tell me what you want."

She wanted to slap his face. She wanted to pull him close.

"I want to make you feel good."

"One wish and you want to use it to give me an orgasm?" Aidan shook his head. "Forget about me. What do *you* want?"

"I want you inside me." She spread her knees apart. Liked that his gaze dipped between her legs. Desire ratcheted higher and her fingers tightened on the edge of the table.

"Why?"

"I don't understand what you're asking."

He stepped closer. "It's not deep. It's not a mystery. You know exactly what your body is craving right now. Why your muscles are quivering and you're breathing harder. All you need to do is admit it, and I'll make it happen for you."

Jesus. Her breasts were heavy with want, her nipples so tight it almost hurt.

"You want me to make you come, KJ?"

Yes. All the yes. The answer shuddered through her, loosening her limbs, sparking a heat in her belly. She managed a nod.

"Then fucking say that. Own it."

She was so wet. So desperate that her inner muscles clenched, and she whimpered at the pressure. "I want to come."

"How?"

The question invaded her blood.

"I want your mouth on me."

He invaded her space, placing his hands on the table on either side of her hips. Leaned in close. He smelled warm and primal, like the promise of sex.

"Here?" He brushed his lips over hers.

She shook her head.

"Here?" He dragged his mouth across her cleavage and her head tipped back at the delicious sensation.

"Lower."

"Tell me what you want," he challenged again, lowering her onto the table. She shivered as the cool steel pressed into the hot skin of her back.

"Lick me."

He ran his tongue along the crease of her hip and she shifted restlessly. Unsatisfied. He was so close to where she needed him. She moved her hips, but he just chuckled and dragged his tongue a little farther from the mark.

Frustration made her bold.

"Lick my pussy." She'd never said the word before. Not aloud. But it felt a little bit shocking on her tongue, risqué for her, one step past her comfort zone. And she found it exhilarating. Especially when Aidan swore under his breath and pushed her back against the table.

"Don't ask me," he growled. "Make me."

She fisted her hand in his hair and pushed him right where she needed him. The first brush of his mouth made her hips buck.

Her mind went blank with pleasure, and it took her several moments to realize that whenever she quit directing the action, the action quit.

"Don't you dare stop now."

He chuckled as she tightened her fingers in his hair. Her breath came sawed from her lungs as he worked her over with lips and tongue, responding perfectly to her hand on his head. It was a revelation, being in charge of her own pleasure, taking what she wanted. What she needed.

Having Aidan's head between her legs was almost too much, and the need inside her spiraled out of control in record time.

The sharp catch of her orgasm tugged her under, and her back arched off the table as she drowned in the waves of pleasure racking her body.

The satisfied grin that tilted Aidan's sinful mouth made her feel wanted and wanton and a little bit wicked.

"That was…" She didn't really know how to finish the thought as she reached behind her to grab the T-shirt.

"It definitely was," he agreed.

God, he was beautiful. Broad shouldered and slim hipped, his arms corded with muscle.

Kaylee hopped off the table. She dropped her gaze to the substantial bulge in the front of his jeans. Her hands fisted, balling the material of the shirt.

"Looks like it's my turn to ask you what you want," she teased, cocking an eyebrow. He shook his head, surprising her.

"I'm good. That was about you."

She frowned. "Are you sure? Because—"

"You need to be selfish sometimes. That's what being a rebel is all about. Saying what you want. Taking what you want. You know?"

She didn't. Not really. The idea detonated in her brain, leaving her confused, disoriented by how bright and loud it was.

"Be the motherfucking butterfly."

Sage. Profane. Simple. The advice was so perfectly Aidan.

To Kaylee, life was complicated. Intricate. Like making her way through a minefield of people's expectations and feelings and desires. She'd spent her whole life navigating that way, trying to keep the peace, to live up to expectations, to not bother anyone, to earn her place.

Aidan made everything seem so easy. He'd offered to come with her. And then he'd told her not to go. Two choices. Black or white. Nothing gray. No elephants.

All she had to do was pick one.

Her bag was on the couch, where she'd left it the night before. With a gut full of trepidation, she walked over and dug her phone out from beneath her change of clothes. Her fingers shook as she swiped through to her mother's contact information and connected the call.

Sylvia Whitfield picked up on the first ring. "Traffic's a mess. You should probably avoid taking the—"

"I'm not coming, Mom."

Eerie silence, the kind that warned of an impending jump scare in a horror movie, made Kaylee's hand tighten on the phone.

"Pardon me?" Her mother's voice was terrifyingly calm. Never a good sign.

"Something came up."

"Something randomly came up? At the exact same time as our standing weekly brunch?"

Kaylee winced under the censure, but her gaze snagged on Aidan's, and just like that hug he'd given her when she was seventeen and heading off to Oxford, she found strength there that she could borrow. She took a deep breath.

"Are you bleeding, Kaylee Jayne? Is it some sort of emergency? Because a lady doesn't cancel plans without adequate notice unless—"

"There's no emergency. I'm not coming because I don't want to." Finally saying the words aloud was like standing at the edge of a cliff. Terrifying and exhilarating. To be honest. To tell her mother the truth.

"Kaylee, if you do not show up for—"

Static surged over the line and then there was no sound. "Mom?"

Kaylee pulled the phone from her ear, checking the screen. The call time was still ticking away steadily, so she tried again. "Mom? Are you there? Can you hear me?"

There was no response. With a sigh, Kaylee disconnected. For a brand-new phone it sure glitched a lot. "Great. Now she's going to think I hung up on her."

"That's probably the least of your worries after that performance. You did good."

"You won't think so when it starts raining fire and the locusts show up."

His grin made her heart stutter. "C'mere."

He pulled her against his chest and she tucked in, listening to his heartbeat. "I'm proud of you."

Tears formed at the foreign words, at the realization no one had ever said that to her before, but she willed them away. Today was her emancipation, and she wasn't going to spend it crying. "Talk is cheap, Beckett." She leaned back in his arms. "I'm gonna need you to back it up with action."

He lifted his brows. "Name it. Your wish is my command."

"Good. Because I like my omelets made with two eggs."

CHAPTER SIXTEEN

"So? What do you think?"

Kaylee pulled off her motorcycle helmet and stood beside Aidan on the cracked pavement. "When you said you wanted to spend the day together, I definitely wasn't expecting *this*." She cocked her head contemplatively. "It's nice, as far as abandoned buildings go."

Aidan rolled his eyes and grabbed her hand, pulling her with him toward the door. Even now, the thrill of his touch made her skin prickle. She wondered idly if it would ever go away, the jolt of his presence, the way every cell in her body vibrated when he was near.

Aidan let go of her hand and passed her his helmet so he could unlock the door, and then she found herself inside a high-ceilinged industrial space. It still had the faint smell of fresh paint and old sweat. And the front reception area was obviously next on the list for renos, as the walls were stripped bare and there were patches of plaster where repairs were being made.

Aidan relieved her of the helmets, setting them on the counter to the left before ushering her farther inside. "Welcome to Sal's."

Two boxing rings, a gauntlet of heavy bags, an assortment of speed bags, and a bunch of other specialized equipment that Kaylee couldn't identify filled the massive space.

"And Sal doesn't mind us being here?" she asked, meandering toward a wall that had obviously not undergone any recent painting. It was full of names and dates scrawled in black marker, some dating back to the '70s.

"He doesn't have much say considering I own the place."

The announcement pulled Kaylee's attention from the signatures.

"Sal's retiring, so I partnered up with his son to keep it open. Just doing a little cosmetic stuff before it reopens next month. This is where I learned to box."

There was a note of pride in Aidan's voice, a boyish excitement, as he surveyed the wall. "Here, look."

He pointed at one of the lower signatures, and Kaylee did a double take at the boyish printing that read Aidan Beckett.

"Everyone gets to sign when they win their first bout in the ring." He rubbed his finger almost reverently across the date beside his name. Kaylee did some quick math.

"You had your first boxing match when you were twelve?"

Aidan laughed as he walked along the wall. "No. I *won* my first boxing match when I was twelve. After my mom got sick, I developed a bit of an attitude. It was…highly recommended that I find healthier ways to channel my aggression. Sal kind of took me in. I learned a lot from him."

Aidan tapped on the wall. "Check this out."

Kaylee walked over to join him. The sight of her brother's name in his bold, slanting scrawl took her aback. The date beside his name made him fifteen when he'd signed.

"This is the year we met," Aidan told her, making his way toward the closest speed bag.

"At Harvard-Westlake?" Kaylee prodded, naming their high school in a desperate attempt to keep Aidan reminiscing. She'd never actually heard their origin story.

Aidan nodded as he lifted his elbows and sent the speed bag dancing beneath his steadily rolling fists. The rhythmic thwapping echoed through the cavernous space. "I punched a guy for calling me a scholarship kid, and then Max had my back later when a bunch of actual scholarship kids tried to jump me. Which, for the record, I probably deserved. But Max and I held our own against the four of them, and they left me alone after that."

Aidan gave the bag a final punch and turned to face her.

"I remember that day! Max came home with his face all messed up, and my mother was beside herself yelling at him because she was hosting a party that night. 'Do you want the neighbors to think I've raised a common street thug?'"

Aidan grinned at her impression of her mother. Kaylee had to admit, it *was* pretty good.

"He was banned from making an appearance that night. I remember being kind of jealous about that. That was because of you?"

Aidan nodded slowly. "Friendship forged in blood and split knuckles. Max and I used to spend a lot of time here."

"You did?" There was so much she didn't know.

"Max never told you any of this?"

She shook her head. "Max and I aren't close. Not like the two of you were." There was a sadness to her voice, Kaylee realized. One that Aidan had obviously recognized, because when he spoke again, there was a cajoling tone in his voice that she recognized from their past and his youthful attempts to cheer her up.

"All right, KJ. No more talking. Let's get you in the ring and see what you're made of."

"You're never going to make the wall if you keep hitting like that."

She laughed at the smack talk. Aidan liked the way she crinkled her nose before she punched.

"I'm trying. This is harder than I thought."

"Remember, elbows in and hands up."

The stubborn set of her chin when she concentrated reminded him of Max. She reset into the stance he'd taught her earlier.

Aidan slapped the focus pads together with a loud *thwap* and held his hands up as targets. She landed three decent jabs and one really good one. "There you go! Now you're on a roll. Try that again."

His phone buzzed in his back pocket and he dropped

his guard, intending to answer it. Kaylee punched him in the shoulder with a pretty respectable shot. "Whoa. Easy there, Fists of Fury."

Her gloved hands flew to her mouth, eyes wide with horror. "You moved your hand! I'm so sorry."

Aidan grinned as he pulled off the focus pads and tossed them onto the stool in the corner of the ring. "I'll live," he assured her, extricating his phone.

His easy dismissal stoked her competitive streak. "Well, sure, but you might have a bruise, right? That was a solid punch."

"Bloodthirsty," he admonished, but he was still chuckling at Kaylee when he answered the call. "Hello?"

"Just got the results back from the coding analysis. You said you wanted to know right away."

The words stiffened Aidan's shoulders. He nonchalantly angled his body away from his boxing protégée and lowered his voice. "And?"

"Coding bingo, just like you thought. The Whitfield and Cybercore products are both built on the original sample you provided."

His dad's work. Aidan let the news sink in. He had all the proof he needed to ruin Whitfield Industries. To gain control of the patent for code he could put in the hands of Endeavor Tech, the start-up he'd just backed, to give them a foothold in a tough market—one he truly believed they could dominate if given the chance.

"Say the word and I'll turn the results over to the lawyers."

Aidan glanced over his shoulder at Kaylee. Ever

the vigilant student, she was shadowboxing, practicing the combination he'd taught her. "You know what? Hold off on that."

"Sorry?"

"I want to look it over before we take the next step."

"Uh, okay. Whatever you say, sir."

Aidan disconnected the call and shoved his phone back in his pocket. "Sorry. Business," he said vaguely as Kaylee bounced over to him in an exaggerated impression of a boxer.

"Sounds like a convenient excuse from a man who knows he's about to have his ass handed to him," she taunted, raising her gloves. "Jab, jab, hook."

She named the punches as she threw them, and Aidan couldn't help his smile as he raised his bare hands to block.

"I've got you on the ropes now," she jeered when he took a step back. "What are you gonna do?"

God, she was gorgeous. Flushed with laughter and exercise, her dark ponytail swinging, Aidan wanted her more than his next breath.

"That's easy," he said, and in a lightning-quick move he'd reversed their positions, caging her in with her back to the ropes. He captured her gasp of surprise with his mouth, kissing her deep and hard, the same way he wanted to fuck her. Only when she moaned under the onslaught did he let up and break their kiss. "First I'm going to overpower you, and then I'm going to distract you."

Kaylee swallowed as he stepped closer so their chests touched. "I think it's working."

He grabbed the hem of her T-shirt, and she raised her arms so he could pull it off. The sleeves got stuck on her boxing gloves, but it was nothing an impatient tug couldn't fix, and then she was free, despite the protest from the stitching.

He'd buy her a new one later.

The rest of her clothes came off without the slightest objection, and his followed suit.

"Hold on to the top rope," he ordered as he sheathed himself with a condom from his wallet. Kaylee obligingly spread her arms along the top rope and hooked the gloves around it.

Fuck.

Aidan stroked himself at the sight of her, spread out before him wearing nothing but boxing gloves. His blood thundered in his veins as he stepped toward her, so close that his cock rested against her stomach, and her nipples grazed his chest.

Her tongue darted out to moisten her lips and his hips gave an involuntary jerk at the visual stimulus.

"You make my knees weak," Kaylee said softly, and the romantic words, so out of place in the middle of a boxing gym, made him want to claim her more. He pushed down on the white rope, second from the top, and hooked it under the sweet curve of her ass. Kaylee's eyes flew wide as he used the recoil of it to lift her up. Her legs wrapped around his hips instinctually, an attempt to steady herself that aligned their bodies in a way that made his hips jerk again.

Aidan gave her a second to catch her breath and adjust her grip on the top rope. Once she'd stabilized herself, he reached between them, guided his cock inside her, getting off on her dreamy look and the way she bit her lip as her body opened to take his length. She felt so goddamn perfect stretched around him.

"Better hold on tight," he warned before grasping the rope on either side of her hips and giving it a quick bounce.

Their bodies came together with a force that wrenched a startled cry from her lips, and Aidan worked them into a rhythm, pushing down on the rope before pulling her back to him, their bodies colliding again and again, until he couldn't see straight. He was so fucking turned on by her, the bounce of her breasts as she rode his cock, the sound of her pleasure as their bodies slammed together.

"I'm so close, Aidan. I'm going to come. Make me come."

He wasn't sure if it was his name on her lips or the dirty words that followed, but everything in him drew tight in preparation for her orgasm, and the second her body spasmed around him he abandoned his control and let the sparks racing through his veins ignite.

She dropped her forehead to his sweat-slicked shoulder, and he slid his hand under her ponytail, letting the soft strands tickle his knuckles as he processed the fact that she made his knees weak, too.

CHAPTER SEVENTEEN

Kaylee had spent a dreamy weekend in Aidan's arms, wearing Aidan's T-shirts, and eating Aidan's food. The man really was a genius at omelets. And life advice.

This morning, she was going to implement it by walking into Max's office and unquitting.

As she rode the elevator to the top floor of Whitfield Industries, she felt like a new woman. And it wasn't because her muscles were deliciously sore or her smile was sensually satisfied. Well, it wasn't *just* that.

In a single weekend, she'd given voice to her sexual desires and erected a massive boundary with her mother, and for the first time in her life, she wasn't afraid to stand up for herself. To say exactly what she wanted. To claim some of the self-assurance she felt in her job and onstage and translate it into her personal life.

The delightful haze of secret sex and rebellious confidence dissipated the second the elevator doors slid open.

Max was back.

Kaylee could feel the difference in the building the second she stepped onto the floor.

The office was robust with purpose, as though her brother had brought with him a burst of diligence and sharpened focus that had been missing in his absence.

Not that she hadn't done a kick-ass job of handling things while he was gone, because she had. But Max *was* Whitfield Industries. The company in its current form was the result of his vision. And he'd put his blood, sweat, and tears into it. Figuratively, of course. Emotional robots like her older brother didn't lower themselves to such human weaknesses as feelings.

Ignoring her shaking hands and pounding pulse, she strode straight up to Sherri, Max's hyper-efficient executive assistant. "I need to see him."

"So does everyone. But unfortunately for all of you, the FBI has requested the honor of his and Emma's presence today to talk about the case against your father, so you're out of luck. At least until after four o'clock."

Kaylee wasn't sure if her exhale was one of relief or resignation. "I guess I'll check back later, then."

She wished it inspired more shock, the idea that her father had committed a felony, exploited Emma Mathison for information about SecurePay in return for financing hospice care for her dying mother. Sadly, it was far too easy to believe.

Kaylee had always liked Emma. Pleasant, professional, incredibly dedicated.

When the news of her father's indictment had broken, Kaylee remembered the one time she'd seen the two of them together. She'd been down in the lobby, where her father was supposed to meet her so they could go for lunch, and Emma and Charles had stepped out of the elevator together. Her father had looked so... predatory, but it was Emma who really stuck out in her mind. The woman's posture, her smile, her voice. Everything about her had been brittle. At the time, Kaylee had brushed it off, but in retrospect, it never ceased to haunt her.

"Did you need something else?" Sherri's voice startled Kaylee from her thoughts, and she shook her head.

The day sped by with a million fires to put out, so her ability to *check back later* didn't present itself until seven o'clock that evening.

Kaylee made a point of not knocking as she walked into his office. "Got a minute?"

The sky outside had gone dark, and Max had removed his suit jacket, rolled up his sleeves, loosened his tie. Despite the familiar tableau, Kaylee couldn't help but feel that something had shifted in him. He seemed different. And she wondered exactly what had happened while he'd been in Dubrovnik.

"Not really."

"Well, you need to make one."

Max lifted an eyebrow at her imperiousness, and with a deceptively casual flick of his wrist, his computer screen went dark. He gestured at the chair across from his desk before he leaned back in his own.

Waiting.

A frisson tingled up her spine.

Max was most terrifying when he was silent. Still. *Just say what you want. Be the butterfly.*

She was surprised that it was Aidan's voice in her head, and not her mother's.

Kaylee lifted her chin as she strode toward him, pretending that her heart wasn't climbing up her throat.

Show no fear.

"Tomorrow will be two weeks since I quit."

"And?"

The bland question was enough to shake her out of the normal pattern of sit and wait she so often fell into with her brother. She remembered how he used to be, how they used to be together. And sometimes she found herself sitting quietly around him, hoping that one day he might just look over and see her again. Remember how it was when they were kids.

But he never did.

And she wasn't willing to wait for him anymore.

"And you haven't said a word about it."

"You didn't answer any of my texts or calls." His tone was sharp.

Kaylee allowed herself a moment of petty satisfaction. "I've been a little busy around here doing both our jobs. And while you were gone, I realized something. I'm really good at what I do. So I'm here to unquit. I want my job back."

Pride blazed along her nerve endings. She was triumphant and ready for a fight.

"Fine."

"I'm not taking no for an ans—fine? Fine?"

She should have been thrilled. Instead she was furious.

"That's all you have to say? Do you know how much

courage it took for me to walk in here and stand up to you?"

Max dragged a hand down his tie. "I ceded to your demand. Mission accomplished. What more do you want from me?"

"I want you to be a goddamn person instead of a robot for once in your life!"

She'd surprised him. And what shocked her even more was that he let her see it. He didn't temper his flinch at her outburst, the widening of his eyes.

Max's legendary poker face was gone, and years of bearing his cold distance had her ire up, now that she'd pierced his armor. Now that she could watch her barbs land.

"This isn't the time or the place for this discussion."

"That's exactly the problem! It's never the time or the place. You can't put me off because the timing's bad. Because guess what? The timing's always going to be bad. There's always something else that needs taking care of. That's why PR departments exist! And I know this SecurePay stuff is the most important thing in the world to you, but I'm your sister! I know you got stuck with me when Dad retired, but—"

"Fine. You want to have this out now?" Max reached forward, and with the press of a button hidden some-where on the bottom of his desk the glass wall of his office frosted over. "Let's do it."

"You turned Dad in to the FBI and left the country. I've been dealing with the fallout and acting as the de facto Whitfield while you've been on vacation. Everything fell apart, and I got blindsided. And I quit just to make you see me. But you didn't. You just walked out."

Max stared at her, looking a little blindsided himself, but she didn't back down. She wouldn't let him off the hook this time. The six feet or so that separated them felt like an unbroachable chasm. And what hurt most was that he didn't even make a move to try.

"I don't understand you, Max. It's just so easy for you to cut people out of your life, to shut down. Even Dad. I mean, I know all this shit is bad, but he's our father. And you have to accept some responsibility for your crappy relationship because you never tried to fix it. You just…did nothing. Iced over. Like always."

She ignored the sudden sting of tears. He didn't deserve them anymore. She wasn't the little girl he'd cut out of his life. The one who cried herself to sleep. She was a woman. And Aidan was right. She was done letting her family have all of her just because she was too scared to stand up to them.

With as much dignity as she could muster, she stood but his voice stopped her before she took a step.

"Do you remember Arlo?"

Kaylee frowned at the unexpected question. "Our *dog*?" she asked, stressing the words so he knew what a stupid question it was. "The one who died, after which we never had another pet even though I spent the entirety of my adolescence begging for one? Yeah. I remember." Arlo's death was also the last time Max had hugged her. The beginning of the breach that stretched between them now.

"He didn't die."

"What?"

"Dad got rid of him to teach me a lesson."

Kaylee dropped back into the chair. "He was old. He died."

"He was five."

"But you told me…" Kaylee remembered Max's solemn face when he told her that Arlo had died, that she wouldn't see him again. The way she'd crawled into his arms and cried because her chest hurt so badly. She was eight, and she didn't remember a time without Arlo there. Max had been twelve at the time, and she'd thought he was so grown up. He wasn't crying. It had struck her as odd because Max had loved that dog with everything in him.

"I lied to you because I didn't want you to know what had happened. Mom was so hard on you, and I knew you were closer to Dad."

"I was close to you, Max. At least I used to be."

That muscle in his jaw ticked, and Kaylee hated him for his restraint just then. That icy facade that he used to keep her out.

"That's the last day you ever hugged me, do you know that? After that you were different. Distant. You stopped teasing me. You looked right through me."

"I was trying to keep you safe."

She scoffed. "From what? The emotional trauma of being an outcast in my own family? Because you failed, big brother."

"From Dad!"

The heat of his words flared like a volcano, and Kaylee flinched. She'd never seen Max's rage flare hot before. Cold reserve was his MO. But right now, he was here in the room with her. Fighting with her. Seeing her. And as pissed off as she was, it felt good to have this out with him.

"He got rid of the dog because he said it made me weak. I couldn't let him hurt you to get to me. I promised myself I wouldn't let him know that you were important to me."

A little pinprick of hope burned in her chest at the idea that Max cared about her, but she squashed it with brutal ruthlessness. Words were easy to throw out as placation. Action was what mattered. Aidan was right about that.

"Okay, this is getting way too 'poor little rich kid' for me. You were worried he'd send me away? Like, to boarding school in the Swiss Alps? Because I would have loved to be free of the Dragon Lady for ten months of the year. Of feeling so goddamn lonely in my own house that I used to cry myself to sleep."

"I wasn't worried he would send you away."

Something about the haunted look on Max's face checked her sarcasm. She could feel him slipping away, retreating, even though he hadn't moved a muscle.

"So long as he kept his focus off you and on me, I knew he wouldn't take anything out on you."

The weird choice of words penetrated her anger. Something terrifying slithered through her brain. She wanted to ignore it, but she couldn't. "What did he do to you?"

Max dropped his head. It was so out of character

that Kaylee's lungs flooded with dread, pushing the air out of them.

"Max, what did he do?"

She didn't recognize him when he lifted his head. There was anger edging his voice, but it was the shame in his amber eyes that put her heart in a vise. He didn't look like the formidable man he was. Her imperturbable older brother. He looked…haunted. And starkly human.

"First he'd send me to the closet. I always got to pick which belt he was going to use."

Kaylee hands flew to her mouth. *No. Please no.* Her stomach churned.

He relayed the horror with such cold detachment that it made everything worse. Because she recognized it now. The shift that had happened when he was just twelve years old. A boy who had burned so bright in her memory, his fire snuffed out in a cowardly act of violence.

The tears she wouldn't let fall for herself earlier now spilled down her cheeks with abandon. "I didn't know. I swear I didn't know."

Max's expression was glassy-eyed, like he wasn't quite in the room with her. He was staring at memories somewhere over her right shoulder. "I didn't want you to."

"Why not? I'm your sister. I love you."

"Because there was nothing you could have done. And it stopped. I got big enough and it stopped, Kale. I didn't want you to have to worry about me. I know you love him."

"I'm so sick of everyone trying to protect me! What about you, Max? Maybe I could have helped, but you cut me out. He hurt you like that, and you let me go on thinking he was good? Let me pander for scraps of his attention?" She knew her ire was misplaced, but she was so angry. At her father. At her mother. At Max. "I thought Dad was great, and you let me think it! I defended him to you. I took his side against you."

"I just wanted you to have a parent who didn't treat you like garbage."

"I didn't have a parent. I had a monster, and everyone knew it but me. No wonder you pushed me away! You probably see him every time you look at me."

Numbness tingled through her body. She would have picked Max over her father, but she'd never had a chance. Because Max chose to deal with it alone rather than have her on his side. Maybe not in the moment. She understood how a twelve-year-old boy might think he was saving his little sister. But they weren't children anymore.

And it hurt so much to know he didn't trust her enough to tell her the truth, no matter how soul shattering.

"Kaylee…"

She shook her head. "I can't… I'm sorry he hurt you. I'm sorry I…" Oh God. She wanted to vomit at the thought of Max being whipped.

Kaylee lurched to her feet. "I have to go."

"Kale, wait!"

His voice, her childhood nickname, the truth. It all collided in her chest, spinning like a tornado that took all her memories and upended them, reordered them. It was disorienting to see the events that had shaped her though a totally different lens. To realize that her allegiances were based on lies, that the choices she'd made teetered on a crumbling foundation.

"I didn't mean to—"

She blocked out Max's voice. If he apologized for being the victim of abuse she might throw up all over his office. "I have to go," she repeated, a reminder to her stultifying muscles. Now was not the time and this was not the place for her to lose it. *A lady is always in control of herself.*

She made it to the elevator, relieved to see that Max had paused at his office door, that he wasn't going to follow her. She dropped her head in shame at her own cowardice as the silver door slid shut.

Kaylee made it to her car on wooden legs, and when she dropped into the Audi's leather bucket seat, her only thought was of escape. She jammed her key into the ignition and made her way out of the underground parking garage. Max's confession was like a pickax in her brain, and instead of turning toward home when she reached street level, she turned in the opposite direction. She thought she was driving aimlessly until she recognized her surroundings. She'd driven straight to him—to the last person Max would want her to find comfort with.

One more secret between them, but she couldn't help herself.

She was tired and emotionally drained, and her hands were shaking as the adrenaline that had carried her out of her brother's office dissipated. And now, alone, without shock and pride to keep her emotions in check, the tears she'd managed to outrun caught up with her, stinging the bridge of her nose as she did battle with them again.

Her father had hit Max. With a belt. For years.

It was horrifying. Gut-wrenching. And she didn't doubt Max's story for a second.

Her heart twisted. She thought of all the time she'd wasted trying to please her father, to make him proud. And now... Now she questioned those choices. Because her brother wasn't the man she'd thought he was. And her father wasn't the man she'd thought he was. And if all the choices she'd made in life were based on those misconceptions, what kind of woman did that make her?

She unfastened her seat belt. Pushed open the door.

Not the time for thinking, she reminded herself. Action. She wanted action.

She knocked with enough force that her knuckles stung.

It was getting hard to breathe again. The waiting made her restless, like her skin was shrinking. Thoughts crowded her brain, but she pushed them aside. Feelings warred in her chest, but she shoved them down.

I'm fine, she reminded herself sternly, the way her mother would. *A lady never feels too much in public.*

The sound of the door opening snapped her head up, and then Aidan was there.

"Kaylee?" Aidan grabbed her shoulders, searched her face. "Jesus Christ. What happened to you?"

"Max just…" They were the only words that came out before the sobbing broke loose as he pulled her close, cradled her against his chest as she wrapped her arms around him.

He felt solid in a world that had just tipped off its axis. Max. Her father. But even as sobs racked her body and her chest ached so badly she thought she might split in two, there was comfort in having Aidan's arms around her.

He held her close, stroked her hair.

"Breathe, baby. I need you to breathe, okay?"

The rumble of his deep voice soothed her, even though her mind was spinning in a million different directions. She managed to nod, to heed his words. She gulped in some air.

Max had been trying to keep her safe. It was sweet and heartbreaking and infuriating and sad and all sorts of things that she couldn't put a name to.

Because it meant that her father, the man she'd been so desperate to please, was a monster.

Aidan pulled her tighter.

Jesus, she needed him right now. Needed him to stop the maelstrom of colliding facts imploding in her brain. Her brother was a good man. Her father did a bad thing.

She curled into him, tucking her face into his chest, greedily taking all the comfort that came from his heart beating beneath her cheek, the way his hand cupped the back of her head. Safe.

"What the hell happened?" His voice rumbled

through his chest, deep and sure. She knew why she'd come here now. Because Aidan knew her better than anyone. It was an odd realization, that a man who'd only stumbled back into her life by accident after a ten-year hiatus would hold that honor, but he did.

He was the one who'd caught her rolling her eyes when her mother nagged her about her posture or her hair, the one who'd shared commiserating glances when she was being dragged to violin lessons or ballet class. He knew about her secret life as Lola, knew what it took to make her come, knew what she looked like when her heart was broken.

Things she'd never let anyone else see.

Because she trusted him. She always had.

And right now she trusted him to make her feel better. Because no one else could.

Pulling back, she curled her fingers into the softness of his T-shirt. "I don't want to talk, Aidan. I want to forget."

He frowned at that, just the slight dip of his eyebrow and a tightness in his mouth that let her know he wasn't happy with her nonanswer. But she couldn't. Not yet. Not when she didn't understand herself. Everything she'd thought was real had shifted just enough to make her lose her footing. She was too scattered to dissect it right now.

She just needed something solid to hold on to, and Aidan was her anchor of choice.

Imploringly, she lifted her mouth, tasting the salt of tears on her lips a split second before she tasted him. He filled her senses, filled up all the empty spots inside her, and she wrapped her arms around his neck, pressing against him, letting the pleasure of touching him distract her.

To her infinite relief, he accepted that. He didn't protest or push her away. He just let her kiss him, kissed her back as she clumsily yanked off her jacket and they stumbled through his place toward the stairs, banging into the railing as they undressed each other in her quest to get him to the bedroom. She just needed to get to the bedroom.

He left her for only a second, to grab a condom, and then he was right where she needed him, in her arms, between her legs, over top of her, inside of her.

Yes.

He rocked his hips, pushing deep, and her world narrowed to the rasp of his beard against her neck, the rush of his breath across her skin. Kaylee closed her eyes and let herself feel everything, letting the grind of their bodies push her higher.

He made it good for her. Even as she broke, he kept pumping his hips. She couldn't stop kissing him, touching him. She didn't want to stop. She wanted this forever—her body trembling under his, her fingers in his hair, holding him close as he came.

He stayed over her, staring down at her as they both caught their breath. She felt safe there, with his body caging her in, his weight braced on his elbows and forearms, their legs tangled together. There were a million questions in his eyes, but he didn't ask them. And she appreciated that most of all. That he understood she wasn't ready.

And when he lay down beside her, she tucked herself against Aidan's body and stole the warmth and strength of being held by him until sleep came and gave her temporary respite from the horrors of the day.

CHAPTER EIGHTEEN

AIDAN BANGED ON the door, hoping to hell his intel guy had him at the right place. Resting his hands on either side of the jamb, muscles flexing as he tried to stay calm, he reminded himself to breathe.

Just breathe.

Kaylee might have drifted off into a fitful sleep, but Aidan was too wound up to do the same. She'd been shattered when she'd shown up at his place, and he wasn't going to let that stand.

He banged his palm on the door again, jarring the bones in his hand, and he relished the moment of pain.

Then the door opened, and Aidan came face-to-face with his hated nemesis.

His oldest friend.

Aidan had already moved before he realized it, his left hand gripping Max's T-shirt, his right forearm angled across the man's collarbone. He used his momentum and the surprise of his attack to spin Max and shove him hard against the wall beside the door.

"What the fuck did you do?"

Those cold amber eyes clashed with the fire in his

own, once again reminding Aidan how different they were. Every muscle in Max's body was coiled tight but on lockdown.

"You're going to want to back off, Aidan."

"Not until you tell me what you did to her."

"What I did to whom?"

Aidan shoved Max into the wall again before he let go of him.

To whom.

Fucking Max.

"I'm asking why Kaylee came home crying her goddamn eyes out."

Max went eerily still. "What did you say?"

Maybe he should have seen it coming, but in all the years he'd known Max, the guy had never punched first.

Aidan's head snapped back and the familiar crunch of knuckles versus cartilage accompanied the pain that bloomed behind his nose, but he shook it off. Instinct brought his fist up in a right hook that caught Max hard in the jaw and sent him staggering under the weight of the blow. Aidan flexed his hand as he stepped back, lungs heaving thanks to the cocktail of adrenaline and testosterone that had flooded his body like a shot of nitrous oxide. He shifted his weight to the balls of his feet, ready if his opponent wanted to take this to the next level.

Max drew up to his full height, also sucking in oxygen. His bottom lip was busted up and starting to swell. "You want to come after me, that's fair game. But stay the fuck away from Kaylee, you son of a bitch. Don't drag her into this."

Aidan smirked at the warning because he knew it would piss Max off.

"What the hell is going on? It's after midnight and—oh my God, Max! You're bleeding."

Both he and Max turned their attention to the gorgeous blonde in the tank top and boxers who'd just emerged from what Aidan presumed was the master bedroom.

"I'm fine," Max told her, wiping his mouth with the back of his hand. It came away smeared with blood.

"You're not fine," she said pointedly, the slight rebuke obviously aimed at Aidan. Not that he gave a damn if Max's latest piece of ass didn't approve of his manners.

"Aidan's always had shit for timing, but we have some things to discuss. Go back to bed."

The animosity cooled, but her look turned speculative. Instead of following orders, she headed toward the tricked-out kitchenette and pulled open the freezer.

Aidan frowned at that. Conquests, as a rule, disappeared when you told them to.

So not just a piece of ass, then.

Interesting.

Aidan sniffed, and the metallic tang of blood registered in the back of his throat. He grabbed the hem of his T-shirt and wiped his face before prodding gingerly at his nose. It didn't feel broken.

The blonde returned with a makeshift ice pack in each hand—ziplock baggie, ice cubes, dish towel—

and, surprising the hell out of him, held one out to Aidan.

"I'm Emma."

Aidan took it, a platitude. She obviously had no idea who he was and how her boyfriend felt about him.

"Max has told me a lot about you."

Or he was wrong on all counts.

He rested the ice on his aching knuckles, his surprised gaze sliding to Max. "I didn't know he'd ever told anyone a lot about anything, let alone about me."

She smiled at that, stepping close to Max, cupping his jaw tenderly as she pressed the ice pack to his injured face. It was almost a protective gesture, and the way Max lifted his hand to cradle hers was not lost on Aidan. It made him uncomfortable, like he was intruding on something private.

He dropped his gaze, focusing instead on the throbbing in his sinuses. Despite himself, he was a little impressed. Max had landed a hell of a jab.

"Okay. You two obviously have a lot to discuss, and since that is the extent of my nursing skills, I'm going to make myself scarce." Emma lifted onto her toes and pressed a kiss to Max's cheek, but when she turned her gaze on Aidan, there was a warning there.

Ballsy as hell. He liked her despite himself.

"I'll just be in the bedroom," she announced, walking away from them. "Watching TV. With 911 on speed dial. Play nice, boys."

Aidan waited until she'd pushed the bedroom door closed behind her before he turned his attention to Max.

"How much did you tell her about me?"

"Everything."

"Are you fucking serious?"

Max shrugged, but there was nothing apologetic about it. "I love her."

The admission caught Aidan off guard. It was totally out of character for Max. Well, for the Max he'd known. But he supposed he wasn't the only one who had changed in the last five years. He because he'd lost his father and his friend in one fell swoop. Max because he'd gained ownership of a multimillion-dollar tech company, finally gotten rid of the son of a bitch who'd raised him, and apparently found true love, as well.

Everything was coming up fucking roses.

Aidan let his anger reignite, tightening his muscles, reerecting the emotional wall he'd had in place before Max had opened the door.

As if Max had read his posture, he sighed. "Am I going to need a drink for the rest of this conversation?"

"Probably."

"You want one?" Max offered, heading for the bar cart on the far side of the room.

Civilized. So very Max. "Sure."

Aidan wandered deeper into the suite, down the three steps that led to the sunken living room, stopping in front of the floor-to-ceiling windows that overlooked the city. Los Angeles looked damn good at night—sexy and inviting, an inky sky twinkling with lights. "So... you live in the penthouse of a hotel? Isn't that a bit pretentious, even for you?"

Max shot him a wry glance as he set down his ice pack and pulled the stopper from a crystal decanter. "I like to stick to my strengths."

Silence stretched between them as Aidan surveyed the city below and Max poured.

"This isn't exactly how I imagined this moment."

Aidan glanced over at him. "Been dreaming about me again, huh?"

"Glad to see you haven't changed." Max grabbed the drinks and joined Aidan by the window. "Still as gloriously humble as ever."

Aidan accepted the tumbler and the gibe with a tip of his head. "Well, if it's any consolation, this isn't how I thought this would play out, either." He took a swallow of scotch, and it went down smooth.

Max had always had a knack for the finer things in life.

"I mean—" Aidan gestured at his friend with the glass in his hand "—I definitely thought I'd throw the first punch."

The corner of Max's mouth pulled up as he took a sip of his drink, and he winced, prodding at his busted lip. For a moment, he stared contemplatively at the cityscape. When he spoke, none of that spark of humor was evident in his voice. "She was crying?"

Aidan nodded.

Max sighed. "Then I guess this is the part where I let you explain why the hell she's coming to you in times of emotional turmoil."

Aidan hadn't dissected it much past he was glad she had. But he should have known Max would parse it for meaning. Aidan rushed in hot, ready for action, and Max hung back, assessing the situation. It was how it had always been with them.

He shrugged, sipped his drink. "What can I say? Ladies love a good listener."

Max's flat, subzero stare got under his skin. Made him want to move, pace it out.

"So after five years of this silent feud of ours, you roll back into LA and just happen to start seeing my sister? Who apparently means so much to you that you've come over here to try and kick my ass? That's what I'm supposed to believe?"

The question hit dead center. Max had the precision of a sniper.

"Just to be clear, if I'd meant to kick your ass, you'd be laid out on the ground right now."

"Maybe. But I swear to God, man, if you're using her to get back at me..." Max let the threat hang as he took a swig of scotch. The accusation prickled along Aidan's spine.

"How long have you two been together?"

Shit. Aidan shifted his shoulders. He should have expected the inquisition. Max liked to dismantle things to find out how they worked.

"I'm through answering questions until you tell me what you did to her."

Max's jaw tensed, and it felt good to shift the momentum. To put him on defense. "Let it go, man."

"You know I'm not going to do that."

The man beside him at the window was quiet for so long that Aidan was surprised when he finally spoke.

"I told her my dad used to hit me and I let him to keep her safe. And it made her feel like shit because apparently it's the only thing I'm good at with her."

"Jesus Christ." Now it was Aidan's turn to take a swill of premium liquor. Pieces of their past clicked into place. Max asking him for pointers after their schoolyard brawl. The way he'd tagged along to Aidan's neighborhood boxing gym, despite the dozen or so snooty health clubs that would have bent over backward to count the Whitfields among their ranks. How hard he worked to bulk up the summer after they met. "While we were in high school?"

"It stopped by junior year. No point mentioning it after that."

"Fists?"

"Belt."

Shit.

"You shoulda told me." Anger tightened Aidan's shoulders, and his hand flexed around his empty glass. "I could've helped."

Max's glance darted to him, then back to the city. "You did help. You and Sal. I took care of the rest. And you wouldn't have understood. You had a great dad. A dad who cared about you. Loaned you start-up capital for your business. Was proud of your accomplishments."

Aidan's laugh was bitter. "What after-school-special version of my life were you watching?"

The question got Max's attention.

"My dad was a drunk, Max. A high-functioning one at work, most of the time. The rest of the time he was passed out or betting on whatever odds he could find. It got really bad when my mom got diagnosed and worse after she died. He started to slide. Lost his job. By the time I was thirteen, I spent more time taking care of him than he did taking care of me."

"How did I not know that?"

"Because by the time we met, he'd started to pull it together a little. He was obsessed with the idea that you two turned into SecurePay. You saw the good part of him. The coding-genius part. He saved the 'passed out in his own puke after dropping fifty grand on the ponies' part for after hours." Aidan ran a hand down his beard. "And he really cleaned his act up when you got him that job at Whitfield Industries. For a while anyway. I could tell things were getting worse toward the end. I knew I should have come back."

The guilt that always flared in Aidan's gut when he remembered that moment—the moment he'd decided *fuck the old man, let him take care of himself for once*—struck again. His dad had been ranting on the other end of the phone, a sure sign he was a few drinks too deep. Aidan had been in Spain, some five-star hotel in Pamplona, celebrating the milestone of making his first million and not in the mood to babysit. It was complicated, loving someone and hating them in equal measure.

"I didn't want to deal with his drunk ass, so I stayed away. And now I have to live with that choice."

Max's face turned stony. Unreadable. "That's on me. That's not on you. I'm the one who put John on my father's radar. You asked me to look after him, and I let you down."

"Turned out okay for you, though, huh? Ended up pushing Charles out of the way and taking over the family business. Now you're going to make millions off my dad, and you don't have to share the spoils or the credit."

Max grew still, but Aidan knew he was leaving a mark. Knew his words were well-placed knives. Knew it cost Max not to wince. Aidan itched to deepen the wound, to get a rise. He was more comfortable fighting.

Max's smile was bitter. "So that's what this is about. Revenge."

"I know that SecurePay and Cybercore's knockoff are built on the same code. That you shared it somehow and violated the exclusivity clause in Dad's contract. And I will prove it in court, Max."

He'd been expecting fury. Threats. Bribes. Another punch. Pretty much anything but the way Max stared out the window, at the ceiling, at his bare feet—anywhere but at Aidan.

After years of covering for his father, of letting people believe what they wanted, of lying by omission or through silence, Aidan recognized the signs. A cold sweat broke out across his back and the world shifted under his feet, the realization making him motion sick. He'd blamed Max and Charles for years for pushing John Beckett past his breaking point, and if that wasn't how it had happened…

He tasted bile as he leaned forward. *Just breathe.*

"What did he do?"

Max shook his head. "Don't do this, Aidan. Don't open this wound. Charles is going to jail. It's over."

The advice didn't make him feel better. *"What did he do?"* he repeated.

Max stared into his glass for a moment, and when he raised his eyes, they were older, calmer than Aidan had ever seen them. Five years hadn't quite made him a stranger, but he wasn't the same man Aidan remembered, either.

"When you asked him for that loan to start your business, John didn't have what you needed. So your dad broke his contract and sold the patented code to Liam Kearney to get the money."

Corporate-fucking-espionage.

"No." That couldn't be true. If it was, nothing in his world made sense.

It's okay, Aidan. I got a bonus at the last minute. Take it. It would make your mother happy.

"When your dad got wasted, told me what he'd done, we tried to cover it up so my father wouldn't find out. And I told John he should tell you, that you'd understand. But he didn't want you to know. He felt losing your mother was hard enough on you, and he didn't want you to feel like you'd lost him, too."

Aidan had poured all his rage and hatred and guilt on Max for so long that it felt weird to believe him. But he knew in his gut that what Max had just told him was the truth. Knew how much it must have hurt Max to discover his mentor had let him down.

"It wasn't until after the accident that I discovered my father knew what John had done, that he'd already taken his revenge. In the original contract, your dad held on to a percentage of the SecurePay profits for as long as the code was exclusive to Whitfield Industries. Since John had violated the agreement, Charles forced him into signing away all his rights to the SecurePay code along with any intellectual property developed during his tenure at Whitfield Industries. Threatened your dad with jail time, and said he'd go after you as well, since your company was founded on dirty money. My father fucked him over completely. That contract is the reason your dad was drunk the night he died."

Everything in Aidan went still, but his heart began to race. His blood thundered in his ears as Max's words landed with all the impact of a detonating bomb.

"You were right when you accused me of being selfish. I didn't want to lose Whitfield Industries. My grandfather built this company, and my father almost destroyed it. I didn't want to let him. I wanted my birthright, my chance at the helm. But I hope you can believe, at some point, that it's not the only reason I didn't turn him in for what he did to John. To you."

Max faced him now. "I didn't want your dad's name dragged through the mud. I didn't want your memory of the man he was to be ripped apart because my father is an asshole. And I didn't want my dad to make good on his threat to come after you."

So like Max, really. Just like he'd protected Kaylee. Taking the brunt of the punishment and the blame.

"I've spent a long time hating you for that."

Max finished his drink. "I know."

Something inside Aidan's chest unlocked. Breathing didn't seem so hard anymore. "It wasn't your job to save me."

"You're not the one I was trying to save. Your father, the version of him I knew anyway, was an incredible man who made a mistake. But he did it for you."

Do this for me, Dad. Ninety days to dry out. It'll go by fast.

Eat something, Pop.

Damn it, Dad. The track? Again?

I'll make it up to you, Aidan. I swear.

He stared at Max, who looked as drained and as bleak as he felt. Five fucking years of secrets had taken their toll.

"I'd rather have had you in my life for the last five years than a slightly less tarnished memory of my dad." The truth of that made Aidan feel better and worse. They'd lost a lot of time, missed out on a lot of things.

The thaw in the room wasn't large, but it was noticeable. And uncomfortable.

"I should go." He placed his empty glass in the hand Max had extended. He didn't want Kaylee to wake up alone after everything she'd been through.

Max didn't say anything, just followed him to the door. Aidan stopped with a hand on the knob, one foot in the hallway, and looked over his shoulder. "This thing with Kaylee? It's new. And I have no idea what's happening. But if you make her cry again, I won't stop after one punch."

Max's answering nod was tight and controlled. "Same goes."

The door snicked shut behind him, and for the first time in years, Aidan let himself miss the friendship that had preceded all the pain and guilt that had consumed him since his father's death.

CHAPTER NINETEEN

AIDAN WAS TINKERING with his bike when he heard Kaylee moving around upstairs. Max's questions had pounded in his brain all night, which, along with the throbbing in his face, made sleep an elusive bitch. He was tired and moody and disgusted with himself.

What the hell was he doing with Kaylee? He wasn't back in LA to stay. He'd come here to fuck Max over and get the patent on his father's code. And now that there was neither vengeance nor legal rights for him to claim, he should get the hell out of Dodge.

Because the one thing he wanted to stay for had *disaster* written all over it.

Aidan sighed and dropped his wrench on the concrete floor with a clatter.

His father had put alcohol and gambling above all else, and it had cost him everything.

And now it had cost Aidan everything, too. His friendship with Max. Any chance of something real with Kaylee.

She trusted too easily, cared too much about people who didn't deserve her loyalty.

And he counted himself among them.

"Morning."

Her voice made his abs draw tight, a kick of lust he'd given up trying to control. He kept his head down, focused on his bike. "Hey. You're up early."

"I have to get home and change before I go to work. You want coffee?"

"I'm good, but thanks."

He ignored the part of him that liked the sound of her in his kitchen, and that she knew which cupboard to open to find a mug. It wouldn't do him any good to realize how long it had been since he'd had someone consistent in his world or how comforting it was to think of a place as *home*.

"Can you believe this battery is dead already? No wonder Wes gave it to me. This phone is a piece of crap."

"There should be a charger in that drawer." Aidan glanced over his shoulder as he pointed at the cabinet closest to the door, not realizing his mistake until Kaylee had already banged her mug onto the counter.

"Oh my God, Aidan! What happened to your face?"

Phone woes forgotten, she rushed toward him and he swore under his breath and straightened up from his crouched position to his full height. "It's nothing," he protested.

"You have a black eye. It's not nothing."

"Tool slipped while I was working on the bike earlier."

"Hold still and let me see." She set her hand on his face, and it was so reminiscent of the private moment he'd witnessed between Emma and Max that he winced.

Kaylee's brow crumpled with concern. "Does it hurt?"

Aidan had to remind himself that she was talking about his eye and not the sudden lurch of his heart.

I love her. Max had said the words so simply. No emphasis. No uncertainty. A statement of fact.

Aidan managed the slightest shake of his head.

"I could get you some ice," she offered, but this time she licked her lips, letting him know that the sudden heat kindling in his belly wasn't one-sided.

Her hand still rested on his cheek.

"I could kiss it better." Her voice was barely more than a whisper, but it didn't lessen the impact on his body. He was ravenous for her, instantly ready, desperately hard.

Aidan ran his hands over her ass and down her thighs before he hitched her up his body and she locked her heels across the small of his back. Kaylee pressed her mouth to his, first sweet, running her tongue along his bottom lip, then not so sweet, catching it between her teeth.

He loved having her mouth on him.

"Is this working?" she asked, dropping a kiss against his jaw and another on the side of his neck. "Because if you don't feel better yet, I do have a couple of more advanced techniques that might help you forget about the pain," she teased.

He wanted to take her up on the offer.

Christ, did he ever.

But he couldn't. Not like this. Not until he made things right.

"You still have to get changed and get to work," he reminded her. "You're going to be late if we try out your advanced techniques. And even later if we try out some of mine."

"My name is on the building. What are they going to do, fire me?"

"All the more reason to set a good example," he joked.

Kaylee gave an exaggerated moan of protest as she unhooked her legs from around his waist so he could lower her back to the floor. "Adulting sucks."

Almost as much as watching her walk away from him, Aidan thought.

"Leave your phone when you go. I'll take a look at it." He did his best to pass it off as a casual offer, hoping the waver his voice didn't betray him.

Kaylee arched an eyebrow at him as she grabbed her purse. "Oh, you fix cell phones now?"

"What can I say? I'm good with my hands."

She grinned at that. "Says the man who clocked himself in the face."

Aidan's response was a wounded frown. "That sounds like both a slur on my manhood and an undeniable challenge. And when you get home from work, I'll be happy to prove just how good I really am with my hands. As many times as you want."

"Well, in that case," she said, grabbing her phone from the counter and handing it to him on her way to the door, "you'd better limber up those fingers while I'm gone, because I feel a bout of skepticism coming on."

* * *

When Kaylee arrived at work an hour later, her heels clicked against the tiled floor that made up the lobby of the PR department. Thanks to the communal working space, it wasn't a sound she usually heard above the day-to-day chatter, and it definitely wasn't a sound she should be hearing now, considering Whitfield Industries was still digging out from the perfect storm of scandals that had plagued them lately. To say the PR department was abuzz with activity right now was a massive understatement. Or at least it should be.

That was why the clack of her pumps unnerved her. Along with the surreptitious glances her team was throwing her.

Things made sense when she arrived at her office. Nothing like an unannounced visit from the boss to put people on edge.

"Max? I thought we weren't meeting until…" She trailed off as he turned from his inspection of one of the paintings on her wall. He was dressed impeccably as ever, his Windsor knot crisp and precise. Even the slight wave of his ebony hair was perfect. Perhaps that was what made his fat lip so out of place.

The sight of it hit her like a bucket of cold water.

Tool slipped while I was working on the bike earlier.

No. Aidan wouldn't have gone to Max. They hated each other.

And she'd made it clear to Aidan that she wasn't ready for her family to know about…whatever was going on between the two of them.

"What happened?" But she knew. God help her, she knew.

The realization that Aidan had lied to her struck hard and with disorienting speed.

Max's eyebrow lifted. "Aidan didn't—well, that's not a surprise, I guess."

"He hit you."

The summation made him frown. "I hit him first," Max clarified before releasing an uncharacteristic sigh. "What are you doing with him, Kale?"

This. This was the very reason she'd wanted to keep Aidan from her family. The inquisition. The censure. The justification.

"You don't get to go all big brother on me now, Max." Kaylee stood her ground as he approached. "I'm sorry about what Dad did to you. Truly I am. And I wish that you'd told me earlier, that I'd been able to help you somehow. But what I do with my life is my own concern. We're long past your chance to have a say in who I date."

Even if she wasn't doing such a bang-up job when left to her own devices.

"I just don't want to see you get hurt. You know Aidan has a tendency to bail. And he came here to ruin SecurePay."

"He told you that?" No wonder they'd come to blows. That goddamn app was the most important thing in Max's world. And right now, Aidan had full access to it because she'd left her phone with him. *Shit.*

She reversed direction, opening her office door

and focusing on the elevator across the sea of worried glances.

"Where are you going?" Max asked.

"I'm taking lunch." Fixing her error. Taking charge of her life. Maybe giving Aidan matching black eyes.

"It's nine in the morning."

"Call it brunch, then. I have something I need to deal with."

CHAPTER TWENTY

AIDAN THUMBED OPEN the spyware app he'd gotten from Cybercore as soon as the phone had enough charge to turn it on. This was it. He was going to end this right now. He didn't want any more secrets between him and Kaylee—he wanted a fresh start. A chance to see if what she made him feel stood a chance at becoming something real or if it was doomed to fail beneath the lies and deceit that had stained their relationship before it had even started.

Only one way to find out.

Aidan hit the uninstall button.

Uninstall failed.

What the fuck? Kearney had assured him that was all he had to do. He touched it again.

Uninstall failed.

And again.

Uninstall failed.

Shit. Shit, shit, shit. He dialed Liam Kearney.

"You said this thing would self-destruct."

"It will."

Aidan's grip tightened on the phone. *Prick.* "I wouldn't be calling you if it had."

"Hey, I get it. My tech's too complicated for a lot of people."

"I can handle the uninstall button, asshole. Too bad I didn't make you prove your garbage tech before I paid for it."

"If I were you, Beckett, I might keep a civil tone. You're the one who came begging favors from me."

Kearney was baiting him and he knew it, but it still took everything in him to keep his cool. "Hey, if I'd begged for this, I'd expect what I got, but since you took my money, yeah, I'm feeling a little uncivil about shitty tech that either sounds like static or cuts out. If my father was polite in his dealings with you, it's only because he didn't know what a hack you are."

Aidan hadn't meant to go there, but some part of him needed to know. Needed to confirm what Max had told him.

"Oh, I see. We've got daddy issues. I'll tell you what, because John was nothing but a gentleman during our dealings and because he was a true craftsman, I'm going to overlook your slur on my tech."

Aidan stood up. He needed to move. An outlet. He started to pace. He felt like a caged tiger—dangerous and inclined to rip someone's throat out but with no chance of getting his hands on his prey. And because he knew it, Kearney was poking a verbal stick through the bars.

"Don't even say his name, you hear me? Now, I think you were about to tell me how you were planning to fix this issue I have."

"I'll take a look remotely after my meeting. It'll be fine."

The word set his fucking teeth on edge.

"Do not tell me this is going to be fine, Kearney. People always say that, and it never is. I want the malware you sold me off Kaylee's phone. Right. Fucking. Now."

He hung up, his blood thundering through his veins. But despite the clamor in his head, a soft sound behind him prickled up his spine, froze him. Time slowed as he turned toward the door. The betrayal on her face almost sent him to his knees.

Kaylee's purse slipped from her limp fingers, and it hit the ground with a thump.

One minute, she was charging back home—back to his place, she corrected herself—to give Aidan hell for lying to her about his black eye, and the next minute her whole world was crashing down around her.

"You've been spying on me?"

The words didn't make sense. It was like parroting a language she didn't actually speak.

"I wasn't spying on you!" His exhalation deflated his battle stance. "I was spying through you."

"What?" She shook her head, but even through her shock, the pieces were starting to click into place. "That's why you wanted my phone. Because you... Oh God. You bugged my phone? When?"

Aidan broke eye contact, looked down. "The night we went for drinks."

The first night. The first fucking night. He hadn't wanted *her* at all.

"My God, Aidan. Do you know what I thought when I turned around and saw you in that coffee shop?" Something—part laugh, part cry, and all self-recrimination—burst from Kaylee's lips. It was a harsh, wounded sound that made her flinch. "I thought it was fate."

And the whole time, she'd just been an easy mark. The weak link. The one who used to hang on his every word. No wonder he'd targeted her. And she'd fallen for it. Hell, she'd instigated it! "Max. My dad. Your dad. None of this was about me at all."

The unthinkable occurred then, and it killed her that—in light of what she'd just learned—it wasn't actually unthinkable anymore.

"Did you hack my brother's company?"

Aidan frowned, gave a curt shake of his head. "I had nothing to do with that."

Emotion bubbled up in her throat. She was vaguely relieved when it manifested as a scoffing laugh instead of a strangled sob. "Forgive me if I don't just take your word on that."

"KJ…"

She stepped back from the pleading tone, the intimacy of the name only he called her. "Just swooping in like a vulture then, biding your time. Waiting for the death throes to end."

"It's not like that. Not anymore."

"Oh? And what's it like now, Aidan? What's changed, besides the fact that I caught you?" She shook her head at her own stupidity. "You were just using me to get information. You wanted the goddamn app." The truth cut swift and deep. There was a moment of blessed numbness before pain bloomed in her heart, almost overwhelming with its intensity. She braced her hand on the counter, lifted the other to massage her temple. "None of this was real." Another laugh escaped her, but this one held an edge of hysteria and burned her throat raw.

"It wasn't supposed to be, but it is now." He stepped closer. His voice was raspy, like he was being tortured to divulge state secrets. "Being with you is the realest fucking thing that's ever happened to me."

"There's nothing real about any of this!" Her attention landed on the dining room table, where things had been so different a few days ago. When he'd made her believe she was worth standing up for. Had that all been part of the ruse?

"Don't say that."

He reached for her. She hated that the brush of his fingers on her skin felt so good. Hated that his touch calmed her. Now was not the time for calm.

She stepped back, and his hand fell away from her arm. Cool air swept over her skin where his fingers had been, and she shivered. "Why were you at the burlesque show that night?"

"I was looking for you."

In any other context, the words would have been a dream come true. But not now. Not this context. "Why?"

"My PI tracked your car there."

"That was your plan all along, wasn't it?" It was hard to breathe through her outrage. "I wasn't just a convenient mark you happened to run across at the coffee shop and chose to exploit. You recruited me. You were just using me, right from the start."

Aidan's eyes flashed fire. "Well, you know all about that, don't you?"

The words cracked through the room with the ferocity of a whip.

"What the hell is that supposed to mean?"

"You knew who I was that night in the supply closet. I'm just one more of your dirty little secrets, right? Who are you using me to get back at? Max? Your mom? Or hell, maybe it's all intensely meta, and younger you is proving something to younger me, punishing me for not seeing what an incredible woman you were destined to become. Maybe D? All of the above?"

The charges punched through her chest with devastating precision. It sounded so ugly when he put it that way. But was he wrong? Hadn't she thought each and every one of those things that night in the club, when their gazes had collided? When she'd acted out her most cherished fantasy in that supply closet? When she'd accepted his offer for drinks, all the while hoping he'd figure out she and Lola were one and the same?

"You want to talk truth? Here's one for you. Are you here with me? Or are you here because they wouldn't want you to be?"

Kaylee didn't want to think about it. Not when it didn't matter anyway. He was here only because he was using her. And she'd let fanciful teenage emotions make her think this was something…what? Real? Special? Fated?

She should have known better. No one who meant anything to her ever felt the same way back.

"Jesus Christ, Kaylee. You say that secrets make you feel alive, but all you've managed to do is set your life up as a grenade, rigged to inflict maximum damage on anyone who's wronged you."

"What?"

He pinned her with a measured look. "Your mom lost her senatorial bid when your dad cheated on her with a stripper."

"She cheated on him first!" The defense of her father was automatic, as old as the scandal Aidan had referenced, and her gut lurched with disgust. She pushed the queasy feeling aside as she remembered the horrors Max had endured at Charles Whitfield's hand. She couldn't think about that right now. "And I'm not a stripper. I dance burlesque, and I'm not ashamed of it. Burlesque is art. It's dance as social commentary."

"Tell yourself that all you want. Hell, maybe it's true. But if this hits the media, you know how it will play."

She hated that she had no defense for that. That maybe it was a little bit true. That she'd taken that burlesque class for the wrong reasons, not the least of which was Sylvia Whitfield's disapproval. But no matter why she'd started, she'd grown to love burlesque. The girls. The art of it. It meant everything to her now.

Kaylee raised her chin. "You're hardly in a position to give me life advice, Aidan. You've never stuck around long enough to deal with the intricacies of relationships. Whenever things get hard, you claim wanderlust and disappear on another adventure."

The barb landed. She could tell by the way Aidan's hands fisted, his automatic reaction to every blow, be it physical or verbal, but Kaylee got no joy from it.

"You know what? You're right." He grabbed his leather jacket from the back of the dining room chair. "It's definitely past time that I got out of here."

Kaylee watched him go, flinched as the door slammed in his wake. Further proof that fight or flight was the extent of Aidan's operating capacity.

The rumble of his motorbike confirmed which option he'd chosen to apply to her.

Kaylee's bottom lip trembled, a precursor to the tears scalding the backs of her eyes. But she blinked them back and swallowed the lump in her throat. She needed to get back to work.

CHAPTER TWENTY-ONE

HEARTACHE HANGOVERS WERE so much worse than their tequila counterparts, Kaylee decided the next morning. Her eyelids felt like they were lined with gravel as she dragged them open to check the time. It took a moment for the numbers to register.

Shit. It was almost eight o'clock! Her alarm was supposed to go off an hour and a half ago.

She grabbed her phone with such ferocity that the charging cable came loose from the wall. Everything looked fine, but three attempted swipes later, Kaylee realized the stupid thing was frozen. No wonder the alarm hadn't rung.

Stupid piece of crap.

She held down the power button, forcing a restart before she dropped the phone on her comforter and got to her feet. If she skipped the shower and breakfast, she could probably make it to the office by—

Her plans were cut off by a cacophony of buzzes and dings as hundreds of push notifications and texts and missed calls flooded her phone.

What the hell?

She walked back over to the bed to investigate, but what she saw on the screen in her hand stopped her dead. A litany of words she'd hoped never to see strung together.

Kaylee.

Lola.

Burlesque.

Whitfield Industries.

Scandal.

Stripper.

The phone slipped from her numb fingers.

Everyone knew. Her parents. Max. The people who worked for her. All of Los Angeles. The world. But it wasn't embarrassment that quaked through her at the realization. It was betrayal.

Because burlesque was the one thing in her life that was just hers.

The one thing she hadn't shared with anyone else... except Aidan.

Her heart keened at the idea that he could be so cruel. Her head told her to grow the hell up. He'd bugged her phone with the express purpose of hurting Max, of ruining her family. It was naive in the extreme to think he wasn't capable of this.

Whitfield Industries had been plagued with disgrace of late.

First a security breach had raised questions about the safety of their flagship product—an app designed to keep information secure.

Then her father, the former CEO, had been turned

in to the FBI by his son, the current CEO, for black-mailing a key member of the SecurePay team.

Somehow, Kaylee and her team had managed to juggle and avoid the full brunt of either crisis, but how long was that going to last now that she was the latest scandal? How did you spin the fact that the woman in charge of spin was about to be shamed for taking off her clothes in public? All the plates she'd set spinning to keep people looking where she wanted them to would come crashing down around her.

And much as it pained her, Kaylee knew there were many who would see her "transgression"—being female *and* embracing her sexuality publicly—as the worst of the three offenses.

If her credibility was shot, she couldn't effectively do her job.

Looked like Aidan was right after all. She was a grenade.

She'd done all the work for him. All he'd had to do was pull the pin.

Boom.

With a resigned sigh, she ignored the part of her that wanted to crawl back into bed and pull the covers over her head and grabbed the phone instead. Between the beeps and the buzzing, she managed to text her assistant.

Announce a press conference at 10 a.m.

Then Kaylee walked over to her closet to pick out some appropriate armor for the battle ahead.

* * *

Aidan wasn't sure what he was expecting to see after the shit show that had erupted overnight, but if he'd thought that having her burlesque career splashed all over the internet and the local papers would cow her, well, he'd been all kinds of wrong.

Kaylee strode toward the entrance of the building, looking every inch the competent PR director in her sleek gray pantsuit and heels with her dark hair pulled back in a no-nonsense ballerina bun, and nothing like her alter ego, the blonde bombshell who'd caused all this trouble in the first place. And while Aidan had enjoyed every second of watching her dance, he found he preferred this Kaylee. Her certainty, her determination, her general kick-assiness. No secrets. No flash. Just her.

She was spectacular.

Her stride faltered as she caught sight of his bike, parked near the entrance of her building. He stepped forward, and their gazes collided. His body came alive as though she'd touched him. But instead of altering her direction to meet him, she headed for the entrance, dismissing him completely.

Shit.

He started toward her, and she sped up, but there was no way she'd make it into the lobby before their paths intersected. She beat him to the door by a fraction of a second, pulling it open without breaking stride, so Aidan followed her into the building.

"I'm not leaving until you hear me out."

She shook her head, kept walking. "There's nothing

left to talk about. You should go. In case you haven't heard, I have a huge press conference to manage this morning."

"I didn't do this, KJ."

She whirled on him, eyes flashing. "Right. You're the only one who knows about…my secret identity."

"Ms. Whitfield? Everything okay?"

Aidan's shoulders stiffened at the threat of confrontation. Some rent-a-cop trying to impress Kaylee was the last thing he needed to deal with.

Kaylee nodded, waving off the approaching security guard. "I'm fine, Roy."

The burly man sent a pointed glare at Aidan before he turned and headed back to the crescent-shaped desk to the left of the elevators.

"That's what I'm trying to tell you. I don't think I'm the only one who knows about Lola." Aidan held a hand out, palm up. The static, the interference, the quick drain on the battery, and now the leak. And all of it would benefit Liam Kearney. "I need to see your phone."

"After what happened last time? No way."

"Give me the phone, KJ. I think someone bugged it."

She frowned at that. "Oh, no kidding?"

"I think someone *else* bugged it."

After a beat of stunned silence, Kaylee took off toward the elevators again, leaving him no choice but to follow.

"If you'd just let me explain, I—"

"Explain what? Some giant conspiracy theory? Do you have an evil twin I don't know about?"

"Hey." He reached for her, but his fingertips barely brushed her arm before he thought better of it, pulled his hand back.

She stopped, though, and dropped her head. Her shoulders curled forward as though he'd popped the bubble of her confidence. It tore him apart.

The pretty, studious girl he'd known had withstood the constant nagging of her mother, the emotional abandonment of her brother, and the calculated disinterest of her father, and still she'd grown into a beautiful, brave woman who continued to believe in people. Who looked at him like he was something special. At least she used to.

And he'd ruined it. He hadn't wanted her trust, had actively warned her not to give it to him. But now that he'd lost it…

It felt like forever until she turned to face him, even longer until she lifted her head. "How could you do this to me?" She shook her head. "How could I let you do this to me?"

That spark of fire in her eyes was a relief, even if it was aimed at him. Mad was better than broken.

"You really think I leaked this to the press? You know me better than that, KJ."

For a fraction of a second she looked like she wanted to believe in him again, but then the elevator dinged and the doors slid open and she was back to glaring at him. He followed her inside. Briefly, Aidan thought they might luck out and get the elevator to themselves so he could warn her about the tech glitch, or beg her to forgive him, or push her up against the wall and kiss her until she was too breathless to be mad at him anymore. But before he could do any of those things, they were joined by three women and two dudes in suits.

Aidan exhaled. Despite the easy chatter of the rest of the occupants, the silence between him and Kaylee was oppressive. Thick. He didn't like being around her without being able to touch her.

Not that he deserved to. Or that she'd have let him, even if they were alone. He'd really fucked things up. But at least if they were unaccompanied he could try to fix it.

Two of the women got out on the sixth floor, the other woman on the fourteenth. The guys, it seemed, were in it for the long haul.

They kept whispering to each other. Shoulders shaking with laughter as they alternated covert looks at Kaylee. And Aidan knew he wasn't just imagining it. He could feel her shrinking beside him. Head down, shoulders hunched, like she was trying get small enough to escape their notice.

By the time they got to the top floor, Aidan was strung tight.

If the guy in front of him had known that, he might not have raised his voice slightly as the silver doors slid open. The words *continuing the family legacy* were unmistakable. His buddy laughed.

Aidan's blood ran hot as he and Kaylee followed them off the elevator. "We got a problem here?"

The guy turned around and smirked at him. "Nope. No problem."

"You sure? Because it sounded like maybe you had something you wanted to say."

The tenseness of the interaction was starting to draw the attention of nearby employees.

"Is this…" The asshole glanced at Kaylee, then back at Aidan. "Are you trying to impress her, tough guy? Is that what this is?"

Kaylee's hand on his arm was all that stopped Aidan from ending him, but his fists drew tight anyway, every muscle in his body aching to wipe that damn smirk off the guy's face.

"Because from what I've heard, you don't have to try too hard to get her clothes off. Like father's hooker, like daughter, I guess."

The asshole's head snapped back as blood gushed all over his skinny hipster tie, and with the amount of satisfaction that roared through Aidan's body at the contact, it took his brain a second to realize he hadn't thrown the punch.

Kaylee cradled her fist in her other hand, swearing softly, and Aidan had never been prouder of anyone in his whole damn life.

"You fucking cow!"

The asshole lurched forward, one hand still cradling his bleeding nose, and this time Aidan did step forward, angling his shoulders so Kaylee was slightly behind him. It was only a courtesy, though. Since her punching hand was sore.

"I wouldn't." Aidan's warning was soft and low.

"Jones, c'mon man." His buddy grabbed him and

pulled him back, and Aidan was a little disappointed in his good sense.

The guy swore again, drawing even more of a crowd. Blood spatter dotted the tiles in the reception area like a macabre Jackson Pollock painting.

"What the hell is going on here?"

The air changed around Aidan at the sound of Max's voice, and the gathered spectators snapped to attention, suddenly remembering everything they should have been doing.

"This crazy bitch punched me!"

Icy rage flattened Max's features. "What did you say?"

"Look, Max. Uh, Mr. Whitfield. I—"

"Security will meet you at your desk, Jones."

Max glanced behind him, but his admin already had the phone to her ear.

"Sir, I think…" Wisely, Jones's sidekick stopped thinking when Max levelled that subzero stare at him.

"I'll be at my desk if you need me," he spluttered before hurrying away.

Fucking coward.

Kaylee's punching bag seemed mostly recovered, though his complexion was mottled with anger, blood still trickled from his swollen nose, and his mouth kept opening and closing like a dying fish's. "Are you kidding?" he finally stammered. "You can't fire me!"

"I just did. Take it up with my lawyer if you don't like it."

Jones bit back whatever else he was about to say

at the deadly look on Max's face—obviously the guy wasn't a complete moron—and turned around.

Aidan needled him with a cocky grin and a casual press of the down button.

Max waited until Jones had disappeared from sight behind the silver doors—united front and all that—before he spoke in that clipped, all-business tone that Aidan had always associated with him, even in their teens. "You two, in my office."

Kaylee bit her lip like she was trying not to cry.

"You okay?" he asked, his hand automatically lifting to her back in a comforting gesture. Relief surged through him when she didn't shake him off.

"I punched him." Her hazel eyes were wide, like she didn't quite believe it.

He was so fucking in love with her in that moment that he thought his ribs might crack. Still, he managed to keep his voice even. "Yeah you did. Like a heavy-weight champ."

Kaylee looked down at her hand, then back at him. "I didn't think it would hurt this much."

Me neither. But it did. It hurt worse than anything he'd ever felt.

Aidan exhaled as they headed for Max's office. "C'mon, Slugger. Let's get you some ice."

CHAPTER TWENTY-TWO

"SOMEBODY HAD BETTER START TALKING."

Kaylee followed Max all the way to his desk, dropping into the visitor chair across from him, but Aidan hung back a little, under the guise of taking in the office's killer view and swanky furnishings.

In truth, he was waiting for Max's executive assistant to show up with the ice he'd asked her for.

"Martin Jones called me a hooker and I hit him."

Max's frown darkened, but Aidan didn't get a chance to revel in it, because Max's EA had poked her head into the office. Aidan grabbed the official first-aid-kit-issued ice pack and strode toward Kaylee.

"Where the hell did you learn to punch like that?"

In answer to her brother's question, Kaylee's gaze met Aidan's as he knelt in front of her chair and reached for her injured hand. She was still pissed at him, not that he'd expected less. But when she didn't pull away, he counted it as a win and pressed the cold pack to her battered knuckles, using the opportunity as an excuse to keep touching her, even for just a second or two longer.

"Never mind."

Aidan could hear the eye roll in his friend's voice. Former friend. Whatever.

"You wouldn't say that if you'd seen her jab. She probably broke that asshole's nose. You didn't even draw blood." Aidan got to his feet and turned to face Max. "You should get her to give you some pointers."

The taunt ran out of heat when his gaze fell on a familiar piece of metal, and it drew him forward.

He picked up the little statue of the horse with the flaming mane. His father had given it to Max, and seeing it here, in this office, surprised him. That Max not only had kept it but had it prominently displayed. Aidan set it back on the edge of the desk and cleared his throat. "Nice digs. Looks like the rumors are true—it's good to be king."

Max opened his mouth to reply, but before he managed a word, the door to his office swung open.

"Would you mind explaining why I just got a call from Martin Jones's attorney about a wrongful termination and assault case? And Kaylee's...extracurricular activity is all over social media. Maybe we should move up the press conference before—oh. I'm sorry to interrupt. Vivienne Grant. Head counsel. You must be the reason I'm earning my money today."

The woman was sharp. Or perhaps *precise* was a better term. He almost expected her hand to feel cold and angular, but her palm was surprisingly warm.

"Aidan Beckett, innocent bystander. Assault is over there icing her knuckles, and the wrongful termination part is all on that guy." He tipped his head at Max. The slight twitch of the man's mouth was not lost on him.

Damn it felt good, the two of them on the same side of trouble again.

Then Max iced over, and Aidan recognized the glint of danger in his friend's expression, the one that always sparked when Max dropped the *civilized* in preparation for battle.

"The press conference can wait until its scheduled time. Have Sherri get you the camera footage from the reception area and tell Jones's lawyer to cool his heels. We'll deal with him tomorrow. Right now, I have important things to worry about."

Vivienne's perfectly arched brow lifted, and her gaze fell on Kaylee. "I don't mean to be indelicate, but are you sure Kaylee is the best person to deal with the fallout from this?"

That same spark of danger was all over Kaylee's face when she stood and stared down Max's head counsel. She was fucking magnificent.

"Are you questioning my ability to do my job?"

Aidan got the impression that maybe Vivienne was a little impressed with Kaylee, too. "Not at all. Merely suggesting that some distance might be the best course of action in this case."

"Kaylee can handle it." Max glanced at his lawyer. "If that's all?" Her dismissal was clear in his tone.

Vivienne's nod was sharp. "I'll take care of Jones."

"You always do," Max added, softening the exchange.

Aidan crossed his arms, surprised. That Emma was

having more of an effect on Max than he'd realized the night he'd met her.

"Now," Max said, taking a seat behind his desk, "where were we?"

Kaylee tossed Aidan a look that dripped with disdain. "Before this morning's brawl, Aidan was telling me how he bugged my phone yet has nothing to do with the burlesque leak."

Oh, she was in the mood for a fight, then. He was more than happy to oblige.

"Hey, you're the one who started throwing punches. And I wasn't telling you that I bugged your phone. I was telling you that I thought someone else bugged your phone. And if I'm right, they could be listening to us right now, so hand it over."

Kaylee frowned, leaned back in the chair, and readjusted her ice pack. "Once again, I respectfully decline."

So damn stubborn.

"Remember what you said to me when you found out about the malware? You asked if I hacked Whitfield Industries. I didn't," he stressed at the identical dark looks of the Whitfield siblings. "But I did get the spyware I used from Cybercore."

"Jesus Christ. Give him the damn phone, Kaylee."

Aidan hated that Max's order held more weight for her than his request, but he supposed he deserved it. She dug it out of her pocket with her good hand and held it toward him. Aidan popped out the battery before placing both pieces on Max's desk.

"The program I uploaded wouldn't uninstall properly, so it should still be on there. But just in case Cybercore removed it remotely…" Aidan reached into his pocket, pulled out the cell Kearney had given him, and tossed it to Max. "Here's what I used to deploy the malware in the first place."

Max caught the phone easily. "And to what do I owe this sudden show of transparency and goodwill?"

"I'm not doing it for you."

"He's trying to save his ass," Kaylee snarked from her chair, flexing her knuckles under the ice pack.

He was trying to save more than that.

"Probably worried you'll charge him with corporate espionage before he manages to tear us apart from the inside."

Aidan hated the hard edge to her words, the grim set to her mouth. He'd done that to her and he accepted the pain under his ribs as his penance.

"That's not why I'm here," he said, focusing on Kaylee, though his words were meant for Max, too. "Not anymore."

He'd come back for revenge, for that damned code, for answers. He'd expected to leave victorious.

Instead, he was broken in every way a man could be.

"Just go, Aidan. Whitfield Industries is reeling. You got what you came for." Her words were harsh, but Kaylee's eyes showed every bit of the hurt and confusion he'd inflicted.

"You're right. I did get what I came for. But I didn't get what I want."

Her laugh was tinged with bitterness. "And what is it you want?"

"You," he said simply.

Her throat worked, and her grip crushed the ice pack.

"I'm in love with you, KJ."

He'd never said those words to a woman, and he hadn't really expected to say them to her now, and certainly not across a fucking office, but if boxing had taught him anything, it was that sometimes you had to improvise and roll with the punches.

Max's chair creaked in the continued silence, and Aidan spared him a glance. "Maybe I should give you two a minute."

Aidan shook off the courtesy. "No. Stay. I'm done with secrets."

He waited until Kaylee looked at him before he spoke again. "I know you think I'm a bad bet. I used you to get back at Max, and I'm going to regret that for the rest of my life. But I swear to you, I didn't leak your burlesque to the press."

Aidan paced the front of Max's desk, three steps one way, three steps back, a futile attempt to burn off the excess adrenaline in his muscles. He needed to get this out.

"I've spent a lot of time running, trying to escape bad situations and avoid dealing with the hard stuff. I always thought that's just how I was built. But I realize now it's because I've never had a home I wanted to be at."

Aidan drew to a stop in front of Kaylee's chair.

"Until you. You feel like home. And I'm going to prove it to you, KJ. The only way I know how. By sticking around and letting my actions speak for me."

Her face had gone slack, and he couldn't get a bead on what she was thinking, but her knuckles were white against the blue ice pack clutched in her hand.

"You can be mad at me for as long as you need to. But I'm not going anywhere. So when you're ready, come find me, okay? I'll be at home."

And with a nod at Max and a long look at Kaylee, Aidan walked out the door.

CHAPTER TWENTY-THREE

KAYLEE DRAGGED A DEEP, shuddering breath into her lungs.

Aidan *loved* her.

It wasn't…she couldn't…he didn't…

Some random beeping pulled her out of the processing loop she was stuck in, and she looked up as Max removed a sleek black cell phone from the bottom drawer of his desk. It wasn't the one he used day to day, the silver one she knew was tucked away in the breast pocket of his Burberry suit jacket.

Desperate for distraction, for anything that would knock the maelstrom that was Aidan out of her thoughts, Kaylee stood and rounded his desk for a better view. "What are you doing? Deploying the Bat-Signal?"

"In a manner of speaking…" Max hit Redial on a blocked number, and after a couple of rings, a woman's face appeared on the screen, her light brown skin wreathed in a halo of bouncy raven curls, already talking as though she and Max were in the middle of a conversation.

"I'm gonna guess you finally read the info I sent you about the real reason the government is putting fluoride in the—"

"Not now, AJ. I need you to analyze some spyware," Max interrupted.

Kaylee had a vague impression of a brick wall behind the woman, similar to the one in Aidan's kitchen, before AJ leaned closer, her face filling up the entire screen as she lowered her voice conspiratorially.

"Uh, boss. You know you're not alone, right? Ixnay in front of your ister-say."

Max glanced over his shoulder, and Kaylee turned away to save him the trouble of dismissing her. She almost jumped out of her skin when Max's fingers brushed her wrist, staying her. She stared at the point of contact, then raised her gaze to his.

"You can speak freely in front of her." Max didn't break eye contact with her as he spoke. "Kaylee and I are trying something new."

"And what's that?"

The question came from the woman on the screen, but Kaylee might as well have voiced it herself.

"Honesty."

AJ scrunched her nose up and leaned back. "Sounds pretty fucked up to me, but whatever floats your ocean liner. I assume that since you're bringing this to me instead of your pet security wizards over at Soteria, you're thinking it's linked to the mole who installed the program on Emma's computer."

Max nodded. "A reliable source tells me that one of

the programs on this phone is Cybercore issue, but the CEO is playing stupid about the competing malware."

"You think Kearney's playing the ol' double cross on your *reliable source* then?"

"It crossed my mind."

"And how did the dueling malware manifest?"

Max gestured toward the phone and moved slightly to his right. Surprised, Kaylee leaned forward so she was fully in the frame.

"Frozen screen, garbled calls, trouble closing apps. The battery life is nonexistent," Kaylee answered.

AJ nodded. "And where'd you get it?"

"The phone? Wes Brennan gave it to me after my old one broke. Said he didn't need it."

"And how soon after you got it did the glitching start?"

Kaylee bit her lip, thought back. "The next day, I guess." Right after Aidan had installed the spyware. She tried to summon some of her earlier outrage at the thought, but it only made her heart feel raw.

"Well, color me intrigued. I'm all over it, boss. Let's nail this bastard."

"I'll leave the phone in the usual spot?" Max resumed his spot on the video call.

"Correct. Give me forty-eight hours with it and you'll be begging me to accept the ridiculously generous bonus I will so rightly deserve." And with that, AJ disconnected.

Kaylee glanced at Max. Who knew the king of stoicism had so many surprises in him? "Do I even want to know that that's about?"

"What are you still doing here, Kale?"

She didn't like the question. Didn't like the meaning behind it, or the concern in her brother's eyes. Kaylee set the mangled ice pack on the edge of his desk.

Work. She just needed to focus on work. It was the one thing in the whole world that made sense to her right now. "What do you mean, *what am I doing here?* We have a press conference in under an hour. And I was thinking maybe we should—"

"I was an asshole the day you quit, distracted. I'd lost Emma."

Kaylee's mouth snapped shut at the interruption. She had to lift her chin to maintain eye contact as he stood.

"I'm in love with her, Kale. I thought I'd never see her again, and I couldn't let that happen. So I just walked out and left you to clean up the SecurePay mess. And I'm sorry about that."

Kaylee's eyes widened with astonishment. Her robotic older brother was in love? And with the woman who'd almost ruined SecurePay, the project Max had poured all of his focus into for the last five years and counting?

"I never would have done it if you weren't so damn good at your job."

Kaylee's heart stopped at the compliment. The one she'd been waiting to hear from him for her entire professional life.

"I know you said it was too late for me to play the 'big brother' card, and maybe it is, but I can still play the 'boss' card. And right now I'm telling you—no, I'm ordering you—to take the rest of the day off work."

"But the press conference is—"

"I'll handle it."

"You don't have any talking points and—"

"Not only is Kaylee Whitfield an adult, capable of making her own decisions, but she's done nothing for which she needs to be ashamed. Her personal life is of no concern to us insofar as it does not affect her job performance. Whitfield Industries stands by our director of public relations. And more important, I stand by my sister."

Tears stung her eyes at her brother's words, even though she didn't want them to.

Max put his hands on her shoulders, and she started at the foreignness of the touch. "Do you love him?"

Yes.

Her heart answered before her brain could kick in, and the realization shook her to her core. "So much it's hard to breathe sometimes."

Max let go of her, tipped his chin in the direction of his office door. "Then go *home*."

CHAPTER TWENTY-FOUR

THE ELEVATOR GODS smiled upon her, and instead of a million stops on her way to the lobby, there was only one. Kaylee silently cursed the giggly girls who boarded on the sixth floor as she pressed the close-door button with the speed and voracity of a particularly single-minded woodpecker. With any luck, Aidan hadn't gotten too much of a head start.

She burst into the lobby the second the doors opened, scanning the anonymous, business-suited workday crowd.

Relief and adrenaline, and maybe a little fear, flooded her veins when she spotted him near the security desk, being hassled by Roy. She had a sneaking suspicion that Max had something to do with the stalling tactic, and she made a mental note to thank her brother later.

"Aidan!"

Her half scream echoed and bounced across every hard surface. Everyone loitering in the lobby turned to face her, whether curious about her outburst or because they recognized her from the burlesque scandal, she didn't know.

Didn't care.

Because right now, she had only one concern—winning back the gorgeous, infuriating badass with the golden-blond hair and the black leather jacket who'd turned to face her at the sound of his name.

Kaylee's fingernails dug into her palms as she stood there, frozen, waiting to see what he would do. And then she realized only an elephant would wait.

And she was a motherfucking butterfly.

Her pulse slammed in her ears, sounding a lot like the speed bag at Sal's, but Kaylee ignored it and walked toward him, one step at a time. She didn't falter, didn't stop until Aidan was directly in front of her.

He was still the sexiest man she'd ever seen, the cocky swagger of his stance, the set of his big shoulders, a slight arch in the eyebrow above his bruised eye. "What are you doing down here? You've got a press conference to—"

He stopped talking when she fisted her sore hand in his T-shirt and yanked him close. There was nothing soft about the way she kissed him, commandeering his mouth with the unrestrained hunger he so easily stoked in her. A clash of lips and teeth and tongues that dared him to keep up. Telling him with her body how much she needed him, how much she wanted him, how much she loved him.

He growled as she licked into his mouth, and his hands came up to cradle her head. It was too tender a gesture for the heat of their kiss, love amidst the rush of lust, and it was almost Kaylee's undoing.

They were both panting when the kiss broke, their

foreheads pressed together, his hands fisted in her hair, destroying her bun.

A slight smile toyed with the corner of Aidan's mouth. "What was that for?"

"For being the one person who always saw me, all of me, and never made me feel like I wasn't enough. It's the reason I had a crush on the boy you used to be. And it's why I'm in love with the man you are now."

She placed a hand on his scruffy jaw. "I always thought the reason I kept secrets was because I got off on the illicit thrill of doing something I shouldn't. But I was just hiding. I see that now. I was too scared to stand up for myself and take what I wanted. But I'm not scared anymore."

His hand came up to cradle the back of hers, and he turned his head, pressing a kiss to the middle of her palm.

"I love you, Aidan. And I don't want it to be a secret."

"I love you, too," he said, lacing his fingers through hers and pulling her hand down from his cheek. "And I intend to spend the rest of my life proving it to you, but right now, you've got a job to do." He made a move for the elevator, but she tugged him back.

"Actually, Max is taking care of that. He owes me a press conference. So I thought maybe you could take me home instead."

A beat slipped by as her words landed, and then he squeezed her hand. "It would be my honor," he said softly as they started toward the exit doors.

"Everyone's staring at us."

He glanced around. "Yeah, well, people are perverts, and you just tongue fucked me in the middle of the lobby."

Kaylee laughed. For the first time in recent memory, she felt light inside. Happy.

"Besides, they've probably never seen a burlesque legend so close up before. With all this publicity, you should have a full house for your show this week."

"Actually, I've been thinking that maybe it's time for Lola to retire, hang up the old pasties."

The announcement stopped him dead. Aidan's frown was full of concern as he searched her face, and it warmed her to know she had that kind of support in her corner.

"What are you talking about? You don't have to give up burlesque. This bullshit media stuff is going to blow over. Even if it doesn't, fuck what they think."

"It's not that. I just don't need her anymore. I don't need to put on a blond wig and blue contacts to feel like myself. Don't get me wrong—I love Lola. I love the confidence she gave me. But right now, I just want to be myself for a while."

Aidan pulled her into his arms, lifted her up his body. Kaylee locked her legs around his waist.

"I love you so fucking much, KJ."

She licked her lips, and his eyes darkened with need as she twisted her hips against his growing erection. "I love you more. And if we weren't in the middle of the lobby, I'd prove it to you."

"Jee-zus. You can't say shit like that to me in public." Aidan's fingers dug into her ass as he did an about-face and headed away from the doors.

Kaylee giggled at the sudden change in direction. If they weren't getting looks before, they definitely were now. "What are you doing?"

"You said Max had everything under control. And just because we're being honest with each other doesn't mean we can't still have some secrets."

She moaned at the delicious friction when he hitched her up his body without breaking stride.

"There's got to be a supply closet around here somewhere."

She was never going to get enough of this man, Kaylee realized, lowering her head until her lips brushed his ear. "Hang a left at the security desk. It's the third door on the right."

* * * * *

COMING SOON!

We really hope you enjoyed reading this book. If you're looking for more romance, be sure to head to the shops when new books are available on

Thursday 27th December

To see which titles are coming soon, please visit
millsandboon.co.uk

MILLS & BOON

LET'S TALK
Romance

For exclusive extracts, competitions
and special offers, find us online:

- ![f] facebook.com/millsandboon
- ![twitter] @MillsandBoon
- ![instagram] @MillsandBoonUK

Get in touch on 01413 063232

For all the latest titles coming soon, visit
millsandboon.co.uk/nextmonth

Want even more
ROMANCE?

Join our bookclub today!

'Mills & Boon books, the perfect way to escape for an hour or so.'

Miss W. Dyer

'Excellent service, promptly delivered and very good subscription choices.'

Miss A. Pearson

'You get fantastic special offers and the chance to get books before they hit the shops'

Mrs V. Hall

**Visit millsandbook.co.uk/Bookclub
and save on brand new books.**

MILLS & BOON